Praise for Mary Jo Putney and her unforgettable novels . . .

"A complex maze of a story twisted with passion, violence, and redemption. Miss Putney just gets better and better." —Nora Roberts

"Mary Jo Putney is a gifted writer with an intuitive understanding of what makes romance work." —Amanda Quick

"Enthralling . . . Mary Jo Putney uses sparkling wit and devastatingly perceptive characterization to paint a compelling portrait of one of the most enduring creations of romantic fiction—the Regency rake." —*Romantic Times*

"Ms. Putney has a gift of nonstop sensitivity, wit, charm, and a sense of vitality for telling a wonderful love story." —*Affaire de Coeur*

"Dynamite!" —Laura Kinsale

The Bargain

Mary Jo Putney

SIGNET
Published by New American Library, a division of
Penguin Putnam Inc., 375 Hudson Street,
New York, New York 10014, U.S.A.
Penguin Books Ltd, 27 Wrights Lane,
London W8 5TZ, England
Penguin Books Australia Ltd, Ringwood,
Victoria, Australia
Penguin Books Canada Ltd, 10 Alcorn Avenue,
Toronto, Ontario, Canada M4V 3B2
Penguin Books (N.Z.) Ltd, 182–190 Wairau Road,
Auckland 10, New Zealand

Penguin Books Ltd, Registered Offices:
Harmondsworth, Middlesex, England

First published by Signet, an imprint of New American Library,
a division of Penguin Putnam Inc.

Originally published in a somewhat different version in a
Signet edition entitled *The Would-be Widow.*

First Printing, October 1999
10 9 8 7 6 5 4 3 2 1

Printed in the United States of America

To my mother, Eleanor Congdon Putney,
from whom I inherited my love of travel, language,
and a good read

Prologue

Charlton Abbey, Spring 1812

The fourth Earl of Cromarty was buried with all the pomp and dignity due his rank. The village church bell tolled solemnly as he was laid to rest in a misty rain, all of the male members of his household dressed in black and suitably somber. The late earl had been a handsome, forceful man, fair of mind and quick to laugh. His dependents had all been vastly proud of him.

Chief mourner was the earl's only child, Lady Jocelyn Kendal. At the postfuneral gathering, she performed her duties with impeccable grace, her pale, perfect features still as a marble angel under her sheer black mourning veil. She and her father had been very close.

This would be Lady Jocelyn's last official act at Charlton Abbey, since her Uncle Willoughby was now the owner. If she resented the fact that she had been transformed from mistress to guest in her childhood home, she concealed her feelings.

Though a few elderly ladies might think her independent streak would be considered headstrong in a less well-bred girl, none of the men minded. At twenty-one she possessed more than her share of beauty and charm, and as she moved about the great hall men looked after her, and briefly dreamed.

The last ritual of the long day was the reading of the will. The family lawyer, Mr. Crandall, had come down from London to perform the duty. It was a lengthy task, with numerous bequests for honored servants and special charities.

Lady Jocelyn sat immobile in the crowd of listeners. A mere daughter could not succeed to her father's honors, but she would still inherit a substantial part of her father's fortune, enough to be one of England's greatest heiresses.

The new earl, a solemn-faced man without a tithe of his late brother's dash, listened gravely. Once it had been assumed that the fourth earl would remarry and get himself a male heir, but his experience of matrimony appeared to have soured him on that state. He had been content with his only daughter, and Willoughby was the beneficiary of that choice. Though the new earl sincerely mourned his brother, he was human enough to be glad for his elevation to the title.

The will presented no surprises—until the end. Mr. Crandall cleared his throat and glanced nervously at the statuesque beauty in the front row before starting to read the final provisions. "And for my beloved daughter, Jocelyn, I hereby bequeath and ordain . . ."

The lawyer's sonorous voice filled the room, riveting the listeners. When he finished, there was a murmur of startled voices and inhaled breath as heads turned to Lady Jocelyn.

She sat utterly still for an endless moment. Then she leaped to her feet, sweeping her black veil from her face to reveal blazing rage in her fine hazel eyes. "He did *what*?"

Chapter 1

London, July 1815

In his dream, Major David Lancaster was galloping across the Spanish hills on his horse, Aquilo, who ran with the grace of his namesake eagle. Between his thighs, the horse's muscles were powerful and responsive to the slightest pressure. David laughed aloud, his hair whipped by the wind, feeling as if the two of them could run like this forever, rejoicing in the exuberance of youth and strength.

A distant scream of agony jerked him awake. Years of war had trained him to leap to his feet and grab his rifle while he scrambled from his tent to ward off attack. But instead of movement, he felt only savage pain as his half-dead body failed to respond. From the waist down, nothing moved, his lifeless legs anchoring him to the bed.

He opened his eyes to the ugly reality of the Duke of York Hospital. Aquilo had died at Waterloo, and so had David, though his body stubbornly insisted on clinging to the last embers of life. The soldier's luck that had carried him through years of war without serious injury had deserted him at the end. A direct artillery hit would have been swifter and kinder than this lingering demise.

But it wouldn't be much longer now. He clamped his jaw as the waves of pain ebbed to a bearable level. Though the dingy room wasn't much, at least officer's privilege gave him the privacy to suffer in solitude.

He recognized the soft, regular click of knitting needles and turned his head on the pillow to see his sister's small form silhouetted against the fading light of the lone window. He felt a rush of tenderness. Sally had come every day since his return to London, arranging her duties so that she could spend as much time as possible with her dying brother. This was so much harder for her than for him. He felt no fear, only stoic acceptance. At the end, he would find peace. For Sally there would be loneliness, and the insecure existence of a governess with no family to fall back on.

Alert to his slightest movement, she glanced up to see if he was awake. Setting aside her knitting, she crossed the room to his bedside. "Are you hungry, David? I brought a nice beef broth from the Launcestons."

He knew he should try to eat for Sally's sake, but the thought nauseated him. His stomach was one of the many parts of his body that had lost interest in life. "No, thank you. Perhaps later." He glanced at the window. "Time for you to go, before it gets dark."

She shrugged her shoulders. Dressed in a plain gray gown, she was the very image of a modest governess. It saddened him to think that when he was gone, there would be no one left who would remember her as a wild little tomboy, racing him on her pony, scampering through the meadows with bare feet and shrieks of laughter. They'd been happy then, growing up in the green hills of Hereford. A lifetime ago.

Correctly interpreting her shrug, he said sternly, "Home, Sally. I don't want you on the streets at night."

She smiled, having known him too long to be intimidated by his officer voice. "Very well. I'll dose you and be on my way." Lifting the bottle of laudanum from his bedside table, she carefully poured a spoonful, then held it to David's lips. He swallowed quickly, scarcely noticing the tastes of wine and spice that disguised the bitter opium that would mitigate his pain.

Sally put an arm under his shoulders and raised his head enough so that he could sip a little water. When he finished, she gently settled him back among the pillows. It had bothered him at first that their roles had been reversed, for it had always been his task to look out for her. But pride had swiftly dissolved in the face of his helplessness, and of Sally's calm acceptance of the sordid realities of nursing.

"Good night, David." She straightened the blanket over his inert body. "I'll see you tomorrow afternoon."

With a glance she confirmed that broth, water, and laudanum were all within his reach. The laudanum, at least would be needed before morning. Then she left, back straight and expression controlled. The room was mercifully too shadowed to show the bleakness in her eyes.

Colors began to intensify, shapes twisted, and pain eased as the opium began to take effect. His lids drifted shut. Thank God for laudanum.

While he wouldn't have minded living a few more decades, he couldn't complain. He'd had almost thirty-two years of mostly rewarding life. He'd traveled, fought honorably for his country, made friends closer than brothers. The only regrets he had were about Sally. She was a highly capable young woman, but life was uncertain. If only he could leave her enough to secure her future. If only . . .

The numbing warmth of opium soothed away the pain, and he slept.

Frowning, Lady Jocelyn glided into her drawing room, her voluminous riding habit belling around her. It was time to confide in her favorite aunt, who might have some useful insight into the situation. "Aunt Laura?"

She was about to say more when she realized that Lady Laura Kirkpatrick was not alone. Helping herself to tea cakes was Lady Cromarty, also an aunt but definitely not a favorite. It was too late to escape, so Jocelyn repressed a sigh and moved forward, saying with patent insincerity, "Aunt Elvira. What an . . . an unexpected pleasure."

The countess smiled back with equal insincerity and an alarming array of teeth. "Since I was in town shopping, I thought I'd call to say hello. I can't stay long since it's a good two-hour drive back to Charlton."

"I am quite aware how long a drive it is to Charlton." Jocelyn seated herself opposite the two older women. She hated thinking of her childhood home. She loved the estate deeply and had even toyed with the idea of marrying her cousin Will, heir to the earldom. Like his father, he was amiable and easily managed, and through him she would eventually become mistress of Charlton again. Fortunately, common sense always prevailed. Will wasn't a bad fellow, but she certainly didn't want him as a husband.

Lady Laura poured another cup of tea and offered it to Jocelyn. "I'm glad you returned in time to join us." As a military wife, she'd become an expert smoother of troubled waters, and where Lady Cromarty went, the waters were frequently whipped into a froth.

As she accepted the tea, Jocelyn hoped as she had often before that she would be as handsome as her aunt when she reached her forties. Both of them had the Kendal looks and coloring, with hazel eyes and chestnut hair gleaming with red highlights, but her aunt was blessed with the serenity produced by more than twenty years of happy marriage. A blessing that Jocelyn might never know.

Elvira, Countess of Cromarty, aunt by marriage instead of blood, was quite a different matter. Though she had not been born to a high estate, she had accepted her elevation to the nobility as proof that God was just. Today, her gaze was moving around the elegant room with proprietary interest as she devoured the cake.

Jocelyn's lips tightened. "Stop evaluating the furnishings, Aunt Elvira," she said in her coolest voice. "You are *not* getting this house."

A lesser woman might have been embarrassed at

such candor, but Lady Cromarty only smiled blandly. "Are you getting uncomfortable with your birthday coming so soon, and you still unwed?"

The subject on all their minds landed in the middle of the room like a cat among the pigeons. Determined to have his own way, even after death, Jocelyn's father had left the bulk of his personal fortune to his daughter—on the condition that she marry by the age of twenty-five. If she didn't, most of the investments and Cromarty House, the magnificent London mansion where they were sharing tea, would go to Willoughby.

"Why should I be uncomfortable?" Jocelyn asked with equal blandness. "I'll admit I'm having some trouble deciding which offer to accept, but never fear. I shall certainly be married in time to fulfill the conditions of my father's will."

"I'm sure you've had your offers, dear," Elvira said, her tone implying she thought nothing of the kind. "But when a woman reaches your age unwed, one has to wonder . . ." She gestured vaguely. "So fortunate that if you prefer spinsterhood, you'll have quite a nice little competence, enough to live in some genteel place like Bath."

"Since I dislike Bath, it is very fortunate that the issue will not arise," Jocelyn said in a silky voice.

Elvira's polite mask slipped into a scowl. "It isn't as if you need the money. *We* have five children to establish. It was quite infamous of your father to leave Willoughby scarcely enough to maintain the estates."

Actually, the fourth earl had left his brother ample income to support his family and maintain his lordly dignity, but the countess was the sort who could never have enough. Before Jocelyn could succumb to the temptation to point that out, Elvira shrieked. A tawny body had streaked over the back of the sofa and plopped onto her wide lap, eyeing the countess with golden eyes and a sadistic feline smirk.

Jocelyn repressed a grin. Isis had the usual cat genius for pouncing on those people who least wanted to be pounced on. Making a mental note to order oysters for the cat's dinner, she pulled the bell cord before crossing the room to scoop Isis from the countess's lap. "I'm so sorry, Aunt," she cooed. "Apparently Isis has conceived a fondness for you. Or perhaps for that cream bun in your hand. *Bad* Isis."

The cat blinked placidly, quite aware that the scolding wasn't real. Isis had been the gift of a naval suitor who claimed to have brought her from Egypt, and her velvety, lion-colored fur and fine-boned elegance did resemble the felines seen in Egyptian temple art. The cat had far more aristocratic style than the Countess of Cromarty.

When the butler entered in response to Jocelyn's summons, she said, "Dudley, my aunt was just leaving. Please have her carriage brought around."

Even Elvira could take a hint that broad, but her expression was complacent when she rose. Clearly she thought that the husband hunting had been left too late. "Good day, Laura. And do invite us to your wedding, Jocelyn. If there is one."

Accurately interpreting the look on her niece's face, Laura hastily escorted the countess from the room. On the verge of one of her rare but incendiary bursts of temper, Jocelyn rose and stalked across the room to stare out at the street as she struggled to master herself. Elvira had always been irritating, and it was a mistake to give her the satisfaction of losing control.

A few minutes later, she recognized Lady Laura's quiet footsteps entering the drawing room. Turning from the window, she said, "I'd marry a beggar from Seven Dials before I'd let the money go to Willoughby and that . . . that archwife."

"One could wish that Willoughby had chosen a woman of more refinement," Laura admitted as she sat down again. "But Elvira is right, you know. Time is running out. I haven't pressed you about marriage because you're no green girl, and you know your own business best. Relinquishing most of your inheritance is preferable to an unhappy marriage, and it isn't as if you'll be left penniless."

"I have no intention of giving up the fortune I'm entitled to," Jocelyn said crisply. "Certainly not to the benefit of Elvira."

"You've had over three years to find a husband to your taste. The weeks left aren't much time."

Remembering what she had wanted to discuss, Jocelyn sighed and resumed her seat. "Oh, I know whom I want to marry. Unfortunately, I haven't yet succeeded in engaging his interest. At least, not the marrying kind of interest."

"How . . . interesting. I hadn't realized you had set your sights on someone. Who is the dense fellow who hasn't yet recognized his good fortune?"

Jocelyn reached into the sewing box by her chair and pulled out an embroidery hoop with fabric stretched across the frame. "The Duke of Candover."

"Candover! Merciful heavens, Jocelyn, the man is a confirmed bachelor," her aunt exclaimed. "He'll never marry."

"The fact that he never has doesn't mean that he never will." Jocelyn threaded a length of pale blue silk through a needle, then took a meticulous stitch. "He and I are very well suited, and his attentions have been quite pronounced in the last few months."

"He does seem to enjoy your company. You were just out riding with him, weren't you? But he has stayed well within the bounds of propriety. Morning calls and dances at balls, with the occasional ride or drive. Unless there is more that I don't know about?" Her sentence rose at the end, turning her words into a worried question.

"He has always behaved as a perfect gentleman," Jocelyn said with regret. A pity that the duke hadn't crossed the line of propriety; he was not the kind of man to do that with her unless he had serious intentions. "But he has spent more time with me than with any other eligible female. He's in his mid-thirties, and it's time he set up his nursery."

Lady Laura frowned. "You've set yourself an impossible task, my dear. Candover has perfectly good cousins, so he has no need to marry to get an heir. He's been on the town for years and has never come close to marrying. He's had his share of mistresses, but always widows or other men's wives, never a marriageable young woman." Her mouth twisted wryly. "If you want him as a lover, marry someone else and he'll probably oblige, at least for a while. But he'll never make a husband."

"Blunt talk indeed." Unnerved by her aunt's assessment, Jocelyn considered the last months for the space of a dozen stitches. Had she imagined the duke's interest? No, he found her attractive; she'd had enough experience of men to recognize genuine admiration. And the attraction was more than simple physical awareness of a member of the opposite sex. "There is a . . . a real sense of connection between us, Aunt Laura, perhaps because we've both been pursued by fortune hunters for years. But it's more than that. I think there could be a great deal more."

"It's possible," her aunt said gently. "But you've run out of time, my dear. If he hasn't offered for you yet, I can't imagine that you'll bring him up to scratch in a mere four weeks. If you're determined to marry no one but him, you'd better start packing. Elvira will want to move in here the day after your birthday. She wouldn't dare put you out, of course, but I assume you have no desire to stay on at her sufferance."

"I will not give her the satisfaction of getting what should be mine." Jocelyn stabbed her needle into her embroidery with unnecessary force. Being no fool, she'd already realized that it was wildly unlikely that Candover would move from admiration to matrimony in the weeks left. "I have an . . . an alternative plan."

"One of your other suitors? Lord MacKenzie would marry you in a heartbeat, and I think he'd make a wonderful husband." Lady Laura dimpled. "Of course I'm biased, since he reminds me of Andrew."

Jocelyn shook her head. MacKenzie was pleasant and good-looking, but not for her. "I'm thinking of accepting Sir Harold Winterson. It's something of a game between us that he proposes to me regularly, but he'd be delighted if I accepted. The man must be seventy if he's a day—too old to be interested in exercising his marital rights. I'd fulfill the terms of Father's will, and it wouldn't be that long until I have my freedom again. If I'm a widow, Candover will regard me in quite a different light."

Lady Laura almost dropped her tea cup. "What an appalling thought! To marry a man while hoping for his death would be *wicked*. Foolish, too. I knew a girl who married a man Sir Harold's age, hoping to become a rich widow soon. That was twenty years ago, and her husband is still very much alive, while she has lost her youth."

As Jocelyn's face fell, Laura added, "Besides, there is *no* age at which one can assume a man will not be interested in exercising his marital rights."

Jocelyn shivered at the thought. "You've convinced me. Sir Harold is a sweet old gentleman, but I have no desire to be a wife to him." She bit her lower lip. "While the idea of marrying a man at death's door has merit, Sir Harold is quite vigorous for his age. One would have to be sure the man was really dying."

"I'd like to believe that I've dissuaded you through moral logic, but I have the dismal feeling that it's only the practical problems that discourage you. If you have any more outrageous schemes in mind, don't tell me." Laura regarded her niece gravely. "Marriages of convenience may be the way of the world, but I'd hoped you would find something better. A true meeting of minds and spirits such as Andrew and I have."

Trying not to be envious, Jocelyn replied, "Few people are so fortunate."

Unable to deny that, her aunt said, "Does it have to be Candover? If not MacKenzie, perhaps Lord Cairn. I'm sure he'd be a kind and loving husband."

"But I *like* Candover, Aunt Laura. Men are not pairs of interchangeable gloves. In the seven years since my presentation, I've met no one except Candover whom I can imagine as my husband. You had plenty of suitors in your day. Would you have wanted to wed and bed anyone other than Uncle Andrew?"

"Not after I met Drew." Lady Laura drew her hands together, as if debating whether to say more. "Darling, I've sometimes wondered. Does your . . . your reluctance to marry have anything to do with your mother?"

Jocelyn said in a tone that could chip ice, "We will not discuss my mother!" Realizing how immoderate that sounded, she said more calmly, "I scarcely remember the woman. Why should she have any effect on my marital choices?"

Her aunt frowned, but knew better than to say more. Willing to change the subject, she lifted a letter from the table next to her chair. "I've just received this from Andrew. He and his regiment are safely installed in Paris now. I imagine the Allies will occupy the city for some time while the French government is restored."

"Did he mention any of the officers I met in Spain?" Jocelyn said with quick concern. She and her aunt had pored over the casualty lists after Waterloo. In the weeks that had passed, some of the wounded would have died.

Laura scanned the letter, reading aloud comments about officers that Jocelyn knew. "Here's a bit of good news. Captain Dalton has been sent to the Duke of York Hospital here in London. He has a severe leg injury, but his life is no longer in danger."

"Good news indeed." Jocelyn smiled reminiscently. "Remember how Richard rescued me when I got lost trying to find Uncle Andrew's winter quarters?"

"Remember!" Laura rolled her eyes in mock horror. "I could show you the exact gray hairs I acquired when you rode into Fuente Guinaldo with all those soldiers and not so much as an abigail to bear you company."

"The maid I had then was such a hen-hearted creature," Jocelyn said defensively. "How was I to know that she would flatly refuse to leave Lisbon?"

"The girl had a good deal better sense than you did," her aunt said dryly. "It's a miracle that you weren't robbed and murdered by French troops, bandits, guerrillas, or heaven knows who else. You were mad to come bolting into a war zone like that."

Privately Jocelyn agreed. That had been one of the occasions when her headstrong streak had erupted, despite her endless efforts to curb it. "I'd made inquiries, and it seemed as if the journey would not be unduly dangerous. I'll admit I was a bit worried when my guide ran off and I had no idea where to find the regiment, but I was well armed, and you know that I'm an excellent shot. After Captain Dalton and his patrol found me, I was perfectly safe."

"All I can say is that you have a highly capable guardian angel." Lady Laura consulted the letter again. "Major Lancaster is at the York Hospital, too, but I don't believe you met him. He was on detached duty with the Spanish army the winter you spent with us." Her eyes became bleak. "He's dying, I'm afraid."

Jocelyn leaned across and briefly laid her hand on her aunt's. The Waterloo casualty lists had been painful for her but far worse for her aunt, who had spent her life as an army wife and now saw her friends decimated.

Having met many officers through Lady Laura, Jocelyn sympathized deeply, because she'd liked the kind of men they were. Unlike the perfumed gallants of London, what they did mattered. Perhaps that was why she was attracted to the Duke of Candover, whose fine tailoring could not conceal his intelligence or air of purpose. He was considered an exemplary landlord, she knew, which spoke well of his character, and he was a force for principled reform in the House of Lords. Political views were another area where they were in tune.

Yes, Candover was the one. She liked him very well—but not *too* well.

If only she had more time for their relationship to grow and deepen. She'd observed the duke carefully and believed he would marry if he found the right woman. A woman of his rank, and a similar steady temperament.

But time had almost run out, and if she waited to

bring him around, she would lose her patrimony. Moreover, if she was reduced to living on the modest stipend she would have left, she would lose most of her opportunities to meet Candover socially. She would no longer be a glamorous, much sought after heiress, but a woman of modest fortune past the first flush of youth. She shuddered at the thought. That was quite, quite unacceptable. Her rank in life was one thing she had always been sure of.

Damn her father! They had been so close—yet in the end, he'd betrayed her as surely as her mother. . . .

She cut off the thought with the skill of long practice. Better to think of what she could do to ensure that she would have both her inheritance and the husband she wanted. She had a month still, and a Kendal of Charlton never surrendered, even if she was of Charlton no more.

Returning to mundane matters, she said, "I think I'll call on Captain Dalton at the hospital tomorrow morning. Will you join me?"

"I can't tomorrow or the next day, but tell him I'll be there the day after without fail." Lady Laura rose and excused herself to write an answer to her husband's letter.

Alone in the drawing room, Jocelyn's mind returned to her dilemma. The obvious solution was to marry one of her suitors and have a fashionable marriage, each of them going their own way after an heir or two had been produced. Yet the idea revolted her. She didn't want to be a brood mare to a man she barely knew, nor did she aspire to become one of Candover's passing mistresses. She wanted to be his wife. She was resigned to the fact that few if any husbands were faithful, but at least if Candover strayed, he would be discreet about it. If she was really lucky, he might realize that his wife was all the woman he needed.

Despite her aunt's revulsion at the thought, a swift widowhood would be preferable to a loveless marriage of convenience, for that would give her freedom and the time she needed to win Candover's heart. But not Sir Harold Winterson. Lady Laura was right about that—it wouldn't do to marry the old gentleman and find herself in the distasteful position of longing for his death so she could regain her freedom.

Jocelyn tilted her head to gaze at the gorgeously painted and gilded drawing room ceiling. As a child she often lay on the floor and made up stories about the paintings in the elaborate medallions. She loved this house almost as much as Charlton Abbey.

The unruly side of her nature surged forth again, and she swore an oath that one of her warrior ancestors would have approved. She might never win the duke's love, and Charlton was forever lost, but Cromarty House was *hers*. No matter what it took, she would find a way to keep her home out of Elvira's grasping little hands.

Chapter 2

The soft footfalls of her maid awakened Jocelyn from a restless slumber. She rolled over with a yawn and sat up so a tray of hot chocolate and bread rolls could be arranged over her lap. "Thank you, Marie." Noticing a small frown on the girl's face, she added, "Is all well belowstairs?"

Welcoming the opportunity to talk, Marie Renault said with an enchanting trace of French accent, "The footman, Hugh Morgan?"

Jocelyn nodded encouragingly. Morgan was a handsome young Welshman who had created quite a flutter among the maids when he started work a few months before. Marie appeared to be the girl who had secured his interest.

"His brother, Rhys, a dragoon who was wounded at Waterloo, has just arrived at the York Hospital here in London. Hugh is most anxious to visit him, but his next half day isn't for almost a week." The girl gave her mistress a hopeful glance.

Had Rhys Morgan come over on the same troop ship as Richard Dalton? So many wounded men. Repressing a sigh, Jocelyn sipped her rich, steaming chocolate. "How convenient. This morning I'm going to call on a friend at the York Hospital. Morgan can be my escort and see his brother while I am visiting my friend."

"Oh, excellent, milady. He will be most happy." Expression lighter, Marie crossed to the wardrobe room to prepare her mistress's morning costume. Jocelyn broke open her warm bread roll, wryly wishing that all problems could be solved as easily as Hugh Morgan's.

The Duke of York Military Hospital was dismal, a drab monolith dedicated to the treatment of seriously wounded soldiers. Jocelyn wondered with black humor if the objective was to be so depressing that patients would do their best to recover quickly.

Steeling herself, she marched up the wide steps, her footman close behind. Hugh Morgan was tall, with broad shoulders and a melodious Welsh voice. He was a pleasant addition to the household, but today concern for his brother shadowed his eyes.

The building was crowded with casualties, and it took time to find Rhys Morgan's ward. Jocelyn experienced sights and smells that knotted her stomach, while Hugh's country complexion acquired a greenish-white tinge.

Rhys Morgan lay in a corner cot of perhaps forty jammed into a room too small for its population. Some patients sat on their beds or talked in small groups, but most lay in stoic silence. The bare walls created an unrestful clamor, and a miasma of illness and death hung heavy in the air.

Hugh scanned the room. "Rhys, lad!" He instinctively started to push past Jocelyn, then glanced back apologetically. With a nod, she released him to his brother.

The wounded man had been staring at the ceiling, but he looked up as his name was called. Though the face was startlingly like his brother's, Rhys Morgan wore an expression of blank despair that was only partly lifted as Hugh rushed up and grabbed his hand, Welsh words pouring forth.

The raw feeling in Hugh's face made Jocelyn uncomfortable. As she shifted her gaze away, her eyes were caught and held at the bottom of Rhys's bed. Where there should have been two legs under the covers, there was only one. The left had been amputated just below the knee.

She swallowed before approaching to touch Hugh's arm. He turned with a guilty start. "I'm sorry, my lady. I forgot myself."

She gave a smile that included both of them. "No apologies are necessary. Corporal Morgan, may I introduce myself? I am Lady Jocelyn Kendal, and I have the honor of being your brother's employer."

Rhys propped himself up against the wall behind his cot, alarmed at the vision of elegance before him. With a bob of his head, he stammered, "My pleasure, ma'am."

Hugh hissed, "Call her 'my lady,' you looby."

A wave of color rose under the fair Celtic skin as the soldier attempted to apologize. Wanting to alleviate his embarrassment, Jocelyn said, "It's of no importance, Corporal. Tell me, are you two twins?"

"Nay, I'm a year the elder," Rhys replied. "But we've oft been taken as twins."

"You are very alike," Jocelyn remarked.

"Not any more," Rhys said bitterly as he glanced at the flat bedding where his leg should have been.

Jocelyn colored with embarrassment. Deciding the brothers would be better off without her inhibiting presence, she said, "I'll go find my friend now and leave you to visit. When I'm finished, I'll return here, Morgan."

Hugh looked uncertain. "I should go with you, my lady."

"Nonsense, what could happen to me in a military hospital?" she replied. "Corporal Morgan, do you know where the officers are quartered?"

He straightened when she asked for help. "The floor above, ma'am. My lady."

"Thank you. I shall see you both later." Jocelyn left the room, conscious of the stares that followed her. Impossible not to remember that while she had been living in comfort in London, these men had been getting blown to bits for their country.

Climbing a staircase to the next level, she found a long, empty corridor with individual doors instead of open wards. As she hesitated, a thickset man of middle years strode purposefully from a nearby room. Guessing he was a physician, she said, "I'm looking for Captain Richard Dalton of the 95th Rifles. Is he in this area?"

"Down the hall." The doctor waved his hand vaguely behind him, then marched off before she could get more specific directions.

Resigned to trial and error, Jocelyn opened the first door. A nauseating stench sent her into hurried retreat. Aunt Laura, who had done her share of nursing in Spain, had once described gangrene, but the reality was far more sickening than Jocelyn had imagined. Luckily, the still figure on the bed was not the man she sought.

The next doors opened to empty beds or men too badly injured to notice her intrusion. No Captain Dalton. More and more unnerved, she opened the last door on the corridor. Several figures stood around a table with a man lying on it. A scalpel flashed, followed by a blood-freezing scream of agony.

Jocelyn slammed the door shut and ran blindly into the open space at the end of the corridor. She'd thought it would be simple to locate a friend. Instead, she was finding the worst suffering she'd ever seen in her life.

Eyes clouded with tears, she didn't even see the man until she slammed into a hard body. There was a clatter of falling wood, then a strong hand grabbed her arm. Jocelyn gasped, on the verge of a hysterical scream.

"Sorry to be in your way," a quiet voice said. "Do you think you could hand me my other crutch?"

Blinking back her tears, Jocelyn bent to pick up the crutch that had skidded across the floor. She straightened to hand it over and was profoundly relieved to see the man she sought. "Captain Dalton! I'm so glad to see you up and about."

Richard Dalton was a brown-haired young man of medium height, with hazel eyes much like her own. Though his face was drawn with fatigue and pain, his quick smile was warm. "This is an unexpected pleasure, Lady Jocelyn. What brings you to this wretched place?"

"You did, after Aunt Laura learned you were

here." She glanced ruefully at the crutches. "I didn't intend to put you back into a hospital bed."

"It takes a good deal more than a collision with a beautiful woman to do me an injury," he assured her. "I can say without reservation that running into you is the most enjoyment I've had in weeks."

Richard's flirtatious teasing helped restore her ragged nerves. Though there had been nothing romantic between them, they had always enjoyed each other's company. Probably the lack of romance had made them friends. "Aunt Laura sends her apologies that she could not accompany me today, but she will call on you day after tomorrow."

"I shall look forward to it." He shifted awkwardly on his crutches. "Would you mind terribly if I sit down? I've been upright for as long as I can manage at the moment."

"Of course," she said, embarrassed. "I'll never make an angel of mercy, I fear. I seem to be causing nothing but problems."

"Boredom is one of a hospital's worst problems, and you're alleviating that nicely." The captain swung over to one of several chairs and card tables set beside a window to create a lounge area. He gestured her to the chair opposite him as he lowered himself with a wince.

Jocelyn examined the drab walls and furnishings and the windows that faced another depressing wing of the hospital. Not a place designed to aid convalescence. "Will you be staying here long?"

"It may be a while. The surgeons periodically poke around for bits of shell and bone they might have missed. We had one long argument about amputation, which I won, but now they are trying to convince me that I'll never walk without crutches again. Naturally I have no intention of believing them."

"In any such disagreement, my money is on you."

"Thank you." Bleakness showed in his eyes. "I'm fortunate compared to many of my fellow patients."

"Aunt Laura mentioned Major Lancaster in particular," Jocelyn said, remembering the letter. "Is there news of him I can take to her?"

"Nothing good. He has grave spinal injuries and is paralyzed from the waist down." Richard leaned against the high back of his chair, his face much older than his years. "He can barely eat, and it's an open question whether he will die of starvation, pain, or the opium they've been giving him to make living bearable. The physicians don't understand why he isn't dead already, but they agree it's only a matter of time."

"I'm sorry. I know the words are inadequate, but any words would be," Jocelyn said with compassion. "He's a particular friend of yours?"

"From the first day I joined the regiment, when he took me in hand to turn me into a real officer." Richard's gaze was on the past, and the days and years that had gone into weaving a friendship. "Even in dying, he's an example to us all. Completely calm, except for his concern for his younger sister's future. She's a governess and well situated for now, but when he's gone, she'll be alone in the world, with nothing and no one to fall back on." He gave his head a slight shake. "Sorry. I shouldn't be depressing you with the story of someone you've never even met."

Jocelyn started to say that he had no need to apologize, then froze as an idea struck. She needed a husband, and the mortally wounded major wanted security for his sister. Unlike Sir Harold Winterson, there would be no question of "marital rights" since the poor man was on his deathbed. In return for his name, she could settle an annuity on the sister that would keep her in comfort for life. It was a perfect meeting of needs: she would retain her fortune, and he would be able to die in peace.

"Richard, I've just had a most bizarre inspiration that might solve a problem of mine while helping Major Lancaster." Quickly she sketched in the requirements of her father's will, then explained the solution that had occurred to her.

To her relief, the captain listened to Jocelyn's proposal with no sign of revulsion. "Your proposition is unusual, but so is your situation. David might well be interested. It would be a great comfort for him if Sally is provided for. Shall I introduce you to him if he's awake?"

"That would be wonderful." Jocelyn rose, hoping the major wasn't asleep. If she had time to think about her idea, she might not be brave enough to go through with it.

Richard pulled himself onto his crutches and led her to one of the rooms she'd glanced in earlier, where the patient had appeared unconscious. After opening the door for Jocelyn, he swung across the room to the bed.

As Jocelyn studied the emaciated figure on the bed, it was hard to believe that a man so thin and motionless could still be living. Major Lancaster appeared to be in his late thirties, with dark hair and pale skin stretched across high cheekbones to form a face of stark planes and angles.

The captain said softly, "David?"

Major Lancaster opened his eyes at the sound of his friend's voice. "Richard . . ." The voice was no more than a low whisper of acknowledgment.

The captain glanced at Jocelyn. "There's a lady here who'd like to meet you."

"Anything to oblige a lady," Lancaster said, a thread of humor in the low voice. "I've nothing pressing on my schedule."

"Lady Jocelyn Kendal, allow me to present Major David Lancaster of the 95th Rifles." Richard beckoned her to his side.

"Major Lancaster." She moved into the injured man's line of sight and got her first clear look at him. A jolt of surprise went through her. Though his body was broken, his eyes were very much alive. Vividly green, they showed pain, but also intelligent awareness. Even, amazingly, humor.

He scanned her with frank appreciation. "So this is the legendary Lady Jocelyn. It's a pleasure to meet you. Every man in the regiment took pains to tell me what I'd missed by spending the winter with the Spanish army."

"The pleasure is mine, Major." Jocelyn realized his eyes were striking not only for the unusual shade of transparent green, but because the pupils were tiny pinpoints, making the irises even more startling. Opium. She'd seen eyes like that in society ladies who were overfond of laudanum.

She had intended to make her proposal without

delay, but as she stood by the wreck of what had been a warrior, her throat closed and left her silent. To look into Major Lancaster's green eyes and say that she was here to make a bargain in anticipation of his death was impossible.

Correctly interpreting her strained expression, Richard Dalton said, "Lady Jocelyn has a most unusual proposition, one I think you'll find interesting. I shall leave you two to discuss it." He shifted his crutches to a more comfortable position, then left.

Jocelyn took a deep breath, grateful that Richard had broken the ice. Where to start? Not wanting to overtire the major, she said succinctly, "My father died several years ago and left me a substantial inheritance, on the condition I marry by age twenty-five. I shall reach that age in a few weeks and am still unwed. Richard mentioned your situation, and it occurred to me that we might make a bargain of mutual benefit. If . . . if you'll marry me, I shall settle an income on your sister to ensure her future security."

When she finished, absolute silence reigned, broken only by the distant sounds of street traffic. It took all of Jocelyn's control not to flinch under Lancaster's startled gaze. Yet when he spoke, his voice showed only curiosity, not anger at the bald implication of his imminent death. "I have trouble believing you can't find a husband in the usual fashion. Are the men of London mad, blind, or both?"

"The man I want has shown an unflattering lack of interest in me," Jocelyn admitted, feeling that nothing less than honesty would do. "Perhaps he may someday change his mind. I hope so. In the meantime, I don't want to marry only for the sake of an inheritance, then regret it the rest of my life. Do you understand?" Her last words were a plea; it was suddenly important that he accept her actions as reasonable.

"It would be utter folly to marry the wrong man because of a ridiculous will," he agreed. His eyes closed, leaving his face alarmingly corpselike. She watched anxiously, hoping she hadn't overstrained him.

His eyes flickered open. "How much of an annuity were you proposing?"

Jocelyn hadn't thought that far. After a swift assessment of her income and the costs of living, she asked hesitantly, "Would five hundred pounds a year be acceptable?"

His brows rose. "That would be very generous. Enough for Sally to live a life of leisure if she wished, though I can't imagine her idle. Perhaps she'd start a school."

He fell silent, the pain lines in his face emphasized as he thought. Uneasily Jocelyn said, "No doubt you'll want some time to consider this."

"No," he said emphatically, his voice stronger. "There is . . . no time to waste."

The words chilled her. For an endless moment, their gazes locked. Jocelyn saw no fear about his impending death, only stark honesty and hard won peace. With every breath he drew, this man humbled her.

Carefully shaping each word, Lancaster said, "Lady Jocelyn, would you do me the honor of becoming my wife?" A faint, wry smile curved his lips.

"Though I have nothing to offer you but my name, for your purposes that will suffice."

His ability to joke under these circumstances almost undid Jocelyn's self-control. Choking back her feelings, she laid her hand over his. It was bone-thin, almost skeletal, but the pulse of life was still present. "The honor would be mine, Major Lancaster."

"David," he said. "After all, we are about to wed."

"David," she repeated. It was a good, solid name that suited him.

His brows drew together in concentration. "We shall obviously have to be married here. I'm afraid that you'll have to arrange for the special license, but if you have a man of business, he should be able to obtain one by tomorrow."

"I'll have my lawyer take care of it. He can also draw up the settlement for your sister. Her name is Sally Lancaster?"

"Sarah Jane Lancaster." He closed his eyes again. "Your lawyer must also draw up a quitclaim for me to sign, relinquishing all customary claims against your property."

"Is that necessary?"

"Legally your property would become mine on marriage, and on my death half would go to my heir, Sally. Since the purpose of this exercise is for you to retain your fortune, we don't want that to happen."

"Heavens, I hadn't thought of that." What if she'd made this strange proposal to a man less scrupulous than Major Lancaster? It might have meant disaster.

In an almost inaudible voice, he said, "If your lawyer is worth his hire, he would have protected your interests."

Recognizing that he was at the limits of his strength, Jocelyn said, "I should be able to have the license and settlements by tomorrow. Will this same time be agreeable to you?" As she studied the spare figure under the blanket, she wondered if he would still be alive in another twenty-four hours.

Uncannily reading her mind, he said, "Don't worry, I shall still be here."

She gave his hand a gentle squeeze, then released it. "Thank you, David. I shall see you tomorrow then."

A little dazed by the speed of events, she left the room, quietly closing the door behind her. Richard was seated in the lounge area at the end of the hall, so she joined him, gesturing for him not to stand for her. "Major Lancaster has agreed. The ceremony will be tomorrow. Thank you, Richard. You . . . you've allowed me to take a measure of control over my life."

"I'm glad I could help two friends at once," he said quietly. "Perhaps providence was taking a hand."

"I'd like to think so." With a slightly crooked smile, she bade him farewell.

Wondering if David looked as shaken as Lady Jocelyn, Richard pulled himself onto his crutches and made his way to his friend's room. "I gather all is well?" he asked as he entered.

David's eyes opened. Though he was gray with exhaustion, there was a smile on his face. "Very much so. Will you stand witness for me?"

"Of course." Richard settled in the chair beside the bed. "Do you need me to do anything else for the wedding?"

"Could you take the ring from my little finger and keep it for the ceremony?" He pushed his right hand over the dingy sheets. "I think it's small enough to fit her."

Richard removed the ring. It came off David's bony finger easily.

"My efficient bride will arrange everything," the major said with a spark of amusement. "Thank you for bringing us together."

"The marriage of convenience is a time-honored tradition, though I've never heard of one quite like this," Richard said. "But everyone benefits."

"There are other men here whose families could use the money more than Sally, but I am selfish enough to be glad she will be provided for. A woman without family is only a step away from potential disaster. An accident or illness could push her into abject poverty. Now that won't happen." David exhaled roughly. "Time for more laudanum. Over there, on the table . . ."

Richard poured a dose of the medicine, then held the spoon so David could swallow. "Your sister is not entirely without family."

"She'd starve to death before she would ask help of one of our brothers. Can't say that I blame her. I'd do the same." David's eyes drifted shut. "Now she'll never . . . have to ask help of anyone."

Thinking his friend asleep, Richard hoisted himself onto his crutches, but before he could leave, David murmured, "I would have helped her even without the annuity. I rather like the idea of being married to Lady Jocelyn, even if it's only for a few days."

His voice faded to a bare whisper. "Something to look forward to . . ."

Richard left the room with satisfaction, grateful that Lady Jocelyn was bringing some pleasure into David's last days. The only person likely to object to the arrangement was Sally Lancaster, who guarded her brother like a mother cat with a kitten. At least the income would give her something to think about after he died.

Chapter 3

After leaving Captain Dalton, Jocelyn entered the enclosed stairwell, then plopped down on a step between floors, heedless of her expensive gown. Burying her face in her hands, she struggled to collect herself, her mind a jumble of thoughts and feelings. She was intensely relieved that her problem was solved—assuming Major Lancaster didn't die in the night—yet she half wished she'd never set foot in the York Hospital. Though neither man had shown disgust at her impulsive suggestion, she felt like a carrion crow feasting on the almost dead.

Well, she and the major had made a bargain, and it was too late to withdraw now. There was comfort in the knowledge that he'd seemed pleased to accept her proposition. Yet when she thought of the major's courage, his amused green eyes, she could have wept for the waste. How many other men and boys had died as a result of Napoleon's ambition, or been crippled like Richard Dalton and Rhys Morgan?

It didn't bear thinking of, so Jocelyn stood and carefully donned her gracious-lady facade. By the time she reached Rhys Morgan's ward, she appeared composed again, though misery still knotted in her midriff.

Hearing an anguished, Welsh-accented voice, she paused in the door of the ward, just out of sight of the Morgans. "Who would ever want a cripple like me?" Rhys said harshly, "I can't fight, can't go down in the mines, would only be half a man working on the farm. I wish the damned cannon had blown my head off rather than my leg!"

Hugh's softer voice started making soothing noises, too low for Jocelyn to hear the words. She squared her shoulders before entering the ward. Here was something she could do for a man who would be around long enough to benefit.

When she approached the bed, both brothers turned to face her. Rhys's face was tense, while Hugh's showed the guilt and misery of a whole man in the presence of one who was maimed.

As Hugh stood, Jocelyn said to Rhys, "Corporal Morgan, I have a favor to ask."

"Of course, my lady," he said woodenly.

"I know it would be very dull after all you've done and seen, but would you consider coming to work for me? My aunt will be leaving soon to set up a separate household, and she'll be taking several of the servants, including one of the two men who work in the stables. As a cavalry man, surely you are experienced with horses. Would you be interested in the position?"

The corporal's face reflected shock, and dawning hope. "I should like to be a groom." His gaze went to his missing leg. "But I . . . I don't know if I can manage the work to your ladyship's standards."

Deliberately she looked to the flat place on the bed where there should have been a strong, healthy limb.

"I see no reason to doubt your competence, Corporal." Wanting to lighten the mood, she said mischievously, "Please say yes, if only for your brother's sake. He is positively menaced by housemaids trying to capture his attention. Having another handsome young man in the household will make his life easier."

Hugh blurted out, "My lady!" his face turning scarlet.

At the sight of his brother's embarrassment, Rhys leaned back on the pillows and laughed with the air of a man rediscovering humor. "I shall be most honored to work for you, Lady Jocelyn."

"Excellent." Another thought struck her. "Why not ask the doctors if you can be moved to my house for recuperation? It's a much more pleasant place than this, and your brother will be glad to have you near."

"Oh, my lady!" Hugh exclaimed, his face lighting up.

"I . . . I should like that very much, Lady Jocelyn." Rhys blinked a suspicious brightness from his eyes at the prospect of leaving the hospital.

"Then we shall expect you as soon as you are released." As she withdrew so that Hugh could have a private farewell with his brother, she thought of David Lancaster, who was so frail that any attempt to move him would probably cause his death. Rhys Morgan was robust by comparison. With a comfortable place to live and a good job waiting, he would adjust to his loss fairly soon. And she would get a fine groom in the process.

A few minutes later the footman joined her, and

they left the building. Jocelyn inhaled the warm summer air with relief. Even with the smells of the city, it was blessedly fresh after the hospital.

Behind her, Hugh said hesitantly, "Lady Jocelyn?"

She glanced back at him. "Yes, Morgan?"

"My lady, I will never forget what you have just done," he said gravely. "If there is ever anything I can do to repay you, anything at all . . ."

"It was easily done, and I'm sure your brother will be a worthy addition to the house," she said, shrugging off his gratitude.

"It may have been easy, but few would have done it. 'Tis said in the servants' hall that there isn't a lady in London with a warmer heart than yours."

She inclined her head briefly in acknowledgment, then turned to scan the street. "Do you see where my carriage is waiting?"

Carriages were easier than compliments.

Before returning to Upper Brook Street, Jocelyn paid a visit to her lawyer and man of business, John Crandall. In the years since her father's death, the lawyer had become accustomed to dealing directly with a lady, but today her requests raised his experienced eyebrows.

"You're going to marry a dying officer?" he repeated incredulously. "It will fulfill the terms of the will, but your father's hope was that you'd find a husband to keep you in line. This Major Lancaster can scarcely do that."

Jocelyn did her best to look soulful. "Why do you think I have not married elsewhere? The attachment between David and me is . . . is of some duration."

It wasn't quite a lie. An hour qualified as "a duration." "He was in Spain when I visited my aunt and her husband. But the war, you know . . ." Also not a lie, though certainly intended to be misleading. "I have never known a braver or more honorable gentleman." That, at least, was the truth.

Mollified, Crandall promised to procure the special license, arrange for a clergyman, and have the settlement and quitclaim documents ready in the morning. On the ride home, Jocelyn pondered whether to tell Lady Laura about her wedding, but decided against it. Her aunt had said in as many words that she didn't want to know about Jocelyn's marital schemes. Far better to explain after the deed was done, she thought wryly. She'd learned early that it was easier to get forgiveness than permission.

Jocelyn awoke the next morning with a bizarre sense of unreality. *Today is my wedding day.* Not that this was a real marriage, of course. Yet that knowledge could not mask the reality that today she would take the step that for most girls was the most momentous of a lifetime, and she was doing it almost at random.

On impulse, she decided to add something special to the tragic little ceremony that would take place later that morning. When Marie appeared with her chocolate and rolls, she sent the girl down to the kitchen with orders to pack a basket with champagne and glasses, and to gather a bouquet of flowers in the garden.

She chose her costume with special care, selecting a cream-colored morning gown with pleats and subtle cream-on-cream embroidery around the neckline and hem. Marie dressed her chestnut hair rather severely, pulling it back into a twist with only the most delicate of curls near her face. Seeing that her mistress looked pale, Marie deftly added a bit of color with the hare's foot.

Even so, Jocelyn thought when she glanced in the mirror, she looked as if she was going to a funeral. And wasn't that almost the truth?

At fifteen minutes before eleven o'clock, Jocelyn's carriage halted at the entrance of the York Hospital. Waiting there was Crandall, a bulging case of papers in one hand and a vague, elderly cleric at his side. The lawyer looked gloomy. Jocelyn considered pointing out that he should be glad that she was keeping her inheritance and her need for his services, but decided that would be vulgar.

As Hugh Morgan helped her from her carriage, she said softly, "You know about my father's will?"

He nodded. She was unsurprised; servants always knew everything that happened in a household. "I'm about to marry. Please . . . wish me well."

His jaw dropped for an instant. Rallying, he said, "Always, my lady."

Crandall joined them, ending the private conversation. With Morgan carrying the flowers and a ribbon-decorated basket, they entered the hospital in a silent procession. No one challenged them or asked their business. Jocelyn had the eerie feeling that she could ride a horse into the building and no one would give her a second glance.

Major Lancaster and Captain Dalton were engaged in a game of chess when Jocelyn arrived with her entourage. She was absurdly pleased to see that her intended husband was not only alive, but Richard had helped him sit up against the pillows so that he looked less frail. She smiled at the men. "Good morning, David. Richard."

Her bridegroom smiled back. "This is the best of mornings, Jocelyn. You look very lovely today."

Hearing the warmth in the major's voice, Crandall unbent enough to smile, his sense of propriety appeased. He introduced himself, then said, "Major Lancaster, if you will sign these, please."

David studied the papers carefully before signing. Ignoring the business aspects of the wedding, Jocelyn arranged the flowers on the bedside table in the glass vase she'd brought. Unfortunately, the brilliant summer blossoms made the rest of the room look even more drab. On impulse, she arranged some of the flowers into a small bouquet and tied it with a ribbon stolen from the basket.

After taking her own turn at scanning and signing papers, Jocelyn moved to the side of the bed and gave David her hand. His grasp was warm and strong on her cold fingers. She glanced down into his eyes and was caught by the tranquillity she saw there. Major Lancaster was not a man who either wanted or needed pity.

She smiled tremulously, wishing she could match his calm. "Shall we begin?"

The details of the ceremony were never clear to her after. She remembered fragments: "Do you, David Edward, take this woman . . ."

"I do." Though not strong, his voice was firm and sure.

"Do you, Jocelyn Eleanor . . ."

"I do." Her response was almost inaudible, even to her.

The vicar's next sentences were a blur, until the words *"Till death us do part,"* jumped out at her. It was wrong, *wrong,* that death should be hovering over what was usually a joyous occasion.

She was drawn back to the present when David took her hand and carefully slid on the gold ring that Richard provided. "With this ring I thee wed, with my body I thee worship, and with all my worldly goods I thee endow."

There was humor in his eyes, as if the two of them were sharing a private joke. Perhaps they were.

In a voice much larger than his diminutive frame, the vicar intoned the last, rolling words of the ceremony, "I pronounce that they be man and wife together."

David tugged at her hand, and she leaned over to kiss him. His lips were surprisingly warm under hers.

Fighting tears, she lifted her head. Softly he said, "Thank you, my dear girl."

"Thank you, husband," she whispered.

She wanted to say more, to tell him that she would never forget their brief acquaintance, but the moment was shattered by a low, intense voice from the doorway. *"What is the meaning of this?"*

Jocelyn jumped as if she had been caught in the act of theft. A scowling young woman stood in the doorway, her fists clenched by her sides. While everyone in the room watched in stunned silence, the newcomer marched to the bed. Her gaze moved from

David to Jocelyn, who saw that the angry eyes were brightly green.

With dry amusement, Jocelyn realized that her new sister-in-law had arrived and was not pleased by what she'd found. Sally Lancaster was a short wiry creature, almost relentlessly plain, her dark hair pulled into a tight knot. Her drab gray dress was unfashionably high at the neck, and she wore a practiced look of disapproval. The fine green eyes were her only claim to beauty, and at the moment they sparked with fury.

Jocelyn inclined her head. "You must be Miss Lancaster. I am Lady Jocelyn Kendal. Or rather, Lady Jocelyn Lancaster. As you have no doubt guessed, your brother and I have just married."

The woman said incredulously, "David?"

He reached out his other hand to her. "Sally, it's all right. I'll explain later."

As she took her brother's hand and glanced down at him, her face softened. She no longer looked like an avenging angel, just a tired woman little older than Jocelyn herself, her eyes bleak with despair.

Jocelyn turned to her footman. "Morgan, the champagne, please."

Opening the basket, he produced a bottle and glasses. Pouring and handing around champagne dissipated the tension in the room. Even Sally accepted a glass, though she still looked like a rocket ready to explode.

Jocelyn realized that a toast was in order, but under the circumstances it would be grotesque for anyone to wish the couple health and happiness. In his capacity as best man, Captain Dalton saved the moment. He raised his glass to the newlyweds, looking quite at ease despite the need to balance on his crutches. "To David and Jocelyn. As soon as I saw you together, I knew you were intended for each other."

Only Jocelyn and David understood the irony of the remark.

After the guests drank, David raised his glass in another toast, saying in a faint, clear voice, "To friends, both present and absent."

Everyone could drink to that, and the atmosphere took on a tinge of conviviality. Jocelyn kept a wary eye on Sally Lancaster, and was not surprised when the governess said with false sweetness, "Lady Jocelyn, may I speak with you outside for a moment?"

Jocelyn followed her out of the room with resignation. She'd have to deal with her prickly sister-in-law sooner or later, and better that she make the explanations than David. He was obviously tiring rapidly and had hardly touched his champagne.

In the hallway, Sally closed the door before asking sharply, "Would you kindly explain what that was all about? Is it a new fashion for wealthy society ladies to marry dying soldiers, as one would choose a new hat? Will you be telling your friends what an amusing game you have found?"

Jocelyn gasped. If her sister-in-law believed the marriage was the result of some bored, selfish whim, it certainly explained the woman's hostility. Jocelyn thought of the major's warmth and understanding touch, and felt angry that Sally dared accuse her of marrying for such a callous reason.

Her irritation tinged with guilt, Jocelyn said in the

icy voice of an earl's daughter, "That is a ridiculous statement and does not dignify an answer. Your brother is an adult. He doesn't need your permission to marry."

Sally's eyes narrowed like a cat's. "I think you forced him to do it. David has never even mentioned your name! I can't believe he would marry without telling me unless he had no choice."

Jocelyn realized that the other woman was jealous of her brother's attention, but was irritated enough to say acidly, "Perhaps he knew that you would throw a tantrum and preferred a peaceful ceremony."

She regretted the comment when Sally's face whitened. More gently she said, "We decided very suddenly, just yesterday. Perhaps there wasn't time to notify you."

Sally shook her head miserably. "I was here yesterday afternoon. Why wouldn't he want me at his wedding?"

Captain Dalton joined them, apparently guessing that the ladies would need a referee. Closing the door with the tip of one crutch, he said without preamble, "Sally, David did it for you. Lady Jocelyn, with your permission, I will explain the situation."

Relieved, she nodded, and Richard described Jocelyn's need to marry, and why David had agreed. Sally still looked mutinous. "He had no need to marry for my sake. I can take care of myself perfectly well."

Richard unobtrusively leaned against the wall, face fatigued. "Sally, it will make David much happier to know that you are provided for. Will you let him have that?"

Sally's face crumbled and she began to weep. "I'm sorry, Richard. It . . . it just seems so strange. What right does she have to sweep in like this?"

Jocelyn looked down at the ring David had put on her finger. A simple, well-worn gold signet ring that had to have come from his own hand. Perhaps the only thing of value he owned. It fit rather well. Aching, she said, "I have the right your brother gave me." Raising her head, she said, "If you will excuse me, I will rejoin my husband."

As she reentered the sickroom, she saw that Sally was now sobbing against the long-suffering captain's shoulder. He put an arm around her and smiled wryly at Jocelyn over the bent head. The man had a real talent for dealing with distressed females.

Someone had helped the major lie down again. His face was gray from the effort expended in the last hour, and he looked so fragile that she feared even sitting up again would be the death of him. But as he had promised, he had survived long enough to become her husband.

"It's time I let you sleep." She leaned over to kiss him lightly for the last time, then whispered one of the Spanish phrases she had learned, "Vaya con Dios, David."

"And to you also." He smiled with a serenity that pierced her heart. "Please be happy in the future, my dear girl."

Their gazes held for a long, long moment. Once more she ached with desolation at the damnable waste of it all. Gently she laid her small bouquet on his pillow, so he could smell the fragrance of the blossoms.

Barely able to school her expression, she straightened and collected her entourage with a glance. Then she left, not daring to look back.

Go with God, David. And may angels sing you to your rest.

Chapter 4

Sally had regained her composure, but her glance was hostile when her brother's new wife emerged. Face expressionless as marble, Lady Jocelyn dug into her reticule and removed one of her cards. "Here is my direction. Let me know when . . . anything changes, or if there is something I can do that will make your brother more comfortable. Blankets, medicines . . . Perhaps I could hire private nurses for him?"

Reluctantly Sally accepted the card since there would have to be some future dealings with the witch, but she snapped, "David needs *nothing* from you."

"As you wish." After a fond farewell for Richard—Lady Jocelyn was much more pleasant to men than women—she swept away with her retinue.

Sally muttered between clenched teeth, "Slut."

Unshocked by her language, the captain merely gave a tired smile. "She isn't, you know. She's a woman trying to find a solution in a world made by men. In the same circumstances, you might do exactly the same."

"I doubt it," Sally said, glad that her ladyship was

gone, and good riddance. Noticing Richard's drained expression, she added, "It's time you rested. I'm sure you've been up much longer than your doctor would approve."

"I haven't listened to him yet, why should I start now? But I am ready to lie down." He regarded her seriously. "Sally, think carefully about what you say to David. He's pleased about this marriage. Don't spoil it for him."

She flushed at the warning. "I suppose I deserve that. Don't worry, I won't distress him. I'll go in now and let him know that I haven't murdered his lady wife."

"He'll be relieved to hear that." The captain pushed himself forward from the wall and headed down the hall toward his own room.

Schooling her face, Sally entered her brother's room. David seemed asleep, but his eyes opened when she sat down beside him. "Forgive me, little hedgehog?"

Her heart nearly melted with anguish when he used the old nickname. "Of course I do. It was just such a shock to come here and find a wedding." She lifted the laudanum bottle. "You must be due for another dose of medicine."

David accepted the spoonful of laudanum gratefully, then relaxed into the pillows with a weary sigh. "You're here early today."

"The children's godmother came this morning and whisked them off on some expedition, so I was free unexpectedly." In a voice carefully purged of accusation, she continued, "Why didn't you tell me you were getting married?"

David smiled with a hint of his old mischief. "Because if I'd told you in advance, you would have given me a lecture on how capable you are of taking care of yourself and said it was quite unnecessary for me to provide for you. Am I right?"

She had to laugh. "You know me too well."

His voice faded as he slid toward sleep. "I know you're very capable, but you're still my little sister. I'm glad to know that you'll have five hundred a year."

Five hundred a year! Sally stared at her dozing brother. No one had mentioned how large the annuity was. Whatever else the arrogant Lady Jocelyn might be, it wasn't stingy. Five hundred pounds was five times Sally's annual salary, and she was reckoned a very well-paid female. She'd be able to live in considerable comfort, and even some style.

Would she still want to teach? Sally enjoyed her job, and the Launcestons were the best employers she'd ever had. Still, five hundred pounds a year would give her choices. She could travel. Buy a cottage in a village and live a life of leisure.

Freedom at the cost of David's life. She shook her head, reminding herself that he would die anyway. At least this way, Lady Jocelyn would have five hundred pounds a year less to waste on frivolity.

Taking comfort in the thought, she dug into her shapeless brocade bag for her knitting. After mending all of David's clothing, she'd gone on to knit four pairs of gloves, three pairs of socks, and two scarves during the hours she sat in the hospital. Though she wasn't fond of knitting, she'd found it impossible to concentrate on reading when David labored for breath beside her. At least the needles kept her hands busy.

Glumly she contemplated the current sock. Three stitches had been dropped, and it would take her half an hour just to repair the damage. Well, she had the rest of the day, and David would sleep most of it. She glanced at the bone-thin figure, then turned away with a shudder. Had it only been two weeks since he had been brought back to London? It seemed that she had been coming to this grim hospital forever, and every day he seemed more frail, until it was hard to understand how he still lived.

Sometimes, God help her, she wished it was over, so she could surrender to pure, primitive grief. Other times she wondered how she would learn of his death. Would she be with him? Would Richard send her a message? Or would she arrive and find her brother's bed empty, and know the worst?

Sally realized that the yarn had broken in her hands. Fingers shaking, she knotted the strand together again. *You must be calm. David doesn't need to deal with your grief on top of his pain.*

She looked around at the dark, ugly room, hearing the distant sounds of suffering men, smelling the countless wretched odors of a hospital. It was a poor spot to die, but she supposed any place was.

That afternoon Jocelyn joined her aunt for tea in the sunny parlor that was Laura Kirkpatrick's special retreat. After they had been served and were private, she announced, "You'll be pleased to hear that my marriage problem has been solved. Aunt Elvira can resign herself to struggling along on Willoughby's present income."

Laura set down her cup, her face lighting up. "You've accepted one of your suitors? Which one? There's just enough time for the reading of the banns, but it will have to be a small ceremony, I fear."

"Better than that." Jocelyn handed her aunt a sheet of paper. "The deed is done. Behold, my marriage lines."

"What on earth?" Laura looked at the paper and became very still. When she glanced up, her face showed the beginning of anger. "What is the meaning of this?"

"Isn't it obvious?" Jocelyn had to pause a moment, remembering her last sight of David, before she could continue. "I found a dying man, and in return for a substantial consideration, he did me the honor of making me his wife."

"But you've never even met David Lancaster!"

"I got the idea when I was visiting Richard Dalton, and he mentioned Major Lancaster's condition," she explained. "It's perfectly reasonable. Major Lancaster's sister will be provided for, and I have fulfilled the conditions of Father's will. Richard wasn't shocked when I suggested it, and neither was Major . . . my husband."

Lady Laura's eyes flashed with fury. "They are men who have lived on the edge of death for years. Of course they will see things differently than society will!"

Jocelyn's mouth tightened. "Is that why you're concerned—because of what others will say? I had thought you were above such things. Besides, most of the fashionable world will be amused if the story becomes known. They'll laugh and think me very clever."

Spots of color stood out on Laura's cheeks, but her voice was level again. "I can't deny that what people say is of concern to me. The Kendal family has already had more than its share of scandal."

As Jocelyn paled at that reminder of the past, her aunt continued implacably, "But what truly bothers me is that you are using a fine man's death for your own selfish ends. Why didn't you discuss this with me first?"

Jocelyn tried to maintain calm, but the fear that her aunt would despise her was overwhelming. "You didn't want to know what I was going to do!" she cried, her voice breaking. "Please, Aunt Laura, don't be angry with me. I wouldn't have married him if I'd known how it would upset you. It was an idea of impulse. Major Lancaster welcomed my proposal, and then it was too late to withdraw. I thought we would both benefit, with no harm done. Please . . . please try to understand."

Lady Laura sighed, her anger fading into disappointment. "Perhaps I wouldn't be so upset if your impulse had fallen on a stranger rather than a man I know and respect. David deserves better than to be used so . . . so carelessly."

"Perhaps you're right," Jocelyn whispered, aching at her aunt's disapproval. "But the deed is done and cannot be undone."

Lady Laura rose to her feet. "Tomorrow morning I shall go down to Kennington. It's time to open the house and prepare for Andrew's return from the

Continent." A trace of acid appeared in her normally soft voice. "Now that you're a married woman, you no longer need me as a chaperon."

"I suppose not." Jocelyn gazed at a cake that she'd mangled into crumbs.

Her aunt paused in the door. "I'll be back in a fortnight or two, and no doubt I'll be over my anger by then." After offering that olive branch, she left.

Shaking, Jocelyn sank into her chair. As if the last day hadn't been difficult enough, now she'd alienated her dearest friend, the woman who was the closest thing she had to a mother. She saw her deed through her aunt's eyes, and felt bitterly ashamed. Once again, as so often in her life, she'd got everything wrong.

Well, there was no help for it. She must lie in the bed she had made, even if it wasn't a conventional marriage bed.

As she searched for something to cheer herself, she recalled that the Parkingtons were holding an informal ball this evening. Not too large and with most guests well-known to Jocelyn, it was exactly the sort of event she liked best.

It would be good not to spend the evening wondering how soon she would become a widow.

The gathering at the Parkingtons' house was small, since most of fashionable society had already left London for their country estates. Yet despite Jocelyn's anticipation, she found herself restless, bored by conversations that seemed frivolous compared to the stark realities of the military hospital.

Then a latecomer arrived, and she inhaled sharply,

her pulse accelerating when she saw that it was Rafael Whitbourne, the Duke of Candover. Just looking at him made her feel better. It wasn't only that he was very good-looking, although he was. What she found irresistibly attractive was the knowledge of how very well they would suit each other.

As she chatted with other guests, Jocelyn monitored Candover's progress as he worked his way around the ballroom. She knew better than to put herself in his path. As a handsome bachelor duke who was rich beyond the dreams of avarice, he'd been pursued by countless females, which had made him justifiably cynical. However, she had a title and fortune of her own and didn't need his. They were perfect for each other. If Jocelyn was to win him, it would have to be because of genuine attraction and a mutual recognition of compatibility.

Her patience was rewarded when Candover sought her out after the small orchestra started playing dance music. "Lady Jocelyn," he said with obvious pleasure. "I'm glad to see that you're still in town. Will you honor me with this waltz?"

"Only if you promise not to step on my toes again," she said teasingly.

"That last time wasn't my fault," he protested, his gray eyes laughing. "When that drunken boor barreled into me, the wonder is that we both didn't end up on the floor in a most undignified tangle."

"I found it quite remarkable how you kept your balance while at the same time leaving the boor peacefully unconscious on the floor where he could do no more damage. How did you manage that?" she asked as he led her onto the dance floor.

"I merely assisted him in a direction he was already going." The music began, and he drew her into waltz position. "Learning how to defend oneself is one of the hidden benefits of an Eton education."

The pleasure she took in his company reminded her why she had refused other suitors and justified the painful ceremony earlier in the day. As they exchanged pleasantries, she studied his face, admiring the firmness of his features, the clarity of those cool gray eyes. He was known as Rafe by the handful of people who were his intimates, but she would never dare call him that without an invitation. Perhaps someday.

She thought she was laughing and talking in her normal manner, so it was a surprise when Candover asked, "Forgive me, Lady Jocelyn, but you appear rather out of sorts today. Is something wrong?"

It was the inquiry of a friend, not a mere acquaintance. Glad to see proof that her interest was not entirely one-sided, she replied, "It was an odd sort of day. I got married this morning and have not yet accustomed myself to the fact."

Surprise showed through his usual detachment. "Indeed? I hadn't heard that you were contemplating the fatal step." His gaze became ironic. "Surely the Parkingtons' house is an odd place for a honeymoon."

The time had come to inform him of her circumstances, and her availability. "It's not generally known, but my father made the most ridiculous will, with the condition that I marry by the age of twenty-five or be largely disinherited."

His brows rose. "How medieval."

"Quite, especially when you consider that we were

on the best of terms. But there was nothing to be done about it, so this morning I contracted a marriage of convenience." A note of bitterness entered her voice. "I had hoped to have a real marriage."

"If by that you mean a love match, you know how rare that is in our order, and how seldom it is successful," he said dryly.

"I didn't mean a love match in the sense of being so besotted that one has no true sense of the other person's character," she explained. "There should be attraction, of course, but from all I've heard, that fades in time for even the most infatuated lovers. Far better to base a marriage on respect and mutual affection. A partnership of friendship and shared values and goals."

"How very reasonable of you," he said, intrigued. "I wish more women had such a sensible attitude. It would make marriage a far more appealing state."

From the approval in his eyes, she knew that she had just risen several steps in his estimation. If he was to marry, it would be to a woman like her, who would make his life run smoothly rather than causing painful, emotional scenes.

But marriage was merely a future possibility. Thinking of her current state, she said with a sigh, "I have had to settle for much less than I wanted." She glanced up at him through her lashes. "I will have to look elsewhere for more rewarding relationships."

"Your husband will not object?" he asked, gaze intent.

"He will not," Jocelyn said firmly. In the arms of the man she wanted to marry, she had no desire to think of the soldier who had touched her life so briefly. "Our marriage is nothing but a mutual convenience."

The waltz came to an end. Both of them lowered their arms from waltz position, but instead of moving from the floor, they stayed still, caught in a moment of acute mutual awareness. Candover's gaze went over her with great deliberation, lingering on her low neckline and the curves visible through the gauzy summer gown.

Jocelyn recognized his scrutiny for a subtle, wordless advance. The implications were almost frightening. With a gesture, a faint withdrawal, she could let him know that she had no interest in proceeding further. Instead, she caught his gaze and smiled.

Expert in the ways of dalliance, he recognized her silent signal. With a slow, devastating smile, he escorted her from the dance floor. "I'm leaving London in the morning, but I look forward to calling on you when I return to town in September."

She would be a widow by then and free to explore the promise in his eyes, though that freedom was coming at a higher price than she had expected. Suppressing the painful thought of the dying major, she replied, "I shall await that with anticipation."

With a last, intimate glance, he withdrew. To dance with her twice in a row would draw attention. Instead, there was a tacit agreement between them that left her breathless with excitement. Finally, the only man she wanted was seeing her as a woman, and all because she was now married.

Coolly planning an affair made her uncomfortable, and she wasn't naïve enough to think his plans went beyond an affair. But she strongly suspected that it would take intimacy for him to fully appreciate how perfect they were for each other.

If she lost her gamble as well as her maidenhead—well, she wasn't made of stone. Though it would hurt badly to have him decide he liked her well enough for his bed but not well enough to be his duchess, there would be compensations. She had a normal woman's curiosity about passion, and she found Candover so attractive that she would surely enjoy what he had to teach.

Would he be horrified or intrigued when he learned she was a virgin? She assumed he was clever enough to understand the implications of her spending her wedding night alone at a private ball. Her hope was that he would be pleased.

The two months until September stretched endless and empty before her.

Chapter 5

Sally tossed restlessly all night after she left the hospital, angry at the memory of the cool society beauty who had so casually used and discarded her brother. Even during her lessons with the Launceston children the next morning, her mind continued to churn.

As she left for her daily trip to the hospital, she realized she had been jolted out of her fatalism. For the last fortnight she had passively accepted the doctors' verdict on David's fate. Now her anger had given her a resolve not to give in so tamely. David was in no condition to fight for his life, but she was. If there was anything or anyone who might offer a chance of recovery, she would pursue it.

Before going to her brother's room, Sally sought out her brother's physician, Dr. Ramsey, determined to question every possibility. Dr. Ramsey was a solid man with an air of permanent fatigue. Unlike many of his colleagues, he was willing to admit the limits of his knowledge.

He blinked warily behind his spectacles when Sally caught him between patients, knowing from experience how persistent she could be. "Yes, Miss Lancaster?" he said with a rising inflection that implied he had very little time to talk.

"Dr. Ramsey, isn't there anything more that can be done for my brother? He's fading away in front of my eyes. Surely there must be something you can do."

The physician removed his spectacles and polished them. "Major Lancaster's case puzzles me. He's holding on to life with remarkable tenacity, but there is so little that can be done in cases of paralysis." He set his spectacles firmly on his nose. "Besides the paralysis, I suspect that he has sustained internal injuries which are beyond our present power to heal. All we can do is make his last days as comfortable as possible."

Sally caught his wandering eye before he could escape. "I don't wish to criticize your care. I know you've done everything you can, and I am profoundly grateful. Still—is there any physician or surgeon in London who might have a different approach, perhaps something that is radical by the usual standards? There is little to lose."

Dr. Ramsey nodded. After a long moment of thought, he said, "There's a mad Scot called Ian Kinlock at St. Bartholomew's Hospital. I hear that he just returned from Belgium and several weeks doing surgery after Waterloo. Very eccentric, but he's done some remarkable things."

The physician glanced at Sally's modest dress. "He's qualified as both physician and surgeon, and his fees for private consultations are very high. Apparently he charges people with money a great deal, then gives free care to gutter scum. Quite, quite mad.

You'll never persuade him to call on a patient at the York Hospital."

"I have just come into some money unexpectedly. We shall see."

She turned and strode down the hall. Behind her, she heard Dr. Ramsey mutter, "God help Ian Kinlock." She didn't dignify the comment by looking back.

Her mind was spinning as she walked to David's room. Consulting a new surgeon was grasping at the thinnest of straws, but as long as there was any hope at all, it was worth trying. Besides, she liked the idea of spending Lady Jocelyn's money in a way that might benefit David. St. Bartholomew's Hospital was one of the oldest and busiest in London, and she recalled vaguely that it was a center for surgery. It was near St. Paul's Cathedral, and she would need to hire a hackney coach. . . .

Distracted, she almost collided with a hefty young man in a powdered wig and blue livery outside David's door. After a moment she recognized him as the footman who had been present at the mockery of a wedding the day before. Morgan, his name was.

"Come to see if your mistress's husband is dead yet?" she asked caustically. She felt ashamed of herself when the young man flushed scarlet. He was too easy a target; it wasn't fair to blame him for Lady Jocelyn's want of conduct.

"I came to take my brother home, Miss Lancaster," he said stiffly. "Lady Jocelyn asked me to inquire after Major Lancaster while I was here."

"Your brother is also a patient?" Sally asked in a more conciliatory tone.

"He was a corporal in the light dragoons, miss. Lady Jocelyn has offered him a position in her household and the chance to convalesce in her home," Morgan explained. "She sent her own carriage to make the trip as easy as possible."

The footman's words were intended to demonstrate his mistress's kindness to a woman who clearly did not value her ladyship. Instead, they sowed the seeds of an idea that burst instantly into full, radiant flower. This ghastly hospital was enough to make a well person ill, and she would have removed David if possible. But she couldn't take him to her employers or have afforded to hire lodgings and servants to care for him.

Now, however, an alternative had presented itself. Under English law, David owned the no-doubt luxurious house in Upper Brook Street that the Lady Jocelyn called home. The witch had no right to refuse him admittance. Sally would take her brother to Upper Brook Street, and if her unwanted sister-in-law objected, she'd bring the place down around her ladyship's shell-pink ears.

"How convenient that you have brought a coach," she purred. "We can use it to move Major Lancaster to Lady Jocelyn's house."

Morgan looked first startled, then alarmed. "I don't know, miss. Her ladyship asked me to inquire after him, but she said nothing about bringing him home."

Fixing the hapless footman with the quelling stare she used on her students, Sally said, "No doubt she was worried about moving him. However, I just spoke with my brother's physician, and he agreed that there was nothing to lose by a change." Which wasn't exactly what Ramsey had said, but she'd sort that out later.

Since Morgan still looked unconvinced, Sally moved in with the killing stroke. "After all, they are married. What was hers is now his. Surely dear Lady Jocelyn cannot wish her husband to stay in this, this"—she gestured eloquently—"unwholesome place."

"It's true that her ladyship and the major seemed very fond," Morgan said uncertainly. "And heaven knows my brother can't wait to leave this hospital. You're right, 'tis not a healthy place." He furrowed his brows before giving a decisive nod. "I'll move my brother to the carriage, then be back for Major Lancaster with a litter and someone to help me carry it. Will you pack his things, miss?"

"Of course." As she watched him leave, Sally marveled at how easily he'd been convinced. She would have thought he'd be more wary of his spoiled mistress's wrath.

She sought out Dr. Ramsey again. That gentleman agreed gloomily that if the trip from Belgium hadn't killed the major, a journey across London probably wouldn't, and if it did, that would just be hastening the inevitable.

Ignoring the doctor's dire predictions, Sally returned to her brother's room. "Good news, David. Lady Jocelyn's carriage is here, and I have Dr. Ramsey's permission to move you to her home. I'm sure that you'll be more comfortable there than in the hospital."

"She wants me to stay in her house?" he said with pleased surprise. "That was not part of our bargain. It's most kind of her."

The idea that his "wife" cared enough to send for him made David look so happy that Sally didn't attempt to correct his misapprehension. Instead, she vowed that Lady Jocelyn would make him feel welcome if Sally had to hold a pistol to her head.

"I shan't miss this place." David's tired gaze flickered over the drab walls. "Except for Richard."

"He can visit you now that he's getting around so well. I'm sure he'll welcome an excuse to get out. I'll give him your new direction before I leave." She began packing her brother's belongings into the box that had accompanied him from Belgium.

After finishing that, she lifted the bottle of laudanum. "Shall I give you a double dose? The trip is bound to be uncomfortable."

"Too right. I think I'd prefer not to be aware of what is going on." It was one of the few references he'd made to what Sally knew was constant pain. She uttered a fervent prayer that the carriage ride would not injure him further. If the strain severed his fragile hold on life, she would never forgive herself.

Hugh Morgan rode on the outside of the carriage, but the vehicle was still crowded with Sally, David, and the shy, crutch-wielding corporal jammed in together. Though Morgan had obtained planks and blankets and rigged a pallet across one side of the vehicle to hold the semiconscious major, Sally still winced as they jolted on every cobblestone between Belgravia and Mayfair.

When they reached Upper Brook Street, she said, "Please wait here until I've informed Lady Jocelyn that her husband has arrived."

She marched up the marble steps and wielded the massive dolphin-shaped knocker. When a butler opened the door, she said, "I am Miss Lancaster, Lady Jocelyn's sister-in-law. Please take me to her ladyship, so I can ask her where she wishes her husband to be carried."

Husband? The butler's eyes bulged; it was a tribute to Hugh Morgan's discretion that none of the servants had heard of the marriage. Pulling himself together, he said, "I believe Lady Jocelyn is in the morning room. If you will follow me . . ."

The house was every bit as luxurious as Sally had expected, a perfect background for its flawless mistress. She glanced around, hoping to find evidence of vulgarity, but to her regret, the house was furnished with impeccable taste.

Refusing to be daunted by the towering, three-story high foyer, Sally set her jaw pugnaciously as the butler ushered her into the morning room. Lady Jocelyn sat at a writing table, her daffodil-colored gown a perfect complement to her warm chestnut coloring. Sitting on the desk was a vase of flowers and a tawny cat. It was no plump cozy tabby, but an elegant, thin-boned feline of obviously aristocratic origins. In Sally's jaundiced view, the creature looked as expensive and unlovable as its mistress.

The butler said, "Lady Jocelyn, your 'sister-in-law' wishes to speak with you." His inflection managed to imply simultaneously that Sally was an impostor, and that if she was indeed genuine, Lady Jocelyn owed her faithful retainer an explanation.

Jocelyn looked up with surprise. It was a rude shock to see an angry young woman intruding on her, a hostile reminder of yesterday's unhappy events. "Thank you, Dudley. That will be all."

Jocelyn's tone produced instant obedience. The butler beat a hasty retreat.

"Miss Lancaster. What an unexpected pleasure," she said coolly. With a sudden deep pang, she wondered if Sally had come to say that her brother had succumbed to his wounds. No, she was unlikely to deliver the news in person. Probably she just wanted to harangue her unwanted sister-in-law again. "What brings you here today?"

The surly creature scowled. "I'm bringing David to your house."

"What the devil are you talking about?" Jocelyn asked, startled.

If Miss Lancaster stuck her jaw out any farther, she was in danger of dislocating it. "A wife's property becomes her husband's on marriage. If you don't let David stay here, I'll . . . I'll make him leave all of your property to the Army Widows' and Orphans' Fund. He will if I ask him to."

Jocelyn could feel her hands curling into fists. She hadn't felt such a desire to visit physical violence on someone since her nursery days. "What a touching example of sibling devotion. However, your brother himself suggested that my lawyer draw up a document waiving any claims against my estate."

"He waived his rights?" Sally said in dismay.

"He did indeed. Obviously your brother inherited all of the Lancaster family honor, as well as any claim to looks." Jocelyn reached for the bell cord. "If you do not leave in the next thirty seconds, I will have my servants remove you."

Sally's face crumpled. "Lady Jocelyn, I know that you don't like me any better than I like you. But haven't you ever had anyone in your life that you loved?"

Jocelyn paused, wary. "How is that to the point?"

"If you had a choice, would you leave someone you loved to die in that vile place?"

Jocelyn winced as she remembered the hospital's grimness.

Seeing her reaction, Sally said, "You wanted to know if David could be made more comfortable. Well, he will be more comfortable here, and surely you have enough space and servants that he won't be a burden. If you want to bar me from visiting, so be it. If you ask me to return the entire settlement, I will." Her voice broke. "But please, I beg of you, don't send David back to the hospital. Even if he has no legal right, surely you have a moral obligation to your husband."

"Send him back—you mean he's here *now*? Dear God, are you trying to kill him?" Jocelyn asked with horror, remembering how frail he'd been the day before.

"He's in your carriage and has survived the trip. So far." Sally said no more, but the implication that a longer journey might drive the last nail into his coffin hung in the air.

Jocelyn gazed down at the ring he'd placed on her finger, exerting himself to the limit of his strength to ensure that he didn't fumble. *Till death us do part.*

Given David's condition and Sally's vehement rejection of any further aid, it had never occurred to her to bring him to Cromarty House. But her unpleasant sister-in-law was right. No matter how disruptive and painful it would be to have him here, he was her husband. She owed him this. Moreover, she found that she wanted to do anything that would ease his final days.

She yanked the bell cord. Dudley appeared so quickly that he must have had his ear pressed to the keyhole. "My husband is in the carriage outside. He is very ill and will need to be carried in. Take him to the blue room."

After the butler left, Sally said brokenly, "Thank you, Lady Jocelyn."

"I'm not doing this for your sake, but for his." Turning to her writing desk, she lifted a jingling leather bag and tossed it to Sally. "I was going to have this delivered, but since you're here, I'll give it to you in person. Your first quarter's income."

Sally gasped at how heavy the bag was. As she tugged at the drawstring to look inside, Jocelyn said tartly, "You needn't count the money. It's all there—one hundred twenty-five pounds in gold."

Sally's head snapped up. "Not thirty pieces of silver?"

Jocelyn said softly, each word carved in ice, "Of course not. Silver is for selling people. Since I was buying, I paid in gold."

As Sally teetered on the verge of explosion, Jocelyn continued, "You may come and go as you please. There is a small room adjoining your brother's. I shall have it made up for your use for . . . for as long as you need it. Does he have a personal servant?" When Sally shook her head, Jocelyn said, "I shall assign him one, plus any other nursing care he requires."

Sally turned to go, then turned back to say hesitantly, "There is one other thing. He thought it was your idea to bring him here, and that pleased him very much. I hope you will not disabuse him of the notion."

At the limits of her patience, Jocelyn snapped, "You shall just have to hope that my manners aren't so lacking that I will torment a dying man. Now will you remove yourself from my presence?"

Sally beat a hasty retreat, shaking in reaction. Any doubts she might have had that Lady Jocelyn was a brass-hearted virago had been laid to rest. But surely she would at least be courteous to David, who seemed to cherish the illusion that she was a good person. Discovering the witch's real character would distress him.

Chapter 6

It took only a quarter-hour to get the major and his few belongings settled in a sumptuous room with a diagonal view of Hyde Park. It appeared to be the best guest chamber, and Sally again conceded, with enormous reluctance, that Lady Jocelyn did not do things by half-measures. David was white-faced with pain from the move, and Sally was grateful that she had carried the bottle of laudanum over in her knitting bag. When the footman had left, she gave her brother another dose of opium.

Burying her own feelings about Lady Jocelyn, Sally said, "Though your wife was good enough to offer me a room here, I think it's best that I sleep at the Launcestons'. But I'll come every afternoon, as I did at the hospital, and Richard said he'll call tomorrow." She straightened the covers over his thin frame. "Time for you to get some sleep. The trip must have been exhausting."

David smiled faintly. "True, but I'm fine now, little hedgehog."

"Now that you're settled, I'm going to St. Bartholomew's Hospital. Dr. Ramsey said there's a very fine surgeon there, someone who might be able to help you."

"Perhaps," her brother said, unimpressed.

She noticed that his eyes kept drifting to the door. Was he expecting his so-called wife to visit him? Hoping that Lady Jocelyn was well-bred enough to do that much, Sally said, "I'll visit again later." She bent to kiss his forehead, then left.

Hugh Morgan was approaching the blue room. "Her ladyship has assigned me to be the major's servant," he said ingenuously. "It's a real honor."

"I'm sure you will suit him very well." As Sally left, she felt unwilling amusement at the perfect poetic justice Lady Jocelyn had visited on Morgan, the accidental instrument for bringing the major to these hallowed precincts. Caring for a gravely injured man would not be easy. Luckily, the footman seemed like a kind, conscientious young man. David would be in good hands.

Now to find the mad Scot at St. Bartholomew's.

It took Jocelyn a good half-hour to calm down. When her appalling sister-in-law arrived, she'd been admiring the flowers Candover had sent that morning. The note read only *Until September*, and was signed with a boldly scrawled *C*.

Holding the note and remembering that wordless but potent interchange between them, she'd been lost in dreams. Perhaps in the enigmatic duke she would find what she had always sought, and never dared believe she would find.

Then that unspeakable female had blundered in with her threats and her emotional blackmail. Except for Sally Lancaster's vivid green eyes, there was no resemblance to David, who was a gentleman to the core.

Jocelyn's mouth curved involuntarily as she remembered her remark about buying the major with gold. Aunt Laura would have gone into a spasm if she had heard her niece say anything so unforgivably vulgar, but Sally Lancaster had a genius for bringing out the worst in Jocelyn's nature.

Jocelyn sighed, her amusement gone, and absently scratched between Isis's ears. How could she have thought getting involved with someone's life and death would be simple? She would rather not think of the major's imminent death, and she certainly had not intended to witness it, but that could not be avoided now.

Whenever she thought of David Lancaster, she wanted to cry. It was like a candle going out, reducing the amount of light in the world.

She pulled her mind back to practical considerations. Fortunately Morgan had welcomed the opportunity to serve the major. The footman had a good heart and a steady hand, and Jocelyn had heard from Marie that he aspired to be a valet. Now he could get some real experience.

Summoning the butler again, she said, "Order two wagon loads of straw and have it spread on the street outside. Make sure that it's layered thickly—I don't want Major Lancaster disturbed by the sound of traffic. Also, tell Cook to prepare food suitable for an invalid." If the major could be induced to eat.

After Dudley left, she ordered herself to be more patient with Sally Lancaster, since it would be impossible to avoid her sister-in-law entirely. Sally's irritability was understandable given that she was devoted to her brother and had no one else to care about. With her looks and disposition, she probably never would again.

Jocelyn did not even bother feeling guilty for the uncharitable thought.

Sally had believed that the York had inured her to hospitals, but St. Bartholomew's seemed ten times as crowded and twenty times as noisy. It had been founded in the Middle Ages by monks and appeared not to have been cleaned since. Bart's treated many of London's indigent and a clamorous, odorous lot they were.

Nonetheless, the hospital trained some of the country's best surgeons. As she passed through endless crowded wards, she supposed that was because the surgeons had so many patients to practice on.

It took half an hour of walking and asking questions to locate anyone who knew anything about Ian Kinlock. At first she was told that he wasn't in the hospital because "this was 'is day for the swells." Another listener chimed in that he'd seen the doctor 'imself that very day.

Another half hour of searching brought her to the dingy little room where Kinlock was alleged to be found after he'd done his day's work in the cutting ward. She settled down to wait on an uncomfortable wooden chair. A jumble of books, papers, and anatomical sketches covered the top of the battered desk and bookcase, with more tottering in stacks on the floor. Brilliant Kinlock might be, but neat he definitely wasn't.

After an hour of increasing boredom, Sally's basic fondness for order asserted itself, and she began to straighten the books and papers. A small, grubby towel that had fallen behind the desk was pressed into service as a dust rag. Remembering how her scholarly father had felt about people who re-arranged his books, she took great care not to shift anything to a new location. Nonetheless, simply squaring up the piles neatly and removing the dust did wonders for the appearance of the office.

After tidying the desk, she started on the bookcase, working from top to bottom. On a cluttered middle shelf, her fingers brushed what felt like a china mug. She pulled it out and found herself holding a hollow-eyed, grinning human skull. She gasped and hastily replaced the ghastly relic, rather proud that she hadn't dropped it from shock.

An impatient voice with a definite Scots burr growled from the doorway, "That skull belonged to the last person fool enough to meddle with my office. Are you trying to become a mate to it?"

Sally jumped and spun around, making a sound regrettably close to a squeak. The owner of the voice was a man of middle height with massive shoulders and a blood-splashed smock. His bushy dark brows provided a strong contrast to a thick shock of white hair and added impressively to a scowl that was already first class.

"I . . . I didn't actually move anything from its place," she stammered. "You're Ian Kinlock, the surgeon?"

"Aye. Now get the hell out of my office." He dropped into the desk chair, unlocked one of his drawers, and pulled out a bottle of what looked like whiskey. Ignoring his visitor, he uncorked the bottle, took a long, long draft, and slumped against the chair back with his eyes closed.

When Sally approached, she realized that he was younger than she had first thought, certainly under forty. The hair might be prematurely white, but the lines in his face were from exhaustion, not age, and the compact body had the lean fitness of a man in his prime. "Dr. Kinlock?"

His lids barely lifted to reveal weary blue eyes. "You're still here? Out. Now." He took another pull of whiskey.

"Dr. Kinlock, I want you to examine my brother."

He sighed, then said with an elaborate show of patience, "Miss Whatever-the-devil-your-name is, I have seen over fifty patients today, performed six operations, and just lost two patients in a row under the knife. If your brother was Prinny himself, I would not see him. *Especially* if he were Prinny. For the third and last time, get out, or I will throw you out."

He ran a tired hand through his white hair, adding a smudge of blood to its disarray. Despite his profanity, there was a forceful intelligence about him, and Sally felt a breath of hope. Even more determined to get him to David as soon as possible, she said, "My brother was wounded at Waterloo. He's paralyzed from the waist down, in constant pain, and wasting away like a wraith."

Kinlock's eyes showed only a bare flicker of acknowledgment. "With that kind of injury, he's a dead man. For miracles, try St. Bartholomew's church across the street."

Sally caught his gaze with her own. "Didn't you take an oath, Doctor? To help those who are suffering?"

For a moment she feared that she'd gone too far and the surgeon would murder her on the spot. Then his anger dissolved. "I'll make allowances for the fact that you're concerned about your brother," he said with great gentleness. "I should even be complimented by your touching faith that I might be able to help him. Unfortunately, the amount we know about the human body is so minuscule when compared to the amount we don't know that it's a wonder I can ever help anyone."

She saw the bleakness in his eyes and remembered the two patients who had just died. No wonder he was in a foul mood.

Kinlock took another swig of whiskey, then continued in the same reasonable tone. "Waterloo was fought when? The eighteenth of June? So it's been almost five weeks." He shook his head, talking to himself. "How many bedamned operations did I do over there? And how many men did I lose?"

"You care about your patients," she said quietly. "That's what I want for David—a surgeon who cares passionately."

Scowling, he gulped more whiskey. "With a spinal injury severe enough to cause paralysis, the surprise is that your brother is still alive. Half the bodily functions are destroyed, there are infections and ulceration from lying still too long. A man doesn't survive long like that, and from what I've seen in such cases, it's a mercy when they die. So take my advice: say good-bye to your brother and leave me alone."

He started to turn to his desk, but Sally reached out to touch his sleeve. "Dr. Kinlock, none of those things have happened to my brother. It's just that he is in such pain and is wasting away. Couldn't you just look at him? Please?"

At her words, Kinlock's dark, bushy brows drew together thoughtfully. "A great deal of pain? That's odd, one would expect numbness . . ." He pondered a moment longer, then rattled off a series of medical questions, his gaze sharply analytical.

Sally could answer most of the questions due to her badgering of the doctors at the York Hospital for information.

After ascertaining what David's condition and treatment had been, Kinlock asked, "How much laudanum is your brother taking?"

Sally tried to estimate. "A bottle of Sydenham's every two or three days, I think."

"Bloody hell, no wonder the man can't move! Opium is a marvelous medication, but not without drawbacks." He folded his arms across his chest as he thought. Finally, he said, "I'll come by and examine him tomorrow afternoon."

Her heart leaped. "Could you make it tonight? He's so weak . . ."

"No, I could not. And if you'd want me to after I've put away this much whiskey, you're a fool."

His hands looked steady enough, but she supposed he was right. "Then tomorrow morning, first thing? I'll give you one hundred twenty-five pounds." Reaching through the side slit in her dress to the pocket she wore slung around her waist, Sally pulled out the pouch of gold and handed it to him.

Kinlock whistled softly at the weight of the bag. "You're a determined little thing, aren't you? However, I have patients to see tomorrow morning. Afternoon is the best I can do, and I won't make any promises about the precise hour. Take it or leave it." He tossed the bag back to her.

Stung by the dismissive phrase "little thing," Sally said tartly, "I've always heard surgeons are a crude, profane lot. So good to know that rumor spoke true in this case."

Instead of being insulted, Kinlock gave a crack of laughter, his expression lightening for the first time. "You forgot to mention abrasive, insensitive, and uncultured. That's why surgeons are called mister instead of doctor—we're a low lot, lass, and mind you remember that." He corked his whiskey and set the bottle back on his desk. "By the way, what is your name?"

"Sally Lancaster."

"Aye, ye look like a Sally." His Scots accent was thickening rapidly, probably because of the whiskey. "Write down your brother's direction, and I'll come by tomorrow afternoon. Probably not early."

While Sally wrote the address, Kinlock crossed his arms on the desk, laid his head on them, and promptly fell asleep. She carefully tilted the slip of paper against his whiskey bottle, sure it would be found in that position.

Before leaving, she studied the slumbering figure with bemusement. What the devil did a Sally look like? A mad Scot indeed, abrasive, insensitive, and all the rest. But for the first time in weeks, she felt a whisper of hope that David might have a future.

* * *

Lady Jocelyn threw her quill across the desk in exasperation, leaving a scattering of ink blots on her account book. Isis raised a contemptuous nose at her lack of self-control. All afternoon she'd tried to attend to correspondence and monthly accounts, but she was unable to concentrate for thinking of the man lying upstairs in the blue room.

She rested her chin on her palm and thought how ridiculous it was to be so shy about visiting him. After all, she was his hostess. Lord, his wife! His prickly sister had gone out and not returned and had reportedly turned down the offer of a bedchamber, for which Jocelyn was thankful. At least the wretched female wasn't entirely lacking in sense. If they had to meet daily over the breakfast table, there would be murder done.

"You're quite right, Isis. Since I'm not getting any work done anyhow, I might as well check that the major is comfortable." Or alive, for that matter. Jocelyn pushed herself away from the desk. "Do you think he'd like some flowers?" The cat yawned luxuriously. "So pleased you agree with me. I'll go cut some in the garden."

After gathering and arranging an armful of cream and yellow roses, with some greens for contrast, Jocelyn took the vase of flowers up to the blue room. She knocked lightly on the door, entering when there was no response. The major appeared to be asleep, so she set the flowers on the table by the bed, then turned to study him.

In repose, his face reminded her of a carved medieval knight resting on a marble tomb in the village church at Charlton. Gaunt, noble, remote. His pallor was intensified by a dark shadow of beard. Moved by some impulse of tenderness, she reached out to touch his cheek, feeling the rasp of bristles beneath her fingers.

Disconcertingly, his eyes opened. "Good day, Lady Jocelyn."

Hastily she dropped her hand, her fingers tingling. "Good day. Have you been well taken care of?"

"Very. It was kind of you to invite me here."

With that pleasure in his eyes, she could not have disabused him of the idea, even if Sally Lancaster hadn't warned her. Still, innate honesty compelled her to say, "Most of the credit belongs to your sister. It was she who thought of asking your doctor if it was safe to move you."

"Doubtless Ramsey said that it really didn't matter one way or the other." His gaze circled the room with its high molded ceiling and silk-clad walls. "Your house is an infinitely pleasanter place to die than the hospital."

She pulled a chair up to his bedside and sat so that their faces were nearly level. "How can you be so calm, to speak of your death as if it were a change in the weather?"

He gave the impression of shrugging, though he scarcely moved. "When you've spent enough time soldiering, death *is* like a change in the weather. I've been on borrowed time for years. I never really expected to make old bones."

"Your experience goes far beyond my understanding," she said quietly.

"We are all products of our experience. Mine just

happens to be rather melodramatic," he said absently, for most of his attention was on Lady Jocelyn. With the afternoon sun sculpting her perfect features, she was exquisite. Her eyes, a delicate golden brown with green flecks, entranced him, and he found he was a little less resigned to dying than before.

With a pang, he realized that he would have liked to meet and court this lady when he was well and whole. But even then, his circumstances would never have made him a suitable mate for a woman of her station.

There was a glimmer of tears on her cheeks. He found that by concentrating all his strength, he could lift his hand and brush them away, his fingertips lingering on the rose-petal softness of her skin. "Don't weep for me, my lady. If you remember me at all, I would rather you did with a smile."

"I will not forget you, David—I can promise that." The tears didn't entirely disappear, but she did smile, raising her hand to cover his. "It's so strange to think that three days ago we had never met. Now, there is a . . . a unique connection between us. I had thought a marriage of convenience was just a matter of words spoken and papers signed, but it's more than that, isn't it?"

"It has been for me." Too tired to hold his arm up any longer, he let it rest on the bed. Her hand followed, fingers twining his. There was an intimacy in her clasp that warmed his heart. He wished he had had the strength to touch the shining hair, to see if it felt as silky as it looked. That would be high romance, given that no other part of his body was capable of responding. "I am only sorry to be disturbing your peace."

"Perhaps it's time my peace was disturbed. Too much tranquillity can't be good for the soul." She stood, releasing his hand, to his regret.

Her sweet musical voice took on a businesslike note. "Is Hugh Morgan acceptable to you as a servant? If not, I'll find another."

"Perfectly acceptable. I don't mean to be a demanding guest, or to overstay my welcome."

She bit her lip. "If there is anything you wish, you have only to ask. Do you object to my visiting you?"

Amused that she could imagine such a thing, he asked, "Why should I object?"

"The impropriety . . ."

He laughed at the absurdity of that. After a startled moment, she joined in. "That was silly of me, wasn't it? There can be no impropriety between husband and wife."

"Your reputation is quite safe. Even if we weren't married, I'm in no condition to compromise you." He grinned. "More's the pity."

Jocelyn looked uncertain, then smiled and leaned forward to brush a gossamer kiss on his lips before she turned to leave the room. He admired the grace of her walk and the way the sun burnished her chestnut hair to a shade of red that was more provocative than respectable. Did that color hint of a temper concealed beneath her cool, flawless facade? A delightfully intriguing thought. She was not only a lady, but a woman. One he might have loved.

It was ironic to think that if he hadn't been dying, they never would have met.

* * *

Jocelyn closed the door behind her, then leaned against it, feeling as drained as the major looked. Damn the man, why did she have to like him? Every time she saw him, it got worse. Strange, the feeling of intimacy between them, perhaps because there was no time for polite preliminaries.

There was scarcely any time at all. . . .

Chapter 7

Grateful that Lady Jocelyn was out, Sally spent much of the next afternoon hovering within earshot of the front door as she waited for Ian Kinlock to appear, but the knocker stayed infernally quiet. The hour was well advanced when an impatient rap heralded a visitor. Sally reached the door at the same time the butler did.

Sighing with relief, she saw that it was the surgeon, a black medical bag in one hand. To the butler, she said, "Dr. Kinlock is here to examine my brother, Dudley. I shall take him up."

Kinlock stepped inside. In the elegant town house, he looked as out of place as a dancing bear, and as powerful. As Sally led him upstairs, he said dryly, "Quite an establishment." He scanned her drab garments doubtfully. "Do you live here also?"

She considered explaining, but it was just too complicated. "No. My brother is a guest, and I'm a governess in another household. I spend as much time here as I can."

They entered David's room. From her brother's expression, he didn't anticipate anything worthwhile coming from this visit. He was only enduring another painful examination for her sake. After the introductions, the surgeon said, "Out with you, lassie. I'll examine your brother in private. I already know how you would answer the questions. I want to hear what he will say."

Offended, she opened her mouth to protest, then stopped when David, amused by the surgeon's bluntness, said, "Go on, Sally. I'll manage."

Routed, she spent an endless half-hour pacing around the gallery that circled the open foyer. Not a bad place to exercise in bad weather, she decided, though she rapidly tired of the marble busts of boring gentlemen wearing laurel wreaths. Perhaps she should have asked Richard to stay when he'd visited earlier, but she hadn't even mentioned that Kinlock would be coming, from a superstitious fear that talk would take the magic of hope away.

When Kinlock opened the door, she was on him in a flash. His expression seemed lighter than when he had arrived. Hoping that was a good sign, she said, "Well?"

"Come in, Miss Lancaster. I want to discuss this with both of you."

David was white-lipped from the pain of the examination, but his eyes were alert. Sally crossed to his side, seizing his hand and holding it tightly.

Kinlock began to pace around the room. Sally wondered if the man ever relaxed.

"First, Major Lancaster, there is still a shrapnel fragment in your back, positioned lower than the ones removed after the battle. That is the source of most of the pain." The surgeon scowled from under his bushy brows. "Based on your responses, I think you aren't truly paralyzed. Swelling around the shrapnel would have produced that effect in the days after the injury, but the swelling has abated now."

Startled, David said, "Half my body won't move. If I'm not really paralyzed, what the devil is wrong?"

"I think you're suffering from a combination of factors. The shrapnel certainly isn't insignificant, but I believe that the worst of your problems results from too much laudanum," Kinlock said bluntly. "You were given massive doses to dull the pain of the spinal injuries, which must have been excruciating. The opium helped that, and it also kept you from thrashing around and damaging yourself further, but I believe you're suffering from opium poisoning, and you've probably become addicted as well. Overdosing on laudanum can have many possible side effects—including extreme muscular weakness, and the inability to eat properly."

And David had been living on broth and laudanum for weeks, because the doctors saw no reason for him to limit his intake of opium since he was dying anyhow. "My God. What a vicious circle. The worse my condition, the more they encouraged me to take laudanum to alleviate it, and the more I deteriorated."

"By the time the swelling around the fragment subsided to a point where it might have been possible to move, you were starving and so weakened by pain and opium that you seemed paralyzed. As Paracelsus said, 'Dose alone makes a poison.' " The Scot shook his head dourly. "Or as I say, anything potent enough to heal can also harm."

Trying to grasp the magnitude of what Kinlock

was saying, David asked, "If I stop taking the laudanum, will I recover?"

Kinlock frowned. "It's not quite that simple. Reducing the opium would restore your appetite and save you from starvation, but the pain might be unendurable. If you became strong enough to walk, there's a risk the shrapnel would shift and cause genuine paralysis. Still, even if that happened, you could manage in a wheelchair, and your life would be in no immediate danger. That would be the safest course of treatment."

His last words fell into absolute stillness. Guessing what the surgeon wasn't saying, David said, "You're thinking of a more radical treatment, aren't you?"

"The alternative is an operation. Surgery is always dangerous, and removing the shrapnel might cause the kind of spinal damage it's been assumed you already have. In addition, surgery increases the risk of infection, which could be life-threatening, especially weakened as you are now."

"But if it works?"

"If it works—it's possible that you could be walking in a week."

Sally gasped, her hand tightening on his. David tried to imagine what it would be like to live. To have a future again. Enjoy the robust health he'd taken for granted his whole life. Taking a deep breath, he asked, "How soon could you operate?"

Kinlock's brows drew together as he considered his medical bag. "If you're sure that's what you want, I could do it right now. I have all the instruments I need, and the actual operation wouldn't take long."

David and Sally exchanged glances, communicating wordlessly. The longer surgery was delayed, the weaker he would be. Terrified at the risk but knowing it was his last hope, she gave a stiff nod of agreement.

He turned back to the surgeon. "Then do it. Now."

"Very well." Kinlock hesitated. "For what it's worth, in your situation and knowing the risks, I'd make the same choice."

That was some comfort, David supposed. His gaze went to the bottle on his bedside table as he thought about the strange dreams, the distorted colors and sounds, the haziness he'd lived with since regaining consciousness the day after his injury.

If he'd been strong enough, he would have grabbed the bottle and hurled it across the room. Yet for weeks, he'd welcomed the drug as the one thing that made life bearable. "Ever since I started taking laudanum, I've felt like . . . like a stranger has taken over my mind. I thought that was because I was dying." His mouth twisted. "Opium is a damnably treacherous friend."

"Aye, but you'll need it for the operation," Kinlock cautioned. "After, it might be best to cut back on the dosage gradually. If you stop all at once, you'll have several wretched days of craving, shaking, sweating, and God knows what else."

"Have you had enough experience of opium addicts to know if cutting down slowly makes it easier to stop?"

The surgeon looked troubled. "I honestly don't know, Major. 'Tis a hard habit to break. I knew an addict who tried the gradual approach and failed miserably. Perhaps he would have failed anyhow, or perhaps your method will work better. I really can't say. But you don't have to decide right away. Take a large dose now and continue taking it for the next few days. It would be too much strain on your body to withdraw the drug at the same time as surgery. When you're feeling better will be the time to stop."

Though David nodded, he'd already made up his mind to stop taking the medicine as soon as possible. He swallowed the large dose Sally gave him so that he could endure the surgery. But after Kinlock was done with his cutting, he'd never touch a drop of the wicked stuff again.

Kinlock beckoned Sally into the hall, out of David's hearing. "I'll need two men to hold him down, plus someone to hand me the instruments. I also need towels, sheets, and plenty of hot water and soap for washing up." Seeing her surprise, he explained, "I don't know why, but cleanliness seems to reduce infection."

That made sense to Sally. After all, cleanliness was next to godliness, so it ought to help with surgery. "I'll get everything you need right away."

The surgeon grasped the doorknob to return, but paused. "You said your brother is a guest here. Who owns the house—some kinsman?"

"It belongs to David's wife."

"Wife! Why isn't she here?" Kinlock asked.

"The marriage took place only a couple of days ago and was basically one of convenience. They scarcely know each other. Lady Jocelyn doesn't even know you are here." As she explained, Sally thought for the first time of how the witch would react if David made a miraculous recovery. She felt a surge of unholy glee, despite the horrid possibility that Lady Jocelyn might be permanently connected to the Lancasters.

With a snort for the idiocies of the upper classes, Kinlock reentered the bedroom. Putting away the thought of Lady Jocelyn's reaction, Sally hastened to collect supplies. Her regal ladyship had said to ask for anything required, and by heaven, she would.

Sally was grateful that surgical preparations included covering most of David's body with sheets, except for the small, newly scarred area of his back where the actual incision would be made. Looking at a square of skin made it a little easier to forget that the person she loved most in the world was about to be sliced open. . . .

She cut off the thought and took position by the bed. "I'll assist you with the instruments myself."

"Are you sure, lass? It might be better to have someone not related to the patient. It wouldn't do if you faint or have the vapors."

Her chin came up. "I do not have vapors. Don't worry, I shall manage."

He smiled a little. "Very well." Swiftly he named the instruments and the order they would be used in. The scalpels, probes, and more mysterious tools glittered with cleanliness, and razor-sharp edges.

The two servants who were assisting moved into position, Hugh Morgan at the head of the bed, and the wiry, taciturn coachman at the foot. Queasy but determined, they took hold of David, and the operation began.

Sally was amazed at how swiftly Kinlock worked, deftly cutting and blotting blood. Feeling a little faint, she concentrated on the instruments he asked for, not looking at the surgery again until her head steadied.

After a hideously long interval of meticulous probing of the open wound, he made a small sound of satisfaction. With a delicacy that seemed incongruous for such large, powerful hands, he extracted a small fragment of metal. After dropping it in the basin Sally held out, he muttered, "Now we look around a bit more, just in case."

When he was satisfied, he closed the incision. The servants' assistance was barely needed, for David had hardly moved during the operation, except for a gasp and a convulsive shudder at the initial cut.

With the wound closed, Kinlock said. "Give me that jar, lass."

Sally obeyed, opening the jar for his use. The contents were a disgusting gray-green mass that smelled wretched. To her horror, he smeared some of the oozing material over the wound. How could a man devoted to cleanliness use such nasty-looking stuff? She clamped her jaw shut on her protest. It was too late not to trust him now.

With the operation over, the release of tension was so great that Sally was barely aware of Kinlock putting on a dressing and giving low-voiced instructions to Morgan, who would stay with David. Feeling faint again now that her part was played, Sally went outside and slumped bonelessly onto a sofa set against the gallery wall. Kinlock had been right to warn her that surgery was upsetting. Yet it had been fascinating, too.

When the Scot finally emerged from the sickroom, she glanced up fearfully. "Do . . . do you think that went well?"

He dropped onto the opposite end of the sofa, as weary as the first time she had seen him. She was frightened when he buried his head in his hands, until he looked up with a reassuring smile. "Aye, it went very well. The fragment came out cleanly, and from the tests I just performed, he has normal sensation in his legs. There is still a chance of infection, but God willing, I think he will survive, and probably be as good as new."

Sally hadn't cried when they had told her that David would die, but after hearing that he would live, she dissolved into racking sobs that seemed like they would never end. "Thank God," she said brokenly. "Thank *God*."

Kinlock put an arm around her shoulders as she continued to weep. "There, there, now. You're a braw lassie, and your brother is lucky to have you."

She turned into him, burying her face against his chest. He felt so strong, so solid. A faint scent of fragrant pipe tobacco clung to the wool of his coat, taking her back twenty years to when her father had held her close, safe from the problems of an eight-year-old's world.

The thought made her cry even harder. She had lost her father, then her mother, and almost David, too. But now, by the grace of God and this warm-hearted curmudgeon of a Scot, she would not be alone.

Running out of tears, she finally pulled away from Kinlock and fished a handkerchief from her pocket. "I'm sorry to be such a watering pot. It's just that what you did seems so much like a miracle. I . . . I can't quite believe it."

Kinlock gave a tired smile that made him look surprisingly boyish. "Well, you wanted a miracle. Did you stop at St. Bart's church the other day?"

"No, but I certainly will tomorrow!"

"Be sure you do. Even God likes to be thanked when he's done well."

Sally stood. "Time for me to go back to David. Are there any special instructions about what to do for him during the night?"

"My only instructions are for you to get a good dinner and a solid night's sleep," he said sternly. "Doctor's orders. If you don't start taking better care of yourself, you'll be a patient in no time. You needn't worry about Major Lancaster. Morgan will stay with him, and I'll stop by tomorrow."

She opened her mouth to protest, then had second thoughts. With the tension ended, she was weary to the bone. There was nothing she could do for David that couldn't be done as well by someone else. "Very well."

Kinlock got to his feet and rolled his shoulders, loosening taut muscles. "Would this grand establishment run to whiskey?"

If he wanted to bathe in a tub of the best port, Sally would make sure that his wish was granted. "Shall we go downstairs and find out?"

Kinlock collected his medical bag, and they descended to the drawing room salon. Lady Jocelyn's well-trained butler responded to Sally's tug on the bell cord, speedily producing decanters of whiskey and brandy. She had to give the staff credit. Not once had anyone indicated contempt for her lowly self by so much as the flicker of an eye, though no doubt they had plenty to say in the servants' hall.

Noticing that Ian Kinlock's hands were shaking as he poured himself a whiskey, she asked, "Are you always so strained after surgery?"

He looked a little shamefaced. "Aye. My hands are steady as a rock during an operation, but after I have trouble believing I was foolhardy enough to do it. It's uncommonly difficult to cut into a human body, knowing how hard it is on the patient, but sometimes surgery is the only cure. Like today." He tossed back half his whiskey, then replenished it and settled on a sofa, drinking at a more moderate pace.

Sally sipped her brandy. Very fine, as she'd expected. "What was the awful-smelling dressing that you used?"

Kinlock grinned. "Are you sure you want to know?"

"Yes, please."

"Moldy bread and water."

"Good heavens! After making such a point of clean instruments, you put that filthy stuff on David?" Sally exclaimed, genuinely horrified.

"I know it seems strange, but all over the world there are folk traditions of using moldy materials for dressings," the surgeon explained. "In China, they use moldy soy curd. In eastern and southern Europe, I'm told the peasants keep a loaf in the rafters. If someone is injured, they take down the bread, cut off the mold and make a paste with water, then apply it to the wound."

"How remarkable." Sally had always been insatiably curious, a good trait for a teacher. "Do you keep a moldy loaf in your attic?"

He shook his head reminiscently. "This particular specimen was given to me by a Russian sailor who swore that it was the best he'd ever used. I gave it a try and found I lost fewer patients to infection and mortification. I've been feeding the mixture bread and water for the last eight years."

"What made you decide to try something so unorthodox in the first place?"

"I've traveled widely, which gave me an interest in folk medicine. My more traditional colleagues sneer, but sometimes it works. One of my aims in life is to test such practices and discover which are valid." He smiled. "For example, I've seen no evidence that putting a knife under a childbed cuts the pain in half, but willow bark is indeed good for aches and fevers. When I find something that works, I use it."

Now that David had been treated, Sally found herself curious about Kinlock the man rather than Kinlock the surgeon. "What are your other aims in life?"

"To save as many people from the Reaper as I can, for as long as I can. In the end, death always wins. But not without a struggle, by God." His expression was bleak.

Wanting to erase the sorrow from his eyes, she raised her glass. "A toast for today's victory over the Reaper!"

Expression lightening, he clinked his glass against hers, and they drank. Sally poured more for each of them, and they drifted into general conversation, both enjoying the post-surgery euphoria. Sally spoke of her governess job, Kinlock about his training in Edinburgh and London. After training as both physician and surgeon, he'd become a ship's doctor, which had taken him to many strange parts of the world. Later, he'd been an army surgeon, refining his skills in the bloody crucible of battle.

Sally could hear his passion for his calling in every word he said. Mad Scot indeed! She blessed Dr. Ramsey for sending her to this man, who was surely the only surgeon in England who could have saved her brother.

Chapter 8

Tired from a long day away from home, Jocelyn almost walked past the salon when she finally returned, but paused when she heard a woman's voice. Could Aunt Laura have recovered from her anger and returned to London?

Hoping that was the case, she opened the drawing room door. To her disgust, she found not her aunt, but her uncouth sister-in-law in the process of getting drunk with some rumpled looking fellow Jocelyn had never seen before. Her face stiffened at such liberties being taken in her home. However, remembering her resolution to be more patient, she quietly started to withdraw. Sally might be in her cups, but she probably wouldn't steal the silver, which wasn't in the drawing room anyhow.

Before she could escape, Sally glanced up and saw her. "I've bad news for you, Lady Jocelyn."

"Oh, no. He . . . he has died?" Jocelyn froze, chilled to her marrow as sadness and loss swept over her. So David was gone, his wasted body growing cold upstairs, the green eyes closed forever. She had not even been at home. That brief visit yesterday had been good-bye. No wonder Sally had called for the brandy decanter.

"On the contrary," Sally continued in her strong schoolteacher's voice. "Dr. Kinlock here performed a rather splendid bit of surgery, and it seems likely that David will not only survive, but recover completely."

He was going to *live*? The words were an even greater shock than his death would have been. Dizzy from trying to assimilate such contradictory news, Jocelyn moved forward and grasped the back of a chair to steady herself. How wonderful if what Sally had said was true. David deserved life and happiness.

But in the midst of her gladness one powerful thought resonated: A live husband was not what she had bargained for!

"I know you wanted him dead." Sally rose and approached Jocelyn, her eyes glittering. "Perhaps I'd better stay here to guard him until he can be removed from your home. Since he isn't about to die on his own, you may wish to remedy the situation."

Jocelyn felt the blood drain from her face. "What a despicable thing to say! While my intention was to become a widow, I didn't want to see David dead. If you are capable of appreciating the distinction." Blindly she fumbled around the chair and dropped into it, torn between faintness and a desire to claw Sally's eyes out.

She felt something cool in her hand and looked up to see the doctor pressing a glass of brandy on her, his eyes watching with professional concern. "Drink that, Lady Jocelyn. It will help with the shock."

Obediently she sipped from the glass, choking a

little as the brandy burned its way down. But the surgeon was right, for her mind began to work again. She stared down into her glass and tried to sort out her feelings.

Nothing could make her sorry that David Lancaster was going to live. But what would this mean to her plans for Candover? Even if the duke fell in love with her, she couldn't marry him. The knowledge made her want to weep.

Realizing that she was on the verge of drowning in confused emotions, she forced her attention elsewhere. To the surgeon, for example, who improved on closer examination. Rumpled he might be, but his gaze was intelligent and kind as he briefly described why the major had been so ill and what had been done to cure him.

By the time he finished, she was able to manage a genuine smile. "My thanks, Dr. Kinlock. You've done a good day's work. I haven't known Major Lancaster long, but I do know that the world is a better place for his survival."

Before Sally's disgusted eyes, Kinlock almost started to purr under the hundred-candlepower charm of Lady Jocelyn's smile. Even the most intelligent of men seemed unable to recognize a highbred tart for what she was.

As soon as the thought formed in her mind, she was ashamed of herself. The brandy must be working on her empty stomach. Her accusation that Lady Jocelyn might harm David had come from the same source. As soon as she'd said the words, she wanted to bite her tongue, and not only because Kinlock had glanced at her with disapproval. Lady Jocelyn herself had looked startlingly vulnerable, like a kicked child, when Sally had made her unthinking charge. Who would have thought the witch had feelings? Probably she was just upset at the insult to her dignity.

Nonetheless, Sally had been very rude to her hostess. Though apologies were not one of her specialties, she said stiffly, "I'm sorry for what I said, Lady Jocelyn. I'm sure David will be well cared for here until I can move him. I'll start looking for another place immediately so you won't be unnecessarily inconvenienced."

"There's no need to hurry. The house is large enough to house a regiment, or at least a company." Wrapping herself in her habitual coolness, Lady Jocelyn rose to her feet. "Dr. Kinlock, you will send me a bill for your services? I trust you will make it consonant with the results."

He glanced at Sally. "Miss Lancaster engaged me, and I believe that she intends to take care of the bill."

"Nonsense, the responsibility is mine." She gave the surgeon another wondrous smile. Sally had to admit that if a smile like that ever came her way, even she might be willing to overlook Lady Jocelyn's numerous defects of character.

Her ladyship glanced at the mantel clock. "It's getting late. Pray let my carriage take you to your homes. Unless you wish to stay overnight, Miss Lancaster?"

Guilt at her earlier rudeness made Sally refuse. "No need. Dr. Kinlock says David will sleep all night, and Morgan is here to watch him. I'll walk to my employers. It's not far, and it's still light."

She hadn't thought of her job in several hours, but it suddenly struck her that she would have to make sure that the Launcestons continued to be happy with her. Lady Jocelyn was bound to disavow the financial settlement, since she wasn't going to receive the quick widowhood she'd bargained for. No matter. David's life was worth everything Sally owned, and a life of leisure wouldn't have suited her.

After a swift glance at Sally, Kinlock overruled her. "We'll be happy to accept your kind offer, Lady Jocelyn. I shall make sure Miss Lancaster reaches home safely. If you will call the carriage, we will be on our way."

"This isn't necessary," Sally muttered as Lady Jocelyn summoned her carriage.

The surgeon chuckled. "In my professional opinion, it is. How often do you drink brandy?"

"Almost never," she admitted. "But I am not in the least bit foxed." Her dignified statement was undercut by a hiccup.

Eyes twinkling, Kinlock took a firm hold of her arm and guided her outside to the carriage. Sally climbed in and sank gratefully back into the soft velvet squabs. She was unaccountably a little dizzy and inclined to giggle. How odd.

She had no memory later of what, if anything, they talked about on the short ride, but before they reached the Launcestons' town house, Kinlock signaled the driver to stop and set them down.

Sally blinked owlishly out the window, recognizing a tavern about two blocks from her employers' home. "We aren't there yet."

He took her hand to assist her from the carriage.

"Aye, but the food is good, and I intend to see you fed before I return you. Otherwise, your employers will be sacking you for drunkenness and it will be my fault."

His tone was amused, but Sally still took offense. "I am not drunk. Jus' . . . just a trifle well-to-go. Don't need to eat."

He tucked her hand in the crook of his arm. "You might not be hungry," he said diplomatically, "but I am. Will you join me so I don't have to eat alone?"

When he put it that way, she couldn't refuse. In fact, she didn't want to. She was ravenous, now that she thought about it.

The tavern was a clean, well-kept place, with enticing odors wafting from the kitchen. The owner greeted Kinlock like an old friend and seated them in a dark, quiet corner. Sally rapidly put away bread and cheese, a hot beef and onion pie, a peach pudding, and the strong coffee the surgeon ordered her to drink.

After draining her coffee, she said candidly, "I'm sorry to be such a nuisance, Dr. Kinlock. I must have been a bit drunk, or I wouldn't feel so much more sober now."

Smiling, he surgically sliced an apple into eighths. "Relief for your brother coupled with brandy on an empty stomach did have an interesting effect on you."

She relaxed against the high-backed oak settle, feeling very much at peace. "I don't think I've eaten a full meal since I saw the casualty lists after Waterloo."

The spring had seemed endless while England waited for a battle with the Corsican Monster, miraculously returned from Elba and with whole French armies rushing to his support. She'd read the newspapers compulsively, hungry for every scrap of news. Perhaps she'd had a premonition, because she had never worried so much during the years that David had fought on the Peninsula. When the news of his severe injuries finally reached her, she hadn't been surprised. Sick and terrified, but not surprised. And then the waiting had begun. . . .

Reminding herself that was all behind her, she said, "I'm sorry that because of taking care of me you'll have to walk home when Lady Jocelyn's carriage could have taken you. Do you live near Bart's?"

"No, I have consulting rooms just a couple of blocks away, on Harley Street, and live in rooms above. I eat here often." He traced a circle in a small spill of ale. "What's the story behind your brother's marriage? Not the usual arrangement, I think."

Sally sketched out why Lady Jocelyn had wanted to become a rich widow, and how David had become her husband. The story sounded bizarre when she explained, but the surgeon showed no signs of shock. She suspected that it would take a good deal to surprise Ian Kinlock.

When she had finished, he shook his head with a bemused expression. "The poor woman. No wonder the two of you have been at daggers drawn. Your interests in the major's health have been entirely different."

"Do you blame me for wondering if she might put a period to his unwelcome existence?"

"Nonsense, lassie, you don't believe she's a threat

to him any more than I do," he scoffed. "Didn't you see her expression when she thought he was dead?"

"She did look distressed," Sally conceded. "Probably she was afraid a death in the house would upset the servants."

"She may not want to be married to your brother, but he's a likable man, and she was genuinely happy to hear that he would be well. It will be amusing to see how the two of them work this out."

Dealing with life and death all the time must give surgeons a morbid sense of humor. "The thought of having Lady Jocelyn as a permanent sister-in-law has no appeal for me. She's the haughtiest female I've ever met."

"She's not so bad, for all she's a member of a class of useless wastrels." He sliced up a second apple, having finished the first. "Quite a charming woman, actually."

Sally wisely refrained from comment. Lady Jocelyn was not someone they were likely to agree on. Under the circumstances, politics would be a safer topic of conversation. "You sound like a radical."

"If it's radical to despise lazy people who have never done a particle of good for anyone else, I suppose I am. Women who assassinate character and spend more money on one gown than the average family sees in a year, men whose idea of sport is slaughtering helpless animals and gambling away their fortunes." He smiled wickedly. "I've often thought hunting would be a good deal more fair if the foxes and pheasants were armed and could fight back."

Sally pictured a fox aiming a shotgun and began to laugh. "I can certainly think of a few members of the beau monde who would be improved by buckshot in the breeches."

His grin made her recognize the impropriety of her remark. Kinlock was so unconventional that he made her forget to hold her tongue. She studied the craggy face shadowed by the thick shock of white hair, the expressive features that could reflect such extremes of anger and compassion. She would never be able to repay him for what he had done.

Her gaze fell to the remaining apple slices, which he'd pushed aside. Once more forgetting to think before she spoke, she asked, "Are you going to eat those?"

She immediately wanted to hide under the table, but he only slid the apple pieces to her. "You've quite a bit of eating to catch up on. You've grown too many bones from worry."

He thought she was skinny, she realized as she ate the last two apple slices. Her next thought was to wonder why she should care. To her alarm, she realized that she would like him to see her as a woman in her own right, not simply the sister of a patient.

Acerbically she told herself that the stirring of excitement she felt was only because of the intimacy of this relaxed dinner. In the whole of her spinster life, she'd never dined alone with an attractive man like this, except for David, and brothers didn't count.

Of course in Kinlock's eyes, she was a skinny little governess who had become tipsy and insulted a beautiful woman who turned men into entranced slaves. Humiliated at the thought, she swallowed the last of the apple and slid from the oak settle. "Time for me to return to the Launcestons'."

"Aye, I should be getting home as well."

As he got to his feet, she saw that for the first time since she'd met him, he seemed completely relaxed. Well, he deserved to feel good about his day's work.

As he walked her the last blocks to the Launcestons', she luxuriated in the knowledge that tonight she would sleep better than she had in months.

Chapter 9

Jocelyn sat drinking tea for a long time after the surgeon and Sally Lancaster left. Her Aunt Laura would say that ending up with an unwanted husband was a just reward for her improper actions. On the whole, Jocelyn was inclined to agree.

Drawn by instinct, Isis leaped onto her lap and nestled down, purring and bumping her tawny head into her mistress's ribs in a welcome display of affection. Stroking the sleek fur was a good way to quell the panic that welled up whenever Jocelyn thought about the fact that she was married to a complete stranger. An amiable stranger whom she had come to like and admire, but still a stranger. It was enough to give even the calmest female strong hysterics.

Regaining his health might make the major a very different man from the one who had waited for death with such quiet courage. He hadn't bargained on a lasting marriage any more than she had, and might be equally upset at having lost his freedom to marry as he chose. Perhaps there was a woman he loved and would have married if not for the apparently mortal wounds he'd received at Waterloo.

Divorce was out of the question, of course. She'd suffered all her life from the ghastly scandal of her parents' divorce and would never take that path. A bill of divorcement required an act of Parliament and could only be granted after a humiliatingly public airing of the most intimate details.

Even if she *was* willing to take that route, a divorce required cause. Most often, the grounds were adultery by the wife, which she certainly had no intention of committing. Even if she did, Major Lancaster might not want to divorce her if he decided he liked being married to a wealthy woman. Thank heaven he'd signed the papers waiving his rights to her property, so he couldn't bankrupt her.

She gave her head a quick shake. Her imagination was running away with her. A healthy David might be different from one at death's door, but she couldn't imagine that he would turn into a monster. She would wager money on the fact that he was a decent and honorable man. She simply didn't want him for a husband.

Eventually Isis jumped down, hitting the carpet with an audible thump before proceeding about her own concerns. It was time to inquire after the major's health.

In the blue room, Hugh Morgan watched patiently over his sleeping charge. Because of the incision on his back, the major lay on his stomach, his breathing steady and his thin face peaceful.

"He's doing well?" she asked quietly.

The footman rose and joined her at the door. "Sleeping like a baby, my lady," he assured her in a low voice.

"Good." On the verge of leaving, she remembered to ask, "And your brother. Is he comfortable here?"

"Oh, yes. He's like a new man, and thank you for asking." Morgan gave a shy smile. "You were right about the maids, my lady. They're making quite a fuss over Rhys, and 'tis doing him a world of good."

The comment gave her a much needed smile. At least one of her impulsive decisions was having good consequences.

After a solitary dinner, Jocelyn took her anxieties to bed. She tried to be philosophical about her unexpected husband. After all, in a hundred years they would all be dead, and what would all of this matter? Nonetheless, she tossed for hours before falling into a troubled sleep.

She was awakened by insistent knocking. Isis, ensconced in her usual spot at the foot of the bed, pricked her sharp ears toward the door as Marie entered, wearing a simple dress that had obviously been pulled on in haste. "Hugh Morgan asked me to wake you. The major is very restless, milady, and it's that worried Morgan is."

"I'll take a look." Instantly alert, Jocelyn swung from the bed and donned the wrapper Marie held out. After sliding into slippers, she stepped outside, where Morgan waited with a candelabrum. "Did Dr. Kinlock leave his direction?"

"Aye, Lady Jocelyn. He said to fetch him if necessary."

She belted her robe as they hastened along the gallery to the blue room, the flames of the candles flaring behind the footman. It was very late, the darkest hour of the night.

Hoping they wouldn't have to disturb Kinlock needlessly, she entered the major's room. He'd rolled onto his back and was twisting weakly under the covers. She caught her breath as she saw his legs move. Only a little, but genuine movement. Kinlock had been right—there was no paralysis.

Elated by the knowledge, she crossed to the bed and laid a hand on his forehead. If he were feverish she'd send for the doctor immediately because of possible inflammation, but his temperature seemed normal.

His restlessness stilled under her touch. "Jeanette, mignonne?" he murmured with an admirable French accent.

She removed her hand and said crisply, "No, it's Jocelyn. A proper Englishwoman, not one of your French or Belgian hussies."

His lids fluttered open. A moment of confusion gave way to recognition. "How do you know that Jeanette wasn't my horse?"

"You would call your horse 'darling?' "

"A soldier and his horse become very dear to each other," he said gravely, but there was humor in his eyes.

She had to laugh. "I don't think I want to know more." Her expression sobered. "Do you remember what happened? Dr. Kinlock? The operation?"

His expression tightened. With a flash of insight, she realized that he was afraid to ask about the outcome. "The operation went well," she said quickly.

"Kinlock thought you might make a complete recovery."

At first he was so still that she wondered if he'd heard her. Then, his face straining with effort, he moved his right leg, drawing the knee up a few inches. The same with the left. "My God!" he exclaimed, his voice shaking. "It's true. I can move. *I can move.*"

He closed his eyes again before glinting tears could escape. Guessing at how powerfully affected he must be, she sat on the bedside chair and took his hand, then said to Morgan and Marie, "You can leave for a bit. Morgan, perhaps you'd like to find some tea and something to eat."

"I'd like that, my lady," he admitted. He and Marie exchanged a glowing glance as they left. Servants seldom had much privacy, and the opportunity to share a meal in the depths of the night was obviously welcome.

While David struggled to master the dramatic change in his circumstances, Jocelyn calmly repeated what the doctor had told her earlier in the day. When his eyes opened again, she asked, "How do you feel?"

"Compared to the way I've felt since Waterloo, fairly good. By any normal standard, rather rotten."

Smiling at his whimsy, she asked, "Are you in much pain?"

"Of course I am! What kind of a fool do you take me for?" There was a giddy light in his eyes. Not fever, but the exhilaration that came with miracles.

"Major Lancaster, I have a feeling you are going to be very difficult now that you are convalescing."

Jocelyn continued to study his thin face, thinking there was another, subtle difference.

The eyes. For the first time, the green eyes looked almost normal, without the opium-induced pinpoint pupils. The last dose of laudanum must have worn off. She lifted the bottle from the bedside table. "Dr. Kinlock said to give you some laudanum if you woke up in the night. You need rest to recover."

"No!" His arm flailed out with more strength than she would have dreamed he possessed, knocking the bottle from her hand to shatter in a dark stain across the rich Oriental carpet.

She stared at him as the spicy scent of cloves and cinnamon wafted through the room. His usual humor had been replaced by a kind of desperation. "I'm sorry," he said unevenly. "I didn't mean to strike you. But I won't take any more opium. Ever."

"Why not?"

David marshaled his whirling thoughts, knowing that he must make Jocelyn understand, or she would have some of the damned drug down him for his own good. "Did Kinlock explain that I was dying of opium poisoning?"

When she nodded, he continued, "Heavy opium use distorts the mind and the senses. Sight, sound, scent, thought—everything changes. It was like . . . like having my soul stolen. I would rather die than have that happen again."

"Would you really prefer death?" she asked quietly.

He took a long, slow breath. "No. I exaggerate. I suppose that if taking laudanum was the difference between life and death, I'd take it. But tonight, for the first time in weeks, I am not under the influence of the drug, and I feel better than at any time since that damned artillery shell went off beside me. Stronger. Saner."

"What about the pain?"

His mouth twisted. "I'd be lying if I didn't admit that it feels as if a tiger is trying to chew me in half. But even so, I prefer that to drugged delirium."

"Very well, Major, I won't force it down you, though I make no promises about what Dr. Kinlock might do when he calls tomorrow," she said reluctantly. "If he feels laudanum is essential to your recovery, I'll help hold you down while he doses you."

"Yes, ma'am," he said meekly, having won his battle.

"If you won't sleep, will you eat? You must build up your strength."

He took stock of his innards. "Do you know," he said with wonder, "I believe that I am hungry, for the first time since the battle."

"Does the idea of a roast joint with Yorkshire pudding appeal to you?"

The mere thought made his mouth water. "Who do I have to bribe?"

"Prepare yourself for soup," she said sweetly. "If that seems to settle well, perhaps an omelet or a bit of custard."

He laughed, even though it hurt. "You have your revenge for my failings, Lady Jocelyn."

She pulled the bell cord. Morgan appeared fairly quickly, panting a little after racing up from the kitchen. As she ordered food, David admired the pure line of her profile. Though her nightclothes covered more of her than most day dresses, there was an alluring intimacy to the sleeping garments. She looked tantalizingly huggable.

The footman said warningly, "Cook won't like getting up this late."

She raised aristocratic brows. "If Monsieur Cherbonnier objects to the conditions of employment in my house, tell him that he is under no compulsion to continue accepting the exorbitant wage I pay him. I expect to be served within fifteen minutes. Is that clear?"

Suppressing a smile, Morgan bobbed his head and left to obey.

"Lady Jocelyn, if you ever desire employment, you might become a sergeant-major," David observed. "You have a talent for putting the fear of God into your underlings."

She smiled, unabashed. "My servants lead a fairly easy life, I think. There is no great harm in their being challenged occasionally."

"They seem a contented lot." And well they should be. Lady Jocelyn's cool, ladylike exterior couldn't conceal her underlying warmth and fairmindedness.

"Is there someone you would like notified of your improved health?" she asked. "I'll send a note to Richard Dalton in the morning, but who else? Surely there are some relatives who will be glad for the news."

Unthinking, he replied, "My brothers would hardly be interested in my continued existence."

"You have brothers?" she said, surprised. "I

thought you said your sister would be left alone in the world when you died."

Not wanting her to think he'd lied, he explained reluctantly, "Sally and I have three older half-brothers. Mostly we try to pretend they don't exist. My mother was a second wife, much younger than my father. His sons by his first wife despised her because she had no fortune, and by their standards her birth was inferior. They didn't dare insult her in front of our father, so they took out their resentment on Sally and me." He smiled humorlessly. "I learned to fight at an early age, a very useful skill. After my father died, the oldest son threw the three of us out of the family house."

"How despicable to do that to their father's wife and their own brother and sister!" Jocelyn exclaimed. "Your father had made no provisions for you?"

"He was a rather unworldly scholar who assumed, wrongly, that his heir would take care of us. Luckily my mother was entitled to receive a small jointure. It was enough for a cottage, and a decent education for Sally and me." He thought nostalgically of the cottage, where the happiest days of his life had been spent. "The income ended with her death, of course, but by then I was in the army and Sally was almost through school. We managed well enough."

"No wonder you and your sister are so close."

"Growing up, we were each other's best friends. We played together and studied together." He smiled. "She was even more fun than my pet pony."

Looking envious, she remarked, "I always wanted to have a brother or sister."

"I'd offer you one of my half-brothers, but I doubt

you'd get on with them. They don't even get on with each other. They were a quarrelsome lot when I knew them, and I doubt they've improved." Immaturity could have been outgrown, but not the mean-spiritedness that was so much a part of his elder siblings. "They must have resembled their mother, for they were nothing like our father."

"I see why your sister wouldn't feel she could call on them in time of need." Jocelyn's mouth tightened. "Betrayals by family members are the cruelest, I think."

He wondered whose betrayal had put that shadow in her eyes. Perhaps she was thinking of her father, who had sought to rule her from the grave. "A pity we can't choose our relatives as we do our friends."

"My family has its share of dirty dishes." She smiled self-mockingly. "If I hadn't been so angry with the way my Aunt Elvira was coveting this house, it might not have occurred to me to make such . . . such an impulsive marriage."

David exhaled roughly. Her words were a sobering reminder that the intimacy of this late night interlude was only an illusion. There was nothing between them but a legal contract meant to be fulfilled and over in a matter of weeks at most. Instead, they were in a situation neither of them had bargained for.

Though he knew that the topic must be addressed soon, he was far too tired to discuss it now. "Don't worry, Lady Jocelyn. I think this . . . unintended marriage can be sorted out without damage to either of us."

She looked so pleased it was almost insulting. "Really? How?"

Before he could reply, Morgan entered carrying a tray. Curbing her curiosity, she said, "We can discuss this tomorrow. Or rather, later today. Now it's time for you to eat."

Despite the convenient legged tray designed to be used by someone in bed, that proved harder than expected. What little strength David possessed had been expended on his conversation with Jocelyn. When he tried to raise a spoonful of chicken and barley soup to his mouth, his hand was so weak and uncontrolled that it slopped onto the tray. The footman had already been sent back to his own interrupted meal, so Jocelyn matter-of-factly took the spoon and dipped it into the bowl.

"You shouldn't be doing this," he protested.

She gave him a reproachful look. "Don't you think I will do it well?"

"You know that's not what I meant." Before he could say more, she stilled him with a spoon in the mouth. He swallowed slowly, savoring the flavors and textures. Soup had never tasted so good. "It isn't fitting that you perform such a menial task for me."

She shook her head mournfully. "Just because I have a title, no one thinks I'm good for anything. Perhaps you should just call me Jocelyn." As he opened his mouth to reply, she popped the spoon in again. "That should remove any exaggerated respect."

Mouth full, he could only roll his eyes. He got a chuckle in response. After he swallowed, he said, "You're good at this. Have you done nursing before?"

Her smile ebbed and she looked down, dipping the spoon into the bowl with unnecessary care. "My father, in the last weeks of his illness. He'd always been robust and energetic, and he made a terrible patient. He behaved best when I was with him."

And in return for her daughterly devotion, the earl had left that outrageous will. No wonder she felt betrayed.

He wouldn't have done justice to roast beef and Yorkshire pudding. He didn't even finish the bowl of soup before his shrunken stomach decided it had enough. "I'm sorry," he said, eyeing the other covered dishes with regret. "I haven't the appetite for anything more."

She grinned. "I didn't think you would. To be honest, I ordered the omelet and custard for myself. Being up at this hour makes me hungry."

She lifted the tray away from him and set it aside, then made short work of the omelet. He enjoyed watching the gusto with which she ate. Was it true that a woman who enjoyed her food had equally strong appetites in other areas? It was a pleasant thought to ponder as he faded into the first natural sleep in weeks.

In the hazy land between waking and oblivion, he thought that Jocelyn's hand brushed his hair, but surely that was only a last trace of delirium. . . .

Chapter 10

Jocelyn had suspected that within a week Major Lancaster would be impossible to keep in bed, but she was wrong. The very next morning she stopped by his room and found him sitting on the edge of his bed as Morgan helped him put a dressing gown over his nightshirt. "Major Lancaster!" she exclaimed. "Are you out of your mind?"

Morgan said plaintively, "After he ate his breakfast, he insisted on sitting up, my lady. Refused to listen to reason."

Perhaps the major and his sister did have a resemblance that went beyond eye color, she thought dryly. She wasn't sure whether to be impressed, alarmed, or amused by his determination. "Kinlock will have your head for a haggis if you don't show some sense, Major. Remember that twenty-four hours ago, you were on your deathbed."

He gave her an uneven smile. "If you want me to call you Jocelyn, you'll have to call me David." The words were light, but his voice was strained and his face was sheened with perspiration.

Thinking he looked very unwell, she approached

the bed to feel his forehead. "Has the wound become inflamed?"

He halted her with a raised hand. "Not . . . not feverish. Kinlock warned me that there would be a reaction when I stopped the opium. It's . . . beginning."

She frowned. "Wouldn't it be better to continue taking laudanum until you're stronger? Surely recovering from surgery is enough for now."

"The longer I take opium, the harder it will be to stop," he said tightly. "I want to do it now, before the addiction becomes any worse."

She hesitated, seeing his point, but vividly aware of how near death he'd seemed less than a day before.

Seeing her doubts, he caught her gaze with his. His pupils had expanded until his eyes were nearly black. "Jocelyn. Please trust that I know how much I can endure."

He deserved the dignity of being treated like a man, not a child. "Very well. Just . . . don't overestimate your strength and waste all Kinlock's good work."

"I won't." He took a shuddering breath. "I . . . I'd rather you left now. Withdrawing from the drug isn't a pleasant process. I don't want you to see me at my worst."

She would feel the same in his position; one's darkest moments were best kept private. "Very well." She glanced at the footman. "Inform me at once if you become concerned about the major's condition, Morgan."

"Aye, my lady."

The young Welshman's eyes showed his awareness of the responsibility he bore. Odd that he'd worked for her more than a year, and she'd never suspected the depths of his caring and compassion. Quiet daily life didn't require the display of such qualities, she supposed.

As she exited, the major whispered, "Thank you, Jocelyn. For . . . everything."

She hoped she wouldn't live to regret allowing him to go to hell in his own way.

He exhaled with relief after Jocelyn left, knowing he'd gained a formidable ally. "It's a rare woman who knows when not to argue."

"She's rare indeed, Major," Morgan said fervently.

David glanced at the footman, wondering if he was in love with his beautiful mistress. No, it wasn't romantic love in the young man's eyes, but devotion to a woman he respected profoundly. Though wages could command a servant's duty, it took character to inspire true loyalty.

A chill shivered through him. Knowing what lay ahead, he said, "Help me into the chair, please."

"Wouldn't you be better off lying down, sir?"

"Later. For as long as I can manage, I'd rather face this sitting up."

The footman obligingly took an arm and helped him to his feet. His weakened legs almost collapsed under him, and at first he just stood swaying dizzily. Without Morgan's help, he'd have fallen in a heap on the floor.

When his whirling head steadied, he managed to stagger three steps to the wing chair, with Morgan's considerable help. He sank into the chair and leaned his head against the back, tremors in his limbs and pain blazing from the surgical incision. But at least, by God, he was no longer lying in bed as helpless as a kitten.

Sitting in a chair, helpless as a kitten, seemed like an enormous improvement.

Jocelyn had sent a note to Richard Dalton about the major's health, but the messenger crossed him, and the captain arrived in midmorning not knowing of his friend's miraculous improvement. Too discreet to offer information himself, Dudley left Richard in the morning room and notified Jocelyn of the visitor.

She found Richard standing by a window, his knuckles white on his crutches. Expecting the worst as she herself had done yesterday, he asked, his face a taut mask, "Is David . . . ?"

"Richard, he's much, much better," she said quickly. "He was operated on yesterday, and the surgeon thinks he has an excellent chance of full recovery."

His eyes widened. "David is going to *live*?"

"With luck, he'll be as good as new."

The captain swung to face the window and stared out, his shoulders rigid. To allow him a private time to collect himself, she scooped up Isis, who had followed her in from the study. The cat could absorb infinite amounts of petting.

When Richard finally spoke, his voice was so low it was barely audible. "When your butler brought me here, I was sure you would tell me that David had died last night. You . . . you can't imagine what this means. When so many have died, to know that at least one friend will survive, against all the odds."

"I think I can guess, a little," she said quietly.

Richard turned to her. "What will this mean to you?"

"I honestly don't know," she said wryly. "But I hope that unlike Sally Lancaster, you will acquit me of a desire to slip poison into David's soup."

"Sally never said that!"

"She implied it quite strongly." Jocelyn scratched Isis's chin and got a rumbling purr in response. "To be fair, she was foxed at the time and probably didn't mean it."

"If you were going to murder someone, I assume it would be very direct, perhaps pistols in Bond Street. Not something sly like poison," Richard said with a grin that made him look years younger, the way he'd appeared when they first met in Spain.

"It would be a pity to waste my marksmanship," she agreed.

He shifted on his crutches. "Is David well enough to receive visitors?"

"Since I'm a mere frail female, he threw me out of his room this morning, but I expect he'll be happy to see you." As they left the morning room, she repeated what Kinlock had told her.

"So it was the opium that brought him so near death," Richard said, amazed. "Lord, when I think of how much I gave him with my own hands!"

"Everyone, including David, thought that for the best. But now that he knows better, he's flatly refusing to take any more laudanum." She glanced at her friend worriedly. "Do you know anything about opium addiction? I'm concerned that he might endanger his health by stopping so abruptly."

"In Spain, one of our officers became addicted after a severe wound. He was unable to stop taking opium no matter how hard he tried. His state was . . . unenviable," the captain said bluntly. "Having witnessed that is surely a good part of the reason that David wants to stop the drug as soon as possible. But he's not a fool. He wouldn't insist on doing something that would destroy him just as he is on the verge of recovering."

She must hope that Richard was right. "I'm told you were here yesterday, so you can find your own way up. Please feel free to visit David at any time and to stay as long as you want. I'm sure your presence will speed his recovery."

Understanding her unspoken suggestion, he smiled warmly. "And your home is a much more pleasant place to spend time than the hospital. Thank you, Lady Jocelyn."

Assuming he wouldn't want her to watch him struggle up two long flights of stairs, she draped Isis over her shoulder and returned to her study. She had letters to write. Laura Kirkpatrick would be delighted to hear about Major Lancaster's improved health. And her other aunt, Lady Cromarty, would be *enraged* to learn that her niece's fortune was forever out of reach. A pity Jocelyn wouldn't be there to see the reaction.

She was sealing the note to Lady Laura when Dudley appeared. "The Misses Halliwell are here, my lady."

The Misses Halliwell? Damnation, in the midst of

so much high drama she'd forgotten this was one of her regular at-home days. There would be fewer visitors than during the Season, but she still faced several hours of being charming. It would not be easy today.

With slightly gritted teeth, she went off to receive the Misses Halliwell, three harmless but slightly addlepated spinsters much given to incomplete sentences and pointless stories. Time moved with treacle slowness. On a superficial level she offered tea, cakes, and amusing stories with practiced ease, but underneath ran a river of anxiety. How was David managing? Had he collapsed from pushing himself too hard? Was he enduring ghastly torments from the drug withdrawal?

Glad when the last pair of guests left, she told Dudley to deny her to any latecomers and marched up the stairs to see what was happening. Her knock was greeted with a cheerful, "Come in."

She entered to find a gentlemen's card party in full swing. Hugh and Rhys Morgan had joined Richard Dalton and David around the table, and a game was in progress. Only Richard accepted her appearance casually. Hugh jumped to his feet while Rhys ducked his head with paralyzing shyness. David, sunk deep in the only wing chair, aimed a smile in her direction. He looked as if he ought to be lying flat in his bed, yet a hectic light in his eyes suggested that he would be unable to rest.

Suspecting that Richard had started the card game as a way to distract David from his miseries, she said with mock reproach, "I'd been imagining all manner of disasters! Instead, you gentlemen have been amusing yourselves while I've been playing hostess to half the bores in London."

Hugh Morgan stammered, "I'm sorry, my lady, but Major Lancaster insisted that if I was in the room, I must join the game."

Keeping her tone light, she said, "Major, I fear that you are corrupting my servants."

Matching her tone despite the tremor in his hands, he answered, "On the contrary, I'm participating in a salutary lesson on the evils of gambling. Never play with Richard, Lady Jocelyn. We are using buildings for stakes, and by now he is in possession of the Horse Guards, Carlton House, St. Paul's, and Westminster Abbey."

"Who has won the York Hospital?" she asked with interest.

"None of us wanted it," Rhys blurted out, then blushed so hard his ears turned red.

She was pleased to see how much happier and healthier the corporal looked than he had in the hospital. Perhaps she should turn Cromarty House into a convalescent home, since wounded soldiers seemed to flourish here. "This is clearly no place for a mere female. Enjoy yourselves, gentlemen. I'll send up refreshments."

She withdrew, thinking that she was beginning to understand the comradeship of arms, and how men who had fought together looked out for each other. There was a tangible bond between the three military men, even though two were officers and old friends while the third was a stranger and a common soldier.

Some fusty fellow, perhaps Samuel Johnson, had once said that every man was sorry if he hadn't been a soldier. She hadn't understood the remark before, but now she had some inkling of what it meant.

What a pity that men couldn't find such satisfactions without killing so many of their fellows.

"Craving, shaking, sweating, and God knows what else . . ." David realized that he could no longer keep up even a semblance of playing cards. Instead of hearts and spades, he was seeing shifting patterns that wouldn't hold still long enough to define.

Time had slowed down until it ceased to have meaning. An eon ago, Lady Jocelyn had paid an amused visit. Food had appeared shortly thereafter. The appetite he'd experienced during the night had vanished, and he could neither eat nor drink.

After his companions finished the light meal, he said, voice metallic in his ears, "Sorry, gentlemen, it's time for me to withdraw from the game." Sweat dripped from his hand, staining the cards as he laid them down, and the skin of his wrist had prickled into gooseflesh. With a supreme effort, he managed to add, "Richard, you'll have to win the Tower of London another time."

"Just as well. I could never afford to maintain it." Richard's voice was wonderfully soothing, and it must have been his hand warm on David's shoulder. But surely it was Hugh that got him onto the blessedly soft bed. Neither Richard nor the corporal would have been able to offer much help from their crutches.

He lay shaking as the sheets dampened with sweat. Time would pass more quickly if he could sleep, but his guts were tied in knots and his mind wandered in a peculiar waking dream, where present surroundings mingled with the past, and with the worst nightmares he'd known, fresh as when he'd first experienced them.

Sally appeared, her face anxious even after he assured her that he was fine and she needn't stay. Kinlock was there too, frowning over his pulse rate and saying he was a thrice-damned fool. Hazily he agreed, but argued that since he was already well into the withdrawal period, why waste the suffering if he would just have to do it again later?

His logic must have worked—Kinlock didn't force any more laudanum on him. A reasonable man for a quack.

Hours dragged by as muscles spasmed with pain and he shook with cold no matter how many blankets Hugh piled on him. During a dark hour of the night, he almost broke. His craving for the velvet numbness of the drug was so fierce, so all-consuming that he buried his face in the pillows to keep himself from begging for laudanum. Just a little, to soothe the ache of bone and muscle.

Someone sponged his face with blessedly cool water, and he knew from the jasmine scent that it must be Lady Jocelyn. He tried to turn away, to tell her that she shouldn't be here, but her clear voice told him firmly not to be a lackwit. A strong-minded woman, his wife. Wife? Impossible. Sadly, impossible.

Then black depression seized him and sucked him into endless dark. Perhaps it was night, or perhaps the sun had died. He fixed his gaze on a candle, sure that if he blinked there would never be light again.

Dawn came, tangible evidence that time was indeed passing. He had survived this long, he could continue to endure.

His mind conjured feverish visions of the burning interior plains of Spain, glittering cruelly brown, then breaking into hard yellow shards under the impact of monster raindrops. They washed away in a flash flood of jangling pieces, leaving the green, beloved hills of Hereford, the hills he hadn't seen in twenty years.

He had been twelve, still bearing the marks of a beating from one of his brothers, when the carrier's wagon had come for him and Mother and Sally. Though he had loved Westholme as much as he had hated his brothers, he refused to look back in case anyone watching would think it weakness.

He rolled from the bed and staggered toward the window, knowing that outside he would see Westholme, but Hugh Morgan caught hold of him. Though he struggled desperately, sure that salvation was near at hand if only he could reach it, he was no match for the young Welshman's gentle strength.

He was lying down again. If only he could sleep. . . .

Chapter 11

For two and a half days, the pain radiating from Major Lancaster filled the whole house. Jocelyn's nerves frayed under the strain. Though David had asked her to stay away, she sat with him often, since he seemed unaware of her presence. Hugh Morgan undertook the bulk of the nursing chores, but Jocelyn and Sally and Rhys took turns, too, so that the chief attendant could have a break from the demands of the sickroom. Though she offered to hire another nurse, the footman had refused, saying that he could do what needed to be done.

How long would such torment go on? She'd asked Kinlock, who had no clear answer. It depended on how strong a grip the addiction had on David's constitution. At worst, perhaps five or six days. With luck, less time would be required.

It was a relief to go out to a small dinner party that Jocelyn had promised faithfully to attend. ("My dear Lady Jocelyn, it will be all of my husband's dire relations. I simply must have someone to lend some charm!") She wondered ruefully if her hostess had received as much charm as she hoped for. Jocelyn's shimmering green taffeta dress was probably livelier than the woman inside it.

Still, it was good to get out. During the course of the evening, she managed sometimes not to think of her suffering major for as much as thirty seconds at a time.

It was after one in the morning when she let herself in her front door, waving away the carriage that had waited until she was safe inside. She'd told her servants not to stay up for her. As always, she'd had an argument on her hands. From butler to abigail, the staff appeared to think her incapable of turning a key in a lock or undressing herself.

It never occurred to any of them that sometimes she might prefer to be alone.

As she paused at the foot of the stairs, her absent gaze fell on the door to the salon, reminding her of the nasty little scene that had taken place there earlier in the day. It had been another clash with her sister-in-law. Sally had urged that her brother be given laudanum, to keep his mind from snapping or his heart from giving out under the strain.

Jocelyn understood Sally's concern; indeed, she shared it. But the other woman hadn't been present when David had smashed the bottle of laudanum to keep it away. She hadn't heard the desperation in his voice.

Rather than trying to explain something so profoundly private, Jocelyn had coolly pointed out that David was an adult and his decisions should be respected. Sally again accused her of hoping David would die, her words spitting out like hornets. Only when Richard sided with Jocelyn had Sally retreated, her eyes dark with the fear behind her fury.

Jocelyn found she was gripping the newel post so hard that her fingers were imprinted with carved acanthus leaves. With an effort, she released the post and started up the two long flights of stairs.

Strange how quiet the house was at this hour, the dark three-story high foyer lit only by landing lamps. It was almost possible to believe she lived here alone rather than sharing her roof with ten other people. Eleven, counting her newly acquired husband.

She reached the bedroom floor and walked the length of the gallery to her room. She was almost there when she saw a shadow, a darker shape in the night, moving ahead of her. She froze, her heartbeat quickening as she wondered if a burglar had broken in.

No, the unsteady figure belonged to the man who'd been at the center of her thoughts for these last endless days. Major Lancaster was weaving uncertainly, one hand sliding along the railing that ran around the gallery to protect people from the lethal drop to the foyer far below.

She stared, amazed that he could make his way so far alone. Probably an exhausted Hugh Morgan had fallen asleep during his long vigil, and the major had wandered off without waking him. Blast it, the footman should have called someone to relieve him. Devotion was all very well, but good judgment mattered, too.

Kidskin slippers muffled by the carpet runner, she walked toward him. "Major Lancaster, you really must go back to bed."

He swung around at the sound of his name. His gaze was blank, as if he was sleepwalking. She sighed, her hope that he was through the opium withdrawal fading. "Come along now," she said, her voice low but firm, as if he was a wayward child. "You must go back to bed."

"Who . . . who is there?" His head moved back and forth as he tried to locate her in the shadows with his unfocused vision.

"Jocelyn."

Reassured by her voice, he moved toward her, but his lurching steps sent him crashing into the railing that guarded the gallery. She gasped in horror as his unbalanced upper body swayed outward over the deadly marble floor far below.

Terrified, she darted across the dozen feet separating them and wrapped her arms around him, using her momentum to shove him away from the treacherous railing. He gasped and stumbled backward at the unexpected impact, and the two of them reeled across the gallery and into the wall. As he wavered on the verge of falling, she tightened her grip, taking advantage of the fact that he was pinned between her and the wall.

He was so thin his ribs could be counted through the blue dressing gown and she could feel his heart beating, but his body felt surprisingly solid. And tall. His height hadn't been apparent when he was lying down. He was easily six feet, and with an impressive breadth of shoulder.

As she caught her breath, his arms circled her strongly and he murmured with pleased surprise, "Jeanette!"

"*Not* Jean . . ." She looked up to correct his misapprehension, and his lips descended on hers.

She gave a strangled squeak of surprise at the sheer uninhibited sensuality of the embrace. Their tongues touched, wickedly erotic, and one large warm hand slid caressingly down her bare arm. She felt . . . ravished. Cherished.

Desired.

Her knees weakened and she clung to him, the wall supporting them both. From sheer curiosity, she'd occasionally allowed suitors to steal a kiss, and been pleased to discover that she felt little response. Waltzing with Candover was far more provocative than anyone else's kisses. Until now, when the heated intensity of a soldier's mouth burned away past and future, leaving only the searing present.

Was this how her mother had felt when lust engulfed her, turning her into a harlot with no thought for anything but her own selfish needs?

The thought revolted her, jerking her back to an awareness of her situation. She was tempted to pull away and let the blasted man collapse onto the floor, but settled for turning her head and saying in her most aristocratic voice, "Major Lancaster. Control yourself!"

His arms loosened and he blinked down at her, as if waking from sleep. "Good Lord!" he exclaimed as he registered the fact that they were pressed body to body. "I . . . I'm sorry. I appear to have . . . have behaved very badly."

"So you did."

With a small choke of laughter, he said, "And I'm

also sorry that I didn't appreciate my misdeed when I was misdoing it."

He really had the most appalling sense of humor, but it was hard to be severe with a man when one's arms were wrapped around him. She settled for saying tartly, "Why are you wandering around at this hour? And in a house full of servants, why is this little drama taking place in complete solitude?"

His brow wrinkled as he gave her questions serious thought. "Perhaps everyone is in bed? It must be very late."

She sighed with relief. The clarity of his mind indicated that the drug withdrawal was over, and he had survived. "A profound observation, Major. So pleased you are back in the land of the living."

But what now? She could yell until someone woke and came to help put the major in bed, but she wasn't sure how much longer she could support his substantial weight, and his room was at the far end of the gallery. The door to her own chamber was only a few feet away. "If I help, do you think you can make it to the next room?"

He carefully levered himself away from the wall. After an alarming sway, he caught his balance. "I believe so."

With some awkwardness, they rearranged themselves, with his left arm draped across her shoulders, then lurched into Jocelyn's room, the major opening the door with his free hand. Soft lamplight helped guide them across the chamber. Turning him around so their backs were to the bed, Jocelyn let go and allowed gravity to take over. He collapsed onto the bed like a marionette whose strings had been cut, his legs trailing over the edge of the mattress.

She turned and saw that he was trembling from the effort expended, but he managed a twisted smile. "I appear to be in your debt once more."

"Think nothing of it, Major." Jocelyn lifted his legs up onto the covers and helped straighten his lanky form. Luckily, she had placed him so that his head landed near the pillow. "You have no idea how boring my life was until our paths crossed."

She straightened, panting a little. Even half starved, the man was no lightweight.

To her dismay, he had already fallen asleep. She supposed it was not surprising after three days and nights without any real rest, but the fact that he was on her bed was a blasted nuisance.

She could wake the footmen and have him carried back to his room, but that would be a noisy, time-consuming process. Worse, the major was bound to wake up, which would be a great pity when he needed rest so badly. She winced at the thought of dealing with sleepy, apologetic, and distressed servants when all she really wanted to do was go to sleep herself.

Yet she couldn't retreat to a guest room to spend the night, because none of the other chambers were made up. The major's room was the only one kept always at the ready. She glared at his peacefully slumbering form for a moment, then yanked the pins from her hair. So what if he was in her bed? After all, they were married. More or less.

She undressed behind the screen usually used around the hip bath. It felt odd to be naked in a room with a man, even one who was dead to the world. After donning her most opaque nightgown and wrapper, she pulled a lightweight quilt from her wardrobe and spread it over her guest. Then she crawled under the other half, her back turned to him and her body as close to the edge of the bed as she could safely manage.

Fortunately, it was a very large bed.

David awoke slowly, so warm and at peace that at first he wondered if he was floating in another dream, kinder than the ones that had gone before. But no, his heart beat steadily and his lungs expanded and contracted with convincing reality.

Cautiously he wiggled his toes, wanting confirmation that all his parts were working. Though he ached all over and was exhausted from the last crazed days of drug withdrawal, there were no more agonizing muscle cramps. Best of all, not a trace of paralysis. He'd never take toe wiggling for granted again.

He lay with his eyes closed, not wanting to lose such a delicious feeling of well-being. The scents of clean linen and jasmine, his arm draped over a pillow—a pillow that breathed? His eyes shot open, and he found that he was lying face to face with a sleeping Lady Jocelyn, his arm around her.

Paralysis of another kind struck. He lay absolutely still, scarcely breathing as he tried to remember how he'd arrived in what must be Jocelyn's bedroom. It was very early morning, and the light played over her lush, loosened hair, accenting the red tones. In sleep, she looked young and vulnerable, not at all like the highly competent woman who had swept into his hospital room, and his life.

No wonder he felt so well. There was nothing like waking up with a lovely lady, even if he couldn't quite remember how he'd come to be in—no, on—her bed.

With reluctance, he removed his arm. The motion woke her, and her eyes opened. The changeable hazel color was flecked with gold, and her skin had the flawless purity of an English rose. At this range, the impact rivaled that of a cannonball.

His heartbeat accelerated as they gazed at one another. She looked like a wary songbird who would fly away if he made the wrong move, yet there was no surprise at his presence. What the devil had happened the night before?

Her voice morning husky, she said, "You're back from the abyss, aren't you?"

The abyss. How accurate a description. "Yes. God willing, I'll never have to go there again." He made a gesture that encompassed the room. "Dare I ask how I came to be in this enviable position?"

Her eyes narrowed with amusement. "I imagine that you would dare anything, Major."

He grinned. "Very well. What *did* happen?"

"Not much. Do you remember wandering out onto the gallery?"

Her words recalled images of lurching unsteadily, the railing cool under his hand as it guided and supported him. A woman's light, clear voice. He'd turned . . .

His stomach lurched. "Damnation, I remember hanging over the railing and thinking how very far down the floor was, but my wits were so scrambled that I didn't really care." The memory was more upsetting than the experience had been. Falling off the gallery would have been an unforgivably stupid way to die after all he'd been through. "You dragged me back to safety, didn't you?"

As she nodded, an interesting hint of pink colored her lovely creamy skin. Abruptly he remembered why. He'd kissed her, and for a few incredible moments she had responded wholeheartedly. Then common sense had returned, and Jocelyn had ended the embrace.

Suspecting that she would prefer to pretend that kiss hadn't happened, he said with gentlemanly tact, "I presume you guided me in here, and I fell asleep right away."

"Exactly," she said, looking relieved. "My room was closest, and the only one made up. I didn't want to be driven from my own bed, especially since there was room enough for two."

Which is why they were now lying together with such provocative intimacy. He stroked her chestnut hair, the silky strands twining around his fingertips. "You saved my life last night. Saying thank you seems quite inadequate."

Without moving a muscle, she retreated slightly, as if alarmed by the warmth in his voice. "If you'd fallen, you'd have made the most dreadful mess on the marble."

"Which would be unmannerly, when you've been so kind." Feeling that he had been politely chastised, he withdrew his hand. Lady Jocelyn might be his wife in law, but they were virtual strangers, and he saw no evidence that she was as attracted to him as he was to her. And attracted he was, in a powerful but oddly nonphysical way, since he was still a long way from fully recovered. Desire was dormant. A powerful yearning for greater closeness, to understand her life and mind, was not.

If he was this attracted when he was only a few days off his deathbed, what would he feel when he became a well man again?

She interrupted his thoughts. "You seemed very determined last night. Do you remember where you were heading?"

Glad to be on safer ground, he replied, "Hereford, I think."

"Why Hereford?"

"Why not? It's a very lovely county." Before he could stop himself, he added, "Almost as lovely as you are."

She sat up in the bed, trying to look severe. "I am beginning to think you are a practiced flirt."

"Not in the least." He studied her graceful form, which her loose nightwear only hinted at. "I'm merely stating the truth. Surely you know that you are beautiful."

Her gaze dropped and she looked uncomfortable. He wondered why. In his experience, most women loved being admired. Perhaps Jocelyn was interpreting his comments as a husbandly advance to a woman who had no interest in being his wife.

That sobering thought was interrupted when Jocelyn's maid, Marie, hurried into the room. "Milady, the major is missing . . ." Her eyes rounded as she took in the picture before her. "Mon Dieu!"

As cool as if she was sitting in her parlor rather than in dishabille on her bed, Jocelyn said, "As you can see, the major is not missing. He was wandering last night and it was easier to bring him here than to rouse the whole house. If your slumbering swain is awake, inform him that he can assist Major Lancaster back to his own room."

Marie bobbed her head and backed out of the room, still staring, but with a hint of smile playing around her lips.

Repressing a sigh at the intrusion of reality, David cautiously swung his legs over the edge of the bed, then stood, bracing a hand on a bedpost. "I think I can make it back to my own room without assistance."

She climbed from the bed also. "Best wait for Morgan, Major Lancaster. You've been very ill and are probably still unsteady on your feet."

"I thought I had persuaded you to call me David the other night."

She tightened her wrapper around her, an unconscious act intending to cover her more, though in fact it accentuated her shapely figure. "It will be easier to keep you at a distance if I call you Major."

Using the bedpost as a pivot, he swung around to face her. "I won't do anything that you don't want."

"I . . . I didn't really think you would." She sighed. "But we are in the very devii of a bind."

When the subject had first been raised, he'd avoided it by going into opium withdrawal. This time, the situation must be discussed. "I believe there is a way out of this . . . unintended marriage that will preserve your inheritance and allow both of us to go our separate ways."

She regarded him with great, hopeful eyes. "You really think so?"

"I'll have to look at the will. Do you have a copy in the house?"

"I believe so."

He rubbed his chin and felt a heavy rasp of whiskers. Lord, he was a mess, unshaven, unwashed, and surely showing the effects of his days of delirium. "After I've had a chance to bathe, shave, and breakfast, I'll take a look at the will. One should never look at legal documents on an empty stomach."

She made a wry face. "Just thinking about my father's will gives me indigestion."

Hugh Morgan rushed in, his expression showing the fear he'd felt on waking to find his patient gone. Gushing explanations and apologies, he took David's arm and assisted him from the room.

After the door closed behind the men, Jocelyn glanced up to find Isis sitting on the windowsill where she had spent the night after her spot on the bed was usurped. "Well, puss, it appears that our major has definitely recovered. But what are we going to do with him?"

Isis yawned disdainfully. Cats arranged their relationships much more neatly.

Chapter 12

When Jocelyn joined Major Lancaster some two hours later, it was hard to recognize the man who had been at death's door a handful of days before. Bathed, shaven, and sitting at ease by the window, only his dressing gown indicated his convalescent status. He stood as she entered and executed a commendable half-bow despite the recent surgery on his back.

She seated herself, placing a sheaf of papers by the coffee tray that rested on the small table between them. "Major, you're a wonder. Even Dr. Kinlock thought it would be a week until you were up and about."

"Healing quickly is an excellent trait to have in the military, where time is often in short supply. Care for some coffee? Hugh Morgan just brought a fresh pot."

"Thank you, I believe I will." She studied him as he poured two steaming cups of the fragrant brew. Though he was still very thin, his cheeks almost hollow, his color was healthy. She was amused to see that even though his thick brown hair had been combed into a semblance of military order, it was rapidly, and charmingly, reverting to an unruly natural wave. He was younger than she had supposed, closer to thirty than forty.

When he handed her the cup, she asked, "Speaking of Morgan, where is he now?"

"I thought he might wish to catch up on his other duties, or spend some time with his brother." Correctly interpreting her raised brows, David said reasonably, "I really don't need a full-time nursemaid anymore."

"I suppose not. He hasn't much catching up to do, though. London is very thin of company at this season, so the servants haven't been busy."

He added cream to his cup, pouring it over the back of his spoon so that it covered the surface of the coffee in a rich layer. "When your maid came earlier, you referred to Morgan as her swain. Are they courting?"

"I believe so. The housekeeper assures me that they are behaving with discretion, but there is clearly interest on both sides."

"You're a liberal employer to allow such goings-on in your house. Many prefer their servants not to keep company."

"It's human nature for males and females to be drawn together. Employers who deny that merely force their servants into slyness. As long as no one's work suffers, it would be foolish to issue commands that won't be obeyed."

He smiled. "Lady Jocelyn, I do believe that you are a romantic."

"Not in the least. Merely pragmatic." Although she must have a romantic streak, or she wouldn't be yearning for the Duke of Candover, which had led her into this distressing situation. She handed over the papers. "Here is the copy of my father's will that you requested."

"With your permission?" David began scanning the document. The last will and testament of a wealthy peer was necessarily long, but he made short work of it, returning to study only one section with greater care.

He laid the document on the table. "There are no conditions attached to your inheritance apart from the simple one of marriage by your twenty-fifth birthday. Even divorce or murder would not disinherit you now that you've married."

"Are those the only two options?" she asked, alarmed.

"Not at all. We could live in a state of permanent separation, but that would be very unsatisfactory for both of us. Certainly it would be for me. The best solution is to have our marriage annulled."

Her brows drew together. "What does that mean?"

"Annulments are granted by ecclesiastical courts, and they dissolve the marriage, leaving both parties free to marry again later," he explained. "They are very rare, but if grounds are sufficient, an annulment would be faster and less expensive than a divorce, and far less scandalous, since no misconduct is involved."

"That would certainly be desirable, but what grounds are required? They must be stringent, or annulments would be very common."

He regarded her steadily. "A marriage can be annulled because of lack of consent, bigamy, lunacy, being under the age of consent, and several other reasons. What would work in this case would be—impotence."

It took a moment to absorb his words. Then she stared at him, her eyes rounding with shock. "You mean that because of the paralysis, now you can't . . . ?"

"You needn't look so appalled, Lady Jocelyn. In fact, I have no reason to believe that is the case, but given the nature of my recent injuries, it will be simple to claim that the marriage cannot be consummated and should be annulled. The incapacity must have existed at the time of marriage, and medical witnesses would have to swear to my injuries, but that shouldn't be a problem."

Blushing, she applied herself to the coffee. She hadn't realized how uncomfortable this discussion would become. She was dimly aware that men took their amatory performance very seriously. Surely David was unusual in his matter-of-fact offer to claim an embarrassing disability. "You wouldn't mind making such a claim?"

"Though I'll admit it's legal hairsplitting, as long as I have no clear evidence to the contrary I'll be able to swear to being . . . incapacitated with a clear conscience."

She made herself look up and meet his gaze. "It's very gallant of you to be willing to do something that will surely be humiliating."

"There will be enough embarrassment to go around. Among other things, you would have to be certified as virgo intacta." He hesitated, then said, "Forgive me, but . . . would that be a problem?"

"Of course I'm a virgin!" she exclaimed, flushing

violently. Though there was no "of course" about it; even among her own class, it was hardly unknown for brides to go to the altar when they were already breeding. But Jocelyn had preferred to hold to a higher standard. Besides, she'd never really been tempted.

Charitably overlooking her fluster, he said, "Then I think it very likely an annulment will be possible."

She certainly hoped so. Ready to change the subject, she asked, "How did you learn so much about the law?"

"I read law for two years. It was thought to be a suitable profession for me."

Intrigued, she asked, "Why didn't you continue in the profession?"

He grinned. "I decided that I quite literally preferred death to life as a lawyer, and joined the army."

"You're confirming my prejudices. Since lawyers are usually prosy old bores, the law must be boring."

"Not at all. The great body of Anglo-Saxon common law is part of what makes our nation unique. It's derived from precedent and common sense and is quite different from the French Code Napoleon, for example, which was based on the Roman Justinian Code. Common law has the admirable ability to grow and change with the times. I have no doubt that a thousand years from now our descendants will still be governing themselves with a recognizable form of the law that rules us today."

"What a wonderful thought," she said admiringly. "You've also just done the impossible, and made the law sound romantic. Perhaps you should have become a barrister or advocate after all."

"The day-to-day practice is an indoor, paper-shuffling business. I would have hated it." He tapped her father's will. "Though this is certainly an interesting document. What on earth was your father thinking of?"

"Isn't it obvious?" she said tartly. "I believe he described me as 'a headstrong wench, and too particular in my tastes.' "

"Most unhandsome of him," the major said, voice sober but eyes laughing.

She didn't blame him for being amused. The situation was hilarious for everyone except her. "In fairness, I know my father was sincerely concerned for me. He really believed that for a woman not to marry was a ghastly fate. Also, while he was perfectly happy to see the title go to his brother, Willoughby, he didn't want his own line to die out if I chose not to marry."

"That's understandable."

"Perhaps, but it doesn't mean I will accept coercion tamely." Her mouth twisted. "It's paradoxical. Because of the way he raised me, I can never be content with the ladylike life he wanted me to have."

David lifted the coffeepot and poured more for both of them. "How were you raised?"

"He treated me as if I would be his heir. We rode the estate together discussing drainage and livestock and crop rotation, all the things the lord of the manor must know. The Kendal estate, Charlton, is in my blood and mind and soul." Her voice faltered. "But . . . Charlton can never be mine."

"It won't be the same, but now you are in a position to buy another estate. With time and love, you can make it as much your own as Charlton was."

She glanced at him shyly. "You understand, don't you? I've seldom talked of this. Mere females are not supposed to be so attached to the land."

"Anyone who says that is a fool."

"To be honest, I've always felt that, but few men agree," she said candidly. "Now that my inheritance has been secured, I shall start watching for a suitable estate to come onto the market. It may take years, but in time, I will find what I'm seeking."

"Becoming a woman of property is a worthy ambition, and I don't doubt that you shall achieve it." He studied her face. "But what about marriage? The first time we met, I believe you said there was a man you had hopes of."

She concentrated on mounding the sugar lumps high in the bowl with the little silver spoon, wondering how much to say. Confining herself to the bare facts, she said, "The relationship was only just beginning to develop. I ran out of time before I could determine if we might have a future together."

"What is the gentleman like?"

"Very grand and worldly, and very unimpressed by people who worship his title and wealth. He has a great deal of wit, but kindness, too. He's an admirable landlord and a much respected member of the House of Lords." She hesitated, knowing that she couldn't, and shouldn't, explain the yearning she felt whenever she thought of Candover. "I . . . I enjoy his company greatly."

"He sounds like a worthy and suitable husband."

David scanned her, his gaze enigmatic. "And he'd have to be a complete fool not to appreciate you."

"He seems to enjoy my company, too, but he's always behaved with the utmost propriety because I am, or was, a well-born spinster," she said wryly. "He has a reputation for preferring women who are as . . . as worldly as he is."

Understanding her implication, the major said, "Such behavior is not uncommon among men who are not yet ready to marry. No doubt he has been waiting for the right woman."

"That's what I have believed." She toyed with her delicate china cup in an uncharacteristic display of nervousness. "No doubt I sound very foolish, to be so interested in a man who may never return my regard."

"Not at all. Interest is the essential first step, and if you're right, the interest is mutual."

"You're a very understanding man. I wish you were my brother, but I suppose Miss Lancaster would be loath to share you."

His smile was wry. "You would like me for a brother?"

"I know that's impossible, but I would hope we can be friends. Too much has happened in these last days for us to be strangers."

"You're certainly correct about that." He offered her his hand. "Friends, then."

She was struck by the warmth and strength of his clasp. In fact, she felt something akin to the tingle experienced after crossing a carpet on a cold day. He was well on the road to recovery.

After their handshake, he said, "Speaking of my

sister, I presume that you'll want to revoke the annuity you settled on Sally, since I didn't fulfill my half of the bargain."

For a moment she was tempted. Five hundred pounds a year was a considerable sum, and Sally Lancaster was hardly an endearing object of benevolence. But she had made a bargain. "Of course I won't revoke it. You married me, which was the essence of our agreement."

"You're very fair."

His gaze was approving, but his face and posture were showing signs of fatigue. "I'm tiring you," she said apologetically. "I'm sorry, you seem so well that I keep forgetting how ill you have been. Do you wish to lie down?"

"Perhaps I should." He levered himself carefully from his chair. "I imagine I shall do little but eat and sleep for the next week or two."

She rose also, wondering if she should summon Morgan. "Do you need assistance?"

"I can manage, Lady Jocelyn. Thank you for your concern."

The atmosphere had become oddly formal for two people who had just pledged friendship. "Until later, then."

Her hand was almost on the knob when the door swung open and the Countess of Cromarty exploded into the room, her flushed face a close match for the fuchsia plumes bobbing over her head. Fixing Jocelyn with a fulminating stare, she snarled, *"What is the meaning of this?"*

Chapter 13

Startled, Jocelyn said feebly, "I beg your pardon?"

"You shameless baggage! What's this nonsense about you having married? Just last week you hadn't brought anyone up to scratch!" The countess's eyes narrowed to slits. "Or did you buy a husband, some fortune hunter willing to take you in spite of your sly ways and wicked temper?"

Jocelyn gasped at the wave of vitriol. Though she and the countess had never been fond of each other, they usually maintained at least the appearance of civility. But then, Elvira had never been deprived of a fortune before.

Her aunt was drawing her breath for another barrage when a cool voice cut across the room. "Would you be so kind as to introduce us, Jocelyn?"

She'd forgotten David's presence, but now she stepped aside so that her aunt could see that she had invaded a gentleman's bedroom. Unfortunately, the countess was beyond questions of propriety. The sight of Major Lancaster produced a low growl in the back of her throat.

Wishing she could spare him this scene, Jocelyn said, "David, this is my aunt, the Countess of Cromarty. Aunt Elvira, Major David Lancaster." She deliberately introduced her aunt to David, knowing that the status-conscious countess would see it as the insult it was.

"So you're the one taking part in this farce," Elvira bit out. "I've never even heard of you. You're *nobody*!"

David gave the countess an impeccable bow. "Of course you can't approve of the fact that your niece has thrown herself away on someone of no great rank or wealth. With her beauty, birth, and charm, she could look to the highest in the land. Indeed, I have pointed that out to my dear girl many times."

Looking very tall and very distinguished, he stepped forward and put his arm around Jocelyn's shoulders. "I could not agree with you more about the unsuitability of the match. However, the attachment has stood the test of time. Since our feelings were unaltered, I succumbed to temptation and asked Jocelyn to marry me."

His dear girl was staring at him with blank astonishment, so he gave her a doting smile and an unobtrusive wink. "It's a tribute to your perception that you realize no man could be good enough for your niece, Lady Cromarty. I can only swear I will spend my life trying to be worthy of her."

Jocelyn's astonishment almost turned to uncontrollable giggles. With heroic willpower, she cooed, "David, darling, you do say the sweetest things! As if any woman wouldn't be proud to be your wife." Turning to her aunt, she said soulfully, "Such nobility of nature, such high principles, are beyond price. And the heart of a lion—he is a hero of Waterloo, you know." She slipped her arm around his waist and laid her head against his shoulder. "I am the most fortunate of women."

Elvira stared in stupefaction. Whatever she had expected, it was not this picture of mutual adoration. And while she might not have heard of Major Lancaster, he was undeniably a gentleman. "You have been attached for some time?"

"Oh, we have known each other this age," David said blandly. "But the difference in our stations and the war conspired to keep us apart." He gave Elvira a seraphic smile. "I hope you will wish us happy."

"It seems like a deuced hole-in-corner business to me," Elvira snapped. "No announcement, no banns, no one from the family present. At the very least, you should have invited Willoughby and me. As head of the family, he should have given you away."

Jocelyn let her mouth droop tragically. "Please tell my uncle I meant no slight. There was simply no time to arrange a larger wedding. David was so ill. Indeed, had his life not been despaired of, I believe that his sense of honor would never have allowed him to marry me."

Unconvinced, Elvira said, "This is all very pretty, but how did you two meet?"

Deciding the performance had gone on long enough, Jocelyn said firmly, "It was very thoughtful of you to pay your respects, Aunt Elvira, but I cannot allow you to tire my husband any longer." She stepped away from David to pull the bell cord.

Dudley arrived almost immediately. Jocelyn assumed that close inspection would reveal the shape of a keyhole imprinted on his ear. "Please show the countess downstairs. I am sorry not to accompany you, Aunt, but my husband and I were discussing matters of some importance." She took David's arm, batting her lashes outrageously.

Routed, the countess turned and brushed by Dudley so quickly her plumes hit him in the face.

Jocelyn waited until the footsteps had died away before collapsing into a chair and giving in to whoops of laughter. "I know now why you didn't die of your wounds, Major," she gasped. "You were obviously born to be hanged. I have never heard such a string of half-truths in my life. 'We have known each other this age,' indeed!"

"It's the advantage of legal training, my dear. Any lawyer worth his salt can choose words so effectively that he can convince a reasonable man that black is white. If you think back, you'll see that I didn't actually tell any lies." David sat on the edge of the bed, a smile lurking. "If I was born to be hanged, you were born for Drury Lane. You entered into the spirit of things rather quickly."

"It was very bad of me," Jocelyn said without regret. "But that Aunt Elvira should speak to me so in my own house!"

"Do you always clash?"

"She married my uncle when I was two. I'm told that when we first met, she scooped me up in her arms in an effort to prove her maternal instincts, whereupon I bit her on the nose. Our relationship has been deteriorating ever since."

He grinned. "Lady Cromarty was right. You're a shameless baggage."

Jocelyn smiled back, unabashed. "While the desire

to buy land was the strongest reason to retain my fortune, honesty compels me to admit that wanting to thwart Aunt Elvira came a close second." A thought occurred to her. "If we get an annulment, can she contest my inheritance on the grounds that I was never really married?"

David shrugged. "On a given day, anyone can sue anyone for anything. I don't think she would win, but you will want to discuss the whole matter with your solicitor. Is your uncle the sort to challenge you in court? Even if the suit fails, fighting it would be expensive and painful."

"Willoughby will probably do whatever Elvira wishes. He's a pleasant man, but thoroughly under the cat' s paw." Uneasily she confronted the possibility of a lawsuit. It was time to consult with John Crandall, her lawyer. At least a civil suit wouldn't be as horrible as a divorce.

Elvira's visit had made her think of the future. "What will you do after you are free of our improbable marriage?"

"I'm not sure. Return to the army, probably. The thought of garrison duty doesn't excite me, but I'm not sure what else I'd be qualified to do." He smiled without humor. "Of course, the army might not want me. There are bound to be troop reductions now that Bonaparte is gone for good."

She scowled. "It seems so unfair that the men who saved England will be discarded like . . . like old shoes now that they are not needed."

"Life is a good deal more comfortable if one doesn't expect it to be fair."

A knock sounded at the door, and Dudley entered. "Dr. Kinlock is here to see Major Lancaster."

Moving with his usual impatience, Kinlock entered on the butler's heels. His bushy eyebrows raised at the cozy scene in front of him. "I thought I'd better stop by early today, but it looks like my concern for your welfare was misplaced."

David rose at the surgeon's entrance. "I may not be ready for riding or twenty-mile marches for another few weeks, but I feel well. Whole."

Kinlock grinned. "Your opinion doesn't count, Major. I'm the doctor, so I'll tell you whether or not you're well."

Seeing that the surgeon wanted to perform an examination, Jocelyn rose. "I'll see you later, Major Lancaster. Shall I ask my lawyer to call on us tomorrow?"

He sighed. "The sooner the better, I suppose."

As she left, she realized that she'd spent much longer with David than she had intended. He was very easy company. A pity that she couldn't adopt him as a brother, but that would make Sally Lancaster her sister, which would never do.

David and Kinlock both admired the elegance of Jocelyn's departing figure as she glided from the room. "She's a braw bonnie lassie," the surgeon said in one of his stronger Scottish accents before he began poking and prodding his patient.

After a thorough examination that included listening to the heart through a rolled tube of heavy paper, Kinlock said, "You have the constitution of an ox, Major. The surgical incision is nearly closed with no sign of infection and you've come through the opium withdrawal without damage. I'll admit that I was quite concerned yesterday."

"So was I," David said wryly.

"I won't waste my breath on instructions for your convalescence since you will do as you please no matter what I say." The surgeon scowled from under his bushy brows. "I trust that you have enough sense to eat well, rest often, and not push yourself beyond your strength?"

"Don't worry. I've had some experience with wounds and recovery. I won't do anything foolish." He regarded the surgeon gravely. "I owe you more than I can ever repay. I hope you know how much I appreciate what you have done."

"Don't thank me, thank your sister. When everyone else had given up on you, she didn't. She's a fearsome lass. Had me trembling in my boots." Kinlock smiled, warmth in his eyes. "I did nothing special, except to examine you closely. Unfortunately, the doctors at the York Hospital had already decided you were hopeless."

"You undervalue your own skills." David tied the sash of his robe, glad the examination was over. The fact that he was healing well didn't mean that poking didn't hurt. "I presume you won't be calling again?"

"I'll remove the sutures next week, but apart from that, you have no need of me, Major." Kinlock closed his medical bag with a snap. "I must be off to Bart's. I have several surgeries to perform today."

David offered his hand. "It's been a pleasure."

The surgeon's grip was powerful. "The pleasure was mine. Among all the failures of a physician's life, it is rewarding to have a splendid success now and then." He gave a quick, boyish grin. "Besides, Lady Jocelyn has already paid the outrageous bill I sent her. It will keep my free surgery supplied with medicines for the next year. Good day to you."

After Kinlock left, David stretched out on the bed, careful of his still-sore back. So Lady Jocelyn had even paid the medical bill. The money itself might be insignificant to a woman of great wealth, but it was another sign of her good sportsmanship in the face of the jest fate had played on her. She was a lady in every sense of the word.

He closed his eyes, feeling enormously weary. She was everything he had dreamed of in a woman, she was his wife—and he was helping to rid her of his unwelcome presence. He was a damned fool.

But he had no choice, really. The Lady Jocelyn Kendal, only and wealthy daughter of an earl, was not for a half-pay officer without property or prospects.

When Sally Lancaster entered her brother's room in midafternoon, she was so delighted to see him up and well that she barely refrained from giving him a hug altogether too energetic for an invalid. She settled for grabbing his hands and holding them tightly. "You're going to be all right now, aren't you?"

He chuckled. "As of this morning, I am far too healthy to interest Dr. Kinlock any longer. A few weeks of serious eating and I should be as good as new. And I owe it all to you, Sally. Everyone else had given up, me included. But you didn't."

She smiled teasingly. "I helped you for my own

benefit, David. Who else would tolerate me as well as you do?"

"Plenty of men would be delighted to do so." He gestured for her to take a seat. "Now that you have an independent income and don't need to teach, what do you want to do? Have you ever considered marriage?"

Surprised at the question, she said, "Surely the annuity will be canceled, since dear Lady Jocelyn didn't get the dead husband she had bargained for."

"We discussed that earlier today. She does not intend to revoke the settlement. The marriage accomplished her goal, which was to retain her fortune. My continued existence is a complication, but not one that was covered in our agreement."

"Is marriage just a matter of contract law?" Sally asked indignantly. "That woman has ice in her veins."

David's brows drew together at her vehemence. "Do you dislike Lady Jocelyn?"

Remembering that her brother hadn't seen the blasted woman's true nature, Sally said stiffly, "We've had little opportunity to become acquainted." She searched for something positive to say about her sister-in-law. "Lady Jocelyn has been most considerate about the use of her house and her servants. She also very kindly sent me a note this morning to inform me that you had recovered from the opium withdrawal, which was a great relief."

In spite of her resolution to be high-minded, Sally could not help adding, "But honestly, the thought of being related to her for the rest of my life makes the blood curdle in my veins."

David frowned, but before he could reply a cool voice sounded from the doorway. "You need have no fears on that score, Miss Lancaster." Lady Jocelyn entered the room carrying a newspaper. "Your brother and I have already discussed seeking an annulment, so your blood may continue to flow uncurdled."

Sally flushed beet red, feeling horribly gauche. Unfortunately she'd always been better at attack than apology, so her wicked tongue spat out, "Splendid. If an annulment is possible, I presume David is in no danger from you."

"Sally!" he exclaimed.

"Don't worry, Major," Lady Jocelyn said with a maddening display of tolerance. "It's not the first time your sister has made such accusations. Her concern for you seems to have overstimulated her imagination." She placed the newspaper on the table. "I thought you might enjoy catching up on the news. Excuse me for the interruption."

David said, "A moment, please, Lady Jocelyn."

Responding to the note of command in his voice, her ladyship turned her cool gaze back to her guests. "Yes, Major Lancaster?"

Sally had to admire Lady Jocelyn's bone-deep haughtiness. One could almost see invisible ranks of long-dead Kendals lined up behind her, all of them masters of pride and vastly pleased with their descendant.

David, however, was not easily intimidated. "Why are you two at daggers drawn?"

An uncomfortable silence fell, until Lady Jocelyn said, "Your sister has taken it into her head that I am a danger either to your continued existence, or possibly to her relationship with you. Apparently she enjoys seeing threats where none exist."

Sally's precarious hold on her temper snapped. "'Threats where none exist!' David, I hadn't meant you to know, but I had to force her to let you come here. Once she was in possession of her marriage lines, she was perfectly willing to let you die in that ghastly hospital, so you wouldn't trouble her selfish existence."

David turned his dispassionate gaze to his wife. "Is that true?"

Jocelyn gave a reluctant nod.

Sally wasn't finished yet. "When she gave me the first quarter's allowance, I asked why it wasn't thirty pieces of silver." She glared at her sister-in-law. "Your dear wife told me that silver was for selling people, and since she was buying, she paid gold!"

"Did you really say that?" David asked in astonishment.

Jocelyn's face flamed. "I'm afraid so." Suddenly she looked more like a child caught in mischief than a proud lady with ice in her veins.

To Sally's shock, her brother burst into laughter. "Really," he gasped as he attempted to collect himself, "I have never seen such foolish females."

Both pairs of watching eyes grew frosty. Sally asked in a dangerous tone, "Just what do you mean by that?"

"You are two of the most capable, not to mention imperious, women I've ever met. Naturally you bring out each other's worst natures." He shook his head in mock bemusement. "Whoever claimed females were the weaker sex didn't know you. All a poor male can do is agree quickly and hope to escape unscathed."

"Don't believe a word of it," Sally said acidly to her ladyship. "David is generally quite reasonable, for a man, but whenever he has an object in mind, one might as well wave the white flag immediately because he is going to do exactly what he wants, and the devil take the hindmost."

"I have seen signs of that." Jocelyn's mouth quirked up. "I believe that is the first time you and I have agreed on anything."

Sally felt an answering smile tug at her lips. "What an alarming thought."

David took his sister's hand. "Sally, I gather that because of the circumstances of our wedding you've assumed that Lady Jocelyn is my enemy, but she's not. If she had meant me ill, she could have allowed me to fall over the railing outside my bedroom last night, which would have made her a widow on the spot."

Sally gasped as she envisioned the lethal drop. "You would have been killed!"

"My wits were wandering, and apparently I decided to follow them. Jocelyn pulled me clear and put me to bed safely." He beckoned his wife forward, taking her hand as well. "During the worst of my illness, she tended me with her own hands even though we were almost strangers. She could not have behaved better had we been married twenty years."

Incredulous, Sally asked, "You really helped nurse my brother, Lady Jocelyn?"

"Yes, though I'm surprised he remembers," Jocelyn admitted. "He was out of his head for most of the time."

Sally's mind snapped back to the morning of the wedding, when she had flatly refused all future help from Lady Jocelyn. Under the circumstances, it was hardly fair to blame the woman for not having thought of taking David into her home. Sally had been a thrice-damned fool. With effort, she forced herself to meet her sister-in-law's gaze. "I owe you an abject apology. What I said was quite abominable."

The evil-tempered aristocrat of Sally's imagination would have rubbed salt in the wound. Instead, Lady Jocelyn said ruefully, "Yes, but you had considerable provocation. I should not have spoken as I did."

Warily the two women regarded each other over the head of the man who still held both of their hands. Jocelyn broke the silence. "You have the most magnificent talent for causing me to lose my temper and say dreadful things. If my Aunt Laura had heard me, she would have sent me to bed without any supper for a month. Shall we pretend that the last week never happened and begin over again?" Smiling, she held out her hand. "Good afternoon. How nice it is that you could visit."

Sally had been right in her previous speculation: Lady Jocelyn Kendal was irresistible when she unleashed the full power of her smile.

Smiling back, she took the proffered hand. "Good day, Lady Jocelyn. My name is Sally Lancaster. I believe you are married to my brother. So pleased to make your acquaintance."

As the two women clasped hands, Sally silently

thanked her brother for giving them the chance to start over. Already she could see that it would be much nicer to have Lady Jocelyn as a friend than an enemy.

Chapter 14

The cessation of hostilities was celebrated with tea and cakes. Now that they had decided not to be adversaries, Sally recognized the warmth under Jocelyn's cool manner. To her shame, she realized how much of her original bad opinion stemmed from her own prejudices. Being well-born didn't necessarily make someone selfish and cruel, any more than poverty created nobility of spirit.

After an hour Lady Jocelyn excused herself, claiming obligations out of the house. Sally stayed with her brother a while longer, but rose to leave when she saw that he was tiring. "Did Dr. Kinlock say when he would come again, David?" she asked as she picked up her reticule.

"He'll remove the stitches in a few days, but otherwise he won't come again unless I have a relapse, which I have no intention of doing."

Crossing to the bed, David didn't notice how her face fell. "Oh. How unfortunate. I . . . I never properly thanked him."

"You can be sure that I did." Her brother lay down, wincing a little. "He's an interesting man as well as a fine surgeon. I'll be sorry not to see him again, but he's not the sort to waste time on healthy people."

"I suppose not." She brightened as a thought struck. "I'll stop by his surgery to settle the account with him. He lives only a few blocks from Launceston House."

"Lady Jocelyn has already taken care of what Kinlock assures me was an outrageous bill."

"That doesn't seem right. We should pay it." Sally bit her lip. "Though I would have to use the money Lady Jocelyn gave me."

"I'm inclined to agree with you, but I'm not up to arguing with her at the moment. You may quarrel with her about the bill if you wish." His eyes drifted shut.

She shouldn't be tiring him with trivial matters. "No more fighting. Besides, I find that I object to her ladyship's generosity much less now that I've made my peace with her." She kissed her brother on the forehead. "I'll see you tomorrow afternoon."

Sally turned left to Hyde Park when she exited Cromarty House. The Launcestons believed that during the summer the children should have lessons only in the morning, so she didn't need to return to work. She was very fortunate in her employers. Nonetheless, now that she had a choice, it was only a matter of time until she gave notice. There was much she had enjoyed about being a governess, but she was ready for something different. What, she didn't know.

Despite the beauty of the summer day, as she strolled through the park's green expanses she brooded about the sharp pang of regret she'd felt when David said that Kinlock would not return. Why had she reacted so strongly? Miss Sarah Lancaster was a paragon of the practical virtues, without a romantic bone in her body.

To be sure, she kept thinking of the doctor's powerfully muscled figure, the large hands that could move with such delicacy, but that was merely admiration for the surgeon's strength and skill. And while the image of his prematurely white hair and its contrast with his dark, shaggy brows kept recurring to her, that was only because his appearance was so striking.

She gave a snort of exasperation. Who did she think she was deceiving?

Her steps had led her to the Serpentine, so she found an unoccupied bench and gazed unseeing over the placid waters of the little lake. She was not in the habit of hiding from unpleasant truths, so she must face the fact that Ian Kinlock appealed to her in ways that had nothing to do with his remarkable skills. She liked the man. Liked his passionate commitment to his work, liked his rough tongue, and deuce take it, liked the way he moved, the quick, impatient strength of him.

She sighed. How typical that the first man to take her fancy since she left the schoolroom was so inappropriate. Ian Kinlock lived for his work. As David had said, he had no interest in healthy bodies. And even if he did, plain brown Sarah Lancaster was not the woman to distract him from the serious business of saving London from the Reaper.

Was that one of the reasons she had resented Lady Jocelyn, whose beauty and charm even the good doctor noticed? Sally twisted her gloves into knots as she realized that envy had contributed to her hostility. How disheartening to admit that one was not really a very nice person.

It had been gratifying to scorn Lady Jocelyn as a cold-blooded femme fatale, but based on the last few days, her brother's wife was superior in character as well as in looks. That flawless society beauty had cared for David with her own hands, even though he was virtually a stranger. It was a sobering lesson in not being ruled by appearances.

Sally flattened her gloves on her knee and tried to smooth out the wrinkles. Ian Kinlock might not find a plain brown governess attractive, but surely now and then he needed a friend. From what she had seen of his life, he continually took care of others. It was time that someone took care of him.

Rising from the bench, she tried to remember his schedule. This was one of his days at Bart's, and she had seen how exhausting that was. How might she help alleviate that?

A moment's thought told her exactly what to do.

When Ian Kinlock returned to the grubby little cubicle that was his Bart's office, he was so depleted he could barely open the door. After leaving Major Lancaster, he'd examined a roomful of hospital patients, followed by tragedy on the cutting ward as one woman had died under surgery. Another wouldn't last the night despite his best efforts. At times like this, he wondered why he didn't pursue a fashionable practice that wouldn't demand such reserves of emotional and physical strength.

As soon as he entered the room, he headed toward his desk and the locked whiskey drawer even though he knew that spirits were a damned poor antidote for what ailed him. He didn't realize that he had company until a light, feminine voice said, "You'll be able to drink more if you eat something first."

Blinking, he turned and discovered that Miss Lancaster was sitting in the only visitor's chair. Setting aside the book she'd been reading, she lifted a basket. "I thought you would be hungry, so I brought some food."

Bemused, he pulled out the desk chair and sat down. "At the end of a day at Bart's, I generally can't remember when I ate last."

She handed him a meat pie still warm from the oven. The crust crumbled into rich flakes as he bit into it. Beef and mushroom pie. Delicious. He took another bite, and could feel strength returning. It was food that he'd needed, not whiskey. Nourishment instead of oblivion.

As she produced a jug of ale and poured him a tankard, he said, "Aren't you going to eat, too?"

"I was hoping you'd ask me to join you."

Together they explored Sally's capacious basket. Besides meat pies and ale, she had brought bread, cheese, pickled onions, and warm peach tarts. All were excellent and designed for easy eating.

After finishing the last of his tart, Ian replenished his tankard of ale. "Now that I'm halfway human again, it occurs to me to wonder what you're doing here."

Sally began to clear up the remains of the meal. "When David said you wouldn't be coming back, I realized that I hadn't properly thanked you for saving him."

"I like thanks that take a practical form." He smiled, more relaxed than he had been in weeks. "What you said at the time was quite adequate. I was just the instrument, you know. I do my best, but healing comes from a level beyond my skills."

"I wouldn't have expected such a mystical statement from a man of science."

"I may be a rationalist on the surface, but underneath I'm a wild, mystical Celt." He surveyed her neat, well-groomed figure. "A respectable English lady like you wouldn't understand that."

Sally closed her basket and got to her feet. "Watch whom you call English, laddie. My mother was Welsh, and as true a Celt as you." She walked to the desk with a package. "I've wrapped the bread and cheese in paper so they should keep for several days. It wouldn't hurt your patients if you ate now and then."

She was looking for a clear spot on the cluttered desk to put the food, not wanting the cheese to stain his papers, when her eye was caught by an envelope. Her brows rose as she read, "The Honorable Ian Kinlock."

She lifted the envelope and tilted it toward him. "Sorry, I couldn't help seeing this. Are you sure you're a wild Celt?"

The surgeon actually blushed. She wouldn't have believed it possible.

"My mother insists on addressing me that way," he explained. "My father is the Laird of Kintyre. My mother writes regularly to suggest that I give up this medical nonsense and come home to live like a proper Kinlock."

"So you can slaughter helpless animals and gamble away your fortune?" she remarked, remembering what he had said the night they dined at the tavern.

"Aye, my brothers are a dab hand at that sort of thing. To be fair, none of them have actually gambled away a fortune, and they are very good fellows in their way. Two are army officers like your brother. But we're as unlike as chalk and cheese."

"I can well imagine." She was fascinated by this unexpected glimpse of the gruff doctor. "I should think that the gentlemanly life would cause you to perish of boredom in a fortnight."

"Exactly. My mother has never understood that." He sighed. "She is also convinced I'll succumb to the charms of some hopelessly ineligible female. Bless her, she assumes that all of her five sons are irresistible. She's never really accepted that I am out of leading strings, even though I've more white hair than my own father."

"She sounds rather dear."

"She is. Hopeless, but dear." He tucked the food packet into a drawer. "Shall we go outside and find a hackney? I'm too tired to walk you home."

Not wanting to be a burden, she assured him, "You needn't concern yourself. It's still light out, and I've lived in London for years."

"I may have no talent for being a gentleman, but I certainly won't let a lady walk home in the dark." He grinned. "Besides, you only live three blocks from me."

"Yes, Dr. Kinlock," she said demurely, though inside her pulse quickened at the prospect of more time with him. Just breathing the same air made her feel more alive.

"Call me Ian. Hardly anyone does anymore," he said as he ushered her outside. "Sometimes I get very tired of being Physician and Surgeon Kinlock, one very long step removed from God."

"Just as I grow weary of being Miss Lancaster, paragon of virtue and highly qualified governess." She gave him a slanting glance. "By the way, what does a Sally look like?"

He chuckled as they stepped into the mild summer evening. "Look in the mirror, lass, and you'll find out."

He flagged down a hack and handed her into it. As she settled on the dingy seat, she felt well pleased with her expedition. There was nothing loverlike in the surgeon's attitude and probably never would be, but he seemed willing to be friends.

As they rode through the London dusk, she unobtrusively studied the craggy face under the shock of white hair. He might be willing to accept her friendship—but would that be enough for her?

Chapter 15

Jocelyn's lawyer called the next day. She gave him credit for nobly refraining from saying "I told you so" about the trouble caused by her impetuous marriage, though his expression was gloomy. The lawyer brightened when David outlined his thoughts on annulment. When he discovered that the major had read law, his expression became positively approving.

"I shall have to discuss the situation with a proctor—that is, a lawyer licensed to practice in the ecclesiastical courts," Crandall said thoughtfully. "I believe that the canon law covering this situation requires that the suit be brought by you, Lady Jocelyn. You must cohabit for a time first to . . . umm, verify that the problem is permanent. However, once the process is started, an annulment could be granted in five or six months, since the suit will be uncontested."

The better part of a year before she would be free? That would raise merry Hades with her plans, but she supposed it could be worse. "Very well, Mr. Crandall."

With a return of gloom, he said, "You understand that while your legal position is secure, an annulment will leave you vulnerable to a lawsuit claiming that you were never really married, and hence have not fulfilled the terms of your father's will?"

"I'm aware of the potential problems."

"Though you should win any such suit, the legal fees would be considerable, and there could be unwelcome notoriety." He peered at her over his spectacles. "You would not consider remaining married? It would be by far the simplest solution."

Patience at an end, she said briskly, "Simple answers are seldom the best, Mr. Crandall, especially in regards to something as important as marriage."

With a sigh, the lawyer left. After the door closed, Jocelyn asked, "Do you suppose he became a solicitor because he's glum by nature, or that being a solicitor has made him glum?"

The major smiled a little. "Some of both, perhaps. The practice of law is sobering, since one tends to have to always be dealing with life's problems."

"Then I'm glad you chose the army. Risking death seems to be much better for the disposition than drawing contracts."

A knock at the door heralded the arrival of Richard Dalton. After greeting him, Jocelyn excused herself to leave the two men together.

As Richard lowered himself into a chair, David rose and began to move restlessly around the room. "Don't mind me—after meeting with Lady Jocelyn's lawyer, I feel the need for activity." He stumbled and had to make a quick grab at the nearest bedpost to save himself from falling. "I'll have to see if Morgan can find me a cane to use until I regain the knack of walking."

"Good idea." Richard offered one of his crutches.

"In the meantime, take this. Jocelyn will be most displeased if you break yourself while I sit idly watching."

The crutch helped his balance considerably. He fell into a regular circuit around the room, grateful for the chance to use his weakened muscles.

With less of his concentration on staying upright, David noticed that his friend looked strained. "Is something wrong?"

Richard grimaced. "I decided to visit your miracle-working surgeon to see if he can do more for my blasted leg than the surgeons at the hospital have managed. Kinlock says he might be able to help, but the procedure he has in mind would be an experiment."

"Even with Kinlock, I'm not sure I'd volunteer to be a test case," David said with a frown. "What was his diagnosis?"

"The bones in my leg were badly set after the battle. No surprise, I suppose, given how overworked and exhausted the surgeons were." Richard surveyed his twisted right leg without enthusiasm. "The leg is so crooked that I'll be seriously crippled for the rest of my life. If I'm very, very lucky, I might be able to manage with a cane instead of crutches on a good day. And . . . it hurts like hell."

David winced. They'd never discussed Richard's injury, and he'd assumed it was only a matter of time until his friend recovered. "What does Kinlock suggest?"

"Break the bones where they're crooked and reset them. It's a radical approach, but he thinks there's a good chance that the leg will heal straight enough to allow me to walk and ride and be reasonably active. Though he makes no promises of eliminating all the pain, there would probably be significant improvement in that area as well."

David swore under his breath. Kinlock's suggestion made sense, but surgery was always a risk, and even if it was a success, Richard would have to endure long months of difficult convalescence. "Are you going to do as he recommends?"

"Yes. God knows that I'm not looking forward to the process, but Kinlock is the first surgeon to hold out any hope that I might get rid of these damnable crutches," Richard said vehemently. "Another operation, maybe two, and a few more months in hospital are a small price to pay for the chance to live something close to a normal life."

David was shamed by his own lack of perception. Over these last wretched weeks, Richard had always been there with a ready hand, a quip, or undemanding silence as required. He'd accepted that steadfast good nature at face value, never really thinking about his friend's private anxieties about his future.

Resolving that over the next difficult months he would be as good a friend to Richard as the other man had been to him, David said reassuringly, "Based on my experience with Kinlock, your leg will be perfect by the time he gets through with you."

"It needn't be perfect. I'll settle for ninety percent or so." Dismissing the topic, Richard continued, "What about you? You seem a bit blue-deviled for someone who has just stepped into a fairy tale complete with a miracle and a beautiful princess."

David walked to the window, leaning heavily on his borrowed crutch. "Fairy tales end with 'happily ever after.' The real world is a good deal more complicated."

"Meaning?"

Needing to unburden himself to someone who would understand, he replied, "Meaning that I find it vastly frustrating to be married to a fairy-tale princess who sees me as a brother, and who is pantingly eager to disentangle herself as quickly as possible."

"I've wondered if you might be falling in love with her," Richard said quietly. "Jocelyn is a lovely woman, as kind and intelligent as she is beautiful."

David gave him a sharp glance. "Are you in love with her, too?"

Richard shook his head. "No, but I can tell quality when I see it."

When David looked skeptical, Richard said apologetically, "I realize that not falling in love with her shows a dreadful lack of judgment on my part, but there it is."

David had to laugh. "From what I have heard about her winter in Spain, you were one of the few officers who didn't offer for her."

"Probably true." Richard's expression turned pensive. "That may be why she and I became friends. She seemed to—not exactly despise, but at least not take seriously—the men who became besotted. She'd tease them about being volatile, saying they'd fall in love with another woman in a fortnight. I actually spent more time with her than any of her suitors. Perhaps she's been courted so often that she's bored by it."

"That doesn't bode well for me," David said, trying to keep his tone light. "As soon as I saw her, I was ready to lay down head, hand, and heart, just like all her other volatile suitors."

"You're not volatile. If you feel that strongly, it's not mere infatuation." Richard hesitated. "Do you remember the wedding toast I made? When I said that you seemed to belong together, it wasn't mere rhetoric. I think you would suit each other very well."

David stared at him. "Good Lord, you have a devious mind! You couldn't possibly have foreseen how this would turn out."

"Of course not. You seemed unlikely to survive the week." Richard shrugged. "It just seemed right to bring you together, like one of those battlefield instincts that says when to duck."

"I should have ducked sooner this time." David ran the fingers of his free hand through his hair. "Lady Jocelyn never bargained for a live husband, and it would be dishonorable to try to hold her against her will. Her lawyer is already looking into the procedure for annulling the marriage."

"Surely an annulment will take some time."

"Several months at least."

"That gives you time to try to change her mind."

"Blast it, Richard, look at the disparity in our fortunes! She is rich, I most certainly am not. She's the daughter and niece of an earl, I have no relatives besides Sally that I'm willing to admit to."

"Are you going to give up without a fight because of pride?" Richard asked with maddening calm. "You may not be of equal rank, but you're a gentleman, and you've had a distinguished military career. You'd make a perfectly acceptable husband."

Thinking of the one insurmountable barrier, David retorted, "She's in love with someone else."

That gave Richard pause, but only briefly. "He must not be in love with her, or she wouldn't have proposed to you. Unless he's married, but surely she has better sense."

David shook his head. "From what she told me, the relationship was promising, but still in its early days." His hand tightened on the crutch. "I gather that the blasted man is handsome, wealthy, titled, of admirable character, and in all ways qualified to make Jocelyn an ideal husband."

"Perhaps, but it's quite possible that she'll never bring him up to scratch," Richard countered. "While you are available, interested, presentable, and not without a certain ability to charm the opposite sex. Those are considerable advantages. Why aren't you using them?"

"I suppose I've been waiting for someone to tell me that it's all right to take advantage of my position to try to win her heart," David said slowly. "But it still seems wrong. She could do so much better than me."

"In a worldly sense, maybe, but I think you'd make a better husband for her than a man whose greatest challenge has been the cut of his coat." Richard absently rubbed at his aching leg. "If you're concerned about being thought a fortune hunter, no one who knows you would believe such a libel, and who else's opinion counts?"

"You make the situation sound simple."

"It *is* simple. Lady Jocelyn is unlikely to consider you as a serious candidate for husband if you seem to want to end the marriage as much as she does. Give her the chance to make her own decision. She is quite capable of sending you packing if she feels the need. But the choice should be hers. Don't assume you know her mind, or that it isn't possible that she might come to care for you as much as you care for her."

Excitement quickened David's pulse. Richard was absolutely right. "Thank you for saying what I wanted to hear. I think I knew that you would, or I would never have raised the subject."

Richard laughed. "Glad to oblige. Lady Jocelyn is worth fighting for."

"That she is," David said softly. He'd have to tread a careful line to court Jocelyn without abusing the situation. God forbid she should consider him just another volatile suitor. He must be patient, let her come to know him. Living under the same roof should give him an abundance of opportunity.

And while his rival might have greater fortune and rank, David had the advantage of being a skilled campaigner who was determined to win.

Chapter 16

Jocelyn awoke at dawn after a night of restless dreams. The only one she could remember was her last waltz with the Duke of Candover. The exciting possibilities of that encounter hummed through her, until she remembered the awkwardness of her current situation.

When Candover returned to town in September, she would still be legally married to David Lancaster instead of an eligible widow, which meant that she couldn't begin an affair with the duke. Even though her marriage would be in the process of annulment, an affair would still be adultery. Unthinkable.

With a sigh, she rose from her bed, careful not to disturb Isis, and drifted to her window, which overlooked the garden behind the house. All her dreams must be delayed. What if Candover found another woman while Jocelyn was waiting for her freedom? He might be lost to her forever. Unlike her parents, she was not fickle, and she might never find another man who would suit her as well.

A curious calm fell over her. If she lost him, so be it. She could square an affair with her principles, but not adultery, not even with the man she had sought for years.

A glimpse of movement in the garden caught her attention. Was that the major? Lord, it was. Dressed in civilian garments, he was wavering his way along the path that circled the perimeter of the garden, leaning heavily on a cane.

The possibilities for hurting himself were minor compared to his midnight stroll along the gallery, but she still felt anxious. Walking alone might lead to a fall on the damp ground. If he couldn't get up, he might lie there for hours before someone found him. Perhaps take a chill and die of lung fever.

Wryly she recognized that she was allowing her mother cat instincts to run away with her. The major had survived years of warfare in a foreign country, and would probably come to no great harm in an English summer garden.

Still, it wouldn't be a bad idea to check up on him. She dressed swiftly, choosing a simple morning gown that could be donned without assistance from Marie. After tying her hair back with a ribbon, she descended the narrow backstairs.

Tantalizing scents of baking wafted from the kitchen, so she made a quick stop. Under the startled gaze of the cook and scullery maid, she collected two currant buns hot from the oven, wrapped them in a napkin, then left with a jaunty wave.

By the time she caught up with the major, he had circumnavigated the garden and started on another circuit. He smiled at her with friendly welcome. "You're up early, Lady Jocelyn."

She smiled back, the tension of her uneasy night fading. "And you aren't?"

She fell into step beside him. The garden was large enough to provide a good walk, and she often strolled along this path herself. The early morning was lovely, with dew sparkling like crystals on blossoms and leaves.

"I like this time of day. It's peaceful." He grinned. "I'm also a firm believer in trying to be as active as possible when convalescing, and it's easier to exercise when there is no one around to stop me."

"When I glanced out and saw you, I had instant visions of you collapsing among the rose bushes," she admitted. "It would have upset the gardener to find you like that, especially if you damaged any of his flowers."

"So naturally you came to see if the bushes and I were all right." His voice was warm with approval. "You're very thoughtful."

Embarrassed, she turned her gaze to the path ahead. "There's nothing unusual about looking out for one's guests."

"I was thinking more of the gardener, actually. Good ones are hard to find, I'm sure." His tone was solemn, but his eyes teasing.

She laughed. "Lewis has worked here for at least thirty years. It would be a shame to drive him away in his old age."

"He does a beautiful job." David's gesture encompassed their surroundings. "It's hard to believe that we're in the heart of London. The garden is so well planted that it seems much larger than it is."

"The gazebo at the far end is one of my favorite

places. Perfect for a meal or a quiet read on a summer day." She handed him a hot currant bun. "Since you show no signs of slowing down for breakfast yet, have one of these."

He bit into the bun and a blissful expression appeared on his face. "In case I've forgotten to mention the fact before, your cook is a treasure."

"I'm fortunate in my household," she agreed. "Since I can't have Charlton, I've concentrated on making Cromarty House as pleasant as possible."

He slanted her a glance. "Based on what Crandall said, I'll be enjoying your cook's skills for some time. I'd planned on looking for rooms soon, but that won't do since you and I must continue to share the same roof. I'm sorry for the inconvenience."

"No need to apologize." She swallowed a mouthful of bun, fragrant with plump currants. "I have plenty of space. Actually, I rather enjoy having the company." Particularly since David was the most comfortable of companions. She glanced at his strongly cut profile. He was better than a brother, since she might have had one she didn't like half as well.

"Have you never had a companion living with you?" he asked. "Surely it's unusual for an attractive young woman living alone in London."

"Aunt Laura Kirkpatrick was staying with me until her husband returned from the Continent, but she became exasperated with my outrageous conduct and decided to visit their estate in Kent," Jocelyn said wryly. "She'll return to town eventually, but I don't know when."

"Soon, I hope. I should like to see her again."

"You will. Cromarty House has always been home to my aunt and her family when they are in London. Since my father died, she's stayed with me when she is not following the drum. I've had other companions when Aunt Laura was with Uncle Andrew, but she's far and away my favorite."

"You are very like her."

"I hope so. Since her own children are sons, she has treated me like a daughter."

"Your mother died when you were young?"

Jocelyn tensed, as she did whenever her mother was mentioned. Avoiding a direct answer, she replied, "I scarcely remember her."

"I'm sorry," he said quietly. "It was fortunate that I had my father for enough years to know him well. He was something of a scholar and enjoyed teaching Sally and me. Some of the best memories of my childhood are of sitting with him in the library while he taught us geography from his great globe or going for walks with him through the countryside around our home."

A sudden memory struck Jocelyn—her mother weaving a wreath of spring flowers, then placing it on Jocelyn's head with a laugh and a kiss. She swallowed hard, fighting back the tears that sprang from nowhere. "Your father sounds like a gentle soul. Quite unlike your brothers."

"The difference was enough to make one think of changelings," he agreed. "My father's first marriage was arranged by the two families. My mother was his own choice. The wife of his heart."

They continued in amiable silence as they finished their buns. She kept an eye on the major's progress. While this lengthy walk clearly took effort, he was holding up well. Perhaps he was right to push himself with as much activity as he could manage. The civilian clothing that had accompanied him home from Belgium hung loosely from his gaunt frame, and he leaned heavily on the cane, but he no longer looked frail. In fact, with his height and broad shoulders, he was an impressive figure of a man.

"I've been thinking about what Crandall asked yesterday," David remarked.

"So have I. I noticed he didn't ask if the grounds for the annulment were valid. He restricted himself to discussing the best strategy for obtaining a favorable ruling."

Her companion shrugged. "His job is to represent your interests. It's probably easier not to know the whole truth in this case."

She felt a pang of guilt that David was having to walk a thin line between truth and lie because of her. She wasn't happy about the fact that they were shading the truth, either, but it was by far the simplest solution to their mutual quandary.

"There's something else Crandall said that I've been thinking about, Jocelyn," David said, his voice grave.

When he didn't say more, she murmured, "Yes?"

He took a deep breath. "I'm no great matrimonial prize, but—we are legally husband and wife. Have you considered the possibility of staying married, as he suggested?" He halted and turned to her. "I don't know what you hope for in a husband, but if it is to be loved . . . well, I think it would be very easy to fall in love with you."

She stopped in her tracks. "No," she whispered. They had become such good friends. She trusted him and was so comfortable in his presence. How could he suggest something that would change everything, and not for the better?

The silence between them throbbed with tension. She wanted to look away, but couldn't. He loomed over her, his hands folded over the head of the cane, his gaze searching. He was a strong man, with humor, intelligence, and honor. What would it be like to be loved by him?

Suffocating distress rose in her at the thought. She didn't want his love. Friendship was safer, and far more enduring. "No," she repeated. "I . . . I'm very fond of you, but not as a husband."

He became very still, and she feared that he was angry. Instead, after an endless hesitation, he smiled with no apparent distress. "I rather suspected that would be your reaction, but it would have been foolish not to at least consider the possibility." He offered her his arm. "Shall we see if we can charm more currant buns from your cook?"

Light-headed with relief, she took his arm and they turned toward the kitchen. She had not realized how much she valued his friendship until the frightening moment when she thought she had forfeited it.

Jocelyn had been correct in saying that the gazebo was a delightful place to read in the heat of a summer afternoon, but David wasn't looking at his *Morn-*

ing Chronicle. Instead he gazed at the roses and remembered how Jocelyn had looked that morning when they had walked together. Simply dressed and with bright tendrils of hair catching the sun, she'd been deliciously happy and relaxed.

Knowing it was time to test her feelings, he'd raised the issue of having a real marriage—and her expression had changed instantly to that of a vulnerable, haunted young girl. He'd been trying ever since to understand her reaction. She hadn't been offended. Surprised, yes, even shocked, but there had been something else.

Fear? Surely he was wrong about that. But whatever had shadowed her eyes, it was not the expression of a woman who was in love with one man and must regretfully tell another suitor that he was unsuccessful. Her objections came from some deeper, more mysterious source.

He'd had to fight the impulse to draw her into his arms and tell her that she would always be safe with him. Such a gesture would have been utterly wrong, so he had lightened the mood and been rewarded with her smile.

Winning her would be like coaxing a butterfly to land on his hand. Patience, gentleness, and perhaps a prayer or two would be required.

Would that be enough? He could only hope, and pray.

Lady Laura Kirkpatrick stretched luxuriously, then seated herself at the table by her bedroom window, her silk wrapper falling around her. The tray she had ordered sat on the table, the morning mail stacked neatly beside the gently steaming coffeepot. The top letter was addressed in Jocelyn's elegant, impatient hand.

She slit the seal, smiling as she heard the sounds of splashing water in the adjoining room. Kennington lay just off the main Dover to London road, and Colonel Andrew Kirkpatrick had arrived very late the night before, just off a cross-channel packet. Neither had expected to find the other at the estate, which made their meeting a special delight. Travel-stained and unshaven though he was, Andrew had wasted no time in joining his wife in her bed for a reunion that made her blush to her toes when she thought of it.

Beaming like a romantic schoolgirl, though with much less innocence, Laura scanned the first sheet of her niece's jasmine-scented paper. As she exclaimed with pleasure, her husband entered the room, toweling the last moisture from his freshly shaved face. He was a broad, powerful figure in his velvet dressing gown and moved with the vigor of a man much younger than his fifty years. "Good news, love?"

"The best, Drew. Did you receive the letter I wrote you when Jocelyn married David Lancaster?"

Her husband dropped his towel. "Good God, no! When did that happen? The last I heard, Lancaster was mortally wounded and had been sent back to die in London."

Over coffee and fresh bread served with sweet butter and honey, she explained her niece's creative solution to the need for marriage. "David had an operation, and Jocelyn writes that he is recovering well. I am so glad. He was a favorite of mine."

"Mine, too." The colonel sighed. "So many fell at Waterloo. But British officers are a tough lot. You might have heard that Michael Kenyon was dying? Like Lancaster, he has also pulled through against the odds, thanks to Catherine Melbourne, who nursed him in Brussels after the battle."

"Wonderful!" Mention of her friend Catherine reminded Laura of the long hours they had worked side by side in makeshift hospitals on the Peninsula. God willing, neither of them would ever again have to bandage bullet holes in dying boys.

As she and Drew broke their fast, they traded stories of mutual friends, mourning or rejoicing as appropriate. In the aftermath of the great battle, information had been hard to come by, but gradually the final toll was becoming known.

After they had caught up on the news, Drew asked, "Since your minx of a niece is not going to be a widow, what are her intentions toward Lancaster?"

Laura glanced at the letter again. "She hopes there will be some way to end the marriage. What a pity. I think David would make a wonderful husband for her, but I've sometimes wondered if she fears marriage too much to ever make a commitment."

"I've suspected that is exactly the reason your brother wrote his will the way he did," Andrew said shrewdly. "To force her into marriage because he feared that the great family scandal would turn her into a lifelong spinster."

Laura blinked. "Drew, that's brilliant. I'm sure you're right. That explains everything. How very devious of Edward!"

"When you're dead, it's devious or nothing," her husband said with dark humor.

She said with regret, "I suppose I should go back to London to chaperon." She'd much rather stay at Kennington. Her husband had several weeks free before he needed to return to duty, and a second honeymoon in the country would be delightful.

"Why on earth would a newly married couple need a chaperon?" Andrew grinned. "If you aren't present, their acquaintance may progress to the point where they decide to stay married."

She frowned. "Perhaps. But I'm afraid the outrageous way Jocelyn used David may have given him a disgust of her."

Her husband's thick brows arched. "You think your niece is outrageous? Is this the same Lady Laura Kendal who begged me to carry her off to Gretna Green when her father refused my suit?"

"For heaven's sake, don't ever tell Jocelyn that! I've spent years presenting myself as a pattern card of propriety, and she would never let me forget it if she knew how impetuous I had been." Her eyes gleamed. "Though if my father hadn't relented, it would have been Scotland if I'd had to abduct you myself."

Their gazes caught and held for a moment of deep intimacy. For more than twenty years of military life, their marriage had survived and flourished. Together they had danced at balls in Portuguese palaces and dined on scrawny Spanish chickens in mud-floored huts. Alone, she had sometimes waited in wrenching fear to learn if her husband still lived. Once she had defended herself and her small sons from bandits with a pistol held in two shaking hands.

It had all been very exciting, but she was ready for a new phase of life. With peace, there would be time for lazy breakfasts and long rides across the Kentish hills. And when the boys married and produced grandchildren she fully expected to spoil them shamelessly. Andrew, bless him, would spoil them even more.

Pulling her fond thoughts back to the matter at hand, she observed, "It certainly would be nice if Jocelyn and David fell in love with each other. She needs a man who won't try to change her, but won't let her walk over him, either."

"You may take it from me," the colonel said as he rose and came to stand behind her chair, "that David Lancaster is half in love with her already."

He wrapped his arms around Laura's waist and began to nibble delicately on her earlobe. "The Kendal women are absolutely irresistible to military men. It will take another twenty years for Jocelyn to become as beautiful as her aunt, but she's pretty enough to capture young Lancaster. I just hope she doesn't break his heart. He's not the sort to love lightly."

His hand slid sensuously down the silk of her wrapper, coming to rest on one breast. "Now, shall we stop talking about your tiresome niece?"

Laura laughed and turned her face up to her husband's. "Tiresome?" she said teasingly. "But you have always been very fond of Jocelyn."

"I find her distinctly unwelcome at the moment."

He accepted her offered lips, murmuring, "Remind me where we left off last night."

Laura decided that Andrew was quite right: Jocelyn had no need for a chaperon. She and Major Lancaster could work out their situation in their own way.

Her aunt had better things to do.

Chapter 17

Having seen Ian Kinlock's office at St. Bartholomew's hospital, Sally wasn't surprised to arrive at his private consulting rooms on Harley Street and find the reception room disorganized. She hadn't expected utter chaos, though.

She halted in the doorway, unnerved. The benches that lined the walls were filled to overflowing with waiting patients. Children crawled across the floor, a pair of boys lounged on the battered desk, and two men were arguing loudly about who was to see the surgeon next.

Swallowing hard at the smell of inadequately washed humanity, she asked the nearest patient, a vastly pregnant woman with an infant at her side, "These are Dr. Kinlock's consulting rooms?"

The woman nodded as if too tired for speech.

Sally's gaze scanned the reception area. "Is his clinic always like this?"

"On his charity days, aye. 'Tis quieter other days."

Sally had brought a picnic basket in hopes of another meal with Ian, but clearly he wouldn't be free any time soon. She was debating whether to leave when the voices of the two arguing men rose to shouts. Fists were clenched, and a fight seemed imminent.

Not wanting to think what a brawl might do to the women and children packed into the crowded room, she set her jaw and moved forward. "I *beg* your pardon," she said in freezing accents. "If you insist on behaving like barbarians, go outside."

Both men swung around in surprise. The taller, a burly laborer, said belligerently, " 'E says his wife is to see the surgeon next, but I'm in greater need. See?" He thrust a bloody, crudely bandaged hand at Sally.

" 'E can wait his turn, like the rest of us," the other man retorted. "Me wife was here first."

Other voices rose, either contributing opinions or stating claims for precedence. So much for the quiet evening Sally had hoped for. Repressing a sigh, she stalked to the desk and deposited her basket behind it. "Off," she ordered the sprawling boys.

One elbowed the other, snickering. She fixed him with a glare that could freeze an errant schoolboy in his tracks at thirty paces. "Must I repeat myself?"

The boys exchanged alarmed glances, then scrambled from the desk. Still standing, Sally announced to the room, "As an associate of Dr. Kinlock's, I shall determine when patients see him. Does anyone here have a true emergency? That is, an injury or condition that might cause death if treatment is delayed?"

The laborer started to lift his hand, then let it drop when Sally's gimlet gaze touched him. Patients shuffled and mumbled, but no one claimed an emergency.

"Very well." Her glance scanned the room. "Who arrived here first?"

Several people tried to speak at once with conflicting claims.

"Silence!" Despite her small size, Sally had learned to control a group by sheer force of personality in her early days of teaching in a school. Quiet descended instantly.

"This surgery will run much more smoothly if everyone cooperates," Sally said in a steely voice. "Dr. Kinlock is generously offering his skill and time. You are not entitled to try his patience as well. Is that understood?"

Heads nodded. It was understood.

"I will make a list of the order in which you arrived," she continued. "Who has been waiting the longest?"

After a pause, a frail old woman shyly raised her hand. Sally suspected that she had been waiting while more aggressive patients pushed their way ahead of her. Finding a sheet of paper in the desk, she wrote the woman's name down.

She was just finishing the listing of patients when the door to the inner office opened. A woman came out, holding the hand of a boy with his arm in a sling. Behind them was Ian, face tired. "Who's next?" he said gruffly.

"I am, sir," the elderly lady said in a whispery voice

As she rose to enter the office, Ian's gaze swept the waiting room. His jaw dropped. He must not be used to finding such a well-behaved group.

Then he saw Sally, and enlightenment dawned.

"Miss Lancaster. I'm so glad you could help out today." His words were formal, but his eyes glowed with amusement and appreciation.

She would walk across Wales barefoot to gain such approval. "I'm sorry that I didn't arrive earlier, Doctor. However, everything is under control now."

"So I can see." Eyes twinkling, he took the old woman's arm and gently helped her into his office.

Thinking it might be useful, Sally began questioning patients about what had brought them to the surgery. She soon learned that half the people present were merely accompanying someone who needed treatment. Others had minor problems that could be solved with common sense, or perhaps a listening ear. For example, there was the young mother who explained tearfully how much work an infant was, and how she worried she weren't takin' care of her babby right.

Sally held the baby and listened sympathetically before assuring the girl that her child was plump and beautiful and obviously well cared for, so her mama must be doing a fine job. Cheered, the mother decided that the baby's occasional cough was no great matter and left without seeing the doctor.

The surgery passed with surprising swiftness. As the crowd thinned out, Sally explored the desk and discovered a ledger book in a lower drawer, along with scraps of paper with names and sums jotted on them. She was not surprised to see that Ian's accounts were in grave disarray.

She was trying to make sense of the figures when the last patient left the surgery. Ian appeared in the doorway and leaned against the frame, his arms folded across his chest. "I'm through early tonight. How the devil did you manage to thin the herd?"

"Not everyone really needed a doctor. Some people just need to be listened to for a bit." She leaned back in her chair, stretching tight muscles. "How have you managed to survive without an assistant?"

"I had one, but he left. I haven't had time to find another." He looked hopeful. "I don't suppose you'd be interested in the position? No, I suppose not."

She wondered what she would have replied if the offer had been serious. All in all, she'd had a very satisfying afternoon. Organizing Ian's patients had given her wonderful opportunities to both act as a tyrant, and to offer good advice. Irresistible.

Reminding herself that she didn't need to work at all, she said, "I can help out here until you find a new assistant. In fact, I can assist you in the hiring."

"You're an angel," he said fervently. "I shouldn't question my good fortune, but what brought you here today?"

She gestured at her basket. "I thought I'd bring a cold supper, but I gave the food away. A woman with four children needed it more than you or I."

"A true angel, as generous as you are capable," he said softly. He raised a hand and touched her cheek, his strong fingers light as gossamer.

She caught her breath, wondering how a touch could affect every fiber of her being. For a moment they simply gazed at each other, the air between them throbbing with mutual awareness.

Perhaps her heart was too visible in her eyes, because he cleared his throat and his hand dropped.

"Allow me to buy you dinner. It's the least I can do."

"I expect to be very well fed indeed," she agreed, proud of how steady her voice was despite that moment of unnerving intimacy.

As she got to her feet, there was one thing she knew for sure: For an instant, at least, Ian Kinlock had truly seen her, and liked what he saw.

Chapter 18

Jocelyn surveyed her breakfast companion. Three weeks after his surgery, David was flourishing, scarcely needing his cane anymore. Another month of serious eating and exercise, and he'd be as good as new.

She grinned as he covertly slipped a piece of ham to Isis, who waited beside his chair with transparent anticipation. After gulping down the tidbit, the cat rubbed shamelessly against his leg. "Cupboard love, Major," she said with amusement. "She'd love Bonaparte himself if the price was right."

"I've heard the emperor couldn't stand cats." David fed Isis another shred of ham. "Clear proof of bad character."

She laughed. "Aunt Elvira loathes cats."

They shared an amused glance. The last days had been as peaceful as if the two of them had been stranded on a desert island, like Robinson Crusoe. With Aunt Laura in Kent with her husband and most of the members of the beau monde flown from the city, there had been few callers except for Sally and one or two of David's military friends. David was the best of companions, and Jocelyn enjoyed their long, lazy days, with strolls in the garden, meals in the gazebo, and lively discussions about books and newspaper articles.

As she watched David scratch Isis's head, she wondered for the first time if he might be finding their life a bit dull. His stay in London had been limited to the hospital and her house. "Would you like to go for a drive today?"

"I'd enjoy that."

Glad she'd made the suggestion, she said with mock warning, "I will drive my phaeton and shall be most displeased if you clutch your seat and mutter about harebrained female drivers."

"Anyone who has faced Napoleon's Imperial Guard is inured to lesser hazards," he said, amusement glinting in his eyes.

She smiled, enjoying his teasing. She should have adopted a brother years ago.

It was a sunny August day, and a brisk breeze blew away the less pleasant scents of the city as she drove through the park, then south toward the river. They were in the village of Chelsea when she finally drew the phaeton up in front of a livery stable. She gave the major credit for not demanding to know their destination. He was so *restful.*

"I want to show you my favorite place in the London area," she explained as an ostler emerged from the livery stable to take the horses.

David swung from the carriage and came around to her side to assist her. She took his hand and was climbing down when a gust of wind wrapped her skirt around her ankles. Losing her balance, she stumbled and fell forward into him.

David caught her before she could even gasp and lowered her so that her feet were safely on the ground. For an instant they were pressed together, her nose against his navy blue coat, which was subtly scented with the lavender it had been stored in.

She was searingly aware of the strength and warmth of his body, the beating of his heart against her cheek. Her mind leaped to the night he had kissed her on the gallery. The memories of his mouth on hers, the feverish heat of his body, were so intense that she feared he might pick them from her mind.

"Were you testing how much I've recovered?" he asked, his voice lightly amused in her ear.

She colored and stepped away, embarrassed. "If so, you've passed, Major. A few days ago, we'd have both been flat on the ground if I'd stumbled like that."

"It's nice to be able to rescue you this time." He bent to retrieve his cane, which had fallen when he caught her. "Of course it would have been more impressive to save you from villainous highwaymen, but lacking that, I shall settle for preserving you from a tumble."

She firmly suppressed her strange reaction to the incident. "We must walk down that road, beside the yellow brick wall."

"Is this a private estate?" he asked as they started down the road.

"You'll see." A few minutes' walk brought them to the property's entrance. On one side a brass plate read HORTUS BOTANICUS SOCIETATIS PHARMACEUTICAE LOND. 1686.

"This is the Chelsea Physic Garden," she explained as she rang the bell. "It's owned by the Worshipful Society of Apothecaries. Herbs and shrubs have been brought here from all over the world so that they can be studied to find new medications."

The gatekeeper arrived in response to her ring, greeting Jocelyn with easy familiarity. Once they were inside, she guided David toward the river, which bounded one side of the property. "The Physic Garden isn't open to the public, but an old friend of my father's is in the Royal Society. He brought us here once. I enjoyed the visit so much that he secured permission for me to come whenever I wish."

The garden covered perhaps five acres, and the unusual flora made it seem exotically un-English. Together they explored the winding paths, admiring such rarities as the cedars of Lebanon that flanked the water gate on the Thames and the rock garden that had been created from Icelandic stones. Eventually they settled on a bench in the shadow of a statue of Sir Hans Sloane, an early benefactor.

Relaxed again, Jocelyn inhaled the rich scents with pleasure. "Isn't the Physic Garden wonderful? Many of the plants are found nowhere else in England."

"I never knew this place existed. Just as Kinlock pushes the boundaries of surgery, the apothecaries are pushing the boundaries of medicine," David remarked. "I'm not too fond of opium at the moment, but the drug has been a blessing for countless people. Who knows what other wonders might emerge from here to serve mankind?"

She liked that he understood the drama, the romance, of this peaceful garden. His mind worked much like hers did.

He reached down and picked a flower with a cluster of tiny golden blossoms from a large clump beside the bench, then turned and tucked it behind her ear. "Your eyes turn this shade of gold when you wear yellow."

As a tangy herbal scent wafted from the plant, Jocelyn stared at her companion, her heartbeat accelerating strangely. The light brush of his fingers on her ear had started a tingling that spread in all directions. Once again, she could not imagine why she was reacting so strongly to a casual gesture.

What the devil was happening? This was her friend, her honorary brother, not one of her tiresome suitors, and definitely not the man she wanted to marry. She jumped up nervously. "It's time we were getting back, or we'll get caught in heavy afternoon traffic, and my horses hate that."

Together they left the garden. Yesterday she would have casually taken his arm, but not today, when touching was fraught with unexpected hazards.

As the ostler brought her carriage, she asked, "Would you like to drive?"

"Was my longing that obvious?" he asked ruefully. "I'd love to take the reins, if you're sure you trust me not to ruin their mouths."

She chuckled with a creditable show of casualness. "I'd be surprised if you turn out to be a ham-handed driver. And if I am wrong, I'll simply snatch the ribbons back."

As she expected, he was an excellent whip, effortlessly controlling her horses with a light but firm hold on the reins. She found herself watching his hands. They were large and capable, callused from honest work, not the pale hands of a dandy.

A thin scar ran from his left wrist to his ring finger. She wondered what had created it. A bayonet, perhaps, in a skirmish with a French soldier? That hand had been warm and steady when it held hers during the wedding ceremony.

Till death us do part . . .

She whipped her gaze forward. Her heart pounded as if she'd been running, and would not slow down until she fixed her gaze on the sleek rumps of her horses. Candover had chosen them for her, since females weren't allowed to attend the sales at Tattersall's. She liked the fact that the duke listened to her opinions on horseflesh with respect.

David always listened to her with respect.

She made herself think of Candover again, and the light that sometimes showed deep in his gray eyes. "Until September . . ."

Yet she could not remember exactly what his face was like. Handsome, yes, but the features would not quite come clear in her mind.

She could visualize David's face perfectly. Of course, she'd been around him constantly for several weeks now, so that meant nothing. *Nothing.*

She glanced at David again, glad his attention was absorbed with driving. He had a strong profile, but lines of humor were drawn around his mouth and those striking eyes. In spite of the weeks he had been hospitalized, his face had the weathered tan of a man who had lived outdoors for much of his life. A strong face, remarkably attractive, really.

Damnation, she was doing it again. In Candover's absence, Jocelyn's thoughts were beginning to focus on David. She really needed to see the duke again, to remind herself how special he was.

But it would be at least another month until he returned to London—and when he did, she would be in the beastly position of having to explain that she could not become involved with him then, but would be willing to do so later, when she was free. Would the fragile, budding relationship between them survive such awkwardness?

Bleakly she wondered if she'd ever get her life untangled again.

Perhaps it was mere coincidence that Jocelyn returned home to find a gift from the Duke of Candover. It was a slim, handwritten book that contained several poems by Samuel Taylor Coleridge.

The duke's note said:

I thought you might enjoy these. The poems have not yet been published, though I believe Coleridge's friends are encouraging him to make them generally available. I was particularly struck by the imagery of "Kubla Khan."

Until September—
Candover

Her throat tightened as she leafed through the volume. It was an exquisitely chosen gift, sensitive to her interests, rare and special, yet completely suitable for a gentleman to give to a lady.

Coincidence? No, the gift was a sign. She had needed to be reminded of where her heart lay. David might be her husband, but Candover was her future. The evidence now lay in her hands.

Chapter 19

It was a measure of the friendship that had grown between the two women that Sally decided to bring her problem to Jocelyn. It was late in the afternoon when she called, and her ladyship had just ordered tea in the morning room.

Jocelyn looked up with a smile when Sally entered. "What wonderful timing. I do hope you will join me for tea. But I'm afraid David isn't here. He's gone to visit Richard Dalton, who has had another operation and will be completely immobilized for the next several weeks."

"I know. Ian Kinlock told me he had broken and reset Richard's injured leg, and the prognosis is promising." Sally looked down at her hands and found that she was twisting her gloves nervously. "Actually, I knew David would be out. It was you I wanted to talk to."

Tactfully ignoring her guest's fidgeting, Jocelyn poured tea and offered cakes, keeping up a light patter of conversation. After a scintillating discussion of how gray the weather had been for several days, so dismal for August, Jocelyn finally said, "Is there something I can help you with? I should be delighted to try."

Sally swallowed hard, the delicious cake sawdust in her mouth. "I don't really think you can help, but I don't know who else to talk to."

Jocelyn made an encouraging sound. Unable to meet her gaze, Sally stared at a landscape painting. "How does a woman get a man to fall in love with her? I'm sure you've had a great deal of experience in that area, and some advice would be very welcome. Though it might be wasted on someone like me," she added bitterly.

Jocelyn set her delicate Sevres teacup down with a clink. "I . . . see. Not an easy question to answer."

At least she wasn't laughing. Sally was grateful for that.

"I doubt if there is any one method to inspire love." Jocelyn frowned. "Actually, I'm not sure how many men have really fallen in love with me. They say all heiresses are beautiful, so I think my fortune has inspired most of the admiration I've received."

"Nonsense. No doubt you've attracted some fortune hunters, but most of your admirers are seriously smitten. Look at David, and Richard Dalton."

"Sally, are you feeling unwell?" Jocelyn exclaimed. "You can't be sun-touched when the weather has been so gray. Perhaps some out-of-season oysters? I like David and Richard enormously, and I hope they feel the same way about me, but no one is in love with anyone."

Sally reconsidered. "Perhaps Richard isn't, though he could be with any encouragement. But David is certainly very taken with you."

To her surprise, Jocelyn appeared genuinely distressed. "David and I are *friends*, Sally. There's nothing the least bit romantic between us."

Did the lady protest too much? Not wanting to upset her sister-in-law any further, Sally shrugged. "No matter. If you don't know how you do it, there's no point in asking your advice. I'm sorry to have troubled you."

"You haven't troubled me." Jocelyn broke off the corner of a cream-filled pastry and offered it to Isis, who had been watching the platter with gimlet eyes. "I'd be honored if you would tell me what is on your mind. Even if I can't help, sometimes talking to a friend brings insight."

"If you laugh at me, I shall never forgive you!"

"Of course I won't laugh," Jocelyn promised. "I gather that you are interested in a man who is not responding as you would wish?"

Sally twisted her fingers together anxiously. "I . . . I seem to have fallen quite hopelessly in love with Ian Kinlock. We live near each other and often have dinner together. Sometimes I'll meet him at Bart's, and several times I've helped out at his consulting rooms, receiving patients and organizing the business end of his practice, which he completely ignores."

"I hadn't realized you've been seeing so much of him. Presumably he must enjoy your company," Jocelyn said encouragingly.

"He always appears happy to see me, and he seems to like our conversations, but that's as far as it goes. I'm not sure he's even noticed that I'm female. And if he has . . . well, that fact doesn't interest him."

Jocelyn frowned, understanding the problem.

Would Ian Kinlock ever look up from his work long enough to notice an available female? "A surgeon as dedicated as Kinlock might not make a very good husband."

Sally gave a crooked smile. "I'm well aware of his shortcomings. A wife would always come second with him. I can accept that. I admire his commitment and selflessness. That kind of passionate caring is unique in my experience."

Jocelyn thought of the doctor's compact power and craggy, appealing face. "I hope it's not only his character you admire. He's really a most attractive man."

"Believe me, I've noticed," Sally said with wry humor. "If I hadn't, my admiration would be more detached. Instead, I . . . I think about him all the time. How can I persuade him to treat me as someone other than a younger brother? I can bear to come second, but I want to at least be on the list of what's important to him!"

Jocelyn studied her guest. As usual, Sally wore a loose, high-necked gown with not so much as a ribbon to reduce the severity. Today's dress was navy, not her best color. Her thick hair was the same rich brown as David's, but it was pulled back into a tight knot from which no curl dared stray. Though her features were regular and she had wonderful green eyes like her brother's, no one would ever take her for anything but a governess. "If you don't want to be treated like a little brother, don't dress like one."

"I beg your pardon?" Sally said, offended.

"I don't mean that you look like a boy. I suspect that you might have quite a good figure if you ever wore a dress with any shape to it. But you seem determined to be as respectable and invisible as humanly possible."

"I suppose you think I should cover myself with ribbons and lace?" Sally said tartly. "I would look quite ridiculous. Besides, all that frippery is so—so superficial. A relationship between a man and a woman should be based on respect and mutual affection, not shallow appearances."

"That's very true and admirable," Jocelyn agreed. "But while affection and respect are the essential foundations of a good relationship, the fact remains that much of life is lived on the surface. For every hour that one discusses ethics or philosophy, there are a good many more spent in dining and driving and the trivia of day-to-day life, and there's no denying that a pleasant appearance adds to one's enjoyment of a companion." She had a brief, distracting thought of the hours she'd been spending with David. He was very nice to look at.

"Perhaps you're right," Sally said reluctantly. "But I would look utterly ridiculous rigged out in something like what you're wearing."

Jocelyn glanced down at her peacock-colored gown with its delicate French lace trim and appliqué work around the hem. "This may not be your style, but there are other modes available."

Sally sniffed, unconvinced.

A thought struck Jocelyn. "Do you dress so plainly because of your principles, or because you're afraid you can't compete?"

She half expected her sister-in-law to explode, but Sally considered the question seriously. "Some of both. I have held posts where it was wise to be invisible because of men who might have made my life difficult if they'd found me attractive."

"I hadn't thought of that," Jocelyn said, a little shocked at Sally's matter-of-factness about situations that must have been upsetting.

Sally absently scratched Isis's neck when the cat head bumped her leg. "Even before I became a governess, I found it wiser to dress severely. David joined the army when he was nineteen, leaving it up to me to run the household. My mother was a lovely lady, but not very practical. Because I was small, I did my best to look and act older when I dealt with tradesmen. After she died, I had to seek employment. My first position was as a schoolteacher, and I might not have been hired if I hadn't made myself look prim and older than I was. The habit of invisibility has served me well, until now."

Jocelyn nodded, understanding better why Sally was so stern, so protective of her brother. No wonder David was tolerant of her sometimes sharp tongue. Rising, she said, "The time has come for a change of style. Come upstairs and we'll see what we can find in my closet."

Sally looked at her with surprise and a touch of anger. "I didn't come to beg clothes from you."

"Of course not." Jocelyn swept her sister-in-law from the room. "But I always adored playing with dolls and haven't had the opportunity to do so in years."

Sally had to laugh. As they entered her spacious suite, Jocelyn continued, "My maid Marie is quite choosy about which of my castoffs she will accept.

She's easily as well dressed as I am, and it costs her next to nothing."

Sally's mouth quirked up. "You're saying that if I work at it, I might become as well dressed as a lady's maid?"

"Oh, not that well. Marie has that matchless French sense of style. I envy her." Jocelyn dived into the large closet, which had been built along one wall of her dressing room. "Will you feel better about my frivolity if I tell you that, pound for pound, I match my wardrobe costs with contributions to an orphanage? I have other charities, but this particular one benefits very specifically from how much I spend on clothing."

Sally looked startled. Apparently it had never occurred to her that Jocelyn might have charitable interests. Taking a mischievous pleasure in upsetting her sister-in-law's preconceptions, Jocelyn rang for her maid.

Marie appeared promptly. She was small, no taller than Sally, but with a more lavishly endowed figure. Wearing a gown of Jocelyn's that she had altered with her skilled needle, she was very well dressed indeed.

"Marie, we are going to discover what style best suits Miss Lancaster," Jocelyn explained. "The hair first. While we're working on that, think about which of my gowns would look well on her."

Sputtering half-hearted protests, Sally was placed in front of the dressing table. Marie unpinned her hair and brushed it out. "Excellent hair," the maid said thoughtfully. "But something softer is needed, eh?"

Working together, the three of them devised a style where most of Sally's hair was pulled back into a gentle twist that waved softly over her ears. With trepidation, Sally also allowed Marie to do some cutting. The result was a fringe of delicate curls around her face. While not inappropriate for a governess, the hairstyle made Sally appear years younger, and much prettier. Under Marie's tutelage, Sally soon learned how to create the style herself.

Beginning to get into the spirit of things, Sally didn't object again when Jocelyn and Marie started digging through the closet. Jocelyn pulled out a simple muslin gown in a shade of dark peach. "I'm tired of this one. Try it on, Sally."

Marie opened her mouth, probably to point out that the gown had never been worn, but Jocelyn silenced her with a glance. Her sister-in-law's need was greater.

Sally obligingly donned the gown. Marie pinned it at the back and hem, then said, "The mirror, mam'zelle."

Sally turned to look into the tall dressing mirror, then gasped. "Is that really me?"

"It certainly is. You've been hiding your light most effectively," Jocelyn replied, regarding the results with satisfaction. Her sister-in-law's figure possessed a slim elegance that her normal garments had effectively disguised, and the warm peach tones of the fabric emphasized her fine complexion. While she would never be a classic beauty, she was now a young lady who would draw admiring glances anywhere. Even Ian Kinlock would surely notice.

She turned to her closet again, her lips pursed thoughtfully. "What else would suit you?"

As Isis curled up on the discarded navy blue dress, four more gowns joined the gift pile. When the selection was complete, Sally gazed a little helplessly at the sumptuous array of fabrics. "I can't accept so much, Jocelyn."

"Consider the orphans. They'll benefit when I replace the gowns."

Sally laughed. "Since you put it that way . . ."

The two of them had more tea while Marie altered the peach gown. Since Sally wouldn't see Ian Kinlock until later, she brushed the cat hair from her navy dress and donned it again. Studying herself in the mirror, she said, "It's amazing what a different hair style will do. Even in my governess gown, I look much nicer than before."

"One more thing." Jocelyn opened a dresser drawer and brought out a cashmere shawl patterned in russet and gold. With touches of dark blue and brown, it could be worn with almost anything. She felt a faint pang at the thought of parting with the shawl, but it was perfect for Sally. "Take this, too."

"Oh, Jocelyn." Sally made a soft sound as she touched the luxurious fabric. "This is the loveliest thing I've ever owned. Thank you again. Your generosity shames me."

Jocelyn shook her head. "For true generosity, look to a woman who shares her family's soup with a hungry stranger. I've never lacked for anything, so I deserve no credit for giving away what I don't need."

"The richest family I ever worked for was also the

meanest when it came to helping those who were less fortunate." Sally gave her a shrewd glance. "Why will you never except compliments, Jocelyn?"

The unexpected question rocked her. Worse was the instant, unnerving answer. *Because I don't deserve them.* She had known that ever since—ever since . . .

Changing the subject, she asked, "Who is Jeanette?"

"How did you learn about her?" Sally draped the shawl around her shoulders, checking the mirror to see how it hung.

"David mentioned her name when he was out of his head," Jocelyn said, carefully casual. "Later I asked who she was, wondering if I should send a note about his recovery, but he avoided answering. Is she the sort of female men won't talk about?"

"No, she's not of the muslin company. To be honest, with so much happening in the last months I'd almost forgotten her existence." Sally tweaked a stray curl into place. "According to David's letters, Jeanette is from a French Royalist family and very lovely. I suspect he meant to offer marriage, but then he was sent to Brussels. He hasn't mentioned her to me since returning to England."

"I see. No doubt he thought it best to write her personally." Jocelyn carefully folded the peach gown to prevent it from wrinkling when Sally took it home. So David had plans of his own to marry. No wonder he'd suggested annulment as the swiftest way to end their unintended marriage.

Thinking back to the time he'd asked if she'd considered allowing their union to stand, she realized that he'd been tense when he raised the subject. As soon as she rejected the possibility, he'd relaxed again. Clearly he'd only made the suggestion because of the lawyerly practicality he shared with Crandall. His own attentions were fixed on someone else.

God and the ecclesiastical courts willing, by spring both of them would be free to follow their hearts. She was glad that his feelings were engaged. Probably that was why it was so easy for them to be friends. She just hoped Jeanette was good enough for him.

But why, she thought wryly, did a man seem more attractive as he became less available? How humbling to think one had so much in common with a cow stretching its neck through a gate for better grass.

Before leaving to face the world, Sally studied her image one last time. Her cheeks glowed pink with excitement above the vividly colored shawl. "Will I do?"

"Perfect. You look lovely, but still yourself," Jocelyn pronounced. "Remember, though, fine feathers are only part of what is required. More important is to *feel* that you are attractive. You must believe that it's only right and proper for Kinlock to find you irresistible."

Sally laughed. "So there is a secret to making men fall in love with you after all, and you've just explained it to me."

"Perhaps I did," Jocelyn said with surprise.

Sally hugged her hard. "Thank you for everything. Wish me luck, and not a word to David unless I am successful!"

Chapter 20

Sally was supposed to meet Ian at his consulting rooms that evening, but she wasn't surprised when there was no response to the bell. Probably he'd been called to a patient. She let herself in with the key he'd given her, her hands unsteady. He trusted her to enter and work on the accounts, but that was no guarantee that he'd even notice her enhanced appearance. Yet if this didn't work, she had no idea what would.

The reception room looked much better than on her first visit. Sally had arranged for one of Ian's patients to come and clean regularly. With several children and little money, the woman had been delighted to barter her labor in return for care and medicines when her brood needed them. Ian would have treated the children for nothing, but now the woman could keep her pride.

On the desk was a note in his surgeon's hasty scrawl. *I've been called out to an emergency. Don't know how long I shall be, but will understand if you don't wish to wait. Sorry! Ian.*

She smiled fondly. The words sounded just like him.

Willing to wait, she sat at the desk and pulled out the ledger. While she admired his willingness to treat charity cases for free, she saw no reason why his more prosperous patients shouldn't pay their bills.

It was a mixed blessing that Ian had a small independent income from his family. The money kept him from bankruptcy, but also permitted him to ignore his business. The man definitely needed a keeper, she decided. The trick was to convince him that she was the best one for the position.

After she finished writing invoices for overdue bills, she checked the examining room to see if anything needed to be done. She was always amused by the contrast between his jumbled reception room and the impeccable neatness of his surgery.

A quick glance indicated that all was in order, except for a heel of bread lying by the ceramic jug where he kept his nasty Russian dressing mixture. She lifted the lid and peered inside. Vile the stuff might be, but it had helped David and countless others. It looked a bit hungry. Probably Ian had been interrupted just before he could feed it.

She tore the bread into pieces and added it to the jar. Unknown to Ian, she'd also taken a sample home. The principle was the same as for yeast, where women cultured the same strain for generations, daughters taking a sample of their mother's yeasty bread dough to their new homes when they married.

Might yeast be the ingredient that made Ian's mixture so potent? Perhaps, though the smell was different from the yeast she was used to. Maybe that was because it was Russian. At any rate, if something happened to this original mixture, her daughter brew would be available for his patients.

She was adding water to the jug when she heard the outer door open. "Ian?" she called. "I'm back here."

He entered, a grin on his face as he saw what she was doing. "Is there another woman in England who would give such tender care to a mess of moldy bread?"

She turned so that he could see the peach dress in all its glory. His smile faded, and he stared at her as if she'd just crawled out from under a rock.

Chilled at his reaction, she stammered, "What's the matter?"

"Nothing." A muscle in his jaw worked. "Except that it has just struck me how very improper it is for a young lady to come here alone. I don't know why it's taken me so long to realize. After all, I was raised as a gentleman, even if I have fallen from that standard."

"Since when has visiting a doctor been scandalous behavior?" Sally said, trying to conceal her anxiety under a light tone.

"But you aren't here as a patient. You're a young, attractive woman. This could ruin your reputation. What if your employers took exception to your seeing a man without any chaperon? You could lose your position."

"The Launcestons are very liberal and have the radical view that employees are entitled to some privacy. They trust me never to do anything detrimental to the children," she said stiffly. "Besides, I'll be giving notice soon. With Lady Jocelyn's annuity, I have no need to continue as a governess."

He set his medical bag on the table, not looking at her. "All the more reason for you to take care of your reputation. I never should have allowed you to come here."

Hand shaking, Sally set the lid on the bread jug. "Are you saying that you don't wish to see me again? I . . . I had thought we were friends." Despite her best efforts, she couldn't keep a quaver from her voice. Ian had never said she was attractive before, just as it had never occurred to him that there was anything improper about her presence. Dear God, but she never would have changed her style if she had known it might drive him away.

His voice softened. "We *have* been friends, and I shall miss you a great deal." The Scots burr was becoming very noticeable. "But my office and Bart's and the tavern are no places for you. How often have I kept you waiting? Three times out of four?"

The question was rhetorical; they both knew the answer. Medical work was unpredictable, and more often than not an emergency or an unexpected number of patients would delay him. "I'm not sure which is worse, having you wait for me in a tavern or meeting me here privately," he continued. "Neither is right for a lady."

His blue eyes were troubled, and she had the horrible feeling that his attack of nobility would take him away from her forever. Desperate, she blurted out, "There is a time-honored method for a man and woman to be together with complete respectability. It's called marriage."

She froze, utterly aghast at what she had said.

Ian stared at her. "Sally, have you just proposed to me?"

She nodded mutely, her face hot with embarrassment.

Unable to face her, he crossed to the window and stared into Harley Street, where the oncoming dusk cast long shadows. He should have known something like this would happen, with her heart so open and ready to give love. He *had* known, and had refused to think of the consequences. It had meant so much to have Sally's companionship that he had denied, even to himself, how much more she had become.

"I had a wife once," he said abruptly, pain tight in his chest. It had been years since he'd spoken of his marriage, but time had made it no easier.

Behind him, Sally said quietly, "Tell me about her."

"Elise and I were childhood playmates. She was the loveliest creature, delicate as a fairy." It was becoming dark enough outside to see his own haunted reflection in the window glass. He'd been a mere boy when he'd married. A lifetime ago.

"I had always known I should study medicine. It was a calling as strong as a priest's. I read books, cared for injured animals, traveled with the local physician on his rounds. But medicine is not the occupation of a gentleman. Elise was a lady, and deserved better. We married after I finished at Cambridge, and lived in Edinburgh, where I had taken a government post." He drew a deep, shuddering breath. "Four months after the wedding, Elise fell down the stairs of our little house. She seemed unhurt at first, but that afternoon she collapsed. A hemorrhage of the brain. She died twelve hours later."

"I'm so sorry," Sally said, her voice soft with compassion. "How ghastly for you and the rest of her family."

He sensed her close behind him, knew the sympathy he would see in her eyes, and wasn't sure he could bear it. She was so good, so true, and believed that he was, too. "I don't know if any surgeon in the world could have saved Elise. Certainly I could do nothing." Steeling himself, he turned to face Sally. "But I do know that if I hadn't married her, if I had trusted my deepest instincts and studied medicine instead of taking a wife, Elise would not have died. She would have chosen a different path. Married a better man and had bonnie bairns and been happy. She . . . she was born to be happy."

Sally shook her head in disagreement. "You're too hard on yourself, Ian. You can't know what Elise's fate would have been if you hadn't married. Loving you, she might have chosen four months as your wife over a lifetime without you."

"I can't know about her fate," he agreed, bitterness in his voice. "But I do know that I used her ill by choosing love over my calling. After her death, I studied medicine and surgery with a vengeance. I sailed all over the world, became an army surgeon, learning and practicing everywhere. Sometimes I think doctors do very little good, but there are times when I know I made a difference. That is what my life has been about: making a difference. Not marriage, not money, not ambition as most men know it."

"Has it also been about loneliness?" Her voice was very gentle.

He wanted to bury himself in the softness of her hair, find solace in the warmth of her spirit. Instead, he must reveal how very unnoble he was, the sins he had committed despite the scourge of his Presbyterian conscience. "Of course I have been lonely. Sometimes there have been women who have been grateful for what I have done for them, or for their loved ones, and who have wanted to express their gratitude in a very personal way. Most of the time I have refused. As I have said, I was raised as a gentleman. But other times . . . I am only a man, with a man's weakness."

Her expression showed that she understood what he was saying, yet she didn't turn away in revulsion. "And with a man's strengths. Don't forget that, Ian."

Driven to bluntness, he said harshly, "You are grateful that I helped your brother. Don't make the mistake of confusing gratitude with love."

Surprisingly, she smiled. "Give me credit for some sense, Ian. Of course I'm grateful for what you did. I'd have happily given you every penny I ever possessed to save David." She reached out and laid her hand on his arm. "But gratitude would not have made me love you as I do. Love was inspired by what you are—the good, the bad, and even the foolish, which is what you're being now."

He jerked away from her touch, trying to maintain a scientist's detachment about his body's reactions, but his voice was rough when he replied, "I'd make the very devil of a husband, Sally. I become absorbed in what I'm doing and forget the time. I have no financial sense whatsoever and will never earn more than a modest living. I get irritable and bark at everyone, and I think about my work sixteen hours a day."

"I'm perfectly aware of how important your work is to you and would never interfere with that," she said crisply. "Look at me, Ian. I'm tough and practical, not a fragile plant in need of special attention. Work as late as you like, as long as you eventually come home to me. And I'll work beside you, because my talents will free you to spend more time doing what you do best."

Impossible to argue with that. Since she had started quietly organizing his life, he'd been both happier and a better doctor. The prospect of a lifetime spent with her companionship and strength was almost unbearably tempting.

Perhaps seeing the conflict in his eyes, she said quietly, "I love you as you are and haven't the least desire to change you. I am simply making a modest proposal: you will continue to be in charge of saving the world, and I will be in charge of saving you."

He had to laugh despite the ache of emotion. "Sally, you minx, haven't you heard anything I've said?"

"I've heard every word." She stared up at him, challenging him to match her honesty and vulnerability. "The one thing you haven't said is that you don't care for me."

"Of course I care for you!" he retorted, wondering how she could doubt that. "When we're together, I'm relaxed and happy as I haven't been since I was a bairn. You . . . you fill up holes in me that have been empty so long I had forgot what it felt like not to have them."

No longer able to resist his need to touch her, he traced the delicate lines of her face, the firm jaw and silken skin, the provocative softness of her lips. "And when I look at you, I think of what a wondrous and beautiful creation the female body is, in a way that has nothing to do with my profession," he said quietly. "I hadn't dared put a name to my feelings, but since you deserve the truth, I have no choice but to say that I love you."

With a smile that transformed her small face to heart-stopping beauty, she whispered, "Since we seem to be in agreement, why don't we do something about it?"

With a burst of gladness, Ian Kinlock surrendered to his fate, wrapping his arms around her in an embrace that nearly lifted her from her feet. Small she was, but every ounce was choice. "Ah, Sally, sweetheart, you're a Welsh witch. I thought I was too old and crusty to fall in love again. Then you swept into Bart's looking for the mad surgeon, so adorable I could hardly keep my hands off you. And so brave, helping me with your brother's surgery even though you were white as a Scottish sheet. I kept thinking how lucky your brother was to have earned such loyalty. I just hope to God you don't live to regret this."

Adorable? Sally thought about that for a moment; it wasn't a word she had ever associated with herself, but she liked it. She liked it very well. "I won't. You may think of your work sixteen hours a day, but that still leaves eight hours for me, and I don't expect that you'll be sleeping for all of them."

He burst out laughing, his face boyish under the white hair. "No, I don't suppose I shall, not with you around to keep me from my rest."

He bent his head to hers in a kiss that began in tenderness, and rapidly developed into a hunger of both body and soul. For a long, long time they stood in front of the window, making a spectacle of themselves for anyone who might be passing by in Harley Street. Dizzily it occurred to Sally that of course one would expect a doctor to kiss with great skill, since his knowledge of anatomy was profound.

She would have cheerfully gone upstairs to his rooms, but he finally released her, his white hair disordered where she had buried her fingers, and his breathing ragged. "I owe you a dinner, lass. Then we shall go to Cromarty House to break the news to your brother. I have no intention of asking his permission, because if he has any sense at all, he would refuse it."

"He'll be glad to have me off his hands before I dwindle into a maiden aunt." She fluttered her lashes outrageously, feeling giddy and desirable, because the man she loved also loved and desired her. "Shall I draw up a lineage chart for your mother's approval? I am not without respectable connections, and I'll have five hundred pounds a year."

"The annuity is that much?" Ian asked with interest as he escorted her to the door. "If you'd told me you were a wealthy woman, I would have proposed earlier."

"I proposed to you, remember? And don't worry,

by the time I have your office in hand, you'll be making quite a good living. After all, aren't you the finest physician and surgeon in London?"

On the steps outside the door he stopped and brushed her cheek with the back of one strong hand. "Not the finest, perhaps," he said, his voice very tender and Scottish. "But certainly the luckiest."

Regardless of who might be watching, Miss Sarah Lancaster, former prim governess, pulled her fiancé's head down and kissed him with great thoroughness.

Chapter 21

David felt as if he was living in an enchanted bubble, untroubled by the normal cares of the world. He and Jocelyn spent most of their waking hours together, and every day he wanted her more. After visiting the Physic Garden, they began making regular expeditions around London. They hadn't gone out together socially, though. It was easier not to have to explain their relationship.

The hard part was concealing his attraction. Jocelyn was a delightful companion, except on the few occasions he'd shown some sign of interest. Her withdrawal was always swift and complete. She tended to avoid even the most casual of touches, such as being helped from her carriage. Perhaps she sensed his desire and wanted no part of it.

But enchanted bubbles must eventually burst. It was mid-August and summer was at its heady best. All too soon the birds would be flying south, the beau monde would return to London, and Jocelyn would formally file for an annulment. Intuitively he felt that if he didn't change her mind by then, it would be too late. He would lose what he'd never truly had, despite her obvious pleasure in his company.

The day was warm, so they were lunching in the gazebo at the bottom of the garden. Both had brought books, and they might end up spending the entire afternoon with no more company than Isis, who sat with her paws demurely tucked in front of her, her gaze alert for any bird foolish enough to venture into her range.

"More coffee, David?"

"Please."

He watched as she poured for each of them, wishing he could lean forward and kiss her graceful nape, visible under the casually twisted richness of her hair. As he recovered his strength, it was becoming increasingly difficult to conceal such thoughts.

Better to think about how Sally and Ian Kinlock had announced the news of their engagement. David had been amazed. How had Sally managed to fall in love and captivate an admirable husband under his very nose without him noticing?

Jocelyn hadn't been surprised, though. With a smile that reminded him of Isis, she'd ordered champagne, and they'd toasted the betrothal. He wouldn't have believed that the intense surgeon could ever be so relaxed, but clearly love had worked magic on both Sally and Ian. He'd been envious as well as genuinely pleased for the happy couple.

Pulling his gaze away from Jocelyn, he remarked, "Not only will Kinlock make Sally a worthy husband, but I keep thinking how convenient it will be to have a good doctor in the family."

She laughed. "I've thought of that. May I borrow him if needed?"

He looked away at the reminder that Jocelyn didn't

intend to remain part of the Lancaster family. His gaze fell on Dudley, who was approaching with a tall, serious-faced man who looked as if he might be something important in the City. The butler looked disapproving, but then, he usually did.

Reaching the gazebo, Dudley said, "Excuse me, Lady Jocelyn, but this person claims to have extremely urgent business with Major Lancaster."

The fellow must have been persuasive to talk Dudley around. David studied the newcomer, but was sure they'd never met.

The man stepped forward and bowed. "Forgive me for disturbing you, but I have urgent business with Major Lancaster." His intent gaze went to David. "You are the Honorable David Edward Lancaster, born at Westholme in the county of Hereford in 1783?"

David's neck prickled. Such a legalistic introduction did not bode well. "I am," he said coolly. "Forgive my rudeness, but what business is it of yours?"

"Permit me to introduce myself. I am James Rowley. You may not remember my name, but the Rowleys have represented the Lancaster family in its legal affairs for three generations."

He should have known the man was a lawyer. Struggling to control the anger that Rowley had triggered, David said tersely, "No doubt my brothers heard I was near death and sent you to confirm the happy event. You may inform them that they are out of luck. My health is now excellent, and I have no intention of gratifying them by dying any time soon. May I look forward to being ignored by them for another twenty years?"

Startled and uncomfortable, the lawyer protested, "That is not why I'm here. Indeed, I'm delighted to find you recovered"—Rowley paused, then said with emphasis—"Lord Presteyne."

David went cold, as numb as when the lethal shell fragments had struck him down. On the other side of the table, Jocelyn gasped, her gaze going to his face as she recognized what had just been said.

After drawing a deep breath, he said, "You'd best sit down and explain yourself, Mr. Rowley."

The lawyer stepped into the gazebo and took a chair, setting his leather portfolio on the floor. "It's a straightforward matter. Your three brothers are all dead without heirs, so for the last several weeks you have been the seventh Baron Presteyne."

Unable to escape the belief that this was a jest in incredibly bad taste, David retorted, "All three of those brutes met their maker at once? Someone must have burned the house down with them in it."

"It wasn't that melodramatic. Not quite." The lawyer cleared his throat. "Your middle brother, Roger, drowned three years ago in a boating accident. Then this year, early in July, your other brothers, Wilfred and Timothy, engaged in a drunken brawl." He glanced at Jocelyn, who was listening in fascination. "The cause is unimportant. They chose to duel on the South Lawn to settle the matter. Whatever their defects of character, both were excellent marksmen. Timothy was killed outright. Wilfred lingered for some days before succumbing."

"Dare one hope that he suffered a great deal?" David said, unable to control his bitterness.

Eyes enormous, Jocelyn reached across the table to

him. He caught her hand, holding on as if she was his lifeline. Perhaps she was, as he fought a flood of long-buried memories.

"You have every right to be furious. Your eldest brother in particular acted abominably when he evicted your mother, your sister, and you from Westholme. It was most unfortunate that your father did not make clearer provisions for his second family, but he was too trusting," Rowley said soberly. "But that was in the past. They are dead, and you are alive. You are now the seventh Lord Presteyne, with all that implies."

With effort, David masked his roiling emotions. "From what I remember of Wilfred, what's implied is a large number of debts. Will there be anything left after settling them? It would be just like him to gamble Westholme away."

"The estate is encumbered, but not hopelessly so," the lawyer replied. "The trustees, of whom I am one, would not allow your brother to mortgage the property as heavily as he would have liked."

That was good news. Westholme had been in the family for over three centuries. It would have been bitterly ironic to inherit the title without the estate that had been the heart and soul of the Lancasters. Beginning to absorb the magnitude of the news, he said, "I don't suppose there's any money, but as long as the estate survives, there is hope."

"I could not in conscience wish for your brothers' deaths, but I am most pleased that you have inherited," Rowley said austerely. "I kept in touch with your mother after she left Westholme, and I followed your army career. You and your sister are cut from very different cloth than your half-brothers."

"That's obvious," Jocelyn said tartly. "Those brothers sound dreadful."

"There was madness in their mother's family," the lawyer said. "They were more than just disagreeable. I think they were mentally afflicted."

David laid his left hand on the table, palm down. A thin white scar ran from wrist to finger, paralleled by several lighter scars. "Do you see those lines? Timothy cut them with an Italian stiletto he was very proud of. He said he would keep cutting until I said my mother was a whore. I was six years old."

Jocelyn gasped, her horror and revulsion mirrored by the lawyer. "Did someone come along and stop him?" she asked.

"I fought as best I could, given that he was thirteen and easily twice my size. My chance of winning was nil, but the noise attracted two footmen, who separated us."

"Was he punished?" Jocelyn's face was pale.

"Wilfred told him not to play childish pranks," David said dryly.

"Childish pranks!"

David studied the scars, remembering the vicious pain, and the even more painful humiliation of the older boy's insults. "My father wasn't told. Neither my mother nor I wanted him to know how wicked his older sons were. It would have hurt him terribly."

Rowley shook his head in amazement. "I had no idea the situation was so bad."

"Sorry, I didn't mean to give you nightmares. It's

ancient history. Mother and Sally and I were happy in our cottage, and grateful to be away from Westholme. It would have been impossible to stay after my father died."

The lawyer leaned forward intently. "I can understand that you might not wish to return to the scene of so much unpleasantness, but Westholme needs you. The estate has been neglected, the tenants are demoralized. I'm here today not only to tell you of your inheritance, but to urge you to take control as soon as possible. When you do, the other trustees and I will release what money remains toward immediate improvements."

David almost laughed. The lawyer seemed to think that he might want nothing to do with Westholme. Getting to his feet, he said, "You need have no fears on that head. It was my brothers I hated. Westholme"—he hesitated—"Westholme I have always loved. Give me your direction, and I will call on you tomorrow to discuss the situation further. For today, I have quite enough to think about."

Rowley stood and gave a rare smile. "On behalf of the tenants and employees of the Westholme estate, may I congratulate you on your new honors, Lord Presteyne?"

David smiled faintly and offered his hand. "You may."

"Lady Presteyne." The lawyer inclined his head to Jocelyn, then made his way up the garden path.

Struggling to absorb the enormity of what had happened, David resumed his seat, saying with an attempt at humor, "Now you know my guilty secret."

"That for all of these years you were 'honorable' but hiding the fact? It didn't work—I knew you were honorable from the beginning." Jocelyn laid her hand over his, her eyes intent. "How do you feel about this, David? You've just inherited a great many demanding responsibilities that you never expected."

"You're right. It quite literally never occurred to me that I would ever inherit, not with three older brothers." He smiled wryly. "I guess Wilfred and company have just disproved the old saying that only the good die young."

"Either that, or it proves that sometimes divine justice takes a hand." She looked thoughtful. "The morning you recovered from the opium withdrawal, I asked where you had been trying to go, and you said Hereford. Does that mean you'll be happy to return?"

"In spite of everything, I will," he said quietly. "There is no lovelier place on God's green earth."

Her smile was generous and full of understanding. "As I feel about Charlton."

"Precisely." He withdrew his hand as some of the repercussions of his inheritance struck him. "I'll have to go to Westholme soon to determine what needs to be done. Will you come with me? I suspect that you're more knowledgeable about land management than I, and I'd value your opinion."

He held his breath as surprise, pleasure, and wariness rippled across her face. Was she uneasy about being with him on his property rather than in her own home, where all of the servants were loyal to her?

Making up her mind, she said, "I'd enjoy that."

Before he could feel too pleased, she added, "Since we're supposed to appear properly married before I can file for the annulment, I'd better behave in a wifely way."

Not as wifely as he'd like, alas. He stood. "I'll go break the news to Sally. It may be a while before the money is available, but she will eventually have the portion she should have inherited when my father died." He hesitated, then said, "Would you mind terribly if I call on Richard alone? I know we had planned to go together, but there are some things I would like to discuss with him privately."

She looked a little hurt, but covered her reaction with a sunny smile. "Of course not. Give him my best wishes. I do wish he had come here to convalesce from the operation. It would have been no trouble."

"He had his reasons, I'm sure." With a nod, he left the gazebo. In fact, Richard had said that a guest in the house might interfere with any relationship that might develop between David and Jocelyn. Though for all the progress David was making, Richard might as well have accepted Jocelyn's invitation.

Chapter 22

David chose to walk to the York Hospital, both to build his strength and to give him time to sort out his chaotic emotions. In most ways, his unexpected inheritance was a great blessing. Certainly he no longer need worry how to occupy himself for the rest of his life; from the sound of it, Westholme would require major attention.

He had a lot to learn about agriculture, since he hadn't been trained as the heir and had left the estate when only twelve. Still, learning to run his estate was a relatively straightforward challenge. Less certain was the troubling question of how his inheritance would affect his relationship with Jocelyn.

The York Hospital was as dismal as ever, though less crowded now as patients either died or left. When he entered Richard's room, his friend looked up from a book. His injured leg had been splinted and bound, and it would be weeks before he could use crutches again. But his prospects for recovery were excellent, which kept him in good spirits. "Hello. No Lady Jocelyn today?"

David shook hands with his friend. "No, I decided to walk over on my own. She sends her best wishes."

"Please thank her for the books she sent. With these and the flowers and food she sends regularly, I'm the most pampered patient in the hospital."

"She's regretting that she doesn't have you at Cromarty House, so she can pamper you more thoroughly." David sat in the single wooden chair. "There's been a remarkable amount of news since I visited yesterday. To begin with, my sister and Ian Kinlock are to marry."

"Excellent!" Richard chuckled. "That's quite a job of matchmaking you managed from your deathbed."

"I hadn't thought of it that way. I shall tell Sally that she must thank me for getting mortally wounded." He paused, surprisingly tongue-tied about his other news. "That's not all that's happened. I'm going to be selling my commission after all. I've found another situation outside the army. Or perhaps I should say that it found me."

"Is that an oblique way of saying that your relationship with Lady Jocelyn is progressing satisfactorily?"

"No such luck." He ran restless fingers through his windblown hair. "I've told you about the three half-brothers that I didn't get on with. What I didn't mention was that our mutual father was the fifth Lord Presteyne. This morning I learned that all three brothers have shuffled off this mortal coil. I have suddenly become a baron."

"Good God!" Richard said in blank astonishment. "Will you still talk to us commoners?"

David looked up with a flash of real anger. "Richard, don't ever say anything like that again, even in jest."

"Sorry. I know you would never drop your old friends for such a reason." He studied David's face. "You look like you've been struck by lightning."

"That's how I feel." He grimaced. "I'm not unhappy about inheriting, but the idea will take getting used to."

"I can well imagine. Luckily my father was an itinerant fencing master, so I have no such surprises in my future. Being a lord strikes me as a very confining occupation."

David turned one hand palm up. "Confining, yes, especially since the estate isn't in good financial condition. But . . . my roots are at Westholme. Nowhere else could ever be home in the same way."

"Then I'm glad for you." Richard's brows drew together thoughtfully. "I assume this eliminates your worries about your station being too far beneath Lady Jocelyn's."

"Her rank and fortune are still greater than mine, but the differences are minor compared to before." David drummed his fingers on the arm of his chair. "The drawback to my change in circumstances is knowing that she has a passion for land. I wonder if she might choose to remain married because of Westholme. Sentimental fool that I am, I'm not sure I would want her to stay for such a reason."

"If she did, would that be such a bad thing? You get on very well already. A mutual passion for your estate might be a good foundation on which to build a deeper relationship."

"That's a very cold way to look at marriage," David observed. "I don't think you'd be so practical if you'd ever fallen in love."

"Probably not," Richard agreed. "But I do think you're worrying too much. If she is really in love with that mysterious other man, your inheritance won't make any difference. If she does stay with you, it will be for a good reason."

David sighed. "You're probably right. I must say, this inheritance is giving me new insight into why Jocelyn has so little use for fortune hunters. It's only been a couple of hours since I inherited, and I'm already thinking the worst."

"You'll get used to it, Lord Presteyne."

It was odd to hear the title on his friend's lips, but as Richard said, he'd get used to it. "She's coming to Hereford with me. The next few weeks should tell the tale."

"You'll carry the day. You've always been a first-class campaigner."

"I wish I had your confidence." David thought of Jocelyn's graceful figure, the tenderness of that morning they awoke in the same bed. His jaw tightened. "But if I fail, it won't be for lack of trying."

Tired by his long walk, he hailed a hack, but instead of going directly to his sister, he gave the address of John Crandall, Jocelyn's lawyer. Talking to Richard had helped clarify his thinking. Now it was time to take some precautions.

Luckily Crandall was free when David arrived. His habitual gloom lightened when he heard of the inheritance. "Does this mean that you and Lady Jocelyn will remain wed? It would be so suitable."

"That decision must be the lady's. So far, her preference is for annulment," David said with careful neutrality. "She and I will be traveling to evaluate my estate in Hereford. I think it best to file for the annulment before we leave."

Crandall frowned. "Do you think that necessary?"

"I do." David volunteered no more information. Though his will had always been strong in the past, he feared that spending so much time with Jocelyn might warp his honorable intentions of letting her leave him. Far better to institute annulment proceedings now, so that he could not stop the process even if he wanted to. The power *must* be in Jocelyn's hands, since he didn't trust himself.

Seeing that David was not going to elaborate, Crandall said, "I have conferred extensively with the proctor—that is, the ecclesiastical lawyer—who will present the case to the consistory court. Church courts are different from king's courts in that the principals do not testify. Evidence consists of depositions from witnesses." He gave a dry little cough. "Two medical affidavits certifying the extent of your injuries will be required. I presume that you have doctors who will bear witness to that."

David nodded, reasonably sure that wouldn't be a problem. And if he later decided to marry to get an heir, well, he could always claim a miracle had occurred. "What about the evidence concerning Lady Jocelyn?"

Looking embarrassed, Crandall said, "There must be an examination, of course. Perhaps a midwife can be brought in, in deference to the lady's sensibilities."

That was a good idea, though the examination was sure to be unpleasant no matter who performed it.

"Do you think that the court will be sympathetic to our case, given the unusual circumstances?"

Crandall leaned back in his chair and steepled his fingers, more at ease now that the conversation had returned to legal issues. "I believe so. It would be considered only reasonable for the late Earl of Cromarty to hope his daughter would carry on his blood, if not his name. The fact that the lady followed her heart to marry a gallant hero of Waterloo, then found herself in a position where she might be deprived of children . . . yes, I believe the court will take a compassionate view of the issues."

The lawyer's florid description made David suspect that the man secretly read Gothic novels, but no matter, as long as he was accurate in his reading of the legal situation.

After the remaining points had been discussed, David left, secure in the knowledge that the annulment would proceed with maximum efficiency. *Hell.*

The evening before Sally had mentioned that she would be at Kinlock's consulting rooms in the afternoon, so David sought her there. He found her with her head bent over a ledger and a quill in one hand, but she glanced up when he entered. "Behold your sister, the clerk," she said gaily.

He kissed her cheek, then sat on one of the benches. "The work seems to suit you. Or is that the glow of new love?"

"Both. I'm managing by nature, so I quite enjoy seeing that Ian's office runs smoothly. It's better for him, better for the patients. As to Ian himself—well, I'm pinching myself hourly to see if I'm dreaming."

Her happiness lightened his mood. "It doesn't sound as if it took you long to accept when he proposed."

She blushed. "Actually, I asked him. He took some persuading, too!"

After an instant of surprise, David laughed. "You *are* a managing woman. But by the time the two of you broke the news, he was obviously entranced by the prospect of marrying you." His amusement faded. "Today I was visited by a Mr. Rowley, the Lancaster family lawyer."

Sally tensed, as wary as he had been. "Yes?"

"Our three brothers are dead. All of them," he said baldly. "I'm the seventh Lord Presteyne."

The quill snapped in her fingers. "Good God! How . . . remarkable. What happened?"

After he explained, she said, "I suppose I should make a show of good Christian regret, but I can't. They reaped what they had sowed."

He and his sister shared somber glances. In all the world, only the two of them would ever know the whole wretched story of abuse. Their parents had prevented the worst excesses, but hadn't been aware of the small daily humiliations Sally and David had endured. That shared persecution was the foundation of their unusual closeness. Someday it might be possible to pity the three older Lancasters, but for the moment neither of the younger ones had any desire to try.

David broke the silence. "The estate is short of money now, but eventually, you'll receive the marriage portion that should have been settled on you."

"Good. Betrothal is making me amazingly practical." Sally chuckled. "Ian hates to admit it, but he's the son of a Scottish baron. He once mentioned that his mother worried that he'd fall prey to some totally ineligible female, so she should be happy to know that I'm the sister of Lord Presteyne."

"You always were."

Her face hardened. "I'd rather have been an orphan than claimed Wilfred as kin."

Kinlock chose that moment to return from his call on a patient. He entered the reception room with his medical bag swinging in one hand as he whistled like a schoolboy. Impending marriage definitely agreed with him.

The surgeon greeted his visitor jovially, then perched on the desk, one hand on his fiancée's, while David told him about the barony. Kinlock was intrigued, but not particularly impressed. Pedigrees interested him much less than people did.

After explaining his inheritance, David asked, "May I talk with you privately, Kinlock?"

"Of course."

Seeing his sister's raised eyebrows, David assured her, "Nothing to do with you, Sally. Remember, I'm a former patient."

Kinlock gestured him into the inner office. When they were private, he said, "You look hale enough. Do you feel as if something is going wrong with your recovery?"

"This concerns a different aspect of my injuries." David hesitated, wondering how best to broach the subject. "I don't know if Sally has told you that Jocelyn will be seeking an annulment on the grounds of impotence."

Kinlock's brows shot up. "It's too soon to be thinking like that, lad. You're not fully recovered, and I don't think that the injury you suffered will have that kind of long-term effect. Give nature a chance to take her course. Worry itself can cause exactly the condition you're worrying about."

David raised a hand. "You're right, it's too early to be sure. That's why I thought it best to obtain medical depositions now, when they won't present a challenge to the conscience."

"I . . . see." Kinlock folded his arms. "Then again, maybe I don't. Perhaps you'd better explain."

David paced across the room to the window, hating that such private issues must be discussed, though he supposed that with a lawsuit pending, it would only get worse. "Miracles can have unexpected repercussions," he said stiffly. "Our marriage . . . was never intended to last."

After a long silence, Kinlock said, "Serious spinal injuries like yours can be braw tricky. It's certainly not beyond the realm of possibility that sexual function could be affected. Send your lawyer, and I'll make a statement to that effect."

"Thank you." David turned away from the window, feeling tired. "As long as you feel you can do so honestly. I don't want to abuse the fact that we are soon to be brothers-in-law."

Kinlock shrugged. "The law may be full of hard and fast lines, but medicine isn't. It's not my place to say whether or not you and Lady Jocelyn should stay married. Though my personal opinion is that you're making a big mistake."

David smiled without humor. "Would you want to hold Sally in a marriage against her will?"

The other man frowned. "No, I suppose not."

David took his leave, choosing to walk again despite his fatigue. Perhaps the late afternoon sunshine would dispel some of his gloom.

It was ironic, really. Here he was doing his damnedest to ensure Jocelyn's free choice—yet in his heart, he wished that annulment wasn't possible, and that he and his wife would have to make the best of their marriage.

Chapter 23

Three days later they set off for Hereford. Jocelyn was glad to leave London. She supposed David was wise to put the machinery of annulment into motion, but the physical exam to prove that she was *virga intacta* had been humiliating in the extreme. She found the whole subject of annulment distasteful. The best that could be said about it was that it was not as bad as divorce.

Rhys Morgan rode on the box with the driver and acted as guard, an excellent use of his military experience. Though it would be a while before the stump of his leg healed enough for an artificial limb to be fitted, he had already made a place for himself in Jocelyn's stables, working with the horses and tack.

Marie had nearly purred when she found that she would be sitting next to Hugh Morgan for several days. Hugh had easily shifted from being the major's nursemaid to his valet. Though his skills were still imperfect, his enthusiasm more than made up for that. All in all, it was a happy expedition. The only discontent was manifested by Isis, who had yowled plaintively when Jocelyn left, apparently recognizing from the piles of luggage that a long journey was contemplated.

They took an indirect route, swinging west into Wales to drop the Morgan brothers off at their family's home near the market town of Abergavenny. It had been years since Rhys had seen his parents, and he planned on staying with them at least a fortnight. Hugh would also stay for a week, then travel to Westholme to join his master.

Jocelyn had never visited Wales before, and was delighted by the dramatic landscape. At her suggestion, they stopped on the crest of a hill overlooking the town as they neared their destination.

While Rhys stared at his home, eyes suspiciously bright, Hugh said to Marie, "My family lives on the mountain just above Abergavenny. See that wisp of smoke coming from the trees? I think that must be the cottage."

Marie shaded her eyes and peered across the small valley. "Such a lovely place to grow up," she said in her charming French accent. "What is the mountain named?"

"Ysgyryd Fawr."

Her eyes rounded. "What did you call it?"

Patiently Hugh attempted to teach her the correct pronunciation, but she couldn't get her tongue around the unfamiliar sounds. As Jocelyn and Marie dissolved in laughter, Hugh muttered something good-naturedly under his breath in Welsh.

To Hugh's shock, David replied in equally fluent Welsh. The valet gasped, "You speak Cymric, my lord?"

David laughed and replied in Welsh again. A look

of horror crossed Hugh's face. "I'm sorry for anything I might have said, my lord." He smiled ruefully. "I should have known you were Welsh when I found your Christian name was David."

"My mother was Welsh, and I was raised speaking both languages," David explained. "Don't worry, you never said anything that I might take offense to."

Jocelyn watched the byplay with amusement, enjoying this new facet of the major. He wasn't the sort of man one would ever grow bored with.

They all climbed into the carriage again for the last stretch, and soon they pulled into the yard in front of the Morgan cottage. Instantly a happy riot broke out. With a whoop, Rhys grabbed his crutches and swung off the box, while Hugh forgot his manners and leaped from the carriage.

"Rhys! Hugh!" A solid woman with apple cheeks rushed from the house and tried to hug both her tall sons at once. Within moments three younger children and Mr. Morgan appeared to contribute to the uproar, along with two dogs, and several chickens whose main interest lay in escape.

Unnoticed by the Morgans, David helped Jocelyn from the carriage. Not wanting to intrude on the emotional family reunion, she admired the glorious view of the Brecon Beacon mountains to the west and the Usk river valley below. "It must be hard to leave here. There can be few more beautiful spots in Britain."

"Beautiful, yes, but there is little work," David said pragmatically. "All the Celtic lands are beautiful and poor. Sometimes it seemed the army was made up of Irishmen, Scots, and Welshmen. Hugh and Rhys must count themselves lucky to have good jobs now. I imagine both of them have been sending part of their salaries home for years."

She bit her lip, "That never occurred to me. Sometimes I feel ashamed to have been as lucky as I am."

"There is nothing wrong with enjoying good fortune as long as one is generous to those less fortunate. And from what I have seen, you have been very generous."

The warmth in his eyes aroused an uneasy mixture of pleasure and embarrassment. He gave her more credit than she deserved.

As the first burst of greetings died down, Hugh took Marie's hand and brought her forward to his parents. "I'd like you to meet Marie Renault."

The French girl looked nervous, but after one swift, shrewd glance, Mrs. Morgan embraced her. "Welcome, child," she said in her musical, Welsh-accented voice.

Beaming, Marie hugged her back. Then Mrs. Morgan turned to Jocelyn and said shyly, "I know 'tis not what you're used to, my lady, but we'd be honored if you and your husband would take tea with us."

"The honor would be ours," Jocelyn said warmly.

With seven Morgans, Jocelyn, David, Marie, and the coachman, there was barely space for everyone inside, but the meal was delightful. Great pots of tea were accompanied by fresh bread, pickled onions, crumbly cheese, and delicious flat currant cakes that had been fried on the griddle. Sitting between his parents, Rhys was full of laughter, as a young man should be, the grim soldier of the hospital only a memory.

As she nibbled on a currant cake, Jocelyn studied the cottage. It was immaculately clean, the warm waxed woods contrasting pleasingly with the white-washed walls. Across the room, Hugh and the three youngest Morgans perched on a carved wooden chest that looked centuries old. Beside it, a well-worn Bible held place of pride on the shelf of an ancient oak china cabinet. She could be happy in a home like this, with the right man beside her. Then she grinned, unable to imagine Candover living in such humble circumstances. He was an aristocrat to the bone.

When it came time to leave, the elder Morgans thanked Jocelyn earnestly for what she had done for their sons. Once more she was embarrassed. It had been so little from her point of view, and yet they were so grateful.

As David handed her into the carriage, Hugh said quietly, "Are you sure you don't want me to accompany you to Hereford, my lord? My Da says there have been highwaymen in the Black Mountains."

David shook his head. "No need to abandon your family. It's scarcely thirty miles to Westholme, and we'll be there by dark."

"Very well, my lord," Hugh said, looking glad that his offer had been refused.

David climbed into the carriage by Jocelyn. "I'm going to have to teach that boy not to say 'my lord' with every breath," he remarked as the coach started moving. "He's taking my elevation far more seriously than I am."

"Naturally." Jocelyn grinned. "A servant's consequence is dependent on his master's. Isn't that true, Marie?"

Her maid, now sitting alone on the facing seat, nodded vigorously. "Mais oui, my lord. You are a credit to us."

David looked amused, but didn't challenge the statement. Jocelyn guessed that he would never take himself too seriously. It was another thing to like about him.

The weather was dry, the road was good, and they made excellent speed on the next stage toward Hereford. They had changed horses for the last time and were somewhere around the border between Wales and England when the highwaymen struck.

David was dozing in the carriage. Though he'd regained normal movement, his strength and energy were still low, and he slept more than usual. The first he knew of the attack was when a voice bellowed, "Stand and deliver!"

As he snapped to alertness, gunshots blasted deafeningly. The carriage shuddered to a stop, nearly tipping over. Marie was thrown across the carriage. Barely in time, David caught her before she could crash into Jocelyn.

"Down!" He accompanied the order with a firm shove that pushed both women to the floor of the coach. Out the left window, he could see two horsemen with scarves tied over their lower faces, pistols in their hands. An unknown voice barked orders in front of the carriage. At least three attackers, maybe more.

Would it be best to allow themselves to be robbed? He rejected the thought instantly. Cooperating tamely could be a disastrous policy since the coach carried two attractive young women.

The alternative to surrender was to fight, and David had learned the hard way that in combat every second counted. The time to act was *now,* while the horses were screaming and plunging in their traces, occupying the attention of the highwaymen as well as the driver.

"Stay down. Don't get out of the carriage." As a precaution, he'd placed his two pistols in the pocket of his door before leaving London. He yanked them out, along with spare powder and shot, then leaped from the right door, out of the view of their attackers.

Once outside, he immediately dropped to the ground and crawled beneath the rear of the rocking vehicle. Praying that a wheel wouldn't roll over him, he primed and cocked both guns. Reloading would take precious seconds, so he must hope to God that his first two shots would be enough to drive the highwaymen away. He'd get no help from the driver, whose hands were full controlling the panicky horses.

Weapons ready, he inched forward until he had a clear view of two of the attackers. His blood chilled as the nearest man vaulted from his horse and tossed the reins to his partner. Pistol cocked, he wrenched open the carriage door. David took aim, but before he could fire, the highwayman dragged a shrieking Marie from the vehicle.

"C'mere, sweetheart," he growled. "I'm sure you've got somethin' we can use." Looking into the carriage, his eyes widened. " 'Ey, Alf, I need yer 'elp. There's an even better bitch in here."

Red rage blazed through David, but he couldn't shoot the bastard without endangering Marie. Teeth clenched, he raised one pistol and put a ball through the second attacker. The man screamed hoarsely, his shirt blossoming with crimson.

The third highwayman appeared, spurring his horse from the front of the carriage as he shouted, "What the bloody 'ell is going on?"

With the cool clarity of battle, David used the second pistol to blast the man from his horse. Panicked, his mount ran off. The horse of the man who held Marie jerked its reins free and followed. With the robbery in a shambles, the wounded man galloped for his life, leaving the third highwayman without a means of escape.

Knowing the last man was as dangerous as a cornered boar, David sprang to his feet, trying to reload a pistol so he could bring the man down before he hurt Marie. Eyes glittering with fear, the man backed across the road, his pistol in one hand and his other arm around her throat as he used her for a shield. He was a muscular brute and could probably break her neck with a single snap if he tried. David checked his attack, not wanting to endanger her.

Halting made him a dead easy target. The highwayman's pistol rose, the steel barrel aimed straight at David's heart. Praying for a miracle, he dived to one side.

As he hit the ground and rolled, a pistol blasted with ear-shattering closeness, but no ball tore into him. Instead, the robber screamed and fell backward. Marie took the opportunity to wrench free of his grip and bolt behind the carriage.

David scrambled to his feet and saw Jocelyn standing in front of the open carriage door, a smoking pistol gripped in trembling hands. Shooting from a different angle, she had saved him and Marie, but she was dead white, on the verge of fainting.

The wounded highwayman was no longer a threat and the driver had the horses under control, so he embraced his trembling wife. "Well done, my dear girl!"

She clung to him as the terror she'd hardly had time to experience swept through her in nauseating waves. She had known soldiers all her life, been dandled on her military uncle's knee, had danced and flirted with officers, and listened to their war stories. But never before had she seen a soldier in action. She had been stunned by David's swift, precise application of violence. For the first time she truly realized that her friend of the laughing eyes and quiet understanding was a warrior, capable of moving with the strength and speed of a striking leopard.

He was a leader as well, from the sheer power of his courage and presence. She burrowed her face into his shoulder, shuddering as she remembered the horrific moment when the highwayman trained the gun on David at point-blank range. Until then, she had been paralyzed by the speed of events, but seeing him endangered had energized her to act. What if she had been an instant slower? The mental image of David lying on the ground, bleeding from a wound that this time truly was mortal, made her ill.

He murmured, "I didn't realize you were so adept with a gun. Where did the pistol come from?"

"My father taught me to shoot, and I always travel

with a pair of coach pistols," she said unsteadily. "But I couldn't have reacted effectively if not for your example."

His embrace tightened. "Whatever the reason, you were very brave."

She closed her eyes as his gentle stroking eased her knotted nerves. This wasn't the first time they'd touched, but there was hot liquid melting inside her, perhaps a reaction to the attack. She wanted to cling to him forever. She wanted to kiss him, lie with him . . .

Alarmed, she recognized that mingled with her shock and fear was desire. Attraction had been building gradually, and today it had burst into full, hungry flower. She wanted David with a power that surpassed anything she had felt for any other man.

Moistening her lips, she looked up at him. Their gazes locked, and David became very still. Then he raised her chin with one finger and pressed his lips to hers.

Her mouth opened under his, and a current of energy scorched through her, searing her senses and scattering her wits. He'd kissed her once when out of his head, and she'd wondered what his kiss would be like if he was fully aware. Now she knew, and the knowledge was shattering.

Her eyes closed, and for precious moments she didn't think, didn't doubt, simply *was*. Here was strength, a safe harbor . . .

No. Safe harbors were a treacherous illusion. She opened her eyes, needing to escape from the frightening intimacy his touch induced.

Sensing the change in her response, he broke the

kiss, his gaze searching. Jocelyn had no idea what showed in her face, but he dropped his arms and stepped away, his expression once more calm and detached.

Jocelyn brushed back her hair with a trembling hand, as if that could restore her fractured composure. "Are the highwaymen dead?"

David crossed to the one he'd shot and dropped to one knee as he checked the throat for a pulse. "This one is."

Looking weary, he went to the other fallen highwayman and pulled off the mask, revealing a youngish, coarse-looking face. The man was unconscious from his fall and bleeding from a shoulder wound, but his breathing was strong. "This fellow should survive to be hanged."

Jocelyn exhaled, though she hadn't realized she was holding her breath. "I'm glad I didn't kill him, even though he probably deserved it."

David glanced up. "I'm glad, too. Killing stains the soul, no matter how justified it is." His voice was bleak.

"Your soul seems unstained," she said quietly.

"I've done what was necessary. It is for God to decide if what I did was right." Dropping his gaze, he pulled out a handkerchief and began to roughly bandage the highwayman's wound.

Jocelyn watched in silence, unable to turn her gaze away. Though he looked no different than before, her perception had utterly changed. She saw not the casually elegant gentleman but the sinewy body, the perfectly controlled strength. She was intensely conscious of his pure masculine power, and had never been so aware that she was a woman.

"Milady?"

Strange mood broken, she turned and saw that Marie had retrieved a flask of brandy from the carriage and was offering it to her mistress. Jocelyn managed a smile. "You first. You're the one who was mauled by that beast."

Not bothering with polite demurral, Marie put the flask to her lips and drank deeply. She choked a little, but her hands were steadier when she poured a measure into the cap, which was designed as a small cup, and handed it to Jocelyn, who swallowed only a little slower than her maid had. She closed her eyes for a moment as the fiery spirit burned through her. Head clearing, she asked, "Are you all right?"

"Better than I would have been if you hadn't shot the swine, my lady." An involuntary shiver went through her.

Jocelyn offered a small smile. "If you wish to finish the flask and become outrageously drunk, I promise to overlook it."

Marie giggled. "That won't be necessary, but I shall have one more swallow."

David called, "Jocelyn, can you hold the horses so the driver and I can load this fellow into the carriage? He'll have to be taken to the jail in Hereford."

Jocelyn took the bridle of the team's left leader, stroking the horse's nose. Warm horseflesh was very soothing after the chaos of violence.

Grimly David and the coachman lashed the dead highwayman's body to the top of the coach, then deposited the living thief into the rear-facing seat of the carriage. Not wanting to sit beside him, Marie chose to join the driver on the box. The last leg of the journey into Hereford was quiet. David kept a close eye on the prisoner, a loaded pistol ready, but the man never regained full consciousness.

Jocelyn withdrew tensely into her corner of the seat, her thoughts whirling. Was there any significance to that kiss? She was inclined to think not. Letters exchanged with her Aunt Laura over the years had made her realize that there was a dark connection between violence and passion.

Exhausted by nursing after the siege of Badajoz, Laura had poured out her horror at the sights she had seen, explaining that if a city gave in to an attacking army easily, it was usually treated mercifully. But if the attackers had been forced to fight a long and costly siege, by the barbarous logic of war the city would be sacked when it fell, its buildings looted and burned, its citizens slaughtered and raped. Badajoz had been just such a bloody victory for the British, and Wellington had stayed his hand for two days and nights as his men avenged themselves for their losses. Rape and murder had been twined together like strands of a hangman's rope.

The brush with danger Jocelyn's party had just experienced was a faint echo of the eternal struggle between the threat of death and the passion for life. David had saved their small party from harm, and in the aftermath he kissed her. A fleeting masculine impulse, indulged and immediately forgotten.

Jocelyn's own reaction was surely rooted in that same disturbing, unfathomable blend of deadly fear and the joy of survival, but as a woman she would not so quickly forget. The embrace had created an intense physical awareness of the man who happened to be her husband. She was burningly conscious of David's shoulder against hers, and she wanted him in the most ancient and primal of ways.

She closed her eyes as if overcome by the attack, and prayed that she would recover from this madness by the time they reached their destination.

Chapter 24

When they reached the town of Hereford, David installed the two women in a private parlor at the Green Dragon, then left to turn the prisoner over to the law. Jocelyn and Marie shared a bracing pot of tea, and Jocelyn was tolerably composed by the time David joined them.

"What will happen to the highwayman?" Silently she offered tea.

Waving away the offer, he replied, "The Assizes are meeting in Hereford at the moment, so he'll be brought to trial quickly. Probably a week from today."

"Will we all be called as witnesses to the attack?"

"That shouldn't be necessary. The coachman and I can testify to events better than you and Marie. Since the man is not known to have a prior record of violence, I'll ask the court for clemency. Highway robbery is a capital offense, of course, but the influence of my exalted rank should get him transportation instead of the gallows." David paced the parlor, unable to conceal his impatience. "It's time we were on our way. I'd like to reach Westholme before dark."

"Of course." As Jocelyn gathered her shawl and reticule, she realized that he was avoiding her eye as much as she was avoiding his. If they didn't manage to bury this embarrassing intimacy, they would have an awkward stay in Herefordshire.

Forty-five minutes beyond the town of Hereford, David began to show signs of tension. Jocelyn asked, "Do you recognize landmarks?"

He nodded. "We're almost there. The oldest part of the estate lies within a loop of the Wye River, though more land was added over time."

The carriage slowed and turned between a stone pillar and an empty gatehouse. In the fading light, the drive stretched away through a long aisle of thick, gnarled trees. Curious, she asked, "What are the trees, David? I don't recognize them."

Not turning from the window, he replied, "Spanish chestnuts, over two hundred years old. This drive is almost half a mile long."

His body was taut as a bowstring. A day earlier, she would have laid her hand on his to show her sympathy at what he must be feeling on this return to a long-lost home. Now, she didn't dare touch him.

When they halted in front of the house, David climbed from the carriage, his expression shuttered. Jocelyn followed, scanning the rambling structure with interest. The house had been expanded in a variety of styles, but the native stone, warmed by a hint of red, tied the sections together. Though lacking the grandeur of Charlton, it was attractive, and the surrounding hills and woods were as lovely as David had promised.

The grounds had been dreadfully neglected, though. Catching movement from the corner of her eye, she spotted several small ornamental deer that had escaped from the park and were now happily nibbling on the shrubs.

David's expression was remote, and Jocelyn could only guess at his thoughts. With the lightest of touches on his sleeve, she said, "Shall we go in?"

Mood broken, he nodded, and they climbed the broad stairs side by side. David gave the lion's-head knocker several sharp raps. The sounds echoed hollowly inside the house. While they waited for a response, Jocelyn asked, "Were we expected today?"

He scrutinized the facade of the building. "I sent a message, but from the look of the place, Westholme is badly understaffed."

After several minutes of waiting, the door swung open to reveal a balding man of middle years. His face broke into a wide smile. "Master David! Welcome home." He executed a low bow. "Or rather, Lord Presteyne. Everyone in the household has been eagerly awaiting your return."

As they stepped into a high, paneled hall, David stared at the man, then exclaimed, "Stretton, by all that's holy! Are you the butler now?"

The man bowed again. "I have that honor, my lord."

David explained to Jocelyn, "Remember the fight with my brother that I told you about? Stretton was one of the footmen who rescued me." To the butler, he said, "It's a pleasure to see a familiar face. I didn't think anyone would remember me. I'm glad to see that you have advanced in the world."

He offered his hand. After a startled moment, the butler returned a firm handshake. Jocelyn guessed that in the future the two men would stay within the roles of man and master, but for today, recognition outweighed protocol.

David continued, "This is my wife, Lady Presteyne, and her maid, Mademoiselle Renault. I trust rooms have been prepared for us?"

"Yes, my lord, but I'm afraid you will not find things as they should be. Your brother, the late lord, was loath to spend money on the household. Also"—Stretton coughed delicately—"because of the, err, proclivities of Lord Presteyne and Mr. Timothy, it was difficult to persuade decent young girls to work here."

David's brows arched. "Are you the only servant left?"

"Not quite, sir. The lawyers didn't want new staff hired until you arrived, but my wife, who is a good plain cook, is in the kitchen, and a couple of village girls come every day to help with the cleaning." He sighed. "I fear it will take some time to put the house properly to rights."

Jocelyn glanced around, seeing the dullness of the woodwork and the shabbiness of the furnishings. The general air of neglect was enough to make any self-respecting butler apologetic.

"I'm glad the kitchen is operating. Could your wife produce a light meal in, say"—David glanced at Jocelyn questioningly—"half an hour or so?"

She nodded, glad for the chance to rest and regroup.

"It shall be done." Stretton pulled a bell cord three times, perhaps in a prearranged signal to his wife, then led David and Jocelyn upstairs.

Her bedchamber was as shabby as the rest of the house, but the proportions were gracious, and the worn draperies and bedding had recently been cleaned. She had stayed at inns that were far worse. Marie was less charitable, muttering under her breath in French as she unpacked for her mistress.

Jocelyn paused by a window to study the estate. The house stood on a rise that offered a lovely view of fields and woodlands, now glowing with golden light from the setting sun. The sweep of the Wye River showed in the middle distance. Though the landscape was not so dramatic as the Welsh mountains to the west, it was vastly welcoming. No wonder David had wanted to come home to Hereford when he was out of his head.

He would be a fine landowner, very like her father. Less flamboyant in style, but knowing his crops and stock and people, taking the time to share a tankard of ale with a tenant, and never afraid to dirty his hands if a job needed doing.

Smiling a little at the image, she explored the rest of the suite of rooms. To the left, she found a small sitting room in a corner of the house, with views in two directions. Another door led to a large dressing room that contained several empty wardrobes. She opened the door in the far wall and discovered another bedchamber. David's bags were by the bed, though luckily he was not in the room himself.

Hastily she closed the door. Of course they would have been given the master and mistress's suite. She considered checking the door to see if it had a lock, then told herself firmly not to be a lackwit. She would be as safe from David here as she had been in her own house.

The question was, given her alarming reaction to him, would he be safe from her?

David swallowed hard when Jocelyn joined him in the small salon outside the family dining room. Looking fresh as a spring flower, she'd changed into a green muslin gown that brought out the green flecks in her eyes and revealed her slender throat and a tantalizing amount of creamy shoulders. From her smile, she had recovered from the attempted robbery. On the drive into Hereford, she had been taut as a drumhead.

Reminding himself that a gentleman really shouldn't look down the front of a lady's dress—or at least, shouldn't be caught doing so—he pulled out her chair. Stretton had wisely set their places at right angles to each other rather than at opposite ends of the table. Having to speak across six feet of mahogany tended to limit conversation. As David took his own seat, he said, "If I'd realized how rundown the place was, I wouldn't have asked you to come with me."

She laughed. "This is a palace compared to the house I shared with my aunt and uncle in Fuente Guinaldo."

"I had forgot that you are a hardened veteran of the Peninsula." He wondered if things would have been different if they had met then. Might her heart have been more available? Of course, two years earlier he'd had no prospects beyond that of dying of fever or wounds, and probably wouldn't have dared to court her.

It had been a long time since tea with the Morgans,

so they applied themselves to the meal. As the butler had said, his wife was a good plain cook, and the food was solid and satisfying. After the plates were removed, Jocelyn remarked, "Good food, and really excellent wines."

"I'm not surprised," David said dryly. "I imagine the horses will be equally good. Apparently the late lord lavished money on his pleasures and ignored everything else."

Jocelyn selected a fresh peach from a fruit bowl and began to peel off the fuzzy skin with a thin, sharp knife. "Has the house had no mistress since your mother left?"

"Not for some years. My middle brother, Roger, had married, but he lived in London rather than here. There were no children, and his widow has since remarried. Wilfred also had a wife, but she died in childbirth some years ago, along with the baby, and he couldn't find another female desperate enough to take him."

"Is there enough money to take care of what needs to be done here?" She cut a slice of juicy peach and ate it with obvious enjoyment.

Wishing he could kiss that peach-flavored mouth, he replied, "Rowley thinks so, if I live frugally and invest every penny I can spare in the estate. It will take years to return everything to order, but it can be done, which is all that matters." He swirled the wine in his glass absently, thinking of his childhood at Westholme. The good times far outnumbered the bad. "I can't think of a task I would enjoy more."

"Shall I get together with Stretton to hire some

housemaids? With your lecherous brothers gone, it shouldn't be hard to find women to work here."

"That would be very helpful, if you don't mind."

She grinned. "I love hiring people and giving orders. You said yourself that I was one of the most managing females you've ever met."

"It was rather a compliment, you know." He'd never understood why some men were attracted to women who were as helpless as fluffy chicks.

For an instant, intense awareness thrummed between them. Then she dropped her gaze and said randomly, "This is the strangest birthday I have ever had."

"Good God, this is the infamous twenty-fifth birthday? Why didn't you tell me?" he exclaimed. "I knew it must be around this time, but I don't recall ever hearing the exact date. August twentieth. I shall have to remember for the future."

Though perhaps it was foolish to mention a future when their marriage would soon vanish like the morning mist. He wondered if they would occasionally see each other in London and nod politely, or perhaps exchange notes once a year, as if they hadn't once, briefly, been husband and wife.

Grimly reminding himself that the marriage hadn't been annulled yet, he said, "Westholme has a famous wine cellar, and I'm sure that would include champagne. Shall we go down and see what Wilfred left?"

"Lead the way." She swallowed the last of her peach. "Better to celebrate a birthday with champagne than bullets and bandits."

Chapter 25

Stretton produced two branches of candles, a corkscrew, and a pair of goblets, then escorted them down to the wine cellar. "This is one part of Westholme for which no apologies are needed," the butler said as he unlocked the heavy, iron-banded door. "I had standing orders from the late Lord Presteyne that the wine came before general duties. I became quite an expert at feeding claret." From his sardonic tone, it was clear he thought the time could have been better spent.

When Stretton swung the door open, David gave a low whistle. "The Prince Regent wouldn't be ashamed of this cellar." He accepted one of the branches of candles, leaving the butler the other to light his way up the dark stairs. "You may return to your duties. Lady Presteyne and I will explore on our own."

Stretton handed Jocelyn the two wine glasses, then left. Raising the candlestick high so that she could see her footing, David invited her in with a courtly gesture. "Welcome to what was surely Wilfred's favorite part of Westholme."

"Heavens!" she exclaimed as she stepped into the

cool, dry air. "I believe this surpasses the wine cellar at Charlton. I wouldn't have thought it possible."

He was impressed himself. Many things seemed larger to a child than to an adult, but not the Westholme wine cellar. The space was immense, with row after row of silent casks. Over each hung a neat sign that described the date, quality, and origin of the wine inside. Along the wall were racks filled with bottles, carefully tilted to keep the corks moist, and in one corner a worktable stood beside a closet that probably held equipment such as tubs and corks and funnels.

Jocelyn drifted down the nearest aisle, her slippers muffled by the thick layer of sawdust that covered the floor. "This place is cleaner than the cutting ward at the hospital."

"Sadly true." He followed her. "Even the sawdust is fresh, as all serious wine stewards demand. Maintaining this must have taken quite a bit of Stretton's time."

"What did he mean by 'feeding the claret?' " She glanced teasingly over her shoulder. Her naked, softly inviting shoulder. "I imagined tossing it pieces of bread and cheese."

He chuckled. "Claret hasn't much body, so it's recommended to occasionally add small amounts of good French brandy to the hogshead. The same thing is often done to burgundy, while sometimes new milk is used to sweeten white wines."

"How did you learn so much about wine?" she asked curiously, her fingertips trailing over the oak staves of a cask of finest Spanish sherry.

"Wine was something of a hobby of my father's.

That's why the cellar is so large. He used to bring me down and explain how to rack the wines, how to mellow those that were too raw, and other tricks of wine handling." David had enjoyed those sessions with his father, but he shivered as a less pleasant memory surfaced.

Noticing, Jocelyn asked, "Are you cold?"

"Just thinking of the time Wilfred locked me down here. I wasn't found until the butler came down the next day for the dinner wines."

Aghast, she exclaimed. "What a vile thing to do! How old were you?"

"Eight or nine. It really wasn't so bad. One of the kitchen cats was trapped here, too. She kept me company." Kept him from going crazy in the dark by curling up in his lap and purring. He'd liked cats ever since—and had made damned sure none of his older brothers learned that, for fear of what they might do to the kitchen and barn cats if they thought it would upset him.

Jocelyn's eyes narrowed. "I'm really quite sorry that I wasn't the one to shoot Wilfred. It would have been a pleasure."

"Better the sin be on Timothy's shoulders." He resumed his survey. "There's a good supply of Westholme cider. I'm glad to see that's one tradition that has been kept."

"You have a cider press on the estate?"

"Yes, Herefordshire is known for its cider. Westholme has acres of apple orchards." He patted a cask. "These hogsheads are for household use. Servants have their choice of cider or small ale to go with their meals, and when I was boy, chose cider more often than not. Would you like to try some?"

She held out a wine glass. "Please."

He turned the cock, and Jocelyn collected a small amount of clear brown cider in each wine glass. He tasted his. The rich apple scent instantly invoked his childhood, taking him back to the bright autumn days when the first cider was pressed. The occasion had always been an estate holiday, with dancing and feasting in the orchard. He made a mental note to institute the custom again if Wilfred had discouraged the celebrations.

After a cautious sip, Jocelyn finished the rest of hers in one swallow. "Nice. Not too sweet, and just enough alcohol to make it interesting." Her gaze traveled over the wine cellar. "You'll never have to buy wine again even if you live to be a hundred."

"These wines must be worth a fortune. Selling them could raise some money for the estate."

"As long as you don't sell everything," Jocelyn said, a little taken aback. "My father always said that good wine was the mark of a gentleman's table."

"I shall retain enough to keep up my reputation. Now, where is the champagne? Or do you think that was too frivolous a drink for Wilfred?"

"Perhaps in a wall rack?"

Sure enough, one whole rack was devoted to champagne. He surveyed the choices, dizzying reflections of candle flames sliding over the rows of glass bottles. "Blessed if I know the best vintage. I'll have to assume that Wilfred wouldn't have anything that wasn't first rate. My lady, take your choice."

She considered, then tapped a bottle. "That one."

He set the candelabrum on a nearby worktable, then opened the champagne. Despite his care, wine fizzed from the bottle as the cork shot out.

Laughing, Jocelyn held out the glasses. "I'm sure a purist would be horrified that we are drinking out of glasses just used for cider, but I won't tell anyone if you don't."

"Done." After pouring the bubbly wine, he raised his glass to her. "Happy birthday, my dear girl. And may this next year bring your heart's delight." He swallowed the champagne in one long draft, thinking that if it wasn't for the deadline of this birthday, he would never have met her.

"Ahhh . . ." Jocelyn said with giddy pleasure after downing her drink. "The cider was good, but I prefer champagne."

"There is enough here for you to bathe in if you choose."

"What a waste that would be!" She held out her glass for more. In the dim light, her hair appeared dark, except where candlelight sparked red highlights. Though the air was cool, there were no goosebumps showing on the exposed curves visible about her décolletage. As for him—he didn't feel cold at all. Quite the contrary.

Warm and a little reckless, he topped up their glasses. "Sometimes late in the evening in the officers' mess, when men are feeling foolish, they'll bend their arms around each other's to drink a toast." He grinned. "Possibly it's to save themselves from falling. It's part of the ritual to empty the glass with one swallow."

"Sounds interesting." Jocelyn raised her right arm

and hooked it around his. The difference in their heights made her laugh when their arms linked. "You are too tall, sir."

"Between a man and woman, adjustments can always be made." He bent a little to reduce the difference in height. Oddly, though she might think him too tall, he'd never thought she was too short. She was . . . exactly right.

Gaze holding hers, he said. "To you, my lady."

Her laughter died, and her eyes watched him, huge and vulnerable, as they both downed their glasses. The bubbles tingling in his mouth were nothing compared to the sizzle in his blood as he inhaled the scent of jasmine, champagne, and woman. They were so close that the folds of her pale muslin gown brushed against his thighs.

Pulse pounding, he took her glass and his and carefully set them on the table by the candlestick. Then, with even greater care, he cupped her face in both hands and kissed her with gentle thoroughness. She gave a breathy little exhalation and retreated two steps until her back was against the wall, but her soft lips welcomed, and her hands opened and closed restlessly on his arms.

Their tongues touched, and the hammer in his blood became the pounding of battle drums. "You taste of peaches and champagne," he murmured as he slid his fingers into her hair and removed the pins that held it up. One after another, they fell with bright pinging sounds until auburn hair cascaded over her shoulders in a sudden rush. He rubbed his face into the silken mass, intoxicated by jasmine.

"This . . . this isn't right," she whispered even as

she arched her throat so that he could trail his lips over the pale, sensitive skin.

"We are husband and wife, Jocelyn." He traced the arc of her ear with his tongue. "How can this be wrong? Do I repulse you?"

"No. Oh, no." She drew a shaky breath. "But . . . there is someone else. You have known that since the first time we met."

He transferred his attention to her other ear, and felt her breasts press against him as she inhaled. "This someone else—what may I call him, for the sake of convenience?"

Her eyes closed. "Call him . . . the duke."

He repressed a sigh. It would be a duke. "Are you truly in love with this duke?" His hands slid down her sides, following the sleek shapes of waist and hips as he tried to caress every inch of her.

"I love him a little," she said, a catch in her voice. "That's . . . just enough."

Interesting that she wanted to be only a little in love. Later, he would think more about that. His hands stroked down her back, a buffer between ripe, soft curves and the rough stone wall. "You said once that he liked worldly women. If you come together, will he be disappointed, even angry, to find that you are less worldly than he supposed?"

From the length of time until her reply, he knew that she had wondered about that herself. "I thought men enjoyed innocence," she said uncertainly.

"It depends on the man, and the circumstances." He cupped her lovely full breasts, rubbing his thumbs back and forth until the tips pebbled under the fabric. "You are a passionate woman, Jocelyn. You should learn what that means."

She stiffened. "I won't be passionate! My mother was, and she destroyed us all."

The pain in her voice struck to his heart. Tenderly he smoothed back her hair and brushed his lips over hers, delicate and unthreatening, until her stiffness faded. "I tell you as God's own truth," he whispered, "if you allow an experienced man of the world to introduce you to passion when you want him more than he wants you, he will own your soul, but you will not own his. Is that what you want?"

"No. Never that," she replied, her pulse accelerating under his lips.

He tugged at the ties that secured her gown in the back. "Then you must let me teach you something of passion first, so that you will be stronger. Safer."

She made a sound between laughter and tears. "You are *unscrupulous*!"

"Of course." The gown undone, he slid it down her shoulders, exposing her lace-trimmed chemise. Since the thought of love alarmed her, he murmured, "I am a man and I desire you, so of course I am unscrupulous. I want you, and you are in want of an education. Surely we can come to terms."

Her short stays took only a moment longer to loosen. He swallowed hard as they fell away from her torso, allowing her breasts to soften into their natural, provocative curves. Pulling down her chemise, he closed his mouth over her breast, his tongue flicking across the hardened tip.

"You . . . you are trying to confuse me," she said, trying to sound accusing instead of exhilarated.

"Yes," he said simply, the warmth of his breath flowing down the valley between her breasts. "I want you to think of nothing but here, and now, and us."

He suckled her other breast as one hand raised her skirt, his nails grazing her knee. Then he slipped his hand between her thighs, moving gently back and forth against her most private places.

She had felt disgust and humiliation when the midwife examined her, but his touch was different, so different that it eliminated that earlier memory in a rush of heat and moisture and yearning. She writhed, not sure if she was trying to escape or trying to rub against his knowing fingers. Her hands bit into his waist as she sought support.

Was he right that she must become more experienced to have a chance of holding Candover's interest? If the duke's touch enslaved her more than David's, she would be damned indeed. She couldn't think, couldn't *think*. "This is a mistake," she said, a note of desperation in her voice. "A terrible mistake."

He became utterly still, his gaze searching. "Do you truly feel that?"

"Yes," she whispered, tears stinging as heat and desire and fear scored her veins.

"I'm sorry, Jocelyn." Straightening, he enfolded her in his arms, one large hand caressing the bare skin of her back. "I don't ever want to do anything you dislike."

His body was a warm, strong barrier against the world. She hid her face against his shoulder, the dark fabric cool against her fevered face as hot, urgent blood beat through her. She wanted to bite him and wasn't sure if the cause was anger, or a need to taste him as he had tasted her. To absorb him until they were one flesh.

She squeezed her eyes shut, struggling for composure. "I . . . I did not dislike what you did," she said haltingly, "but I don't know if succumbing to your arguments would be wisdom, or madness."

His fingers lightly stroked her nape, sending shivers down her spine. "I'm not sure, either," he said wryly. "Perhaps it would be best to consider what I said later, in cold blood. I certainly can't think clearly when I'm holding you."

She gave a choked laugh, thinking that after tonight, it was impossible to ever imagine having cold blood again.

He lay awake for a long time that night, his unseeing gaze lost in the night. When leading a patrol in dangerous territory, he'd perfected the art of clearing his mind so that fragments of information could float and spin and combine with intuition to guide him and his men through danger to safety.

Now he tried to do the same with Jocelyn. All along, he'd had the maddening sense that he hadn't grasped the elusive core of her. Tonight, she had revealed some missing pieces of the puzzle. She feared passion, feared love, and the mother she claimed to scarcely remember was part of it. Most divorces were granted because a woman committed flagrant adultery, and that had probably been the case with Jocelyn's parents, destroying the family in a blaze of pain and scandal.

Yet despite Jocelyn's fears, she hungered for warmth and love. She reminded him of a feral kitten that yearned to come close, but skittered off at the first sign of movement. Still, her body responded even when her mind withdrew. He must try to win her with passion and friendship, never using the dangerous word love. A strange way to court his wife, especially since most women craved sweet sighs and vows, but he would do whatever might bring them close enough to create lasting bonds.

He sighed and closed his eyes, tired by the long, eventful day. It would behoove him to remember that he had been on his deathbed a few short weeks ago.

As he rolled over and wrapped his arms around a pillow that was a damned poor substitute for his wife, he prayed that he was guessing correctly about the mystery that was Lady Jocelyn.

Chapter 26

Hot blood produced a very poor night's sleep. Jocelyn tossed and turned, alternately thinking intoxicated thoughts about her encounter with David, and despising herself as a wicked trollop for enjoying his kisses and caresses so much. She had always thought of herself as having a steadfast disposition. She had spent years in her thoughtful search for a man who would be a suitable life partner. Yet having found him, she was allowing herself to be distracted by another man.

Admittedly, David was an excellent specimen of male—kind, funny, and companionable, as well as attractive. But that didn't make it right to have her body involved with one man while her mind was involved with another.

Paradoxically, by the time she rose from her bed, she realized that David was right to say that she must learn about passion, even though his argument had been unabashedly self-interested. If she was to control her body, she must first understand it.

Moreover, having taken a small sip from passion's cup, she better appreciated how her clumsy ignorance was unlikely to charm Candover. It had been her married state that had made her eligible in his eyes, so she had better at least learn how to kiss.

Though her brazenness shamed her, she was forced to admit that learning a few of love's more modest lessons from David would be a great pleasure.

Marie arrived carrying a teapot on a tray. Jocelyn made a mental note to order chocolate, since that was her preference in the morning. As she stirred milk into the tea, she asked, "How is your room in the attic?"

Not a good question. Marie said with an expression of great suffering, "It is not like Cromarty House."

"I suppose not." Jocelyn sipped the tea. "Cheer up. In a week your Welshman will be here to share your exile from civilization."

"Ha! Where was he when I needed him, when I was being attacked by wild bandits?" the maid said indignantly.

"Lord Presteyne proved capable of protecting us all," Jocelyn pointed out.

Marie sniffed. "It would be much more romantic to be rescued by my own man rather than by yours."

She choked on her tea. "He is not 'my man.' "

"He is your husband, is he not? And if you let him go, it will be a stupidity unparallelled." Marie's brown eyes regarded her mistress like a stern nanny.

"That is quite enough from you, mademoiselle!" Jocelyn banged her cup into the saucer, her voice icy. There were times when she thought there might be advantages to having servants who were intimidated by her, and this was one of them.

Totally unintimidated, Marie asked, "What gown will you wear this morning, milady?"

"The dark blue muslin." Jocelyn expected that the day would take her to some dusty places, so she'd better wear something that wouldn't show dirt easily. The morning dress was also rather high-necked and severe, which suited her mood.

After dressing, she went downstairs, quaking inside because she was unsure how she could face David after the intimacies of the previous night. Seeing Stretton, she asked warily, "Is Lord Presteyne about?"

"His lordship went out early, my lady. Would you like breakfast?"

Relaxing, Jocelyn ordered a coddled egg and toasted bread, then settled down in the breakfast room to make a list of questions for Stretton. The butler would be an able ally, but he needed guidance about what would suit David, at least in the early stages of restoring the household to what it should be.

She had finished her breakfast and was leaving the breakfast room when David strode into the house. Wearing riding boots and country buckskins, he was a sight to brighten any woman's morning—unless the woman was feeling embarrassed and guilty.

Before Jocelyn could work up a proper blush, he raised her chin and kissed her, his mouth warm and firm. For an instant she froze in shock. But it wasn't a kiss of seduction, or dominance, or possession. Rather, it was a friendly, uncomplicated expression of affection that made her feel very, very good.

By the time he stepped away, her embarrassment

from the previous night was gone. A little breathlessly, she said, "Good morning. You must have risen early."

"I called on the bailiff to discuss his views on what needed to be done. I'm about to find a horse so I can see everything for myself." Taking her arm, he guided her toward the door. "Come, let us check out the stables together. As a connoisseur of horseflesh, you must be as curious as I am."

His buoyant pleasure in the day was contagious. By the time they reached their destination, they were chatting as easily as ever. However, both fell silent when they entered the stables. Like the wine cellar, the stables were immaculately kept and beautifully stocked. Jocelyn gazed greedily at the sleek hunters, a matched carriage team, and massively muscled draft horses. Even her father would have been impressed.

Stopping at the stall of a lovely gray mare, she said, "This is almost enough to forgive Wilfred his sins." Remembering how he'd locked David in the wine cellar, she added, "A few of them, anyhow."

"My brother did have a good eye for horses." David surveyed the long line of stalls ruefully. "A pity he didn't see fit to invest this sort of money to improving the livestock or planting better crops."

Apparently his visit to the bailiff had been educational. Jocelyn stroked the velvety nose of the gray. "You'll do both, won't you? Farm well and have beautiful horses, too."

"In time, I hope." He sighed, his exuberance diminishing. "But not right away."

With my fortune, he could do it all now, without selling wine and horses, she thought as she made nonsense noises to the mare. Between them, they could make quite a partnership—except that he wasn't the partner she wanted, nor was she his choice.

"You'd be the new lord?" a voice said politely. "I'm Parker, the groom."

She and David turned to the newcomer. Parker appeared nervous, though he relaxed under David's easy questioning. Jocelyn guessed that the late baron had been temperamental, and his servants had learned to walk warily around him.

David asked Parker to saddle a tall dark bay. As the groom obeyed, David said to Jocelyn, "Would you like to ride out with me? The gray can be saddled while you change to riding costume."

She hesitated, tempted, before shaking her head. "It's probably best you first see Westholme by yourself."

"I daresay you're right."

"With your permission, I'll confer with Stretton to determine what must be done in the house."

He gave her the smile that always warmed her inside. "I'd be most grateful. I can command a company of soldiers, but I know even less about running a household than I do farming."

Glad she could be of use, she said, "I'll be off now."

He fell into step beside her. "Parker will be needing help in the stables. Would you let me have Rhys Morgan, if he's willing?"

"A good idea. He's made himself useful, but there really isn't enough work for him and my London groom both. I expect he'll be glad to find a situation so close to his family."

The saddled bay was waiting for David outside, so he mounted and bid her farewell until dinner. She watched him ride away, unsurprised that he was an excellent horseman. He did everything well in a casual, unpretentious way. She wondered how he would do in the beau monde, where pretension was often a way of life. But even there, character and true worth would draw respect from people who mattered. If for some reason he didn't marry his Jeanette, there would be no shortage of young women eager to become Lady Presteyne.

On which remarkably depressing thought, she returned to the house.

David kissed Jocelyn again when they met for dinner. This time, instead of startling, she kissed him back most charmingly. He was making progress. Smiling, he escorted her into the dining room. "Did you have a productive day?"

"The house is in dire need of beeswax and elbow grease, but the structure is sound, apart from a little water damage in the attics. I found some fine older furniture up there, so most of the main rooms can be redecorated for almost no cost. Tomorrow there will be eight or ten women from the village here to help." She grinned as she shook out her napkin. "They are all perishing of curiosity to visit the big house and catch a glimpse of you, if they're lucky."

"They'll be better pleased to see a fine London lady, I suspect. What do you think of the house itself?"

She leaned forward, eyes sparkling. "It's really quite lovely. The rooms are laid out well, and the large windows in the newer sections have fine views. Wonderful sunlight, too. We can . . ." Her voice faltered. "You can make this a real showplace."

Pleased by that unintended "we," he said, "It will be a godsend if you can redecorate with existing furnishings. I'm afraid that for the time being, there won't be much money to spend inside the house."

She swallowed a spoonful of sorrel soup. "What did you discover in your survey of the estate?"

"Rowley and the bailiff weren't exaggerating about what needs to be done." He made a face. "Also, that it's remarkable how much riding muscles will ache after a couple of months without being on horseback."

She chuckled but refrained from comment.

"I'd appreciate your opinion on the estate. When would be good for you to ride out with me?"

She considered. "I should probably be around the house tomorrow, since the cleaning crew will be starting. How about the day after tomorrow?"

He nodded, a little disappointed. He was looking forward to guiding her over Westholme. Surely his love for the place would spill over to her. She already liked the house, and being kissed. If she would fall in love with the estate, perhaps she would end by falling in love with him.

Chapter 27

Finding the house had been pure luck. Sally looked up from her spot on the floor, where she had been making lists, to gaze happily around the empty drawing room. When meeting the Lancaster family solicitor, she'd happened to mention her upcoming marriage. Rowley knew of a vacant house only a block from Ian's consulting rooms, so Sally took her fiancé for a look.

They had both fallen in love with the house and signed the leasehold agreement immediately. The location was perfect—convenient to Ian's business, but mercifully separate, and far more spacious than the cramped rooms above his surgery. Sally liked staying in the same neighborhood so she could continue to see the Launcestons, now as a friend instead of an employee. Though a new governess had started, the Launcestons were generously allowing Sally to stay in their house until her marriage. She spent her days planning for her new home and helping Ian. It was a giddy time, full of possibilities.

Getting to her feet, she drifted across the room, admiring the fine moldings, and the way sunlight glowed across the polished oak flooring. It was nothing like so grand as Cromarty House, which suited Sally very well. There was room enough for gracious living, and someday, God willing, children. She could imagine spending the rest of her life in this house, and being thankful every day for her blessings.

In a burst of the kind of exuberance she hadn't experienced since her childhood at Westholme, she threw out her arms and whirled across the floor as if she were six years old again. The sound of laughter stopped her in her tracks as she neared the far end of the drawing room.

Cheeks burning, she whipped her gaze toward the front door and saw that Ian had just entered, using the other key. With his broad shoulders limned by sunshine, he was so attractive that her heart hurt to see him.

"I'd hoped to find you here." Dropping his hat carelessly on the floor, he walked toward her, his eyes alight. "I see you're having a grand time, lass."

She skipped into his arms, spinning him halfway around in her exuberance. "I am indeed. Oh, Ian, I have trouble believing this is all real. That *you're* real."

His mouth descended on hers in a kiss that felt very real indeed. After an embrace that left Sally tingling clear to her toes, he drew back and surveyed her smudged face. "You've been in the attics, I see, and acquired dust in all sorts of decorative places."

"I shall never be glamorous like Jocelyn, I'm afraid."

"If you had a fondness for glamour, you'd have no use for me." Putting an arm around her shoulders, he ambled with her into the dining room that opened from the drawing room. "Are you done with your list making?"

"Yes. The house is in fine condition. It needs some cleaning, and perhaps some painting, but we could move in tomorrow if we wished."

"Actually," he said hesitantly, "I had in mind getting married tomorrow."

She pivoted to look at him in surprise. "Tomorrow? Not October?"

"I received a letter from my mother today. My brother Diarmid is getting married in a fortnight, and there will also be a family christening or two as well." He took her hands in his. "Late summer is as quiet as my work ever gets, so it struck me that this would be a perfect time to take you to Scotland to meet my family. I'd like to show you off. Besides, I haven't been home in several years."

So Scotland was still home, despite all the far places he'd seen. She found that endearing. "Naturally if we are to travel together, we must be married."

"Aye." A slow smile spread across his face. "And I've discovered that I'm braw bad at waiting."

She almost melted at the warmth in his eyes. The rest of the world saw the brusque and brilliant doctor, but this tender, devoted aspect of his nature was for her alone. Heart brimming with love, she slid her fingers into his thick white hair for the sheer pleasure of touch. "Then by all means, my darling, let us marry in the morning."

Two days of domestic toil put Jocelyn in the mood for diversion. Dressed in her favorite blue military style riding habit, she swept down the Westholme staircase, which was well designed for grand entrances, and now gleamed with polish.

David had been reading a letter, but he glanced up, his gaze arrested when he saw her. "Good morning, Jocelyn. That's a particularly dashing habit. Surely modeled on the uniform of the Tenth Royal Hussars?"

"But of course." She raised her face to receive his greeting kiss. His lips were simultaneously soothing and stimulating. Quite a remarkable effect, really. When the kiss ended, she said a little breathlessly, "So much gold braid was irresistible."

He grinned. "Would it be lèse majesté to say that the uniform looks better on you than it does on the Prince Regent?"

"Not lèse majesté, my lord—treason! But I shan't report you," she said magnanimously.

He raised the letter he'd been reading when she joined him. "This just arrived from London. Sally and Ian are married and on their way to Scotland."

"Really! What made them decide not to wait for autumn?"

"According to my sister," David consulted the page, *"I'm sorry you weren't at the wedding, but this is a good time to visit Scotland, and of course I can't resist the thought of having Ian to myself for a whole month. Perhaps we can stop by Westholme on our journey south."*

"Splendid! So they are getting a proper wedding trip. I'm sure Sally made a beautiful bride."

David looked at the letter again. *"Tell Jocelyn I wore the green silk gown with the remarkable décolletage to my wedding, and Ian was so distracted that he had to be reminded to say 'I do.' I was vastly pleased with myself."*

Jocelyn laughed. "And well she should be. Because of Sally, Ian Kinlock is going to be a happier man, and probably an even better doctor."

Catching up her full skirts, she glided out the door David held open for her, feeling a little wistful. How wonderful it must be to feel as sure as Sally and Ian were. The night they'd announced their betrothal, it had been clear how perfectly they suited each other. They flowered in each other's presence. Jocelyn had never felt so sure of anyone, or anything.

Briskly she told herself not to mope. It was a perfect summer day, and she had a fine horse to ride, a beautiful estate to view, and the best of companions.

Though Westholme had been badly neglected, the land was good, with a healthy mix of crops and livestock. She approved—market prices fluctuated, and variety would keep the income steadier. Besides grain, hops, and apples, there were pigs, a small herd of milk cows, and a much larger herd of the white-faced beef cattle named for the county of Hereford.

As they surveyed the cattle, she remarked, "The stock needs improving. One good bull should do it."

Not a muscle in his face moved, yet her mind leaped to the job that a good bull did. Coloring a little, she shaded her eyes and looked into the distance. "I see a church tower. Have you been to your village yet?"

"No, but this would be a good time to visit."

Ten minutes' ride brought them to the village of Westholme. Built of the local stone, it was attractive, though a practiced eye could see the signs of poor maintenance. Under her breath, she said, "Some of these roofs are disgraceful. I hope they are high on the list of things that will be done?"

He nodded. "I slept in my share of leaking huts in Spain. It's not something I feel others need to experience."

Their conversation ended when every resident from toddlers to octogenarians emerged from the cottages to see the new lord. Experienced at greeting tenants and clucking over babies, Jocelyn accepted the attention easily. Though the role of lord of the manor was new to David, he also handled it well. As Jocelyn's father had been fond of saying, a true gentleman was never at a loss.

As she and David said their farewells, a young girl ran from a house and pressed a bouquet of roses into Jocelyn's hands. "For you, my lady."

"Thank you," Jocelyn said, touched by the gesture. These people hungered to believe in the new Lord Presteyne. Already, he had halfway won their hearts. By Christmas, they would be loyal until death—as he would be loyal to them.

A little sadly, she inhaled the roses, heavy with late summer fragrance. What would the villagers think when she left and didn't return? Would David let it be known that the marriage had ended? It would be easier, surely, to let them think she was dead. Or to simply return someday with a new wife, no explanations offered. That would be the lordly thing to do.

Since they were passing the church, which stood just outside the village proper, she asked, "Shall we stop?"

"A good idea." He dismounted and tethered his

horse, then raised his arms to help her down. His grip was firm and strong, frankly masculine. He held her a moment longer than was strictly necessary. Long enough to remind her of cool wine cellars and fevered embraces.

Blast it, everything reminded her of that encounter! She caught up her skirts and entered the church. It was very old, with a square tower that dated from Norman times. She strolled down the center aisle, glad that the vicar wasn't in evidence. His absence meant she could enjoy the soft light and the faint scents of incense and piety without having to maintain a conversation.

The most striking feature was a large stained glass window above the altar. Instead of an obviously religious subject, the design featured a rising sun casting its rays on trees and flowers, and a soaring white dove to symbolize the holy spirit.

Seeing the direction of her gaze, David said, "The old window was badly damaged, so my father replaced it with this one. He asked my mother to design the window as a tribute to their mutual love of nature. Her initials are at the bottom."

"What a fine honor," she said softly. Charlton contained no monuments to her own mother. Even the echo of the late countess's name had long ago vanished.

Feeling a little melancholic, she pushed a side door open and entered the tree-shaded churchyard, asking over her shoulder, "I imagine your parents are buried here?"

"My brother would not allow my mother's burial, even though our father had wanted it," David said dryly. "In Wilfred's eyes, his mother was the one true wife."

"He might have been able to keep your mother's body from this churchyard, but he couldn't have kept her spirit from your father's." She thought of the radiance of the stained glass window. "I'm sure they are together now."

His eyes softened. "I'd like to think you're right."

A large monument engraved with the name Lancaster stood at the back of the churchyard. Jocelyn moved toward it, then halted when she saw two new graves to the right. Freshly carved stones proclaimed the resting places of Wilfred Lancaster, sixth Baron Presteyne, and the Honorable Timothy Lancaster. Next to Wilfred was a grave established enough to have a blanket of soft grass. The Honorable Roger Lancaster.

Sadly she contemplated the final resting place of the three brothers. Once they had been babies, symbols of hope. Someone must have loved them. Had they loved each other? What fatal flaw in their minds had made them heedless and cruel?

She still carried the bouquet, so on impulse she laid a single rose on each grave. After she had placed the last one, she sensed David come up behind her.

He rested a hand on her shoulder. "You have a generous spirit."

"Easy for me to be generous. I'm not the one who was tormented," she replied. "They are gone, and you are still alive. The time for anger is past."

His hand tightened. "You are wise. I shall try to do as you suggest."

Briefly she rested her hand on his. Wisdom was

always easier to offer than to apply to oneself. If only she could let her past go. "Where does your father lie?"

"Over here." With a light hand at the small of her back, he guided her to the other side of the family monument. He stared down at the stone, expression pensive. "I stopped by here once, on the way to join my regiment. That was the only visit since the day my father was buried."

Silently Jocelyn handed him the rest of the bouquet. He removed a small golden rose bud before laying the rest of the flowers on his father's grave. Then he turned and tucked the bud into Jocelyn's lapel, his palm lightly brushing her breast as he worked the rose into a button hole. The small, unintended intimacy was strangely provocative. Casual acquaintances kept a certain distance between them. She and David had closed that space without thinking.

"I've brought a picnic lunch." he said. "Shall we enjoy it in the orchard?"

With a smile, she took his arm and they returned to the horses. She didn't even notice how easily they matched their steps to each other.

The orchard covered several rolling hills, and David took them to the crest of the highest, with a long view over the Wye and the patchwork fields of Westholme. He wanted to flood Jocelyn's senses with beauty so that she would never want to leave.

He helped her from her horse, enjoying the weight of her hands on his shoulders, the brush of her heavy skirts against his legs. She no longer withdrew from him. Instead, she accepted his touch, perhaps even lingered with conscious provocation.

Moving away, she picked an apple from the nearest tree. "This orchard must be spectacular in the spring, when the trees are blooming."

"It is. I used to love to lie here and listen to the hum of bees. The scent was intoxicating." He unpacked his saddlebags, starting with a blanket to spread on the grass. "The trees haven't been pruned and tended as they should be, but most are still healthy and producing apples. A year or two of proper care should restore the crop to where it was in my father's time."

After feeding the apple to the gray mare, she gazed toward the house, whose roof was visible in the distance. "In the peace of the country, it's hard to believe that the bustle of London even exists."

"London has its charms, but I'll be happy to spend most of my time here." He removed packets of food and a stone jug of cider from his saddlebag. "Everything in our luncheon was produced on the estate."

Gracefully she seated herself in a foam of skirts as he set out cheese and ham and fresh baked bread. Even the onions had been grown and pickled on the estate, in Westholme vinegar. After the morning's riding, they both indulged themselves with country appetites. He liked that she didn't peck at her food like a nervous bird.

"Utterly perfect," she sighed after finishing her meal. "To ride the land, eat the fruits of your own fields—nothing could be more satisfying. My father always said the strength of England was that we are country folk at heart, not like the French aristocrats who lived at court and lost touch with their roots."

"Don't limit it to England. Say instead that it's the strength of the British," he suggested as he finished the last of the cheese.

"Sorry. With true English arrogance, I too often overlook the other peoples of Britain."

"If you'd grown up here, you wouldn't," he said lazily as he lay back on the blanket. "These are the Welsh Marches, the border zones that the English Marcher lords held against the wild raiding Celts. This country was fought over for centuries, and memories are long."

"Where in Wales did your mother come from?"

"Caerphilly. Her father was a schoolmaster. He and my father shared a passion for classifying wildflowers and carried on a scholarly correspondence for years. They met when my father was near Caerphilly and wanted to show his correspondent what he thought was a new species of wild orchid."

He smiled as he remembered the story his mother had told her children many times. "The orchid turned out to have already been classified, so my father collected my mother instead. He was quite unworldly, and perfectly happy to fall in love with someone beneath his station. I think he believed that if he loved my mother, everyone else would."

"That was definitely unworldly," Jocelyn said dryly.

"His first wife was the granddaughter of a duke, and she raised her sons to think that rank was all. My mother never had a chance of winning them over."

Jocelyn took a swallow of cider, then handed the

stone jug to him. "Do you feel more Welsh or English?"

He considered as he drank from the jug. "On the outside, definitely English, a product of where I grew up and how I was educated. But on the inside . . . ," he chuckled. "The Jesuits say that if they have a boy until he is seven years old, he is theirs for life. Most of us have mothers, not Jesuits, so by that measure I'm a fey Welshman under the facade of an English officer and gentleman."

Jocelyn looked away, her profile still, and he remembered that she hadn't had her mother for as long as seven years. How old had she been when her family had shattered? Old enough to be permanently scarred.

While he was wondering if he should ask her about that, she said in the cool, detached tone he hadn't heard much lately, "If you are more Welsh than English, you must love daffodils and leeks."

"Guilty," he said promptly. "In springtime, Westholme is covered with a blanket of daffodils. Sally and I helped my mother plant the bulbs when we were children."

Jocelyn smiled, relaxed again. "And now you have come home. Sometimes life provides unexpected happy endings."

Wondering if their marriage would be one of those, he said softly, "I'm sorry there will be no happy ending for you and Charlton."

She drew up her knees and linked her hands around them. "It's the way of the world for women to be taken from their homes and have to create new ones. Someday I will find another home."

Unable to let such an opportunity pass, he raised himself on one elbow, his gaze intense. "Westholme could be yours."

She swallowed hard and looked away, and he felt the presence of her damned duke sitting down between them to share their picnic. Voice constricted, she whispered, "The price would be too high."

"Would it?" He put a note of command in his voice, and she reluctantly turned to face him. He held out his hand. Uncertainly she took it, and he lay back on the blanket, pulling her down on top of him. Cradling her head in his palms, he drew her mouth to his, murmuring, "Is this a high price?"

"You know it isn't, you wretch," she sighed before their lips met, languorous in the summer heat.

She tasted of sunshine and cider. The kisses of the last few days had made her less shy, and she explored his mouth with an innocent enthusiasm that was deliciously arousing. As the kiss continued, he used his hands to arrange her so that their hips pressed together, her skirts falling around him. "Ahh . . ." he exhaled. "That's a very nice place for you to be."

He tugged her skirt high enough so that he could slide a hand up her stocking clad leg over firm, warm curves. As his fingertips trailed along her inner thigh, she rolled her hips against his. He groaned, hardening against the soft press of her body, and too blasted many layers of fabric between them.

A shiver of laughter in her voice, she said, "I don't think you would be able to convince a court that you are incapable of marital duties just now."

"How fortunate that we've already stated our case,

and there are no judges present." Catching her around the waist, he rolled over so that he was above her, her slender throat perfectly positioned for light, teasing nibbles.

Breathless, she said, "Isn't too much restraint difficult for you?"

It was both question and warning that she did not want to go too far. Neither did he, not yet. "I would rather suffer a little here than be calm and sane anywhere else."

He claimed her mouth again, his hand caressing the hidden swells of her breasts until both of them were panting. Wanting more, he whispered, "You must be warm in that heavy habit."

With one hand he unfastened the gold braid frogs that secured the front of her blue jacket. It opened, the dark fabric making her pale skin seem impossibly soft and delicate. Under the jacket was a simple, low-cut white bodice, which revealed a teasing bit of cleavage. He licked it as if she were an iced cake laid out for his delight.

She stroked his nape with her fingertips, the nails sending sharp little shocks of excitement through him. He moved his hand lower. Her skirt had twisted above her knees, making it easy to caress upward to the juncture of her thighs. She gasped when he touched the sensitive flesh. After the first instant of shock, her legs separated and she began pulsing against his rhythmic strokes.

She made a thick, breathless sound that was unbearably erotic. Feverishly he reached for the buttons of his breeches, wrenching at them until a moment of clarity struck. Damnation, he was forgetting everything but the urgency of burying himself inside her. For a moment he teetered on the brink, the race of his blood fighting his saner, better self.

Sanity won. Jocelyn's body might be eager, but her mind and heart had not yet been won, and seduction might bring a moment's pleasure at the cost of losing her trust.

With a groan, he rolled onto his back, his whole body throbbing so powerfully that he could barely gasp, "Having reached the limits of restraint, it's time to stop."

Lacing her fingers through his, hard, she gasped, "Are you trying to drive me mad?" in a voice choked with frustration and laughter.

"Certainly I'm driving myself mad, without even trying." He turned his head so that they were face to face. As he studied the hazel depths and the unguarded emotion in her eyes, he felt a rush of tenderness. Every day they grew closer, which meant that even madness was worth the price.

Chapter 28

If David's intention was to deprive Jocelyn of her wits, he was doing a good job of it, she thought wryly. The next days were quiet on the surface, but he, and the rapturous sensations she had experienced, were always in her thoughts. Passion was such a dangerous commodity that for the first time she understood why women had chosen to take the veil in earlier centuries.

But she was not cut out for a convent, and besides, that was no place for a modern Englishwoman, especially one who wanted children. No doubt her reaction to David's caresses had much to do with the fact that it was all new to her. And of course she liked him very well. . . .

Whenever her thoughts reached that point, she started to daydream about lying wrapped in his arms, then had to drag herself back to mundane reality, of which there was no shortage. Revitalizing the house and staff was a demanding task.

The industrious cleaning crew banished years of grime in a few days, and several members were hired as permanent staff. Hugh Morgan arrived two days before he was expected. From Marie's satisfied expression, she was the lure that had persuaded him to cut his holiday short. Jocelyn promptly put him to work.

Furnishings that had been battered by years of neglect were exiled to the attics, while well-made items from the time of David's grandfather were brought down for cleaning and repair. Several pieces needed reupholstering, but one of the village women proved to be a wizard with a needle. A set of unused brocade draperies was transformed into handsome chair and sofa coverings.

Besides furniture and draperies, Jocelyn discovered splendid Oriental carpets that had been rolled and put away for some incomprehensible reason. Packed in ancient, crumbling sprigs of lavender to keep moths away, the carpets were intact and beautiful. Combining them with the restored furniture and the best draperies made the main rooms look loved and lived in. A complete transformation would take years, but much had been done in a short time, and she enjoyed the work immensely.

Her only diversions were morning rides with David. Together, they explored the fields and lanes of Westholme. No more picnics among the apple trees, though. She was distracted enough already.

Nonetheless, she welcomed his kisses whenever they met.

At the beginning of Jocelyn's second week at Westholme, Stretton interrupted their morning meeting when he cleared his throat in the way that meant he wished to raise a different, possibly questionable, topic. Having learned his habits, Jocelyn said patiently, "Yes, Stretton?"

"It occurs to me, Lady Presteyne, you being newlyweds and all, you might not realize that tomorrow is his lordship's birthday."

She laid down her pencil indignantly. "Why, the wretch never mentioned it! And to think he chastised me for not mentioning my birthday. August twenty-seventh then. I'm ashamed to admit it, but I'm not even sure how old he is. It . . . it never seemed important." Not when she was marrying a man with no future.

"He will be thirty-two, my lady."

She'd thought David much older when they first met. Now thirty-two seemed just right. "We must do something special for dinner tomorrow night."

Together they worked out a menu of David's favorite dishes, with as many ingredients as possible homegrown. Jocelyn was writing the word champagne—to be served at the table, not stalked in the cellars—when Stretton cleared his throat again. She really would have to train him to just speak out. "Yes?"

"There is something else that might be appropriate for tomorrow," the butler said. "If you wouldn't mind descending to the servants' quarters?"

She had been in the kitchen and pantries, of course, but hadn't seen Stretton's personal sitting room. He stood aside as she entered so that her eyes went directly to a medium-size painting on the opposite wall. It showed a tall, dignified man in late middle age, a much younger woman, and two children about three and seven years old.

As she studied the portrait more closely, she realized that everyone except the man had eyes of the same distinctive green. "David's family," she said softly. "How did the painting come to be here?"

"The portrait was in the old lord's bedroom. After he died, Master Wilfred told me to take the painting and burn it. That didn't seem right to me, my lady, so I put it in one of the kitchen storerooms, knowing the young lord would never enter the servants' quarters. When I eventually rose to the position of butler, I moved it in here."

"You did well." Jocelyn couldn't take her gaze off the portrait. It had been painted by Sir Joshua Reynolds, who was a master at capturing the essence of his subjects. David's father had a scholarly mien, a man who might not be too attentive to daily life. His mother was a small, serene woman with dark hair and rosy cheeks like Mrs. Morgan's. Perhaps that glowing complexion was Welsh. Sally was clearly her daughter, with an air of stubborn determination even at age three.

As for David, he looked absolutely adorable. Would a son of his have that same look of good-natured mischief?

Reminding herself that such speculations were none of her business, she said, "This will mean a great deal to Lord Presteyne." She gave Stretton a curious glance. "Why didn't you leave? Wilfred sounds absolutely dreadful."

"He was," the butler said candidly. "But this is my home. Strettons have always served Lancasters." His tone became ironic. "It is unnecessary that we like them."

"You seem to like David."

"Who would not? He was always very different from his brothers. Most protective he was of his sister, and without a trace of snobbery. His mother's influence, of course. She was a true lady, despite her birth. The stories I could tell you . . ." He shook his head reminiscently.

Jocelyn decided it would be poor policy to encourage Stretton in gossip, fascinating though it was. "Please have the painting brought upstairs so I can decide where to hang it."

After much thought, Jocelyn decided the portrait would look best above the mantel in the main drawing room. She arranged with Stretton to hang it during dinner the next night. Until then, the butler was to keep the painting hidden away. She guessed that it would be the best possible birthday gift.

The next afternoon's post brought a letter from Aunt Elvira. Jocelyn studied the letter with foreboding, sure that she would find nothing good inside. She almost put it aside until after David's birthday, but curiosity won. She slit the wafer. The single sheet read:

My dear niece,

Investigation has proved that you never met Major David Lancaster in Spain, and that your "long-standing attachment" is no more than a cynical marriage of convenience.

My lawyer has also discovered that you are filing for an annulment. Neither of these things is what your dear father had in mind for his only daughter, and I am assured that a court will take an exceedingly dim view of your attempt to circumvent the conditions of his last will and testament.

While I have no doubt that we could win a lawsuit, it would grieve us to have to go to such unpleasant lengths. Also, I am confident that you have no desire to disgrace your family as your mother did.

Therefore, Willoughby and I are prepared to divide the Kendal fortune, with you receiving twenty percent and the balance reverting to my husband, who should by rights have inherited in the first place. You will be left very comfortably situated, so I am confident you will see the justice and generosity of our proposal.

However, should you refuse this compromise, I fear that we shall have no choice but to file suit against you.

I shall expect your response within a fortnight.

Elvira Cromarty

In a rush of fury, Jocelyn crumpled the letter into a ball and hurled it into the fireplace, wishing there was a fire in the grate at this time of year. But her anger swiftly faded, leaving a throbbing at her temples.

She should have known that country idylls couldn't last forever. Once her aunt decided to investigate, the information wouldn't have been hard to find. A few questions to David's fellow officers, who would see no reason not to tell the truth, would establish that Jocelyn hadn't met him in Spain. The annulment wouldn't be common knowledge, but no doubt lawyers and their clerks gossiped among themselves. Everyone else did.

The countess had probably been told her case for a lawsuit was weak and decided to try intimidation instead. Elvira, with a brood of children to establish, would have more to lose if there was a scandal, but if a few threatening letters could gain her a share of Jocelyn's inheritance, it would be time well spent.

Jocelyn frowned. Her instincts said to tell Elvira to sue and be damned. Not only would that be satisfying, but it was quite possible that if she refused to cooperate, Uncle Willoughby would intervene and forbid his wife to file a lawsuit. Though justly wary of Elvira's forceful personality, he had an even greater distaste for notoriety.

But her desire to fight could be wrong, since it probably sprang from the lifelong antagonism between her and her aunt. Perhaps it would be wiser to negotiate a settlement rather than put herself through the pain of a lawsuit.

She shuddered when she remembered her parents' divorce. The adults in her life probably thought they had shielded her from the scandal, but she had known. She'd heard the whispers among the servants. She had watched curiosity seekers standing outside Cromarty House, their expressions avid.

Worst of all was a scarlet image blazed on her mind from the day Aunt Laura had taken her for an ice. They had passed a print shop window displaying the latest political and scandal cartoons. Men stood in front of the window laughing coarsely and reading the captions. Jocelyn had heard the name Cromarty, accompanied by words she didn't understand, and seen vile drawings of men and women doing incomprehensible things.

Aunt Laura, pale and upset, had taken her away as swiftly as possible. Forgetting the ices, they had fled for home and never talked about the episode. The memory was stomach turning even now.

Much as Jocelyn hated to admit it, Lady Cromarty had a point: the late earl would not have approved of his daughter's actions. Giving Elvira perhaps twenty percent of Jocelyn's fortune would still leave more money than she would ever need.

But the thought of letting Elvira win made her blood boil. Perhaps she could assign money directly to several of her younger cousins? She liked them, and that would serve the dual purpose of helping them achieve independence, while not giving her aunt the satisfaction of a complete victory.

She must discuss this with David; his calm, logical mind would help her decide the best course. But not tonight. It was his birthday, not the time for a conversation about something as unpleasant as her aunt's threats.

Chapter 29

Wanting to make dinner special for David, Jocelyn took extra pains with her appearance, donning a gold-colored silk gown with black piping and very dramatic décolletage. Marie dressed her hair high in a tumble of waves and curls that emphasized the graceful length of her neck. For jewelry, she chose earrings and a matching necklace of gold studded with small topazes and emeralds that brought out the colors in her eyes.

The effort was justified by the admiration in David's gaze when she entered the small salon. "You're looking particularly lovely tonight, my dear girl," he said with a smile. "Is it a special occasion?"

Not waiting for an answer, he drew her into his arms for a welcoming kiss, one thumb stroking her bare back above the neckline of her gown in a way that sent tremors through her. She relaxed into the embrace, able to forget the countess's latest gambit. Separating from him with reluctance, she said, "Special indeed, my mysterious friend. It's your birthday."

"Good Lord, so it is," he said as they entered the dining room. "To be honest, I forgot. It's been years since I've taken any special note of adding another year to my dish." After seating her, he said, "I suppose Stretton told you?"

"Naturally. Old family retainers always know everything. You are the center of this particular world, and if I had had more time, I would have organized a feast so all your tenants could have celebrated your birthday with you." She smiled wickedly. "You know the sort of thing. An ox roasting over an open fire, barrels of cider and ale, games, songs, dancing."

He shuddered. "I'm glad you didn't. I'm not yet ready to play the role of lord of the manor quite so thoroughly."

Jocelyn smiled and raised her glass to him. "It's a task you will accomplish to perfection, Lord Presteyne."

He lifted his glass in reply. "I hope so, Lady Presteyne."

The expression in his eyes sent shivers through her. Perhaps she should have suggested that they go to the cellars for their champagne. It could become a Westholme custom. . . .

No. It was not her place to institute new customs. Soon she would leave Westholme, probably never to return. Their lives, which had intertwined in such interesting ways, would separate. But for tonight, they would celebrate a birthday David hadn't expected to see.

The leisurely meal was more elaborate than usual, with two removes and a variety of wines. They chatted back and forth about what progress they were making with their respective projects, trading ideas and offering suggestions. Sometimes their hands would touch, and once she fed him a bite of apple tart from her own fork. It was a lovers' meal, she realized, feeling as bubbly as the wine, where glance and touch were more important than soup or salad. Oh, dangerous, yet she could not bear to end it.

Since there were only two of them, there was no nonsense about ladies withdrawing to leave the gentlemen over their port. They stayed with champagne, their conversation drifting from the upcoming Paris peace conference to the best variety of wheat to plant.

As she studied how the candlelight defined the planes of David's face, she wondered at what point he had become so handsome. When they first met, he had been painfully thin, the tan skin almost transparent over the high cheekbones. He could stand to gain a few more pounds, but now he was a man in the fullness of his strength, radiating a quiet control and virility that were nearly irresistible. Her gaze lingered on his well-cut mouth, remembering the taste of his lips, then lifted to find him watching her as intently as she did him.

For a moment, she felt a tug so hard it hurt her heart. Perhaps she really could stay here, give up the other man in her life as he had given up his other woman. He had made it clear that he was willing to live up to the vows they had made. She could create a place for herself on this lovely estate, spend the nights in his arms. . . .

No. It would be perilously easy to fall in love with David, and she didn't have the strength or courage to risk that. She rose to her feet, saying brightly, "How late it has become! Almost ten o'clock, and suddenly I'm so tired I can scarcely keep track of the conversation."

David glanced at the mantel clock. "You're right," he said with regret. "And I must rise early to go into Hereford for the highwayman's trial. Sweet dreams, Jocelyn."

He stood and made a move to give her a good night kiss, but she eluded him, afraid that she might cry if that happened. She must leave Westholme soon, she realized, before she lost the last shreds of common sense.

Upstairs, a yawning Marie helped her undress, brushed out her hair, and put her to bed before retiring to the despised room in the attic. Despite her fatigue, Jocelyn tossed and turned, unable to sleep. A full moon poured its silver light in the window, stirring her to intolerable restlessness as her mind and body pulsed with longings.

She considered pulling the draperies in the hope that dark would still her unease, but the problem was inside her, not in the night sky. She was uncomfortably conscious of her body, of the gossamer softness of the sheer muslin nightdress against her skin, the light weight of a sheet holding her to the width of the bed, the flood of moonlight that made her crave passion more intensely than safety. She was deeply aware that she was a woman, and that for too long she had held herself apart from men.

Finally she slipped from the bed and walked to the window. The moon that tormented her floated high in the sky, a primitive goddess of femininity that her body cried out to worship.

Deep in the house a clock struck. She counted twelve strokes. Midnight, the witching hour.

It suddenly occurred to her that she hadn't shown

David the family portrait. He hadn't come to bed yet, or she would have heard him through the door that connected their chambers.

On an impulse she refused to identify, she tied a blue silk wrapper over her nightdress and left the room, picking up a three-branched candelabrum in the hall to light her way down the stairs. Fantastic shadows accompanied her through the silent house, adding to her sense of unreality.

David still sat where she'd left him, his cravat loosened and his tailored coat thrown casually over a chair in the warm August night. His hair was tousled as if he had run his hands through it, and a half-filled glass of brandy sat in front of him.

His expression was remote when she entered, but it changed to concern when he saw her. Rising, he asked, "Is something wrong, Jocelyn?"

She shook her head, feeling the weight of her hair heavy over her shoulders. "Not really. I wasn't able to sleep, and I realized I'd forgotten to show you something. It's a gift to you from Stretton, or perhaps from Westholme."

"Intriguing." He smiled lazily, looming over her as they left the room.

Acutely aware of his height and strength, she led him to the main drawing room. Stretton had not failed her, and the painting of David's family now hung above the fireplace. Wordlessly she lifted the candelabrum so that the light fell across it.

He inhaled, his gaze devouring the painted images. "I had no idea this painting still existed. I assumed that Wilfred would have destroyed it."

"He wanted to, but Stretton hid it away." She studied the portrait again, thinking what a fine job Reynolds had done at capturing the sense of family. "It's a beautiful painting. Was your family happy then?"

"Yes, particularly when the older boys were away at school. My father took more pleasure in his second family than his first. I don't think he ever knew the malice his older sons were capable of." His nostalgic gaze traveled to the portrait again. "Or perhaps he didn't want to know. He was a kind man, with no taste for unpleasantness."

"Your strength came from your mother?"

"It must have. She was able to build a new life for her children, and I never knew her to feel self-pity for what she had lost." He touched the frame, his fingertips tracing the gilded whorls. "Perhaps she was happy not to be the lady of the manor anymore."

She envied David that confidence, that he could accept being called strong and never question it. She didn't think she had ever been able to accept a compliment comfortably in her life. Her social rank she was sure of, but praise of her person triggered bone-deep uneasiness. She had become convinced of her unworthiness very early.

His gaze went around the drawing room. She had grouped the furniture from the attic around three oriental carpets, creating comfortable conversation areas to break up the vast expanse. Candlelight shone on polished wood and hinted at the rich colors of the carpets. "This room has never looked better. You have a talent for beauty."

He looked back at her, and their gazes locked. She could not have turned away for all the treasures of

Araby. Softly she asked, "Why were you sitting alone so long?"

"I . . . was thinking. About you." The deep tones of his voice seemed to reach out and caress her. "How beautiful you are. How very difficult it is to restrain myself whenever we touch."

She drew closer, her breasts almost brushing him, her head tilted back to hold his gaze. Amazed at her own brazenness, she asked, "Why do you exercise such restraint?"

He stood absolutely still, making no attempt to either withdraw or reach out to her. "I promised you your freedom, and the promise binds me. I have already gone further than I should."

"We have signed the papers for the annulment, and we will both have our freedom. But what of tonight?" she asked intensely. "Who will know or care what happens between us?"

"I care, and I hope that you would, too." The skin tightened over his cheekbones. "But I'm not sure that you know what you want."

She laid her palm on his forearm, feeling the hard muscles beneath his sleeve. "I know that I want you to hold me," she said, her voice husky with longing. "I know that the lessons on passion you've given me so far are only an overture to one of life's great symphonies."

The civilized mien of an officer and a gentleman vanished. "Are you sure?"

The thought quickened her breath, making her want to run like the wind—and be caught by the lion. "As sure as one can be in this imperfect world."

He took the candelabrum from her hand and

placed it on the mantel, but all vestige of control vanished when his mouth met hers. The yearning they both had been denying exploded into a hunger that would not be satisfied with mere kisses.

He had embraced her before with skill and passion, but this was much, much more, both tinder for the flame and promise of fulfillment. His arms locked around her, drawing her so close that she felt his heart pounding against her breasts, the shape of his buttons pressing into her body through her thin nightclothes.

She tugged at his shirt, yanking it loose so that she could touch his warm skin. Though she had seen all of him when he was ill, now she yearned to rediscover his body in full strength and virility. Her hands opened and closed convulsively on his bare back in a tactile celebration of his flexing muscles. Sliding one hand around his chest, her fingers found the flat circle of his nipple. Wondering if he would feel the same kind of sensations she did, she squeezed the nub between thumb and forefinger.

David gasped, his whole body going rigid. "God help us both." Then, breath ragged, he caught her up in his arms. "This time, we will do it properly."

He carried her from the room as if she were no heavier than a child. As they ascended the stairs, she pressed her face into his shoulder, tears stinging her eyes with the knowledge that what seemed certain and wise in the night was as ephemeral as the moonlight that illuminated their path.

Chapter 30

When he reached her room, he set her on her feet so he could latch the door. She stood and watched him, a curved figure sculpted of moonshine and shadows. He swallowed hard as he saw how the soft folds of her gown draped sensuously over her ripe body. Diana's handmaiden, a nymph of the night who stole men's souls.

He had waited and prayed for this moment, when her heart would open to him, yet this seemed too sudden. Struggling between desire and the fear of doing the wrong thing, he said shakily, "This is the last chance to change your mind, Jocelyn."

"I have no doubts." Gaze intense, she untied the sash of her wrapper, shrugging so that the silk slithered down her body to pool around her bare feet. "Do you, my lord?"

"None at all."

"Then let me see you," she whispered.

His loosened cravat was gone with a yank. Then he pulled his shirt over his head and dropped it on the floor. The admiration in her gaze aroused him to painful readiness. Suspecting that it might not be wise to allow a virgin to see too much of a rampant male, he closed the distance between them and drew her into his arms.

Her hair fell back across his arm as she turned her face up to his kiss. A ribbon was drawn through the neckline of her nightgown, so he untied the bow, then worked the garment over her shoulders and down her body, using it as an excuse to slide his palms over every square inch of warm, yielding flesh.

She leaned into him, her hands caressing, the fullness of her breasts against his bare chest unbearably arousing. Panting, he laid her across the bed, then swiftly stripped off his remaining garments and lay beside her.

The moonlight created madness. Jocelyn should have felt shy, but the heat in his eyes set her ablaze. She loved the sight of him, the hard planes of his body so different from her own in the uncanny light, the scars his marks of valor.

She gasped when he cupped her breasts in his hands, holding them together as he kissed and sucked until she feared they would shimmer into flame. He played her like a master musician who had been given a precious instrument, his warm lips and hands invoking chords of response that resonated through her whole being.

Restlessly her hands danced over him, registering the textures of his smooth skin and lightly tickling hair. There was no time, only sensation. Her fingers brushed the heated shaft that pressed against her leg. He made a thick, rough sound that aroused her as fiercely as the slide of his hand between her thighs. She explored further, clasping the head of the fascinating, firm but resilient, organ.

He jerked, gasping, "If you wish this to last, best have a care, madam."

Hastily she released him, kneading his back and shoulders as he kissed her ears and throat and mouth again and again. She could barely separate the torrent of sensations, until the heat in her loins became an annihilating fire. Nothing existed but the touch of his knowing fingers and the fever of her response. She was falling, falling . . .

She bit into his shoulder, shuddering as convulsions racked her body. She would have been terrified, except for the secure haven of his embrace, and his richly satisfied whisper, "Yes. *Yes.* . . ."

She clung to him, shaking, until she could say dizzily, "So this is the lesson in passion you wanted me to learn."

"Oh, my dear girl, it's only the first step in an endless exploration." He moved between her slack legs, positioning himself at the entrance to her body.

She tensed, wary of invasion, but he was in no hurry, tracing her lips with his tongue, drawing her into another kiss, as if they had all the time in the world. She relaxed and soon desire began flowing through her again. She moved her hips against him in a shy invitation. Pressure and friction created new sensations, aching emptiness and a yearning for completion.

As their tongues twined in an erotic dance, his hand came between them, finding a place of such exquisite sensitivity that her breath caught in her throat. Coiled heat formed around his touch, spiraling tighter and tighter, a promise of madness, but whenever she approached the cliff she had plunged off before, his hand became still, until she thought that desire would consume her very bones.

When she could bear it no longer, she choked out, "What . . . what now, my lord?" as she instinctively arched her hips upward in wordless demand.

He met her movement with a powerful thrust, sliding deep within her. There was a moment of sharp discomfort, which gradually faded as she felt the heated throbbing where they were joined. This was the closeness she had yearned for, the archetypal fusion of male and female that was the ancient ritual of the night.

She rocked against him. He began to move, slowly at first, then faster, until his frayed control abruptly shattered.

"Oh, God, Jocelyn . . ." With a groan, he buried his face in the angle of her throat, spilling himself into her. She cried out his name, ravished by a passion beyond anything she had ever imagined, yet which carried a core of gentleness and caring that made her want to weep with gratitude.

Scoured by emotions beyond her ken, she might have wept, but he cradled her exhausted body against his, smoothing her hair tenderly, as if she was the most precious creature in the world. Soon he slept, but she lay drowsily awake, wishing that the morning would never come. For these few hours, her mind was beyond questions and doubts, and she feared that such peace might never come again.

He woke after moonset and rolled onto his back, bringing her with him so that she sprawled along the length of his body, as at the picnic in the orchard. But this time they lay skin to skin, with nothing to separate them. Sensual strokes and languid sighs led to slow, profoundly satisfying lovemaking as she set the rhythm of their joining.

Finally, her head cradled on David's shoulder, Jocelyn slept with the utter exhaustion of a child.

David awoke very early. The room was shadowy in the half-light, and outside the birds sang their dawn chorus. He felt an absurd desire to join them from his own sense of exhilaration. Jocelyn lay curled under his arm, looking more like a girl of seventeen than a worldly woman of twenty-five.

He kissed her lightly on the forehead, and she turned against him with a soft exhalation. She looked delectable with her auburn hair spread around her, but also hauntingly vulnerable.

He resisted the temptation to wake her. Despite the magic of the night just past, he suspected that by daylight she would feel a certain awkwardness. It would take time for the cool, collected lady to fully accept the passionate moon maiden who was her secret self. It was just as well that he had to go to Hereford for the Assizes. His absence would give Jocelyn time to adjust to the change in their relationship, perhaps to start planning for their life together.

He slipped quietly out of the bed, tenderly pulling the covers around her shoulders. She was still sleeping soundly, so he restricted himself to the lightest of kisses before returning to his own room and dressing for the day.

After leaving a message for her to find upon waking, he set off for Hereford, impatient for the long hours to pass until he could see her again.

* * *

Jocelyn awoke slowly, her body a combination of delicious languor and unexpected soreness. Her cheek felt raw, as if it had been scraped by something bristly. Absently she touched it, and memory flooded through her. David's face against hers, his urgent words in her ear. Passion, submission, and fulfillment beyond her most vivid imaginings.

She turned her head and discovered that she was alone in the bed. Shakily she sat up. The left pillow still showed the impression of David's head, and on it lay a red rose, its stem wrapped with a note. The flower had been plucked at the perfect moment, the petals just beginning to open and a few droplets of dew lying jewel-like against the deep crimson surface. Red for passion. She hesitated before picking it up, warned by deep instinct the message it contained would change the world irrevocably.

But the world had already changed. After inhaling the delicate fragrance of the rose, she unwrapped the note.

Jocelyn—To my infinite regret, I must go to Hereford for the Assizes, and will not see you until evening. I love you. David.

She stared at the note and felt her heart crack into aching pieces. The pain started as small, slow fractures, then splintered in all directions, shattering along the fault lines of terror and loneliness that riddled her spirit.

Grief overwhelmed her. Shaking with sobs, she buried her face in her hands, the rose clenched desperately in her right fist. She had wanted friendship and passion, not the searing agony of love. Unable to resist, she had played with fire, and now she burned.

How could she have been fool enough to think that devastation could be avoided? She had destroyed herself, and grievously injured David in the process.

He couldn't love her, because he didn't truly know her. In the white hot clarity of the marriage bed, where nothing could be concealed, he would swiftly see her flaws. When he did, the illusion of love would vanish, replaced by indifference or worse.

And that she could not bear. She had already fallen into the abyss. Now she must leave, before the final annihilation that would inevitably come.

She was numbly plotting her flight when Marie entered with her morning tray. "Good morning, milady. It is another fine day."

Her cheerfulness vanished when she saw her mistress clearly. "Milady! What is wrong?" Setting the tray on a table, she retrieved the blue silk wrapper from the floor and draped it around Jocelyn's bare shoulders.

Jocelyn stared at the spreading scarlet stains on the white sheet, where bright drops of blood were dripping from her thorn-pierced hand. The stem of the rose had snapped in her spasm of misery.

Becoming aware of the pain helped clear her mind. Shakily she said, "We must leave this morning to return to London."

The maid frowned. "But Lord Presteyne will be in Hereford all day."

"He is not coming with us. Tell my coachman to

prepare the carriage, then pack my things. I want to be gone by midmorning."

Marie bit her lip, her astute gaze interpreting the room's dishevelment. "Milady, are you sure? If there has been some quarrel, would it not be better to wait and discuss it with his lordship?"

On the verge of breaking, Jocelyn said flatly, "Do as I say."

Her tone silenced the maid's protests. Eyes wide and worried, Marie left to inform the coachman of their imminent departure.

Thinking of all that must be done, Jocelyn climbed from the bed and tied the wrapper around her waist, then carried her cup of chocolate to the desk. The warmth cleared her mind a little. Fighting a new bout of tears, she started to compose a note to David.

There would be time enough for desolation on the journey home.

Chapter 31

Within the hour, they were ready to leave. Jocelyn took a last survey of the room. Though she had been here only a brief time, the knowledge that she would never return made her profoundly sad.

Her musings were interrupted by Marie. "Lady Jocelyn, about Hugh Morgan."

Jocelyn turned and saw anxiety on the maid's face. "Yes?"

"Does Hugh work for you, or for Lord Presteyne?"

"Oh. I hadn't thought of that." She frowned. Though she paid the young man's salary, he was David's personal servant. "Ask him to come here."

When Marie returned with her sweetheart, Jocelyn said, "Morgan, since you are Lord Presteyne's valet, it seems appropriate for you to continue in his service. He has been very pleased with your work, and I imagine he will wish to retain you."

She pressed her fingers to her temple, trying to guess how David would react to her departure. "If Lord Presteyne decides to dismiss you because of your . . . your past association with me, you may return to my household. The same is true for your brother, Rhys, if he prefers to work for me rather than here at Westholme."

Hugh stared at Jocelyn, his open face agonized. "Lady Jocelyn, has his lordship hurt you in some way? If he has . . ."

He looked so protective that Jocelyn had to swallow a lump in her throat before she could reply. "On the contrary, it is I who have injured him."

Face set, she walked from the room, leaving Marie and Hugh staring after her.

The Welshman asked, "What has happened, lass? Her ladyship looks like the devil himself has walked on her grave."

"I don't know," Marie said miserably. "Yesterday she and his lordship were smelling of April and May, then this morning she was crying fit to break your heart, and we must leave immediately."

Hugh enveloped her in his embrace. "Good-bye, sweetheart. If I know Lord Presteyne, we'll be following you to London as soon as he gets home."

"I don't want to leave you," Marie cried, tears bright in her eyes. "Let me stay, or you come with us to London. You can be milady's footman again."

"Nay, lass, you saw her face. For now, my lady needs you, and I think my lord will be needing me." He kissed her hard, already missing her. "We'll be together again soon, I swear it."

With an agonized last glance over her shoulder, Marie took her mistress's jewel case and left the room. Hugh found a window where he could watch the two women climb into the waiting carriage, assisted by the unhappy butler.

And then they were gone.

* * *

It was late afternoon when David returned home, impatiently pushing the front door open without waiting for a servant. As he entered the hall, Stretton approached, expression lugubrious. David removed his hat and flipped it to the butler. "Where is Lady Presteyne? In the attics again?"

Looking as if he'd rather be anywhere else, Stretton replied, "Her ladyship left for London this morning, my lord."

Uncomprehending, David repeated, "She left?"

"Yes, my lord."

She must have received an urgent message from a relative. A life or death matter. Yet a premonition of disaster was already knotting his belly when he said, "I presume she left a letter for me?"

"Yes, my lord." The butler handed him a sealed note.

He ripped it open and read: *David—I'm sorry. I never meant to hurt you. It is best we not see each other again. Jocelyn.*

The words struck with the impact of musket balls. He reread the note twice, trying to make sense of it, but there was nothing more to be learned. There was . . . nothing.

He shoved past the butler and climbed the stairs three at a time. Surely this must be some bizarre joke.

Throwing open the door to her chamber, he saw that it had been stripped of all traces of its recent occupant. The elegant clutter of perfumes and brushes was gone from the dressing table, leaving only a lingering scent of jasmine.

Disbelievingly he touched the bare mattress, as if

to find some warmth left from the night before, but there was no remnant of the joy they had shared. The joy he *thought* they had shared.

He scanned the room. The only sign of occupancy was a crumpled ball of paper in the cold fireplace. He picked it up, hoping it might be a preliminary good-bye note that would say more than the one she had left with Stretton.

He almost discarded the letter when he saw that it wasn't in her hand, then read through when he saw it was from Lady Cromarty. *Damnation.* What did it mean that the countess was threatening Jocelyn?

Ice formed in the pit of his belly and spread through his body as different possibilities flashed through his mind. Had Jocelyn decided that she didn't want the annulment after all, since it would make her vulnerable to her aunt's extortion? Freeing herself of her virginity may have been done to undercut Lady Cromarty's case.

Or—God help him—she might have decided that she was ready to go to her duke and didn't want to do so as a virgin. Who better to relieve her of an unwanted maidenhead than a willing, temporary husband? He had cooperated with alacrity. She had been an apt pupil, and could now offer herself as a woman of the world.

Yet it was hard to reconcile such cold-bloodedness with his image of Jocelyn, her warmth and honesty. Had she thought he would gladly bed her for the moment's pleasure, with no emotions involved, then been dismayed by his declaration of love?

Perhaps he had been wrong to think there was

warmth and vulnerability beneath her ladyship's highly polished exterior. She had grown up in a different world than his, where lords and ladies behaved in ways incomprehensible to common people.

He crushed the letter in his hand. Traditionally men were blamed for using and abandoning women, while in this case the reverse appeared to be true. It was an irony he didn't appreciate.

His thoughts ground to a halt when he realized that he had no idea if he was making sense. The only incontestable facts were the note saying she didn't want to see him again, and the letter from her aunt that turned an act of love into a handful of ashes.

He was staring blindly out the window when Morgan entered the room and said hesitantly, "My lord, I want to talk to you about Lady Jocelyn."

"There isn't much to talk about." David swallowed, struggling to put a calm public face on what had happened. "It was . . . kind of her to come and help organize my household here."

Refusing to accept dismissal, Morgan said, "Marie told me that this morning her ladyship was crying as if her heart would break. When I asked my lady if you had wronged her, she said that on the contrary, she had injured you."

Seeing his master's expression, Hugh flushed. "I meant no disloyalty to you, my lord, but she will always have my first allegiance, for what she did for my brother."

Reminded of Rhys, David wondered if a woman who had rescued a depressed, crippled soldier purely from the kindness of her heart could really be a callous seducer. Frowning, he tried to fit this new data with the other facts of Jocelyn's departure. She hadn't been distraught the night before, he was willing to swear to that. Unless she could lie with both words and body, she had come to him from desire, and experienced rapturous pleasure.

Might she be angry with him for consummating their marriage? Too much champagne might have clouded her judgment and left her blaming him for what had happened. Which would be damned unfair considering how often he'd asked her if she was sure, and in his experience his wife had always been fair.

Speculation was useless, he realized; Jocelyn's behavior was unlikely to be caused by anything obvious. Despite her calm, apparently confident exterior, he had known that she was wary of the very concept of love. Somewhere deep inside her she carried scars that had been broken open by the vulnerability of passion and his declaration of love.

His confused thoughts were interrupted by Hugh's determined voice. "Marie says Lady Jocelyn is in love with you. Everyone in the house could see it."

In love with him? David's paralysis broke. He must have been mad to consider abiding by Jocelyn's brief, senseless note. The only way he would let her go was if she would look him in the eye and swear she didn't want him.

Striding to the door, he ordered, "Throw a few of my things in a bag. I'm leaving for London immediately."

"I'll go, too, my lord," the valet said with determination. "I promised Marie I would come to her as soon as I could."

Envious of a relationship that was so much more straightforward than his own misbegotten marriage, David said, "Then we shall have to bring both of them home."

Chapter 32

Jocelyn returned to London as fast as a good coach and hired horses could take her. Throughout the long journey, she studied the gold wedding ring David had placed on her hand, and bleakly thought about her past. Many men had claimed to love her, and she had easily dismissed their declarations as youthful infatuation or fortune hunting.

Yet David had been able to reduce her to cinders with a handful of words. He had insinuated himself into her life with his courage and kindness and laughter. Thinking that another woman had his heart, she had allowed herself to come too close, and now she was paying the price.

They reached London late in the afternoon of the second day. By then, Jocelyn was exhausted by the thoughts that jolted around her head in rhythm with the pounding hooves of the horses. One bitter conclusion was unavoidable: the pain of the present was rooted in the unbearable past that she had always refused to acknowledge.

The time had come to face that past, no matter what it cost her. She might be flawed beyond redemption, but she should not be a coward as well.

Tonight she would sleep in London, and tomorrow she would go on to Kent to find Lady Laura, the only person who could answer her questions.

As she entered the foyer of her home, she scanned the familiar grandeur. Grand, but so incredibly empty. What was one lone woman doing with so much space?

Carrying the jewel case, Marie started up the staircase. Her silent sympathy had made her a welcome companion on the long journey from Hereford. Would she stay with Jocelyn, or return to Westholme to be with her sweetheart, leaving her mistress even more alone?

Feeling unequal to the two flights of stairs, Jocelyn entered the salon, wearily stripping off her gloves. She rang for tea and was sipping a cup and waiting for it to invigorate her when the door opened.

In stepped Lady Laura, strikingly attractive in a modish blue evening gown. "What a nice surprise to have you back, my dear!" she said warmly. "Where is David?"

Jocelyn rose and gave her aunt a heartfelt hug. "I'm so glad you're here," she said, her voice choked with incipient tears. "I was going to travel down to Kennington tomorrow to see you. Is Uncle Andrew in London also?"

"Yes, he had business at the Horse Guards. We are to meet later at a dinner party." Eyes worried, Lady Laura guided her niece to the sofa so they could sit down together. "What's wrong, darling? You look like death in the afternoon."

Jocelyn sat back on the sofa and wiped her eyes

with the back of her hand. "It's . . . complicated. Do you have time to talk before going out?"

"You know that I always have time for you," said her aunt, looking even more worried. "What do you wish to discuss?"

Where to start? With the horrible mess she had made of her own and David's lives? Or earlier, to the tragedy that had warped her life beyond repair?

Face rigid, she said, "Tell me about my mother."

"You've always refused to talk about Cleo," Laura said, startled. "Why do you ask now?"

"Because I must understand," Jocelyn answered harshly. "What kind of person was she? Why did my father divorce her? Was she as great a whore as everyone says?"

"My dear girl, who ever told you that?" her aunt exclaimed, expression horrified.

"Everyone! Do you remember the caricatures we saw in that print shop window?"

The older woman winced. "I didn't realize you were old enough to understand what the pictures and comments meant."

Lady Laura couldn't have been more than nineteen or twenty when that episode had occurred, Jocelyn realized. She must have been as upset as her niece. More, perhaps, because she had to face vicious gossip in the salons and ballrooms of London every day. No wonder she had been eager to follow the drum with Andrew Kirkpatrick.

"That day was hardly the only time." Jocelyn's mouth twisted. "Servants called her a harlot when they thought I couldn't hear. So did the well-bred young ladies at that exclusive seminary in Bath my father sent me to, the one I ran away from. Then there was the noble lord who tried seducing me at his own daughter's come-out ball because he assumed I was no better than I should be. 'Like mother, like daughter,' he said just before he shoved his tongue in my mouth."

"Dear God, why did you never tell me? Or your father?" Laura looked ill. "You always seemed so . . . so unconcerned. You were only four when your mother left, and you didn't seem to miss her. If you ever asked what happened to her, I never heard of it."

"Of course I didn't ask!" Jocelyn began to tremble. "Even a small child knows what subjects are forbidden."

"Cleo was headstrong and she made some terrible mistakes, but she was no harlot," Laura said emphatically. "She and your father had a whirlwind courtship and married within weeks of their meeting. When the first flames of passion burned out, they discovered they really had very little in common."

She shook her head sorrowfully. "They could have lived separate lives, like many fashionable people do, but each wanted the other to . . . to fulfill their dreams. Be a perfect lover. They could not accept each other as they were. The fights were extraordinary. They fought in public, they fought in private. There was some twisted kind of love between them that came out as anger and hatred. You don't remember any of this?"

"Oh, yes," Jocelyn said, her voice a bare whisper.

"I remember." She squeezed her eyes shut as her father's remembered shout sliced through her brain. *"You're a woman, which means you're a greedy liar and a whore. God damn the hour I met you!"*

Her mother had responded with rage and smashed china, cursing her husband for his cruelty and faithlessness. Jocelyn had huddled unnoticed in a corner of the huge Charlton drawing room, riveted at the sight of her parents' fury, too terrified to run away. The fight, and others, were seared into her soul.

She pressed a hand to her midriff, trying to ease the pain that had been there for a lifetime. "My memories are patchy. Tell me what happened as you remember it."

Laura bit her lip. "By the time I made my come-out, your parents had reached the point of doing their utmost to hurt each other. Your father took one of the most notorious courtesans in London as his mistress, which was bad enough. The final explosion came when he dared flaunt her at one of Cleo's balls, in this very house.

"I was chatting with Cleo when Edward brought his mistress into the ballroom. Cleo turned dead white. She was an expert shot, and I think that if she'd had a pistol, she would have put a bullet through his heart. Instead, after a blazing row in front of half of fashionable London, she left the ball with Baron von Rothenburg, a Prussian diplomat who had been pursuing her.

"Cleo and Rothenburg began a flamboyant affair that gave your father an abundance of evidence for a divorce. She never set foot in this house after the night of the ball. Your father refused to allow her back inside, even to collect her personal belongings. He had everything packed and delivered to Rothenburg's, along with a challenge to a duel. Edward wasn't wounded, but Rothenburg took a bullet in the lungs that contributed to his death five years later."

Jocelyn rubbed her aching temples. "Dear God, how many lives did that woman destroy?"

"You mustn't blame your mother for the divorce. It was every bit as much your father's fault. Perhaps more so," her aunt said bleakly. "I loved both Cleo and Edward, but they were bound together in some catastrophic fashion that brought out the worst in both of them."

"So she ran off with another man," Jocelyn said with dripping scorn. "What a wonderfully moral solution to her problems."

"Cleo was no lightskirt. She would never have taken a lover if your father hadn't driven her to it. She came to love Rothenburg, but he was a Catholic and his family wouldn't countenance a divorced woman. Though he would have married her anyhow, she didn't want him to become estranged from his family, so she stayed with him as his mistress until his death."

Fighting a reluctant trace of admiration for her mother's refusal to ruin her lover's relationship with his family, Jocelyn asked, "How did she die?"

"The day after Rothenburg's funeral, she took his stallion out riding and . . . and tried to jump a gully that was too wide. Both she and the horse were killed." Laura closed her eyes, pain on her face. "Please don't think too ill of her, Jocelyn. She might not have loved wisely, but she had a good heart, and she gave it generously."

So that was the full story of the noble, beautiful, passionate Cleo, Countess of Cromarty. The anguish that had lived with Jocelyn since she was a child erupted in excruciating waves. Leaping from the sofa, she paced across the room, her hands tearing frantically at each other. Barely able to speak, she cried out in a voice of raw agony, "If she was so wonderful, then what was wrong with me?"

She spun around to face her aunt, tears pouring from her eyes. "What was so horribly, damnably wrong with me, that my own mother could abandon me without a single word? Without a shred of remorse or regret?"

She tried to say more, but couldn't. Joint by joint, she folded to her knees and crumpled into a crouch, arms clutching herself in a frantic attempt to staunch the primal wound that ravaged her spirit. "What did I do wrong?" she gasped, feeling as if she was being torn in half. *"What did I do wrong?"*

"Dear God in heaven!" Laura exclaimed, her voice shaking. An instant later, she dropped on the floor beside Jocelyn and enfolded her in her arms, rocking her as if she was an infant. "My darling girl, is that what you have believed all these years? Why didn't you ever ask me? I could have told you the truth."

"I knew the truth." Jocelyn's mouth twisted. "That my mother was a whore, and that she left me without a single backward glance."

"That's *not* how it happened! Cleo tried desperately to get custody of you. Once she rode out to Charlton to see you when she thought Edward was in London, but he was home, and he threatened her with a horsewhip. He said he'd kill her if she ever tried to come near you again.

"She tried to convince him that since you could not inherit the title, you should be with her. When he refused, she dropped down on her knees and begged him to let her see you, but he wouldn't allow it." Laura began to cry. "I was horrified, but it wasn't until I had children of my own that I recognized the full depths of what she was suffering."

"It sounds to me as if my father discovered that I was most useful as a weapon to punish his hated wife," Jocelyn said bitterly. "And maybe she wanted me for the same reason—to hurt him. I was the pawn between the feuding king and queen."

"Don't confuse Edward's fury with Cleo with his genuine love for you," Laura said. "He told me later that he was terrified that she would steal you away to the Continent with Rothenburg, and he was right to fear that. In a divorce, a woman has no rights at all. Cleo was branded an adulteress in the eyes of the world, and the law wouldn't raise a hand to help her. If she could have abducted you, I'm sure she would have. For the next five years, until Cleo died, your father made sure there was always a footman or other servant he trusted to guard you."

"Did he discharge my nurse, Gilly, because he feared she was loyal to my mother rather than him?"

Laura sighed. "I'm afraid so. I told him it would be cruel to both you and Gilly, but he was afraid she might take you to your mother. Perhaps she would have. The servants adored Cleo. You are like her in many ways."

Losing warm, nurturing Gilly had been like losing her mother for a second time. Then Aunt Laura had been lost to marriage. By the time Jocelyn was five, she had known that to love someone was to lose them.

Wondering at her aunt's knowledge, she asked, "How did you learn so much about my mother's thoughts and feelings?"

"She had become my sister, and I couldn't bear to lose her. We corresponded until Cleo died. I sent her drawings you had made, told her how you grew. After I married and left Charlton, I had the housekeeper write me about how you were so I could pass on the information to your mother. Cleo would ask if you ever talked about her, but you never said a word," Laura said softly. "I could not bear to add to her unhappiness, so I lied and said that you spoke of her often."

"I thought of her all the time, but I was afraid to ask," Jocelyn whispered.

Laura stroked her head gently. "Why were you afraid?"

Jocelyn squeezed her eyes shut, trying to make sense of this new view of the world. "I think that . . . that I believed that if I ever asked about her, Papa would send me away, too."

"He would *never* have done anything like that." Laura hugged her. "He loved you more than anyone or anything else in his life. Since you never asked about your mother and seemed content, he decided it would be better for you if he never raised the subject. He was grateful because he thought you had escaped unscathed."

"Unscathed?" Jocelyn laughed, an edge of hysteria in her voice. "My whole life has been about their divorce."

"Neither of us dreamed that you took it so badly, or that you were the victim of such taunts and insults." Sitting back on her heels, Laura said gravely, "But never doubt that you were loved. I think the main reason Edward never remarried was to have more time and attention for you."

"And here I thought he just liked having a passing parade of mistresses," Jocelyn said acidly. That, too, had shaped her view of the world: men were fickle by nature. "Has Uncle Andrew been a faithful husband? Does such a thing even exist?"

She immediately wished that she hadn't asked, but her aunt said calmly, "Yes, Drew has been faithful. He gave me his word, and I have never doubted it. Just as he has never had occasion to doubt me."

"Are you two as happy as you seem?" Jocelyn asked in a small voice. "I've wondered if any marriage for people of our order can ever be happy."

"Such a cynic you've become," Laura said with a sigh. "Yes, my dear, Drew and I are happy. Oh, we've had our disagreements—all couples do. But the love that first drew us together has only become stronger with the years."

Jocelyn asked unsteadily, "You think my mother really loved me?"

"I *know* that she did. Cleo wrote me a letter just before her death. Later I realized that . . . that she was saying good-bye." Laura swallowed hard. "She said that the greatest regrets of her life were losing you, and that she would never see you grow up. She sent you a gift, but I hesitated to pass it on. Because you always refused to discuss your mother, I didn't want to risk upsetting you. If only I had been wiser."

She rose and extended her hand to help Jocelyn up. "Come along. It's time to do what I should have done years ago."

Chapter 33

Silently Jocelyn followed her aunt upstairs to the chamber the Kirkpatricks shared whenever they stayed at Cromarty House. And they always did share a bed, not like most couples of their class. More proof that perhaps marriage really could be happy.

Lady Laura opened her jewelry box, removed a flat, oval-shaped cloisonné box about four inches long, and handed it to Jocelyn. It was a portrait case, and an exquisitely lovely one.

Fumbling a little, Jocelyn found the catch in the side and opened the case. Inside was a miniature of a golden-haired woman, a striking beauty with hazel eyes. Set in the frame opposite the portrait was a piece of parchment with a delicate script that said, "To my daughter Jocelyn, with all my love."

Her hand closed convulsively around the cloisonné case as the sight of her mother's face triggered a flood of memories. Playing in the garden, her mother weaving flowers into her hair. Exhilarated rides on her mother's lap on a horse that skimmed across the hills of Charlton. Playing in a silk-and-lace filled dressing room, her mother casually unconcerned when Jocelyn accidentally ruined a new bonnet.

Tears pouring silently down her cheeks, Jocelyn welcomed the good memories she had buried along with the unendurable pain. Her mother had loved her. Though she had left, she *had* looked back, as ravaged by the separation as Jocelyn had been.

Her aunt put an arm around her shoulders and let her cry. When the tears finally stilled, Laura asked, "Do you understand your mother better now?"

Jocelyn nodded. "I don't know if the scars will ever go away, but at least now I know where they are, and how they came to be."

"Shall I stay with you this evening? I can easily forgo the dinner party."

"I'd rather be alone. I have a great deal of thinking to do." She sighed. "Perhaps now I can sort out the muddle I've made of my affairs."

"Trouble with David?"

"I'm afraid so. Serious trouble."

"He's another one like Andrew, my dear," Laura said quietly. "If you make your marriage a real one, David will never let you down."

"It may be too late for that." Not wanting to say more, Jocelyn changed the subject by gesturing at her aunt's gown. "You'll have to change. Your gown hasn't been improved by my weeping all over it."

"A small price to pay for having cleared the air after too many years," Laura said as she rang for her maid. "You're sure you'll be all right tonight?"

"Quite sure." She kissed her aunt's cheek shyly. "I always thought of you as my real mother. Now, I have two."

Laura smiled. "I wanted a daughter, but I could not have loved one of my own more than you."

Tears threatened them both, but her aunt's maid entered before emotion gained the upper hand. As the maid clucked over her mistress's rumpled gown, Jocelyn made her escape. Now that she had recovered her past, she must untangle the complications it had created in the present.

A happy Isis purring on her lap, Jocelyn stayed up very late as she thought about her life, and her parents. Perhaps she should be angry with her father for depriving her of all communication with her mother, but Lady Laura's explanation made her understand his reasons. Though she had always feared that his love was fragile and might be withdrawn if she didn't please him, he had given her the best of himself. That she didn't trust his love was her failing, not his.

She even understood his blasted, manipulative will. Though she had never revealed her reservations about marriage to him, he must have guessed that left to her own devices, she'd probably have died a spinster. Never subtle, the earl had arranged her life so that she had little choice but to confront her fears.

She had always thought of herself as being like Lady Laura, and it was true that the physical resemblance was strong. But there was also much of Cleo in her. That business about pistol shooting, for example, not to mention the intense, headstrong disposition. Jocelyn had spent her life suppressing that side of her nature, but it was an integral part of her. If she was to accept her mother, she must also accept herself.

So be it.

Yet understanding and accepting the past was only the first step. One long, anguished conversation was not enough to make her feel that she was worthy of love. Even with her father and her aunt, she'd never felt fully loved. Always there had been the vague, not quite conscious fear that she was flawed beyond redemption, and that anyone who saw her clearly would leave her.

Yet she yearned for love, which meant she must learn to see herself as lovable. Not an easy task. In her mind, she knew that she was a decent example of womankind. She tried to live up to the spiritual values of her faith. She was generous with her time and money, and tried to be kind. She did her best to value people as they deserved, rather than scorning all but those who were born to the same station in life she was. But it would take a long time to believe in her heart that she deserved love, if indeed she ever succeeded at that.

Lord, she didn't even know what love was. She had thought she was a little bit in love with the Duke of Candover, and even after all that had happened with David, the duke still had a hold on her mind. Was that love, or an illusion she had spun because her rational mind thought he would make a suitable husband—one who would never be overcome by the kind of destructive passion that had doomed her parents' marriage?

David Lancaster called up more complex feelings. She had married him at random, laughed with him, come to think of him as a trustworthy friend, and in a burst of irresistible yearning she had lured him to her bed. She didn't know if that was love, but the thought of not having him in her life produced a gut-wrenching sense of loss.

Would he follow her to London or had she already destroyed what was between them? If he didn't come, would she have the courage to go back to Westholme? She must, because she had spent too much of her life running.

By the time she retired to restless slumber, her mind was numb with wondering.

She awoke the next morning feeling the unnatural calm that followed a tempest. When she joined her aunt and uncle for breakfast, the colonel studied her intently before leaving for the day, but he asked no tactless questions about his former staff officer. Jocelyn was grateful; she would have been quite incapable of discussing David.

Lady Laura invited her niece to join her for a morning at the modiste, but Jocelyn refused, unready to deal with the normal trivia of existence. Instead, she went to her room and started to write an account about her aunt's revelations, and how she felt about them. Perhaps the process of forming vague emotions into words would clarify her understanding.

Late in the morning she stopped for a cup of tea. If David had decided to follow her to London, he could be here as early as that evening. She yearned to see him, but had no idea what she might say. That perhaps she loved him, but she really didn't know for sure? He deserved better than that.

She covered page after page as memories and insights poured through her. Strange how clear her mind had become now that Aunt Laura had given her the key to unlock the past.

She was taking a break and flexing cramped fingers when Dudley entered with a card on a silver tray. "A visitor, my lady."

Lifting the card, she read, "The Duke of Candover." A shiver ran through her. So the man who had occupied her thoughts for so long, who had been her shield against the solid reality of David Lancaster, was here.

"Until September . . ." In fact, he was back in London a few days early. Coincidence, or might he have been anxious to see her? He'd been thinking of her—the gift of poetry he'd sent was proof of that.

Well, she had wanted answers, and here was an opportunity to get some. "I shall be right down," she told her butler.

After Dudley left, she splashed cold water on her face to remove traces of the tears she'd shed, then studied herself dispassionately in the mirror. Marie had done her job well—Lady Jocelyn Kendal was her usual elegant self. Odd how she still thought of herself by that name when legally she was Lady Presteyne. It was a symbol of her skittish refusal to accept the marriage she had made.

She tried a smile. The image in the mirror was not entirely convincing, but reasonable. Feeling fatalistic, she descended to greet her visitor.

Darkly handsome, the duke was leaning casually against the mantel, but he straightened when she entered the drawing room. His cool gray eyes showed open admiration as Jocelyn approached.

"Good morning, Candover. This is an unexpected pleasure."

"I was called back to London by business and saw that your knocker was up as I drove by. To find you like this was more than I had hoped for." He regarded her with the warmth that he had shown when they had last seen each other, at the Parkingtons' ball. "Though it is not yet September, dare I hope you are ready"—he lifted her hand and kissed it lingeringly—"for diversion?"

Despairingly, Jocelyn realized that she was responding to him. She had hoped that she would feel nothing, but he was still deucedly attractive. More than that, beneath his legendarily cool exterior, she had always sensed a genuinely decent man, though it would surely pain him to realize that she thought of him that way.

Knowing she must learn more about what she felt, she smiled with all the charm she could muster. "The subject is open for discussion, your grace."

"I think you should call me Rafe. I much prefer that to Rafael." A slow, intimate smile crossed his face. "Naming me after an archangel was singularly inappropriate, don't you agree?" Then he cupped her chin in his palm, and touched his lips to hers.

Jocelyn experienced the kiss with a curious duality. He was pure male, and her instinctive response made it clear that he had earned his reputation as a splendid lover honestly. This is what she had dreamed of finding with him.

But he was not David. Her reaction to the duke was a frail, rootless thing next to the tempest of love David had kindled in her.

The wonder was that it had taken her so long to recognize an emotion that was now revealed as so powerful, so unmistakable. She had started to fall in love with David the first moment she had looked into his eyes at the hospital. And she had continued falling, always denying her feelings because the thought of being in love was so frightening. All of the time she'd been telling herself that David was just a good friend, the brother she'd always wanted, she'd already been hooked like a brown trout on an angler's line.

David would laugh when she told him that, but it would be warm amusement, not belittling. Now that she understood, she must go to him and ask that he forgive her erratic behavior.

She was about to disengage from the duke's embrace when the door to the drawing room swung open.

Chapter 34

David Lancaster and Hugh Morgan traveled hard through most of the moonlit night, reaching London in early afternoon. When they pulled up in front of Cromarty House, David barely took the time to settle his account with the post-chaise driver before he leaped from the carriage and bounded impatiently up the front steps. Not having a key, he was forced to use the knocker and wait for what seemed forever.

Dudley opened the door, saying with surprise, "My lord! How . . . unexpected."

As Hugh went in search of Marie, David asked, "Where is my wife?" Because, by God, she was still his wife, and she owed him an explanation at the very least.

"Her ladyship is in the drawing room. But . . . but she has company."

The butler's voice rose as David brushed past him and went to the drawing room. Opening the door, he started in—then froze when he saw that Jocelyn was in the arms of a man who must be her thrice-damned duke. Candover was the man's name, according to what Hugh had told him during their journey.

Murderous rage swept over him, surpassing anything he had ever experienced in battle. So the instinct that had guided him with Jocelyn was no more than a treacherous illusion, compounded of his hopes and dreams. The summer over and her unwanted virginity gone, Jocelyn had flown back to London to her preferred lover.

The tableau shattered when she looked up and saw him. He would have thought the situation could not be worse, but he was wrong. Jocelyn cried out, "David!" and pulled away from the other man. Her face glowed, as if she had been longing for her husband's arrival rather than halfway into another man's bed. Or had she moved from virgin to *ménage à trois* in three short days?

She moved toward him, hands lifting with welcome. "How did you get here so soon? I would not have thought you could be in London before tonight." Then she stopped abruptly as she saw his expression.

As always, she looked honest and innocent. David's stomach twisted with the sick knowledge that he had never known her at all. She was indeed the fashionable lady, the perfect hostess even under these circumstances.

His hands clenched, but he managed to control his fury well enough to say tightly, "It's obvious my arrival is both unexpected and unwelcome." His gaze snapped to the dark man who watched with shuttered eyes. No doubt the bastard had considerable experience of angry husbands. "I presume this is the Duke of Candover? Or is my dear wife spreading her favors more widely?"

As Jocelyn gasped, the duke nodded coolly. "I'm Candover. You have the advantage of me, sir."

So they were going to be civilized. Bitterly David reminded himself that Jocelyn had never pretended to want him for a real husband. He had promised she would have her freedom, and their mockery of a marriage carried no license to insult her under her own roof. She had done a great deal for him, and if she was incapable of giving love, that was his loss, not her crime.

Nonetheless, he wanted to take the duke apart, preferably with his bare hands. The fellow looked athletic, but he was no match for a trained soldier. David cursed himself for his damned sense of fairness. Violence would relieve some of his angry pain, but he had no right to murder Candover. The duke was there by Jocelyn's choice.

In a voice that could cut glass, he said, "I'm Presteyne, husband of this lady here, though not for long." His icy gaze returned to Jocelyn. "My apologies for interrupting your amusements. I'll collect my belongings and never trouble you again." He spun around and left, slamming the door behind him with a force that rattled the windows.

Shaking, Jocelyn sank onto a chair, her hands pressed to her solar plexus. She had been so happy in the blaze of her new understanding, so indifferent to Candover's kiss, that she hadn't even considered how compromising her circumstances were—until she had seen the furious revulsion on David's face. If she lived to be a hundred, she would never forget his expression, that combination of anger and raw, betrayed pain.

From that first meeting in the hospital, David had opened himself to her with complete generosity, always giving kindness and comfort. He had even committed near perjury about a humiliatingly intimate matter to give her an annulment.

And how had she repaid him? When he had declared his love and was most vulnerable, she had spurned him and fled without any explanation. When he put aside pride to follow her, he had found her in the arms of a man of greater rank and fortune. Dear God, how he must despise her!

She stared blindly at the door where he had disappeared, knowing that the paralyzed numbness she felt was a tissue-thin barrier against an ocean of pain. He would never believe she loved him now. It was the ultimate irony that in the moment she discovered love, she had destroyed her chance of ever sharing it with her husband.

She forgot Candover's presence until he said dryly, "Your husband doesn't seem to share your belief that the marriage is one of convenience."

Mutely she raised her gaze, deeply ashamed to have involved him in such a scene. "I'm sorry," she whispered.

"What kind of game are you playing? Your husband doesn't seem the sort of man to be manipulated by jealousy. He may leave you, or he may wring your neck, but he won't play that kind of lover's game." His eyes were hard as flint.

With an effort, Jocelyn pulled her disordered senses together enough to speak. She owed Candover honesty. "I wasn't playing a game. I . . . I was trying to discover what was in my heart. Only now do I know how I feel about David, when it is too late."

His expression softened in the face of her stark misery. "I'm beginning to suspect that under your highly polished surface beats a romantic heart. If that's true, go after your husband and throw your charming self at his feet with abject apologies. You should be able to bring him around, at least this once. A man will forgive the woman he loves a great deal. Just don't let him find you in anyone else's arms. I doubt he would forgive you a second time."

She stared at him, torn between pain and hysterical laughter. "Your sangfroid is legendary, but even so, the reports do you less than justice. If the devil himself walked in, I think you would ask him if he played whist."

"Never play whist with the devil, my dear. He cheats." Candover lifted Jocelyn's cold hand and lightly kissed it. "Should your husband resist your blandishments, feel free to let me know if you want a pleasant, uncomplicated affair."

He released her hand. "You would never have more from me, you know. Many years ago I gave my heart away to someone who dropped and broke it, so I have none left." He put his hand on the doorknob, then hesitated, his gaze lingering on her face. In a voice so low she could barely hear the words, he said, "You remind me of a woman I once knew, but not enough. Never enough." Then he was gone.

Startled by the bleakness in his eyes, Jocelyn realized that she had never really known him. What scars did he hide behind *his* polished surface? She had not thought to wonder, because she had been hiding in the shadows and spinning her fantasies. She'd understood *nothing*.

There would be time to berate herself later. Now, she had more important things to do. She bolted from the drawing room and up the stairs at a speed she hadn't achieved since she was twelve years old.

Heart pounding, she burst into the blue room without knocking, and found her husband packing his few remaining possessions into a portmanteau. Breathless from two long flights of stairs, she gasped, "Please, David, give me a chance to explain! That was not what it looked like."

His brows raised sardonically. "Are you trying to say you weren't wrapped passionately in Candover's arms? I hadn't realized my eyesight was so poor."

Jocelyn winced under the lash of his sarcasm. Before today, she had never seen him angry. There had been kindness, intelligence, humor, and heart-melting tenderness, but never this icy, terrifying rage.

Struggling to control her voice, she replied, "Yes, I let him kiss me. I wanted to understand my feelings for him, and it seemed the quickest way to find out." She moved a step closer. "What I discovered was that I don't want an annulment. I want to be your wife."

"Oh? Have you decided that a nominal husband will give you more freedom to cut a promiscuous swath through the beau monde?" He slammed the portmanteau shut. "I regret to inform you that my values are shockingly conventional, and I have no desire for a wife with fashionable morals. If you want a husband for propriety's sake, you can buy yourself a more tolerant one after you regain your freedom."

He lifted the case and looked down at her, his face

expressionless but his lean body rigid with tension. "I will not oppose the annulment. If you try to withdraw from it so you can maintain the fiction of being married, I shall file for divorce. Would your duke find you a suitable mistress then?"

Lacerated by his anger and pain, she begged, "David, please don't go. I kissed the man once, I didn't join the muslin company. I don't want him and a fashionable life, I want *you*! I would count myself blessed to spend the rest of my life with you at Westholme."

His lips tightened, and she realized with sick despair that she had said the wrong thing. "Hungry for my acres, Lady Jocelyn? You could buy my dying body, but not my living one. Now *stand aside.*"

Instead of moving out of the way, she planted herself in front of the door, blocking his escape. With devastating empathy, she recognized that the depth of his anger was a measure of his hurt. She who had spent a lifetime nursing her own feelings of rejection had inflicted the same kind of wounds on the man she loved.

Desperate to break through his anger, she asked unsteadily, "What if I am carrying your child?"

There was a spark deep in his eyes, and for a moment she thought she had reached him. Then his face shuttered again. "If you work quickly, you can use it as a lever to convince Candover to marry you. I believe he needs an heir."

"Stop it!" Jocelyn cried out in agony, twisting sideways to hide her face against the door. *"Stop it!"*

David drew an anguished breath. "Don't make this any harder than it has to be, Jocelyn." His hard hands closed on her shoulders to move her from his path.

A last, frail argument occurred to her. Forcing back her tears, she turned to face him. "You have studied the law and pride yourself on having a fair mind. Will you judge me without hearing all the evidence?"

His mouth twisted harshly. "I found the letter from your aunt. The contents made it seem probable that you decided virginity was no longer an asset, and set out to seduce me for that reason. I arrived here and found you in the arms of the man you claimed to have wanted all along. How much more evidence is there?"

She looked up into his eyes and ached for what she saw there. "Oh, my love, is that what you believed, that I invited you to my bed from cold-blooded calculation? I have been many kinds of fool, but never a calculating one. My heart and my body knew that I loved you long before my mind did. My fears prevented me from recognizing that you were the man I've been searching for my whole life."

A muscle jerked in his jaw. "Then why did you run away and say we should not see each other again?"

"For complicated reasons I am just beginning to understand, I have only let myself become interested in men who were out of reach," she said haltingly. "Men who could be trusted not to care for me deeply. When you left that note saying you loved me, I was overwhelmed with fear and confusion, so I ran."

"I don't understand," he said, expression perplexed. But at least he was listening.

"When I returned to London, I spoke with Aunt Laura to learn more about what I had been hiding from all my life. I was only four when my parents divorced in the greatest scandal of their generation. I never saw or heard from my mother again. Ever since, on a level far too deep to recognize, I have believed there was something horribly wrong with me. My mother had abandoned me, and I feared my father would also if I wasn't the perfect daughter, always bright and pretty and collected. It was a role I learned to play very well, but that's what it was—a role."

Her eyes slid away from his, her words wrenched from her. "If my life was a fraud, that meant that no man could love me, because none of them knew me. Anyone who claimed to love me must be either a liar after my fortune, or worse, a sincere fool who would come to despise me if he knew me better. I could not allow a man to come close enough to discover my fatal flaws. Only after Sally said you wanted to marry someone else could I start to acknowledge my feelings for you."

She gave a humorless smile. "Candover is an attractive man, easy to dream about. But when I kissed him, I realized that what I liked most was that he didn't love me, which was perfect since I never felt that I deserved to be loved."

In the face of her gallant, painful honesty, David's anger began to dissolve. Abandoned by her mother, terrified of losing anyone else she loved—no wonder that under her serene facade lay fear. The pieces she had revealed came together into the whole Jocelyn, the wounded child as well as the bewitching woman.

Overwhelmed with love and compassion, he raised one hand to stop the flow of agonized words. "You don't have to say more, Jocelyn."

She shook her head, eyes stark. "The time for hiding from myself is over. When you left me the note saying that you loved me, I was terrified, because if you loved me, it was just a matter of time until you discovered what was wrong with me." Her voice broke before she finished, "I could survive losing the regard of someone I do not care for deeply, but losing the man I do love would destroy me. So I left . . . before you could send me away."

He enfolded her in his arms, wishing he could heal the wounds she had borne all her life. "I'm sorry for all the beastly things I said," he whispered, his voice husky with emotion. "You did nothing to deserve such cruelty on my part."

As she clung to him, trembling, he kneaded her neck and back, trying to soften the taut muscles. "You see why I try to be a cool English gentleman. When the wild, emotional Welshman escapes, I am immune to logic and good sense. I hadn't known I was capable of such jealousy. But then, I've never loved anyone as I love you." His mouth curved wryly. "It didn't help that Candover is a wealthy, handsome duke. If you need to sort out your feelings in the future, do you think you could experiment with a short, elderly fishmonger?"

Between laughter and tears, she finally raised her face to him. "If you'll give me another chance, there won't ever be any other experiments."

Tears swam in her eyes, but her mouth was warm and welcoming. He embraced her fiercely, using his hands and mouth in a primal need to mark her as his.

For the first time, she kissed him with her whole self, concealing nothing. With all defenses down, they were joined in an emotional intimacy that came from the soul, leaving them both shaken.

Reconciliation flared into passion, the need to be as close as humanly possible. With fumbling hands and ripping fabric, they made their way across the room, leaving a trail of hastily discarded garments. This time there was none of the tentativeness of new lovers. They had learned each other on all levels, and the result was an inferno of desire.

Jocelyn fell back on the bed, pulling him with her. She wanted to absorb every inch of him, to forge a bond that would bind them for a lifetime, and beyond.

They made love with the desperate hunger of two people who had nearly lost what they valued most, staying tangled together even in the hazy aftermath of loving. David released Jocelyn only long enough to pull a cover over them before once more cradling her close. As bodies cooled and breath returned, they talked as lovers do, of how each had begun to love the other, of the small landmarks and discoveries that laid the foundations of their personal miracle. There was no reason to rush, and every reason in the world to savor that sweet sharing.

Much, much later, David murmured, "I'm grateful your servants have the sense not to walk in on us without knocking. I would hate to embarrass one of the maids."

Jocelyn felt so full of joy that anything would have

made her laugh. "If I know anything about my household, they have deduced exactly why we have been closeted in here for hours, and they're celebrating with a champagne toast in the servants' hall. From what Marie has said, they've been worried about my impending spinsterdom, and had decided you were the perfect solution."

Her head was lying on his chest and she could feel as well as hear his laughter. "What excellent servants you have."

Looking up at him, she asked, "Is it safe to assume that Jeanette is no longer relevant?"

The tanned skin around his eyes crinkled mischievously. "To be honest, I'd forgotten that I'd written Sally about Jeanette. It was a lightning-bolt affair that ended when she sorrowfully informed me that a man of greater fortune had offered for her, and she really could not support life on an officer's salary. After the initial shock wore off, I discovered I didn't miss her in the least. Jeanette is entirely ancient history, as is our annulment." He bent to kiss her again. "It's too late to change your mind, my lady wife. I'm not letting you go again."

Jocelyn closed her eyes, hearing once again the echo, "Till death us do part," this time with a resonance of infinite warmth and protection. Hesitantly she said, "I've discovered why I've believed myself unworthy of love, but it will be a long time before all of my fears are gone. I hope you will be patient if I cling too closely."

David rolled over so that he was above her. "If you have trouble believing that I love you, then I will just have to repeat the words every day for as long as we both shall live. I love you, Jocelyn. Does that help?"

Warmth kindled in her heart, spreading until every fiber of her being was suffused with the knowledge that she was loved. She pulled his face down to hers, tasting the salty sweetness of his lips. "It certainly does, my dearest love. It certainly does."

Epilogue

Since David and Jocelyn's wedding had been so hasty and private, they gave a large reception to officially announce the marriage to friends and family. Richard Dalton attended on his crutches, looking justifiably pleased with himself for following his intuition that the two of them belonged together.

Elvira, Countess of Cromarty, went into a hysterical rage when she learned that her wretched niece had withdrawn the application for an annulment. It was bad enough knowing that Jocelyn's fortune was forever out of Elvira's reach. Far worse was discovering that the girl and her husband were besotted with each other. As she told the long-suffering Willoughby, the very least one could have hoped for was that they would be as miserable as most married couples.

When David's letter reached his sister on a rainy day in Scotland, Sally happily reported to Ian that her brother and his wife had fallen in love and were now married for real. He looked up from the anatomy text he was browsing with a twinkle in his eyes, agreeing that marriage was a braw good thing—his Scottish accent was in full flower—because it combined temptation with opportunity in a most satisfactory fashion. Taking that as a challenge, Sally set out to tempt him, which led to an applied anatomy lesson that both of them found a good deal more enjoyable than the one Ian had been studying.

Voice wickedly suggestive, Colonel Andrew Kirkpatrick reminded his wife that he had said the Kendal women were irresistible to army men. She laughed in agreement, and put out the candle.

Delighted not to have to decide which well-loved employer to serve, Hugh and Marie began to plan their own wedding. Rhys would be his brother's best man.

Jocelyn wrote a brief note to the Duke of Candover, thanking him for his forbearance and good advice, and urging him to matrimony as the happiest of all states. He smiled a little sadly when he read her words, drank a solitary toast to the lady and her fortunate husband, then smashed the glass in the fireplace.

Though she took a dim view of sharing her mistress, Isis continued to sleep on Jocelyn's bed. After all, she had been there first.

Author's Note

The idea for David's life-threatening injury came from a Waterloo account that described an operation on an officer who had just been paralyzed by a spinal wound. As soon as a shell fragment was removed, the officer promptly scrambled from the table and escaped from the makeshift hospital, as any wise man would in those days.

Long-time readers will recognize other characters. Richard Dalton is the hero of my very first book, a traditional Regency called *The Diabolical Baron*, which actually takes place a year later, when Richard has recovered from surgery.

The Duke of Candover was created because I needed a super-cool Other Man for *The Would-Be Widow*, the original version of this story. However, Rafe caught my imagination by showing intriguing signs of vulnerability in his last scene, so naturally he had to have a book of his own. Look for Rafe's story in the historical romance *Petals in the Storm* (first published as a Signet Regency entitled *The Controversial Countess*). It's always great fun to see arrogance humbled!

This book contains the first appearance of Ian Kinlock, crusty Scot and brilliant surgeon, whom I have since hauled into service every time I needed Regency medical help. He played vital roles in *Shattered Rainbows* and *One Perfect Rose*, as well as appearing in the Regency *Carousel of Hearts*. It's always nice to see him again.

Traditionally, British surgeons are called Mister while physicians are called Doctor, a difference which goes back to the fact that physicians were considered gentlemen, while surgeons, who worked with their hands, occupied a lower social rung. Since Ian was qualified in both disciplines, I've called him Doctor for simplicity's sake.

A note about lawyers. As most people know, in contemporary Britain lawyers are divided into barristers, who appear in court, and solicitors, who do the majority of legal work in their offices and who engage barristers when cases go to trial.

However, the situation was far more complicated during the Regency, since there were three kinds of law, each with its own court system: equity, common law, and church courts. Worse, each system had two categories of lawyers that dealt with that particular branch of law. This is mind-bogglingly complicated and not especially relevant to my story, so mostly I've just used the term lawyer, which like a basic black dress is always suitable.

I've used the 95th Rifles, one of the most renowned British regiments of the Napoleonic wars, over and over again because it was one of the few outfits to fight both on the Peninsula and at Waterloo. And if it seems as if all of my Regency-era characters know each other—well, fashionable London wasn't too large a place in those days!